The Magic Bi-Scepter

VERITAS GRATIA VERUM AMORIS

EAN

ISBN 978-0-989877-0-5-3   **$14.99 U.S.**/$19.99 Can.

9 780989 877053

51499>

S

The Magic Bi-Scepter

by
Mika Bówyn

based on the 1762 Italian Commedia dell'arte play
"Il Re Cervo" ("The King Stag")
by Carlo Gozzi

 **Cagliostro the Enchanter**
BOOK 1

Library of Congress Control Number: 2019934501

ISBN 978-0-9898770-5-3

10 9 8 7 6 5 4 3 2 1

First United States paperback edition, 2019

ARISTEIA® BOOKS
NEW YORK

for Gnagnarelli

Contents

Yet both before us are already there,
the truth we seek, the true love we desire.
And when we learn to look with wiser eyes
to recognize what once we could not see,
we place ourselves upon a different path
that leads us now to where we sought to be
along a route of unimagined dreams
within the outstretched reach of Fate's kind hand
awakened by new magic that we make.

—from *"Per Vedere"* by Alcina Alberghi

Chapter 1

The Enchanter's Assistant
and
The Map of Here

"**W**here am I…?" Truffaldino wondered aloud. Lowering the map, he put the spyglass back up to his eye and took another long look around. The dusty cobblestones and narrow streets were as unremarkable as a medieval town could be.

He studied the map again for a moment, then peered with frustration back into the spyglass. "Oh, why does the real thing always look so different from the map?" he lamented.

There was a sudden light tapping on his back. Truffaldino jumped in surprise and uttered a startled cry. "What the…!"

Lowering the spyglass in a rapid panic and whirling around, Truffaldino found himself surrounded by a pair of very small monks, no taller than the height of where the bottom button fastened the waist of his jerkin. The two ascetics were clad in drab monasterial robes with pointed-peak cowl hoods hanging back over their shoulders, and were entirely bald save for a single monastic wreath-like ring of tonsured hair encircling each of their heads.

"Oh," exhaled Truffaldino, sighing with relief and wiping the back of his hand elaborately across his brow. "It's two friars."

Both monks shook their heads dismissively.

"We are *not* friars," one of the monks corrected.

"We are *monks*," explained the other monk. "Actually, we're *scribes*."

"Actually, *I'M* a scribe," the first monk clarified with pride. "I am Graphiare!" he added, pronouncing his name as *Graff-eye-AIR-ree*.

"And I am Pentimento!" proclaimed the second monk. "*I'M* a painter. I paint miniature paintings."

"We make manuscripts," they both chorused in cheerful unison.

With momentary interest, Truffaldino regarded the two ascetics. Each monk held a sheaf of vellum sheets in one hand, and in the other a poised quill pen. And each monk had an inkwell ring affixed ingeniously to a finger on the hand that held the parchment, permitting each monk to easily dip a quill tip in and out of the ink as needed to write at will on the stiff pages of handheld vellum.

Truffaldino looked back down at his map, and after checking it carefully scratched his head in confusion. "Hmmm…" he said uncertainly. "I don't see you two anywhere on this map…"

"We are the Royal Manuscript Makers," stated Pentimento, seemingly unconcerned with Truffaldino's inability to put his finger on where they were.

"It is our job," Graphiare added with significance, "to keep track of everything important that happens here in the Kingdom of Benebento."

"And we put it all into a manuscript," said Pentimento.

"I write it all out with beautiful calligraphy," explained Graphiare.

"And I paint beautiful miniature paintings to go with the writing," added Pentimento.

Truffaldino was still studying the map with concern. "That's fascinating…" he said distractedly. "Say," he went on, pointing at the map. "Can you two friars please tell me where I am…?"

"Monks!!" said Graphiare indignantly.

"We're *monks!*" echoed Pentimento.

Truffaldino nodded amiably. "Yes, of course. But seriously, I need some help. Can you tell me—"

Graphiare held up one hand and pointed his quill meaningfully at Truffaldino. "We can tell you nothing, traveler," he stated firmly.

"We," Pentimento added, "have a *Non-Interference Clause* in our contract with the King."

Graphiare pointed the tip of his quill vaguely skyward. "We can observe," he stated strictly.

"But we cannot participate," said Pentimento.

"*Documentation,*" recited Graphiare.

"*Without participation,*" recited Pentimento.

Graphiare aimed the tip of his quill back toward Truffaldino. "Now," he went on formally. "What is your name, traveler?"

Truffaldino looked around, glanced back at the map, then returned his gaze to the eager scribes and sighed. "I am Truffaldino," he acquiesced with resigned civility. "Assistant to the great enchanter Cagliostro," he added, pronouncing the enchanter's name as *Cah-lee-OH-stroh.*

Graphiare had dipped his quill pen into his finger-ring inkwell and was now busily scratching out precise calligraphic text across the parchment page.

"And," Graphiare went on, "how would you describe your feelings at this moment?"

Truffaldino thought for a moment. "Um... Lost...?" he answered. "Hungry...? Impatient...? Annoyed...?"

Graphiare nodded approvingly and continued writing without looking up from the parchment page. "Excellent!" he remarked with satisfaction.

Pentimento had meanwhile been using his own quill and ink to draw some manner of illustration on the piece of parchment atop the sheaf of pages he was holding, and he now paused to gaze intently at Truffaldino's face. "What color would you say your eyes are?" inquired Pentimento.

Truffaldino had to think about this for a moment. "Um... Green?" he said at last.

Both Pentimento and Graphiare were nodding and writing and drawing with industrious enthusiasm.

"Outstanding!" Pentimento declared conclusively.

And having apparently suddenly completed their various documentation, the scribes abruptly halted their work and looked up cordially at Truffaldino.

"Good-bye!" said both scribes in friendly unison. They turned around, and off they went.

Truffaldino watched them depart for a moment and shook his head dubiously. "Documentation without participation..." he muttered. "What a strange place it is here. Now if I could just figure out where 'here' is…"

He discontentedly checked the map again, then put the spyglass back up to his eye. "Maybe if I just focus on something farther away…" he mused, rotating the aim of his body and his gaze to change the view through the spyglass.

"Ahh," he sighed. "How rustic. The sleepy peacefulness of the distant forest…" He continued to turn as he tried to follow what he was seeing. "If only it weren't moving so quickly, I could get a better… Hey! Wait a minute…!"

Truffaldino quickly lowered the spyglass.

"Oh!" he exclaimed. "It's a personage! Colorful-looking, too. Perhaps he's one of the locals. Maybe *he* can tell me where I am…"

Still clutching his map and the spyglass, Truffaldino dashed through the warmth of the leisurely afternoon sunlight and across the dusty cobbles for several dozen steps in the direction he had been looking until he caught up with a short rotund individual who seemed important: a fancifully-clad man whose colorful robes flowed in his wake as he strode with speedy intent while his long whitish hair bounced with each quick heavy step.

"Excuse me," Truffaldino said breathlessly as he tried to keep pace with the man's brisk gait.

"No, I'm afraid that won't be possible," the man said without either slowing his stride or glancing to the side to see who was addressing him.

"I beg your pardon?" asked Truffaldino, getting more out of breath with every step.

At this point, the man partially turned his head for a brief moment to get a glimpse of Truffaldino, but still did not slow his pace.

"No, young man," he said unwaveringly. "I'm afraid I cannot do that, either."

By now Truffaldino had jogged another several dozen steps just to keep up. "I… I don't understand…" he said, panting. "If I could just ask you to—"

The portly man stopped suddenly and turned to face Truffaldino. "Now listen here, traveling fellow," he said sternly.

Truffaldino skidded to a stop and the soles of his turnshoes stirred a flurried cloud of dust from the cobbles.

"You," the man declaimed, wagging a grandiloquent finger, "seem to have confused me with someone else. I am Avogadro, the King's Wise Man."

This pronouncement was delivered with huge importance, and Avogadro lifted his hands with mystical grandeur toward the heavens, opening his arms wide toward the sky and the greater universe.

"I know many things," Avogadro continued with pontifical import, turning his focus back to earth. "I can explain many peculiar phenomena. I can utter whimsical and enigmatic portents. However," he said, looking pointedly and momentarily at Truffaldino, "I can neither excuse you, nor pardon you. You are inexcusable, and your behavior is unpardonable. Good-day!"

And with a magisterial flourish of his exotic raiment, Avogadro turned and strode away.

Truffaldino halfheartedly opened his mouth to reply, but seemed to realize it was futile. For a moment he simply stood in dismay and watched the departing mystic hurry off down a narrow street. Truffaldino looked back down at the map and scanned it again. "Well," he concluded discontentedly, "*he's* not on the map either."

Truffaldino returned the spyglass to his eye, still peeved. "Wise Man…" he muttered. "More like a wiseguy if you ask me…"

Truffaldino again scanned the surroundings until something else caught his gaze. "Oh!" he exclaimed with relieved surprise. "More locals…!"

Into Truffaldino's line of spyglass view had entered a formidable-looking knight and a young lad who seemed to be in the service of the knight. Within moments, the progress of their traverse led them to approach where Truffaldino stood.

"Now see here, Italo," the knight was reprimanding. "That new armor is too heavy. I won't be able to walk five steps!"

"But you won't have to walk, Sir," Italo explained respectfully. "You'll be riding your horse."

"Until I fall off because my armor is too heavy!" the knight exclaimed indignantly.

"But Sir—" Italo tried to continue.

"A fine thing, that!" the knight interrupted. "I, Sir Balzanno, the commander of the King's armies, toppling off my horse into the castle moat. And who would dive in after me? *You*, Italo?"

"Well, I—"

"As I suspected," concluded Sir Balzanno. "And another thing,

Italo. That new armor is too thin. It will never protect me in battle!"

"But Sir Balzanno!" Italo protested politely. "That's why we got the heavier armor!"

Sir Balzanno shook his head dismissively. "Strong and light!" he instructed. "That is the order of the day, squire!"

Sir Balzanno paused in his discourse as he spotted Truffaldino, who was still watching them through his spyglass.

"Ah-HA!" Sir Balzanno declared with satisfaction. "There! Now *that's* what I'm talking about, Italo. Innovation! That's *just* the sort of thing I need. Some sort of glass shield for the visor window on my helmet. How would you feel if I got a piece of dust in my eye during a joust?!"

Italo's shoulders dropped in resignation. "Terrible, Sir…" he said contritely.

Sir Balzanno nodded with large understanding. "Of course you would."

The brisk steadily-walking progress of Sir Balzanno and Italo had by this time brought them very near to Truffaldino, who now lowered his spyglass to greet them.

"Excuse, me…" Truffaldino began.

"Not at all, young man," said Sir Balzanno generously. "Thank you very much. You've been quite helpful."

"Oh!" replied Truffaldino. "Well, you're welcome. No trouble at all, really…"

Sir Balzanno turned formally to Italo. "Come along, squire!" the knight commanded.

"Yes, Sir Balzanno," said Italo with respectful weary obedience.

Sir Balzanno strode off with swift purpose while Italo rushed hastily to keep up with him.

Truffaldino watched them head off, and then remembered the map in his hand. "Oh, wait…!" he called after them. "I need to ask…"

But Sir Balzanno and Italo had gone on their way.

Truffaldino sighed and held up the map, addressing it with annoyance. "Well, you're a big help!" he scolded it with earnest irony.

"What's that you've got there?" said a lovely female voice near Truffaldino's ear.

"It's a—" Truffaldino began as he turned around, but he stopped when he saw the young lady to whom the voice belonged.

"Wow…" Truffaldino said in amazement. "You're beautiful…"

The simply-dressed young lady looked down at the ground for a moment in polite embarrassment. "Oh…" she said shyly. "Well, I…"

"No, seriously," Truffaldino explained. "I mean, I can't fall in love with you because my master, the enchanter Cagliostro, says I'm going to marry a girl with *red* hair. But honestly, I bet you're the most beautiful young lady anyone's ever seen."

"Oh…" the young lady said courteously. "Thank you very much…" She looked at the map Truffaldino was holding and pointed to it. "But, what's that…?"

Truffaldino was having a hard time not staring at the beauty of the young lady. "What…?" was all he could manage for a moment.

The young lady smiled shyly and pointed again to the map.

"Oh," Truffaldino said at last, finally following the aim of her gesture. "This…" He looked down at the map and frowned with disapproval. "It's *supposed* to be a MAP OF HERE. But it doesn't seem to be working right…"

The young lady gave a slight nod and continued to gaze thoughtfully at the map. "I wonder if it would help me find Tartaglia…" she mused, pronouncing the name as *Tar-TAHL-yah*.

"Who's that?" asked Truffaldino.

"The King's Prime Minister," explained the young lady. "I'm trying to find him. I'm *always* trying to find him. He's never trying to find me, though…" The young lady's face took on an expression of melancholy. "He'd much rather find Angiolina…" she added quietly, pronouncing the name as *AHN-jee-yo-LEE-nuh*.

Truffaldino looked at the sad expression on the beautiful young lady's face. "Who are you?" he asked her.

"I'm Nicoletta," she said. "My father is Avogadro. The King's Wise Man? He probably just passed this way recently."

At the mention of Avogadro's name, Truffaldino rolled his eyes ruefully. "Don't remind me…" he demurred. "Well, I'm Truffaldino."

Truffaldino smiled at Nicoletta, who smiled back at him.

"Say," Truffaldino went on. "Maybe you can help me. My master gave me this MAP OF HERE because I'm supposed to meet him, but I can't figure out where I am…"

Nicoletta nodded. "Maybe I can help you with that," she said, extending her hand for the map.

Truffaldino handed the map toward Nicoletta.

She took it from him and considered it for a moment. "Hmmm…" she said thoughtfully. "Let me see…"

Truffaldino watched her hopefully as she studied the elaborate colorful markings on the worn wrinkled parchment.

After a few more moments of inspection, she nodded slightly. "Wave your arms up and down," she instructed him.

Truffaldino collapsed the telescoping spyglass and slipped it into a pouch hanging from his belt, then obediently began to wave his arms up and down in repeated huge motions.

Nicoletta looked around the map more intently, and then suddenly spotted something. "Oh!" she exclaimed with recognition.

Her slender fingers moving with dexterous light agility, she reoriented the map halfway around in her hands as if it had been upside down.

"Here you are," she observed brightly, pointing to a specific place within the parchment's markings. "See?"

Still waving his arms, Truffaldino looked over at the map.

Nicoletta held it so he could see it better, pointing more obviously to a place on the map.

"Oh! Yes!" he exclaimed happily, waving his arms with increased zeal. "There I am! At last!"

Continuing to wave his arms with relieved delight, Truffaldino leaned closer to the place on the map where Nicoletta was still helpfully indicating. "Hello, Truffaldino!" he hailed companionably, calling out a greeting to the representation of himself on the map.

Nicoletta smiled.

Without taking his eyes off the map, Truffaldino directed his appreciative rejoicing to Nicoletta. "It's me!" he proclaimed. "I'm waving!"

"Yes, you are," agreed Nicoletta with amused encouragement. "And doing a fine job, too."

Truffaldino could barely contain the exuberance of his relief and gratitude. "Thank you, Nicoletta!" he exclaimed, still waving his arms and focusing on the map. "Now all I need to do is find the palace, and I can finally be on time to meet my master Cagliostro."

"The palace?" asked Nicoletta. "That's easy."

She slightly adjusted the position of her finger and moved it to indicate a place on the map not far from where she had first been pointing.

"It's right over there," she said. "Come along, Truffaldino. I'll show you…"

Continuing to hold the map so they could both see it, Nicoletta took Truffaldino gently by the arm and began to steer him as the two of them started to walk off together.

With delighted fascination, Truffaldino remained mesmerized by seeing himself on the map, and was unable to take his eyes off that part of the parchment as he and Nicoletta proceeded.

"Oh, look!" Truffaldino exclaimed, watching the map. "Now I'm *walking*!"

Nicoletta smiled with gentle amusement and nodded kindly. "You are a very talented young man," she agreed.

"And look!" Truffaldino said with delight, pointing to the map.

"You're walking, too! Right next to me. See? That's you. You're the one holding the map!"

"Yes, that's me," Nicoletta agreed, making sure Truffaldino did not trip while he remained captivated by the map. And staying focused on the reality of the actual world ahead, she guided them both forward.

Chapter 2

The King's Counsel
and
The Enchanter

At the heart of the kingdom of Benebento was the castello, the glorious and majestic Castle Delprego. Fashioned with precise perfection from countless finely-hewn massive blocks of golden stone, its high walls and towering ramparts shone like the sun. The warmth of steadfast protection, beneficent rule, and the righteous might of royal authority radiated out from its powerful grandeur and bathed the kingdom in the surety of security and constancy.

At the heart of the castello was the Palace Gardens, an expansive private piazza courtyard for the King. This arboreal conservatory was lavishly opulent with a lush abundance of plants and trees and flowers of sundry sizes and species, fertile flora rich with a diversity of vegetational texture and a wealth of varying hues from nature's most subtle and spectacular offerings of organic color.

The central area of the gardens was an artfully manicured glade, a verdant clearing bounded on three sides by an elaborately sprawling yet easily-navigable geometric low-grown hedgerow maze. At the center rose a great circular marble fountain, its ornately sculpted scallop-shell and acanthus-leaf motifs contrasted by the simple trickling and gradual flow of its gently tumbling water. From the highest and smallest of its three elevated round decorative levels, slowly-overflowing water cascaded with glassy smoothness from tier to tier, each circular vasque larger in diameter than the one above it, all spilling endlessly and discreetly into the clear green-blue pool of the fountain's vast ground-level basin with an aqueous aural softness that currently was being drowned out by the impassioned voices of a disagreement.

Mere steps from the fountain, an argument was underway. The mystic Avogadro and the knight Sir Balzanno were engaged in a boisterous and animated four-way debate with two other apparently noble personages: a dignified-looking man, and a tall man with gaunt angry features. All four were gesturing emphatically and talking at once. There was heated dissent, so heated that none of them was paying any attention to the King.

King Theramo was a young monarch, still too youthful and guileless to appear royally handsome, but whose features suggested that he one day might be. For now, however, his expression was one of continual uncertainty. His regal but not overly ostentatious raiment was not necessarily the wrong size, yet it nevertheless did not seem to fit him. Even his imperial crown appeared not quite suited to King Theramo's head. No amount of his periodic adjusting and re-adjusting could set the crown right, and King Theramo seemed as though he would have been far more comfortable simply not wearing it.

Amidst the numerous free-standing architectural accents of the gardens was an elaborately whimsical furnishing in the form of a large outdoor mirror. Flanked on either side by two massive classical-stonework urns with exotic ferns growing from each vessel in healthy abundance, this particular nearby object at the moment was doing nothing to help the king's unsettled demeanor, and the merest glimpse of himself in reflection served only to make him appear more ill at ease.

In proximity to this considerable looking-glass, King Theramo had been pacing back and forth next to a span of one of the royally manicured maze hedgerows, observing the ongoing argument with growing concern. He continued to pace anxiously until at last he stopped and spoke, raising both hands in the air as he addressed the four men.

"My friends!" began King Theramo. "My friends, excuse me! But you must desist! This will never do!"

Upon realizing they were being addressed by their king, the others immediately stopped arguing and quieted themselves to silence with apologetic and respectful utterances of "Your Majesty, Your Majesty."

"Do not talk over each other," instructed King Theramo. "I beseech you. Speak your thoughts in turns." He looked directly at the tall man with gaunt angry features who was dressed in robes of dark subdued hues. "Tartaglia?"

Tartaglia gazed back at King Theramo. "Odds bodkins," he began. "I don't like enchanters, Sire. And as Prime Minister, I am deeply troubled that Your Majesty would embark on such an extreme path of action before discussing it with your most trusted and confidential advisor."

King Theramo unconsciously adjusted his crown and nodded

his head in regretful assent. "Yes... You are right, Tartaglia. I should have consulted you first..."

The King turned his focus to the dignified-looking man who was dressed in more cheerily-colored robes, colors that were nothing like the startling whimsy of the flowing robes of Avogadro, but colors that nonetheless were lively and vibrant. "Lord Pantalòné?" said the King, pronouncing his name as *Pahn-tah-LOH-nay*.

"As your Chancellor," Lord Pantalòné began, "I must say, Sire, I am troubled by this plan. Since the reign of your dear departed parents, Benebento has been a peaceful realm with happy subjects and prosperous citizens. Magic, My Lord? Why, we already have more success as a kingdom than could ever possibly be wished for. What need have we of magic? I am worried that introducing the forces of magic here into this land of light may bring unwelcome darkness."

King Theramo nodded with grave recognition as Pantalòné spoke, uncertainty gathering on his face.

"Hmm..." King Theramo replied at length. "Your thoughts are sensibly spoken, Chancellor," he went on unsurely. "This venture of mine may be too hasty..."

The King turned to Avogadro. "Avogadro, you are my Wise Man. What do you think?"

Avogadro took a deep mystical breath and touched a hand to his forehead before answering. "Your Highness," Avogadro began, gesturing with an open palm. "As you know, one of my only two daughters was lost to enchantment. There is a prophecy that she will one day come home: *New wings shall bring the gift of flight, an old man shall become young, a bird shall disappear, a daughter shall return.* That prophecy is all I have left of my first daughter. Consequently, I can only advise you to stay away from enchanters."

King Theramo nodded gravely as Avogadro spoke, more uncertainty clouding his expression. "Yes, Avogadro," the King acknowledged. "Perhaps you are right... Getting involved with an enchanter could bring unforeseen problems..."

King Theramo turned to the knight. "Sir Balzanno?" said the King. "Your thoughts?"

Sir Balzanno looked squarely at King Theramo and spoke without hesitation. "My Liege, I don't trust magic," he stated simply.

King Theramo nodded knowingly. "Neither do I," he agreed.

"However," Sir Balzanno continued, "as commander of Your Majesty's armies, I feel it is my duty to point out that magic could bring extraordinary unheard-of capabilities to our armed forces. With the right powers of magic at our command, our armies would be invulnerable and undefeatable. Better still, no enemy would dare even attack us at all! With the threat of such overwhelming magical military might to keep our adversaries at bay, this enchanter could very well make it so that not only would Benebento never lose a war, Benebento would never even have to fight a battle!"

King Theramo's face lit up slightly, and his crown swayed as he nodded enthusiastically. "That is a remarkable possibility indeed," he agreed. "For such worthwhile peaceful ends, perhaps any magical means would be justified..."

"No more need to fight, eh, Balzanno?" said Tartaglia suspiciously.

"I'll have you know," Sir Balzanno protested proudly, "that generations of Balzannos have fought and died with honor for their kingdom and their king. Ending all war for all time would in no way diminish the glory of the Balzanno bloodline or the Balzanno name."

"Your Majesty," interrupted Lord Pantalòné. "If Your Highness is of two minds about this issue, might I suggest that we, your advisors, have a vote and provide Your Highness with at least a consensus point-of-view on the matter?"

King Theramo brightened immediately. "Yes," he agreed with relief. "A vote. That is an excellent idea." He turned toward Tartaglia. "Prime Minister?"

Tartaglia seemed darkly unenthusiastic. "I'm not necessarily in favor," he said. "But I vote yes. Some unknown benefit may possibly come from it."

King Theramo turned to Lord Pantalòné. "Chancellor?"

Pantalòné thought for a moment longer. "I suppose we ought not close our minds to new ways of thinking," he mused. "I'll vote yes."

King Theramo turned to the knight. "Sir Balzanno?

Sir Balzanno contemplated hesitantly for a moment, then thrust a gauntleted fist forward in assent. "I vote yes, My Liege. Go boldly forward. Proceed with the plan."

King Theramo turned toward Avogadro. "Avogadro?"

Grave concern furrowed the brow of the wise man, and his

long whitish hair swept back and forth as he shook his head in decided negation. "Too hazardous," Avogadro concluded without hesitation. "I vote no."

King Theramo nodded. "Good," he proclaimed. "It's unanimous, then. Three-to-one. We'll do it. Excellent!"

At that moment a palace guard rushed into the gardens. Entering from the one side not bordered by the hedgerow maze, he approached quickly through the small grove of lofty cypress trees that surrounded the marble walkway of the path back into the castle. A single long curl of his ink-black hair, uncontained by his guardsman's helmet, bounced half coiled across his forehead as he dashed with respectful speed to where King Theramo was standing. The young man halted, bowed, then knelt at the King's feet.

"Your Majesty," the kneeling guard began.

King Theramo nodded. "Arise, Leandro. What news have you?"

Leandro stood up. "Your Majesty," he reported. "Two visitors seek an audience with you. The enchanter Cagliostro and his assistant await, just beyond the grove."

"Perfect!" the King replied emphatically. "Bid them join us here in the gardens."

With a respectful nod and a slight bow, Leandro turned and took a few brief steps back in the direction of the marble walkway, beckoning with polite formality in the direction of the cypress grove. As Leandro gestured courteously, a tall man entered. Following just behind was Truffaldino in his utilitarian jerkin and simple leggings. But all eyes were on the tall man.

King Theramo wearing his crown was nearly the same height

as Tartaglia, but the man who now entered the gardens towered at least a head taller than either of them. His layered robe with shifting ripples of iridescent black and indigo was so long that that it hid his hands and feet from view. As he strode over the marble paving stones, thin nearly imperceptible wisps of smoky vapor continuously wafted off his every movement as though he were a recently materialized apparition that might vanish at any moment.

Everyone present moved apprehensively closer together as they silently took in the imposing presence of the mysterious figure.

The stranger had a thin dark beard, dark hair that was closely cut and slightly white on the sides, and bright penetrating eyes that now looked meaningfully and expectantly at everyone around him.

"I am Cagliostro the Enchanter," said the stranger. He spoke with quiet power in a deep calm commanding voice that seemed to be coming from somewhere else.

For several moments, no one seemed to have the courage to speak.

"Truffaldino is my assistant," Cagliostro went on, one large powerful hand emerging for a fleeting moment from beneath his robes as he gestured toward Truffaldino.

Truffaldino shuffled and fidgeted nervously as he looked uncomfortably around at the King and the panoply of important personages surrounding him. "Felicitations and salutations, Your Various Excellencies," Truffaldino began. "It is an honor and a pleasure to make your acquaintance at last. You have no idea the trouble I had finding this place. Why, I almost—"

Cagliostro interrupted him with a slight glance that was gentle but firm. "That will do, Truffaldino," said Cagliostro.

Truffaldino nodded with apologetic rapidity. "Right," he said in mortified embarrassment. He turned aside and with frustrated disappointment slapped his own head. "Idiot!" he chided himself.

Tartaglia tentatively stepped slightly forward. "Lord Cagliostro," he said cautiously, gesturing toward the King. "You have the honor of standing before His Majesty Theramo, King of Benebento."

Cagliostro and Truffaldino bowed respectfully to King Theramo.

"And I," Tartaglia went on importantly, "am Tartaglia, loyal Prime Minister to the King. We are the King's inner circle of most trusted and faithful counselors. These other three advisors are Pantalòné—our Royal Chancellor, Sir Balzanno—Commander of the Royal Benebento Army, and Avogadro—the King's Wise Man."

At the mention of Avogadro, Truffaldino could not stop himself from rolling his eyes. "Oh, brother…" he muttered to himself.

Lord Pantalòné gave a courteous and appropriately slight bow to Cagliostro and Truffaldino. "Greetings," he said politely.

Sir Balzanno likewise inclined his head to the two strangers and greeted them civilly. "Welcome, good sirs," he said.

Avogadro had closed his eyes and put one of his hands significantly to his own forehead. "I'm getting something…" he announced, his brow furrowed with concentration. "Something that starts with an 'M'… Is it… Magic?" Avogadro opened his eyes and looked directly at Cagliostro and Truffaldino. "Does one of you know something about 'magic'?"

Truffaldino rolled his eyes again. "I'm getting something that starts with a 'P'," he said under his breath, "and it's a great big Pain In My—"

"I know magic," Cagliostro replied patiently. His voice was not loud but somehow seemed to fill the gardens with its sound. "That is why I have come here to serve King Theramo."

With his hand still to his forehead, Avogadro closed his eyes again and nodded mystically. "You are pleased to meet me…" he pronounced.

"Truffaldino and I are pleased to meet all of you," Cagliostro said diplomatically.

King Theramo nodded and seemed ready at last to take charge. He lifted a hand to indicate Leandro, who was standing poised protectively at his side. "And this is Leandro," said the King. "My most trusted palace guard."

Leandro bowed respectfully to Cagliostro and Truffaldino.

The King turned to address the others. "My dearest advisors. I cannot thank you enough for the invaluable benefit of your wise counsel. You have my deepest gratitude. I will now be conferring with Cagliostro alone. You are all excused to go."

Pantalòné nodded and turned to leave.

A look of concern crossed Sir Balzanno's face, and the articulated plate armor of his gauntlets clattered quietly as he clasped his hands together in indecision. "As you wish, My Liege," the knight said reluctantly. "Keeping in mind, of course, that the dictates of due protocol prescribe—for the safety and welfare of the King and the kingdom—that at all times a ranking member of the military is required to be—"

Pantalòné turned back for a moment and put a hand kindly but firmly on Sir Balzanno's armored shoulder. "That'll do for now, Balzanno," he instructed the knight. And to King Theramo, he said respectfully, "Thank you, Your Majesty."

Sir Balzanno nodded grudgingly at Pantalòné and turned back toward the King. "As Your Majesty prefers," the knight continued, "I shall of course take my leave. And in the interest of your safety and personal welfare, I shall position myself in a stance of vigilant readiness just beyond the cypress grove and—"

"No, you won't," said Pantalòné. "You will leave the King with complete privacy as he has instructed, and you will accompany me to the Royal Dining Hall for trencher bread and ale while we await His Majesty's next directive."

"Oh, very well," Sir Balzanno sighed with a resigned shrug. "Thank you, My Liege," he said with respect before turning again and allowing Pantalòné to lead the two of them out of the gardens through the tall trees of the cypress grove.

Avogadro was nodding mystically, and he turned toward the King with a look of deep significance. "Your Highness. Due to my professional expertise in dealing with matters of magic, it occurs to me that—"

"My Lord," Leandro said to Avogadro, hastily interrupting and taking hold of one of the oversized colorful sleeves of Avogadro's robes. "My Lord, come quickly! There is... uh... A portent! Of some sort... In the... uh... In the scullery! It must be interpreted at once!"

Avogadro immediately nodded his head in wise

acknowledgement and touched a hand mystically to his own forehead. "Yes... Yes, I knew that..." he said authoritatively. "Lead the way, young Leandro."

Leandro nodded and quickly began to guide Avogadro away toward the cypress grove.

King Theramo looked at Leandro with deep appreciation, and exhaled gratefully. "For this relief, Leandro, much thanks."

Leandro paused for a brief moment, only long enough to bow to the King. "Thank you, Your Majesty," he said.

"Thank you, Your Majesty," Avogadro said distractedly in parting, as Leandro proceeded to usher the two of them away along the marble walkway back toward the interior of the castle.

Tartaglia stepped closer to the King and addressed him in a confidential tone. "Your Majesty," he said importantly. "Your private discussion with the enchanter doubtless will have profound and far-reaching effects on the future of the kingdom. I expect you will of course be wanting me to remain here with you, by your side."

"My most trusted and faithful Tartaglia," King Theramo said, nodding appreciatively. "What I should ever do without the wisdom and insight of your loyalty, I do not know. For this meeting with the enchanter, however, I will be conferring alone."

"Odds bodkins!" said Tartaglia, offended.

There was an uncomfortable pause.

"As you wish," Tartaglia at last managed to say through his frustration. "Thank you, Your Majesty." Unable to hide his irritation, he turned with reluctance and began to slowly make his way toward the marble path.

Cagliostro turned for a moment to Truffaldino. "Truffaldino—"

"I'll just head back inside the castle for now, Sir," Truffaldino suggested obediently.

Cagliostro nodded. "And Truffaldino—" he went on.

Truffaldino nodded quickly. "I won't cause any trouble, Sir. You have my word!"

Cagliostro gave Truffaldino a kind but firm look.

Truffaldino nodded more emphatically. "That's me, Sir. No-Trouble-Truffaldino. I'll be on my best behavior."

One of Cagliostro's large hands emerged for a moment from beneath his robes with a slight gesture, indicating to Truffaldino the path out of the gardens.

Truffaldino nodded again and turned, bowing, to King Theramo. "It has been my greatest honorable pleasure to make your royal acquaintance, Your High Excellentness. I've always wanted to get to meet a real live king, and—"

"That will do, Truffaldino," said Cagliostro.

"Right," Truffaldino answered hurriedly. He turned aside and slapped his own head with disappointed embarrassment. "Idiot!" he scolded himself as he hastened off toward the cypress grove.

Within a few steps Truffaldino found himself alongside the slowly shuffling Tartaglia who had only just reached the marble walkway. "Say," Truffaldino said breathlessly to the brooding Prime Minister as he caught up with him. "Aren't you Tartaglia? You know, I met someone who was looking for you…"

Whether oblivious to Truffaldino or merely ignoring him, Tartaglia only scowled, lost in his own thoughts, not bothering even to cast a dismissive or uninterested look in Truffaldino's direction as the two of them proceeded through the cypress grove and away toward the interior of the castle.

The enchanter and the King were now together alone.

"You're not an easy fellow to get a hold of, Cagliostro," the King stated simply.

That is by design, Your Majesty," said Cagliostro.

King Theramo nodded. "Your name is not well-known, and your reputation more elusive still. Finding out how or where to contact you has been nearly impossible. Nevertheless, I am grateful you are here, and I appreciate your coming to see me."

"Benebento," said Cagliostro, "is renowned as being a kingdom of peace and goodness. I am happy to be of service, if it is within my means and if the need is just."

For a moment, neither man spoke. The only sounds were the ambient noises of the gardens: the quiet layered-cascade of the fountain water, the barely discernible rustle of the tallest trees from a warm Spring breeze, the intermittent song and chatter of nearby and distant birds.

King Theramo started to pace again, then stopped himself. He turned to the enchanter.

"I'm taking a big risk," the King said at last. "Calling on the services of an enchanter…"

The King looked distractedly around at the gardens, and accidentally caught a glimpse of himself in the mirror. He quickly turned his focus back to Cagliostro.

"It's highly irregular," King Theramo went on. "But I'm desperate…"

The enchanter looked steadily and patiently back at the King. "How may I assist you, Your Majesty?"

Chapter 3

The King's Dilemma
and
The Enchanter's Magic

King Theramo glanced uneasily at the mirror, then looked back at Cagliostro and pointed to the large looking-glass. "This mirror was given to me by my parents, King Bernini and Queen Donatella. I would like to rule as well as they did…"

The King paused for a moment, then went on. "But when I look into this mirror, the king I see looking back at me is not the king that I believe my parents would be proud of."

"And precisely how does that reflection fall short of the exacting standards you set for yourself?" asked Cagliostro.

Turning away from both the looking-glass and Cagliostro, King Theramo started pacing again. "I wish…" he began anxiously. "I wish that I were not so naïve. I wish that I were not so trusting. I wish that I could have the confidence of my own convictions, and not be so easily persuaded by anyone who gives me their point-of-view. I cannot trust my own judgment. Consequently, I cannot make the decisions a king needs to make… I do not take the actions a king must take…"

"Your Majesty is but a young man and a youthful monarch," said Cagliostro. "It is Your Highness's very youthfulness that so innocently desires at such an early age to possess the judgment which is acquired only with experience and the wisdom that comes with the passage of time."

But the King was shaking his head. "You don't understand. In truth, Cagliostro, what I need... What I lack... What I am most missing and most in need of is... The Truth. I need to know the Truth. Is a complex situation truly as I perceive it? Is a trusted advisor truly being honest with me? Is an allied kingdom openly negotiating peace whilst secretly preparing war? If someone says they love me, do they love me truly? Or do they lie to gain the throne next to mine, to deceitfully possess half the kingdom, to crush my heart? I trust *everyone*. My very opinions are shaped simply by the words of whoever has spoken to me most recently. It is a terrible affliction! I cannot trust the power of my convictions because I do not even know what my own convictions are! Decisions of state... Judgments of character... Matters of the heart... With my inability to see the Truth in these realms, I am a hunted animal running toward a dense forest with my eyes blindfolded. I am desperate! I must find some way of knowing the Truth!"

Cagliostro looked kindly at the King and almost smiled. "It is the impetuousness of youth," said the enchanter. "The will of youth is ever driven irresistibly and precipitously forward by the insistent immediacy of Now. What you describe, Your Majesty, indeed sounds dire when framed as you have depicted it. Yet, I am unconvinced that the obstacles placed in your path by the reasoning of your own mind are in any way insurmountable in Real Life. The normal passage of time and the simple persistence of your own determination would be sufficient, in my opinion, to solve all your problems."

At these words, dejected sadness gathered on the King's face, and he began aimlessly pacing again. "Then," he said unhappily, "either you cannot help me, or you will not help me."

Cagliostro's large hands slowly emerged from within his robes and came up together underneath his chin almost as if he were thinking of a prayer. "Your Majesty," said the enchanter. "This *sine qua non* ability you crave, this capability you cannot succeed without, this supernatural means to know the Truth... If you possessed such a power, what would you do with it?"

"I would use it to choose a queen," the King said without hesitation. "This is at the heart of why I wanted to meet with you."

King Theramo unconsciously adjusted his crown and began pacing again. "Although he does not realize it," the King went on, "it is because of the duly appropriate urgings of my most trusted Prime Minister, Tartaglia, that I have now been spurred to seek your help, Cagliostro. Of late, my faithful Tartaglia has been most dogged and resolute in reminding me that I have no queen. Once upon a time, I did endeavor to undertake the process of finding a bride. However, I... I abandoned the process. Without the ability to know the Truth, for me the process is futile."

King Theramo stopped pacing and went to the mirror. "Before they died," he went on, "I swore to my parents that I would never fail them, that I would never fail the kingdom. I vowed that the Benebento they were entrusting to me would—under my reign— continue, in all its magnificence and splendor, to be a kingdom of goodness and peace and prosperity and happiness. Such as it had always been under their rule, so would it always be under mine. That was my pledge. And to stay true to that promise, I cannot rule alone. I must choose a queen. But she must be a good queen. She must be the right queen. She must be the best queen for Benebento. And somehow, I must find her, whoever she may be. From the entirety of the Kingdom of Benebento, I must find the one woman who is the right woman to be my Queen."

Cagliostro nodded. "A noble goal, and a challenging task."

King Theramo let out a great disconsolate sigh. "You have no idea!" he said miserably. "Hundreds of young ladies have sought the job. I have met with all of them. But I have absolutely no idea if any of them is the one who should be Queen. I have talked with all of them. But I have no way of evaluating anything they say because I have no way to know the Truth. I am sifting through precious stones in the dark and trying to determine which is the diamond. Without help, it is an undertaking at which I cannot succeed."

"Interesting…" Cagliostro said thoughtfully. "And what of the complex situation, or the trusted advisor, or the allied kingdom?"

King Theramo adjusted his crown again. "I will always aspire to be as good a man as my father was," he said slowly. "And I will always aspire to be as great a king as he was. But my father's greatest achievement was to make Benebento into the wonderful kingdom it is today. And I believe he was able to achieve that greatness because of my mother, his Queen. My mother and father loved each other very much. I believe it was their love for each other that enabled them to be such great rulers. If I could marry a queen who loved this kingdom as much as I do, a queen whom I loved and who loved me as much as my parents loved each other, I believe that together we then could become rulers worthy of the greatness of Benebento that was created by my mother and father. If I possessed the power to know the Truth, I would use it to choose a queen, to find the right queen for me, to find the right queen for the Kingdom of Benebento. With the right queen by my side, I believe the two of us would find a way to overcome my terrible inability to think for myself, so that I could at last become a king worthy of my parents, worthy of my promise, worthy of this great kingdom."

Cagliostro nodded again and his hands retreated back out of sight within the folds of his robes. "Your Majesty," he said slowly. "Because your desire to use magic comes from the goodness of your heart, I shall provide you with a solution to your problem."

King Theramo immediately brightened with sudden hopeful enthusiasm. "Then you can help me?!"

"Yes," said Cagliostro.

"You will give me the power I seek?!" asked the King.

"I will give you more than what you have requested," said Cagliostro. "You have sought one power, however I shall give you two."

"I am overwhelmed with gratitude, Cagliostro! I am thankful and appreciative beyond my ability to articulate. But, why do you grant me more than what I've asked?"

"The Truth you seek comes in many forms," said the enchanter. "And it can be hidden from view by different means. The two magical powers I shall give you provide two very different ways of seeing the kinds of Truth you wish to know."

Cagliostro's large powerful hands once again emerged from the depths of his long robes, and now they held an ordinary-looking pair of rivet spectacles fashioned from thin simple gold with straight temple-pieces and curved ear-hooks. The circular lenses were connected at the tops of their round rims by the two small oblongs of an inverted-v-shaped hinged-nose-bridge fastened at its apex with a single round rivet pivot. The most distinguishing feature of the glasses was an almost invisible floating cloud of barely perceptible twinkling points of light that whorled and danced languorously about the edges of the glass, sparkling glimmers that winked and shifted and were nearly impossible to see.

King Theramo could barely contain his excitement and he moved quickly to take hold of the gift that Cagliostro was now handing toward him. "Oh!" the King exclaimed in happy exuberance. "Magical Truth glasses! I have *always* wanted a pair of these! You just put them on, and then you know the Truth, right?"

Cagliostro shook his head. "Not exactly, Your Majesty…"

The enchanter walked to the mirror and placed both his hands over the decorative frame at the top as if he were delivering a kind of benediction. There was a distant sound like wind chimes as another nearly invisible swirl of twinkling points of light began to wink and dance across the large surface of the mirror.

"One form of the power of Truth you seek can now be found in this looking-glass," Cagliostro explained. "This gift from your parents, King Bernini and Queen Donatella, is now a Mirror of Truth. When you wish to know if someone speaks truthfully, first put on the spectacles…"

King Theramo nodded and quickly put on the glasses. He immediately winced in pain. "Oh! Ow!" he exclaimed in discomfort. "They're a bit uncomfortable, aren't they?" he went on unhappily, trying unsuccessfully to better adjust them. "Rather painful, in fact…"

Cagliostro nodded. "Sometimes the Truth hurts, Sire. I regret I can do nothing about that."

King Theramo continued to struggle with the position of the glasses on his nose and over his ears before noticing that a trace of a smile had crept onto the enchanter's face.

"Do you take pleasure in my discomfort, Cagliostro?" asked the King.

The enchanter shook his head. "Indeed I do not," he explained earnestly. "Your Highness misunderstands. I regret not only your discomfort, but as well I am now regretting the style of the glasses I have given you. It… It is not your best look, Your Majesty."

"Ah, I see," replied the king. "So, what amuses you is not my pain induced from the spectacles, but merely the unfortunate and unintentionally comical effect the spectacles have on my appearance."

"Yes, Your Majesty," Cagliostro agreed politely.

With more futile re-adjustments, King Theramo attempted for a few moments longer to reduce the pain of the glasses before giving up. "A complication with no immediate resolution…" he sighed, resigning himself to the discomfort. "Very well, Cagliostro. What happens next?"

Cagliostro took a step back and gestured with a large hand toward the mirror. "Wearing the spectacles, you can now see how the Mirror of Truth responds to any statement which is spoken aloud."

"I don't understand…" said King Theramo.

"Observe…" instructed the enchanter, turning to face the mirror and speaking to it directly. "I am swimming in the castle moat," said Cagliostro.

Shimmering instantly into view within the reflection of the looking-glass in large distinct letters were the words: A LIE.

"I am an enchanter," Cagliostro went on.

The previous words faded instantly away, and now shimmering into view within the reflection were the words: THE TRUTH.

King Theramo audibly drew a breath as he gasped in happy astonishment. "It's extraordinary!" he exclaimed. "Unbelievable…!"

"No one else can see what you are now seeing," said Cagliostro. "Only if you are wearing the spectacles can you see what the Mirror of Truth has to tell you."

The King stared at the words in the mirror with elated incredulity. "So, even if someone else were here," he said, "still I would be the only one able to see what the mirror says?"

The enchanter nodded. "Only the person who wears the spectacles can see the message of the mirror."

King Theramo could hardly contain his appreciative delight.

"Cagliostro! You have done it! You have given me the power I so desperately need!"

Cagliostro smiled kindly back at the King.

King Theramo now hastened to remove the spectacles. After taking the glasses away from his face, he began rubbing the bridge of his nose and tops of his ears with his fingers to try to push away the soreness.

"And now," the enchanter continued. "The second magical power…"

Chapter 4

The Bi-Scepter
and
The Invitation

King Theramo carefully folded the magical spectacles flat and slipped them securely into a wide pocket deep within his royal robes, but never took his eyes off Cagliostro.

Cagliostro's powerful hands again emerged from within his own robes, this time holding what at first appeared to be two long narrow glittering cylindrical metal objects side by side in parallel, but was in fact a single object composed of two identical shafts hinged together at one end. The device was elaborately ornate and decorative, crafted from gold and silver, and in length was as long as the span of the King's forearm.

"This," Cagliostro explained, "is a Bi-Scepter. As you can see, it is like a king's scepter, but it is made up of two separate pointing-rods. Thus, it is actually two scepters attached together at one end. The two shafts swivel apart and can be aimed in two different directions at the pointing-ends, while always being still connected and joined at the base end by the hinge."

"It is an exquisitely beautiful object indeed," observed King Theramo. "Magnificent to behold, and truly unique in its design. But... What does it do?"

"Something the likes of which your mind has never before

contemplated," said Cagliostro. "With this Bi-Scepter, you may switch bodies with another creature or person."

"Wait… What?!" exclaimed the King, unable to grasp what he was being told.

"Switch bodies," repeated Cagliostro. "You can leave your body and enter the body of another, while that person or creature leaves their own body and enters yours."

King Theramo was slowly shaking his head in amazed disbelief. "It's… It's extraordinary…! But, how does it work…?"

Cagliostro took hold of the Bi-Scepter so that he grasped one scepter-shaft in each hand, then spread the device apart at the pointing-ends like calipers or map dividers or a drawing-compass. Showing King Theramo how the two pointing-rods were hinged together at the base-end of their handles, Cagliostro continued to swivel the two conjoined staffs apart, moving them so that their aim was angled in two different directions. The same shimmering points of sparkling lights that had danced around the spectacles and the surface of the Mirror of Truth danced about the Bi-Scepter as well, with the same nearly invisible twinkling.

"Aim one pointing-rod of the Bi-Scepter at yourself," explained Cagliostro. "Aim the other pointing-rod at the person or creature whose body you desire to switch into."

The enchanter now indicated a large green gem embedded in the grip-handle of one of the pointing-rods, located just underneath where his thumb currently rested on the shaft.

"By pressing this emerald," Cagliostro went on, "you activate the magic of the Bi-Scepter. You will then transpose a creature or person into your body, and simultaneously transpose yourself into the body of that creature or person."

King Theramo was nearly unable to speak from amazement. "It's unbelievable…!" he managed to exclaim. "But, how will this remarkable device help me? Within this extraordinary magic, where is the power of seeing the Truth?"

Cagliostro swiveled the two pointing-shafts of the Bi-Scepter together, where they interlocked back into each other side-by-side with a soft precise metallic click.

"Sometimes," explained the enchanter, "seeing the Truth means to see the world from the vantage point of another. Sometimes seeing the Truth means seeing when no one knows it is you who are watching. Within the body of an animal, you may go where you will, hear what you will, see what you will. No one could ever possibly suspect that you are you, thus no one will adjust their words for your ears or modify their deeds for your eyes. You shall see things as they are when you are not there, yet you will be there. Whether you temporarily inhabit the body of an animal, or the body of another person, you will learn Truths you could never discover as yourself. You will be present, yet you as King Theramo will be unseen. The body of the creature or person you have transposed into will be your veil, and through that veil you will behold Truths you otherwise would never know.

"Amazing…" breathed King Theramo. "Truly amazing. And, what of the creature or person who is transposed into *my* body?"

Cagliostro nodded. "That creature or person shall live in your body until such time as you switch yourself back," he explained, handing the Bi-Scepter to the King. "The return to your own body is a switch as straightforward as the first. Simply aim the two ends, press the emerald, and the switch will occur."

"It's incredible…" said King Theramo, carefully taking the device from Cagliostro.

"The power of the Bi-Scepter," the enchanter added, "does include one slightly macabre attribute. I hesitate to mention it, and I bring it up only because I know Your Majesty sometimes engages in royal hunts to commemorate certain festive occasions. If you were to transpose yourself into the body of, say, a *dead* animal, the body of that animal would then come to life with you inside of it, and your own body would now be dead, with the deadness of the animal inside."

"That's a rather grisly scenario," said the King.

"Indeed," agreed Cagliostro. "A peculiar situation arising only under very particular circumstances, and thus unlikely to occur. I share the information with you solely in the interest of full disclosure."

The King nodded, captivated by the awesome power and subtle beauty of the Bi-Scepter in his hands, turning it over and marveling at its wonder from different angles, until he noticed a feature he had not previously seen.

"Cagliostro," said King Theramo. "There is a little counter. On the pointing-shaft without the emerald button, here on the handle of the other scepter. What is its purpose?"

"What number does it say?" asked the enchanter.

King Theramo inspected the small counter more closely. "It says… *Four.*"

Cagliostro nodded. "Then you need not worry yourself about it."

King Theramo looked at the Bi-Scepter for a moment longer, then carefully slipped the device into another pocket deep within his royal robes. "Cagliostro," he said. "These gifts you have given me are miraculous. With these magical powers, I shall at last gain control over my life, over my kingdom, over my future. I am indebted to you more than I could ever repay…"

"Your Majesty," Cagliostro said carefully. "With great power comes great responsibility."

King Theramo paused and looked back at the enchanter. "Cagliostro, the very fact that you believe in me enough to entrust me with these wondrous gifts gives me the confidence to know that I will make only prudent use of this magic. Because of your faith in me, I am quite certain that I will not mis-use these extraordinary powers.

"By your own words, Your Majesty," said Cagliostro, "your very opinions are shaped simply by the words of whoever has spoken to you most recently."

King Theramo's air of jubilance became momentarily deflated. "Yes…" he lamented. "Indeed. It is too true, and even now I see that I have once again proved that bleak assessment to be cruelly accurate. But, what am I to do? How can I use magic to change my life if I cannot be trusted to use magic until my life has changed…?"

"There is a way," said the enchanter. "It is simple, but imperative:

you must tell no one of these powers you now possess. If no one knows of the magic you have, you need not fear the words of others manipulating you into mis-using your powers."

"Tell no one…?" the King asked anxiously. "Not even those upon whom I depend to help me make vital decisions about critical matters? The implementation of this magic may involve the most important choices I ever make. How will I get the guidance I rely on in such crucial situations? May I tell no one at all? Not even Tartaglia, my most trusted Prime Minister?"

"Let no one know of the existence of these powers," said Cagliostro. "In success, there will be time enough to share with those you love the knowledge of what you have kept to yourself. But if others learn of the magic you now control, success may never be attained. You have sought these powers to make things better. It would be bitter irony and a tragic loss if ultimately they serve only to make things worse."

King Theramo nodded in agreement. "You are of course completely correct," he said firmly. "No one should know of the existence of this magic until it has successfully served its purposes for the powers of Good."

"Your Majesty must persist in that conviction even when I am not the one who has spoken to you most recently," the enchanter cautioned.

King Theramo nodded with guilty embarrassed understanding. "I… I vow to do my utmost, Cagliostro. It is an endless wrestling match with myself that I never win. But I understand what is at stake, and I am resolved to find a way to persevere…"

Cagliostro nodded. "As you have recognized," he said confidently, "I would not have entrusted you with such potent magic if I did not believe you would use it in good faith. Whatever happens, it is my firm belief that all will turn out for the best."

"Thank you, Cagliostro," said King Theramo. "It is my most ardent wish that you yourself shall somehow benefit from all that you have given me here today."

Cagliostro bowed with polite respect to the King. "Your Majesty is too kind," said the enchanter. "Thank you, Sire."

"And now, to action…!" declared the King with enthusiastic animation. He quickly turned in the direction of the castle and stepped for a moment toward the cypress grove.

"Graphiare! Pentimento!" the King summoned, calling out in a loud commanding voice, before returning toward where he had been standing with Cagliostro.

Even before King Theramo had made his way back to the enchanter, the two scribes had appeared with industrious eagerness out from the cypress grove, scurrying cheerily along the marble walkway. Efficiently wielding their parchment sheaves and inkwell rings, with quill pens poised they swiftly made their way to the King.

"Yes, Your Highness?" they said together in enthusiastic unison.

"Take down this message." King Theramo instructed them.

Rapidly nodding their tonsured heads, they flipped open the caps of their inkwell rings with expert dexterity, dipped the tips of their pens in the ink, and with the quietly coarse scratching of quills on vellum began swiftly scribbling away in calligraphic and pictorial precision even before the King had begun to dictate.

"*Dear Tartaglia, Pantalòné, Sir Balzanno, and Avogadro,*" King Theramo began. "*I am at last ready to resume my mission of finding the right young lady to be my Queen. I am aware that you have family members—daughters and sisters—whom, for a long time, you have rightly believed deserve to be considered in this process. I thank you for your patience and your loyalty. To make amends for the delay, I will be interviewing your family members immediately. If you have a daughter or sister who wishes to become Queen, I hereby invite you to please send them to meet with me right away here in the Palace Gardens. Sincerely, Your Royal Majesty, et cetera, et cetera.*"

Graphiare and Pentimento happily finished their work and looked up at the King with bright-eyed expectancy.

King Theramo looked down at them. "Did you get all that?" he asked.

"Yes, Your Highness!" they said together in proud unison.

"Good," said the King. "Now, go deliver it to my advisors."

"No, Your Highness!" the two scribes said together.

"What?!" exclaimed King Theramo indignantly. "How dare you! This is a direct command from your King! You will carry it out at once!"

"My Lord, we cannot," said Graphiare.

"What do you mean?" demanded the King. "What are you talking about? Why can't you?"

"We have explicit orders, Your Highness," Graphiare replied.

"Not to participate," said Pentimento, "in any events that occur within the Kingdom."

"*Documentation...*" recited Graphiare.

"*Without participation!*" recited Pentimento emphatically.

"It's the *Non-Interference Clause,*" Graphiare explained.

King Theramo was incensed. "Oh, don't be ridiculous," he said with irritation. "Everyone knows there's no such thing as a *Non-Interference Clause!*"

"You wrote it yourself, Your Highness," said Pentimento.

The King paused for moment.

"Oh..." he said at length, remembering. "Oh, yes. I supposed I did..."

King Theramo unconsciously adjusted his crown. "Very well," he sighed. "That will be all. You are dismissed. Please send Leandro in on your way out."

"No, Your Highness!" Graphiare and Pentimento said together.

King Theramo looked down at the two bright-eyed scribes and waved his hands at them in frustrated exasperation. "Oh, good heavens! Out! Out!!"

"Thank you, Your Majesty," Graphiare said politely, bowing.

"Thank you, Your Majesty," said Pentimento, bowing respectfully.

The two scribes flipped closed their inkwell rings, turned, and scampered cheerfully off back along the marble walkway toward the cypress grove and the castle, their fleet feet unseen beneath their monasterial robes, the pointed-peaks of their cowl hoods bouncing jauntily on their shoulders as they went.

With some vexation, King Theramo watched them depart for a moment before again taking several decisive steps in the direction of the castle, toward the cypress grove.

"Leandro!" the King summoned loudly, and then returned to where he had been standing with Cagliostro.

"Cagliostro," King Theramo began cautiously, "I… I expect there is no chance you might be able to stay for a while here in Benebento… To… To make sure I don't get into trouble…"

"No, Your Majesty," said the enchanter. "I'm afraid that would be impossible. As you might imagine, I have other pressing issues elsewhere that demand my presence."

The King nodded. "Of course…" he said. "I suppose I must seem a bit like your assistant Truffaldino, promising you I that won't get into any trouble…"

Cagliostro looked earnestly back at the King. "Your Majesty," he said steadily. "You and Truffaldino have in common only one thing, and that is that I care very much about you both."

King Theramo nodded slowly and smiled. "That is a kind sentiment indeed," he said quietly. "If you would be so good as to please convey to your assistant that I am honored to be in his company in this regard."

Cagliostro nodded. "That is very gracious of Your Majesty," he said. "I will of course share your thoughts with Truffaldino. It will mean a great deal to him, I am sure."

"Cagliostro…" the King went on. "Will I see you again…?"

"There are things even an enchanter cannot know, Sire."

King Theramo nodded with regretful recognition. "Of course. I understand completely."

At that moment, Leandro rushed obediently into the gardens, his single long curl of ink-black hair bouncing half coiled across his forehead as he dashed to where King Theramo was standing, then bowed and knelt at the King's feet.

"Your Majesty," he said dutifully.

King Theramo nodded. "Arise, Leandro. I have need of your assistance, with a matter of utmost importance…!"

Leandro stood up. "Your Majesty," he replied in readiness.

"Please see to it that all necessary arrangements are made to immediately set up this portion of the gardens as an audience area, with chairs, a table, and anything else you deem necessary and appropriate for a series of royal interviews."

"Yes, Your Majesty," said Leandro.

"And I have an extremely specific and important invitation message that must be conveyed to my four closest advisors, post haste."

"Yes, Your Majesty," said Leandro.

"But first, Leandro," King Theramo continued. "You will please be so kind as to show out our esteemed guest, the enchanter Cagliostro. We deeply regret his departure, but we are profoundly appreciative of his visit."

"Yes, Your Majesty," said Leandro, and with a respectful nod and a slight bow, he turned expectantly toward Cagliostro.

Wisps of smoky vapor had begun to faintly reappear around

the enchanter's movements, as if he might be on the verge of dematerializing, or in some other way about to vanish.

Cagliostro turned toward the King. "Your Majesty," he said. "I leave you with these final thoughts of guidance. Truth is but one kind of information, and information alone is not knowledge. Neither Truth nor knowledge alone or even together can engender good judgment. It is only bad judgment—and what ultimately is learned from it—that can truly lead to good judgment. This is a Truth that I hope may lend you reliable footing should you stumble during your climb to success."

The King nodded anxiously. "Without your help, I would be unable even to attempt the ascent. For now, however, for me, the upward journey begins with the first step of a quest for Truth."

"Good luck be with you, Sire," the enchanter said respectfully. "I bid you adieu."

"Good luck be with you, Cagliostro," said King Theramo, nodding gratefully to the enchanter, then turning and nodding to Leandro.

Cagliostro paused a last moment to bow respectfully to the King. "Thank you, Your Majesty."

Leandro, too, paused for a brief moment, only long enough to bow to the King. "Thank you, Your Majesty," he said, before turning toward the cypress grove and proceeding to lead Cagliostro away toward the interior of the castle.

And with that, the enchanter's visit came to an end.

King Theramo watched the two of them depart, then walked

over to the mirror and stood before the reflection. After a moment of contemplation, he reached into one of the deep pockets within his royal robes, taking out the spectacles and putting them on. He immediately winced from the instantaneous discomfort.

"Upon my word," he said with emphatic displeasure. "These are, beyond any comparison, the most painful things I have ever worn…!"

Shimmering instantly into view within the reflection of the looking-glass in large distinct letters were the words: THE TRUTH.

King Theramo looked in surprise at the message that had appeared in the mirror, then touched the side of the glasses as realization came to him, and he laughed.

"Indeed," the King mused aloud. "For a moment I neglected to remember your purpose and your great power…"

The previous words faded instantly away, then shimmering into view within the reflection again were the words: THE TRUTH.

The King laughed again, nodding in agreement with the looking-glass for a moment, until a wave of seriousness washed over his thoughts.

"It is lonely being king," King Theramo said quietly. "And I do not wish to rule alone. Yet, I would rather rule alone than have the wrong Queen at my side."

The previous words in the looking-glass faded instantly away, then shimmering into view within the reflection again were the words: THE TRUTH.

King Theramo nodded and now hastened to remove the spectacles from his face, rubbing his nose and ears with his fingers to again try to push away the ache.

"Verily, that is a uniquely intense discomfort," he said with unhappy amazement, glancing at the mirror and then looking down at the spectacles in his hands. "But to be able to know the Truth at last, that is worth enduring any pain."

Chapter 5

The Parrot
and
The Departure

"**I** didn't do anything wrong!" Truffaldino announced hastily.

Cagliostro had exited the Castle Delprego through the vast arched opening in the towering outer gatehouse and was striding purposefully across the drawbridge to meet Truffaldino on the other side.

"Honestly, Sir," Truffaldino explained as the enchanter approached. "Chancellor Pantalòné and Sir Balzanno *invited* me to join them in the Royal Dining Hall for some trencher bread and ale. Well, they didn't exactly invite me. But they didn't object to me sharing their company and partaking of some liquid refreshment and a few trifling comestibles…"

"Truffaldino—" Cagliostro began as he arrived at where his assistant was awaiting his return.

"And I only had one pint of ale, Sir," Truffaldino went on quickly. "Well, okay, maybe it was two pints. But no more than three. Honestly, Sir. And I hardly had any trencher bread. And I didn't in any way interfere with any of their—"

"Truffaldino," Cagliostro repeated.

Truffaldino paused. "Yes, Master?" he said with guilty apprehension.

"You didn't do anything wrong," said the enchanter.

"I… I didn't…?" Truffaldino asked cautiously.

"No, you didn't," said Cagliostro. "Your brief social sojourn with the two advisors caused no trouble whatsoever."

"Oh, thank goodness," Truffaldino exhaled with considerable relief. He lifted up the map he had been holding and showed it to Cagliostro.

"Look, Sir," Truffaldino said proudly, pointing to a place on the map. "Thanks to the young lady Nicoletta, I've totally figured out how to use the MAP OF HERE you gave me. Look, I'm right over here…" Truffaldino began waving one of his arms and looking at himself waving on the map. "See…? That's me! Waving! Are you impressed?"

"The MAP OF HERE is a tool, not a toy, Truffaldino," said Cagliostro.

Truffaldino stopped waving. "I'm sorry, Master," he said slowly, looking crestfallen. "I just wanted to show you—"

Cagliostro held up one of his large powerful hands and smiled. "You've done a fine job with the map, Truffaldino," he said earnestly.

"Thank you, Master!" said Truffaldino, beaming. "Though," he added, looking back at the map more closely and squinting intently, "*you* don't seem to be here, Sir… You're supposed to be next me. You see? This is me here on the map…" Truffaldino began waving again. "I'm the one waving," he explained. "And this is where you should be, Sir. Right here next to me on the map. But you're not anywhere to be seen…"

Cagliostro nodded. "I prefer to remain more elusive to locate," he said.

"You're hard to find, alright..." Truffaldino agreed, looking up from the map and taking a break from waving. Then he noticed the fresh wisps of vapor swirling around the enchanter's robes.

"Oh..." observed Truffaldino. "Is our work here finished, Sir? Is it time for us to move on? Are we leaving now?"

Cagliostro paused before answering. "Do you like it here in Benebento, Truffaldino?" the enchanter asked.

Truffaldino nodded. "Except for that Tartaglia fellow. He is so grumpy and irritable. I don't think he likes anyone, including himself. He also seems dangerously devious. I wouldn't want to be on the wrong end of his scheming, whatever it is. I don't know what Nicoletta sees in him."

"Love is its own way of seeing, Truffaldino," said Cagliostro. "Love is a common language, but its individual dialects can indeed be mysterious, at times to the point of incomprehensibility."

"Is that how I will be?" asked Truffaldino. "Whenever I finally encounter the young lady with red hair you've told me I'm destined to fall in love with? Will you start to wonder what's wrong with me? Will I be unable to think about anyone or anything but her? I'll behave strangely, but I'll think I'm behaving normally? And you'll wonder what my problem is?"

Cagliostro smiled. "I expect so," he said. "It may not be quite so extreme and debilitating. But yes, I think what you've described is reasonably likely."

"Well," said Truffaldino, "I suppose if someone as decent as

Nicoletta is that much in love with Tartaglia, there must be some good in him somewhere…"

"That may not necessarily be so," said Cagliostro. "Love often is neither clear-eyed nor fact-based. But I agree with you, Love sometimes perceives a goodness that can be seen by no other. We shall wish for Nicoletta that that is the case with her Prime Minister Tartaglia."

Truffaldino eyed Cagliostro with suspicion. "Is there something you're not telling, Sir?" he asked skeptically. "Do you know something about this Nicoletta-Tartaglia business?"

"I know only about issues that involve magic," the enchanter replied vaguely.

Truffaldino's forehead wrinkled in perplexity. "I feel like there's something I'm not seeing…" he mused aloud with dissatisfaction.

"No need to fret, Truffaldino," Cagliostro advised. "The mind often is at its best when left to work on its own. Sometimes the solution to the most inscrutable puzzle will present itself if you just look away from the problem for a while."

Truffaldino nodded uncertainly. "I confess, I do not always understand what you tell me, Master," he admitted. "But you still are my favorite teacher. No one teaches a lesson better than you, Sir. And I suspect that you often secretly hide the real lesson disguised inside of words that seem to be about something else entirely…"

"You continue to be an apt learner," said Cagliostro. "But tell me," he went on. "What other impressions have you of this realm and its people?"

"Master," Truffaldino began, gesturing with one hand toward

the map. "Benebento is such a friendly open kingdom. And everyone is free to come and go as they please from the palace. Townspeople, livestock, even some of the forest animals roam freely and safely. I've seen woodland creatures coming and going from the local forest as if they hadn't a care in the world. What a remarkable welcoming peaceful warm happy place this is."

Cagliostro smiled. "You like animals, Truffaldino," he said.

Truffaldino nodded emphatically. "If the animals aren't afraid of the people, it must be because no one treats the animals badly, and that means the people are good people."

"It is a good kingdom," said Cagliostro. "The King has a good heart, if not yet a good ability to rule. It is the goodness of his heart that guides the land."

"Benebento has a nice feeling to it," agreed Truffaldino.

"And you really like it here?" Cagliostro asked.

"Oh, very much, Master. But, not enough to want to part with you, Sir. My most favorite place still is to be at your side. Or, to be at your beck-and-call, for those times when you need me to just stay out of the way for a while."

"You are a loyal apprentice, Truffaldino."

"Thank you, Sir!"

"I am thoroughly pleased that you wish to continue to be my assistant," Cagliostro said firmly. "That is my preference as well. However, I have a bit of business in another kingdom that is truly of a most ordinary and insignificant nature. And should you wish to remain here in Benebento a short while longer, whilst I attend to these few other rather banal matters, I would grant you permission to stay here without me until such time as I have concluded my other business. If such was your wish."

"Are you sure you can take care of everything without my help?" asked Truffaldino with concern.

"I shall endeavor to do my best on my own," said Cagliostro. "Should the need arise, I shall of course summon you from here without hesitation."

Truffaldino nodded. "Okay, Sir," he replied, rolling up the map and slipping it back into his belt-pouch."

"In my absence," said Cagliostro. "You will need to take initiative and be independent."

"I won't get into any trouble, Sir," said Truffaldino earnestly. "I give you my word."

Cagliostro nodded. "And, I shall be leaving in your charge a companion of sorts."

"Sir?"

"You have countless admirable qualities to recommend you, Truffaldino," said Cagliostro. "Your affinity for animals is among your most noble strengths of character. In that regard, I shall be asking you in my absence to take care of an animal particularly dear to me. And it will keep you company until my return."

"But…" Truffaldino began, extending his left arm toward Cagliostro, palm open in a gesture of apprehensive confusion.

The air over Truffaldino's left hand shimmered and sparkled. Sounds like distant wind chimes twinkled in the air for a moment, then all went back to normal, except now there was a parrot perched on Truffaldino's hand, gently gripping his fingers.

"Oh…!" Truffaldino exclaimed, taking a moment to process what had just happened. He eyed the parrot and brought his hand and the bird closer toward his body cautiously, as if he feared the creature might at any moment take off and fly away.

"But…" Truffaldino now protested. "Sir, I have no leather gauntlet. And the animal has no hood. And no jesses!"

"My heavens," said Cagliostro. "It's not a hawk, Truffaldino. It's a parrot."

Truffaldino looked at the parrot more closely. "Well, Master, whatever it is, it is a particularly calm and pleasantly colorful creature."

"I have always had a strong attachment to this animal," said Cagliostro. "Though I confess, I do not understand why."

The parrot blinked at Cagliostro, then gently and purposefully sidled across Truffaldino's hand onto his sleeve, whereupon it proceeded to clamber upward, making its way up the length of Truffaldino's arm until it reached a more secure and lofty perch atop the left shoulder of his jerkin.

"It's a very personable animal," said Truffaldino. "Wherever did it come from, Sir?"

"I once received it as an odd gift," recounted Cagliostro. "Though, the gesture was secretly ill-intentioned. The poor bird was given to me wrapped in a tangle of evil spells, one of which was designed such that the bird would be an unwitting spy, and unknowingly convey all it saw and heard of my magic back to the one who had set the spell. Though it was no easy feat, I modified that spying spell so that no information was ever conveyed to the evildoer who hoped to receive it. The bird has lived with me for several years now in harmonious happiness, and I have unaccountably become extremely fond of it. I know you will take good care of it, Truffaldino."

Truffaldino had turned his head toward the bird and was trying to focus on it, an undertaking made difficult owing to the close proximity of Truffaldino's face to where the animal was currently perched on Truffaldino's shoulder.

"Sir," inquired Truffaldino. "I wonder why I've never before seen you with this hawk. I mean, this parrot."

"Like information, learning, knowledge, and wisdom," explained Cagliostro, "familiarity must occur at its proper pace and arrive at its proper time."

Truffaldino nodded. The parrot nodded with him.

"That makes sense, Sir," agreed Truffaldino. "I expect there are probably very many things about yourself that you haven't yet told me."

"There is no one I trust more than you, Truffaldino," said Cagliostro.

Truffaldino beamed with happiness. "Thank you, Sir!"

Roiling clouds of vapor now were swirling thickly around the enchanter. "Truffaldino," said Cagliostro. "I will be away at least overnight. You and the parrot will require food and lodging."

There was a distant sound like wind chimes, followed by the abrupt jingling of metal coins clinking together from somewhere inside Truffaldino's belt-pouch, which now suddenly bulged slightly wider and sagged slightly lower on Truffaldino's hip.

"There is an inn next to the taverna in town," continued Cagliostro. "I am confident you will be able to locate it using the MAP OF HERE."

Truffaldino reached down to feel the heft of the newly arrived coins weighing down his belt-pouch. "Thank you, Sir!" he said appreciatively.

"You have achieved resourceful success with mastering the map, Truffaldino," said Cagliostro as the vapor thickened around him. "I rely on you to always be alert and strategically learning, even in my absence."

"I promise I won't get into any trouble, Sir," repeated Truffaldino earnestly. "I give you my word."

Cagliostro nodded, though the vapor clouding around him was now so dense he could barely be seen. "And I," the enchanter said, "shall be periodically giving you *my* words while I'm gone."

A look of confusion came over Truffaldino's face. "Oh, Sir…" he said hastily, eyeing the thickening vapor with mounting anxiety. "Please don't go just yet. I'm not sure I understand exactly what I should be doing while you're gone. I really need some more instructions, Sir. From you in person, before you leave. While you're still here…!"

"King Theramo of Benebento paid you a high compliment, Truffaldino," said the voice of Cagliostro.

"He did…? The King…?" said Truffaldino in amazement.

The swirling smoky vapor churned into a full thick cloud, then dissipated completely without a sound. The last of the foggy wisps evaporated without a trace, and the enchanter was gone.

Chapter 6

The Knight's Daughter
and
The Wise Man's Prevision

"Now how am I supposed to figure out what to do next...?" Truffaldino lamented aloud. He looked back across the drawbridge, up toward the lofty turreted towers and looming majesty of the Castle Delprego.

"My master said I needed to take initiative and be independent..." Truffaldino went on. "But he also promised he would give me his words while he was gone..."

"Inn next," the parrot said matter-of-factly into Truffaldino's nearby left ear. "Inn next."

Truffaldino turned his head to look at the vibrantly colorful bird perched on his shoulder. This brought his face so close to the parrot's that the animal's beak was now nearly touching Truffaldino's nose.

"Yes!" agreed Truffaldino, smiling appreciatively. "Yes, of course. Of course! Thank you, parrot. Thank you!"

The parrot tilted its head to one side and blinked at Truffaldino.

"My master mentioned how well I did with the map..." remembered Truffaldino, and he was reaching down to his belt-pouch to retrieve the map when the warm dusty ground and the quiet afternoon air were disturbed by quick footsteps hurrying closer.

The young lad Italo was trotting rapidly toward Truffaldino and the parrot, looking around anxiously as he approached.

"Greetings, traveler," Italo said breathlessly, skidding to a stop in front of them. "I am Squire Italo, apprentice to Sir Balzanno."

Truffaldino nodded. "Greetings, Italo," he said cordially. "I remember you from this morning. I am Truffaldino, assistant to the enchanter Cagliostro."

Italo nodded politely and wiped sweat from his brow as he continued to breath heavily and work to catch his breath from running. "Truffaldino, have you seen my master come through this way?" he asked anxiously.

Truffaldino shook his head. "Sorry, Italo," he said sympathetically. "I'm afraid I can't help you. I haven't seen Sir Balzanno. Why do masters always expect us to know where they are, but they always make themselves impossible to find?"

Italo nodded his head in emphatic rueful agreement, bending forward and placing his hands on his knees to position himself to breath more easily. "It is rather vexing," he panted unhappily.

"Knight! Knight!" announced the parrot.

Truffaldino turned again toward his shoulder to look the parrot closely in the eye. "No," said Truffaldino. "No, it's way too early for bedtime. And besides, I haven't even found the inn yet…"

Italo stood back up straight, and for the first time noticed the colorful bird perched nonchalantly on Truffaldino's shoulder.

Truffaldino looked away from the parrot and put a hand companionably on Italo's shoulder. "Italo, why not come along with us?" he offered. "We're just about to head into town. We're going to the inn."

Italo was staring at the parrot in amazement. "What... What is it?" he asked.

"You know. An inn," Truffaldino explained patiently. "A little place where you stay and eat and sleep."

Italo looked from the parrot, to Truffaldino, and back to the parrot again.

"Knight! Knight!" repeated the parrot.

Italo shook his head. "I wish *I* were a knight," he said wistfully. "I wish I were a knight. I've always hoped to become a knight one day..."

Truffaldino nodded sympathetically. "Well," he said, "for now, why not come along with us to the inn? You can even show us where it is."

"I'm afraid I can't, Truffaldino," said Italo. "I have too much work to do for Sir Balzanno. Honestly, with all the chores and errands he gives me, I don't think I'll ever get to become a knight. I won't have time! But at the moment, I really do have to find him or I'll be in too much trouble..."

"Two! Two!" declared the parrot, looking off into the distance and blinking.

"You are too, too repetitive," observed Truffaldino. "You are too, too repetitive. Why do you do that?"

"Two! Two!" repeated the parrot.

"Yes, yes," said Truffaldino. "Exactly. Exactly! Why do you say everything two times? Why do you say everything two times?"

Truffaldino in exasperation slapped his hand against his head. "Now you've got *me* talking like a hawk. I mean, like a parrot!" he muttered with frustration.

The parrot continued to look past Truffaldino and Italo, over their shoulders, in the direction of two steadily approaching figures.

Still some distance away, the two figures—Sir Balzanno and a young woman—were having an animated discussion as they walked along the road toward the drawbridge where Truffaldino and the parrot and Italo were standing, as yet unnoticed by the knight and the maiden who were immersed in their own conversation.

"But my dear Smeraldina," Sir Balzanno was saying to the young woman. "It is *because* you are my daughter that this momentous opportunity has presented itself. Per the King's royal invitation, I and Tartaglia and Avogadro and Pantalònè, as valued members of the King's inner circle, are having this prized privilege extended exclusively to our daughters and sisters. It is an extraordinary honor, and an unprecedented opportunity."

"But Father," Smeraldina was saying. "It is so very peculiar to be in competition with my friends. Just look at who is now competing for the job of Queen. Tartaglia's sister, Clarìcé," Smeraldina began, pronouncing her name as *clah-REE-chay*. "Avogadro's daughter, Nicoletta," Smeraldina went on, "and Pantalònè's daughter, Angiolina. We are all friends, Father, yet now we find ourselves all vying for the same position, for the occupation of Queen."

Smeraldina moved her arms with emphatic animation as she talked. A shoulder strap of her dress had slipped down to one side, and eventually she had reflexively pulled it back up, but a moment later it had slipped back down to its previous position halfway down her upper arm, where it seemed to prefer to return to and remain no matter how often she re-adjusted it, which—whether from lack of awareness or lack of concern—was apparently infrequently.

"But my dear daughter," the knight admonished severely. "Just look at your inappropriate attire…! You are dressed more for the taverna than you are for an audience with your King!"

Smeraldina shook her head and tossed her flowing red hair back over one shoulder dismissively. "We each must do the best we can with what we have, Father. My face is not as beautiful as Nicoletta's, my soul is not as lovely as Clarìce's, my heart is not as pure as Angiolina's. But when I walk into the taverna, every young man there wants to marry me. Every young man at the taverna has proposed marriage to me, many times! I have said no to them all. I have broken the hearts of as many young men as King Theramo has dashed the hopes of young ladies seeking to be his bride. Other girls cover themselves not because they are modest or proper but because they have nothing to show off. If I am to seduce the King, I must be dressed for the occasion. Men can dream of what they imagine, but they actively desire to possess that which they can actually see. One cannot sell one's finest wares without bold advertising."

"Dear daughter!" Sir Balzanno exclaimed, mortified. "This is neither a tawdry game nor bawdy sport. This is marriage! To the King of all the land! This is a matter of the utmost gravity. It is not a trifle!"

Smeraldina again shook her head. "Alas, dear Father," she

explained. "To me, it *is* a mere trifle. I can embrace the *challenge* of convincing the King to want me for his Queen, but I cannot take such a marriage seriously. Marriage without love is not a prize one seeks with earnestness to win. It must be approached for what it is: an objective to be attained, not a true aspiration of the heart."

Sir Balzanno looked more mystified than ever. "You do not love our King…?" he asked his daughter in baffled disbelief.

Smeraldina shook her head, again flipping her vibrant red hair back over one shoulder. "Do I need to love him in order to become Queen?" she replied. "Clarìcé, Nicoletta, Angiolina, me… Only one of us is actually in love with King Theramo. And it is *not* me! Yet we are all four of us *all* going to the interview. Does any one of us really have a choice? Say 'no' to our King? Say 'no' to our family when a 'yes' from the King would change our family's lives for the better forever? No. We do not have a choice. As competitors we each shall strive to win the job of Queen, and as friends we all shall cheer whichever one of us triumphs in the contest. Though, dozens if not hundreds before us have undergone this same interview process, and none has ever been selected by the King, so who's to say if it should even be one of the four of us who ultimately prevails in this most peculiar manner of royal marital selection."

Sir Balzanno halted their forward walking progress and turned to confront his daughter, the troubled contortions of paternal anxiety ranging across his face. "My dear daughter," he said gravely. "Should I request of the King to exempt you from this process? If your heart is not in it, how can I in good faith as a father subject you to such a hollow endeavor? The memory of your dear departed mother, Heaven rest her soul, would never forgive me!"

Smeraldina's face softened for a moment into a loving smile and she came to a stop with the knight, turning to place her hand with filial affection on the shining armor of his shoulder. "Dear Father. Look with me for a moment at my current life. Am I now *married* to the man I truly love? Am I now *betrothed* to the man I truly love? Am I now *with* the man I truly love? No, no, and no. Better to find a new path, than stand in place or remain on the same path that has not led to where you want to go. My current course has not brought me to love, nor has it brought True Love to me."

Sir Balzanno studied his daughter intently in further concerned confusion. "But, my dear Smeraldina," he asked, bewildered. "Who is the man you truly love?"

Smeraldina shook her head again, flipping her shining hair over one shoulder. "Either he has never been born," she said, "or else I have never met him. But it is *not* the King. I do not love the King. To become Queen would not be to join myself with the love of my life. It would be to elevate our family status."

"Then surely," Sir Balzanno protested, "that alone cannot be adequate justification for you to proceed on this path toward attaining an outcome you do not truly desire...?"

"Venturing nothing accomplishes nothing," Smeraldina explained simply, re-adjusting the errant strap of her dress, which promptly slipped back halfway down her upper arm. "Although I cannot from here see how going to an interview with the King will bring True Love into my life, it assuredly can do no worse for me than I myself have thus far done. And what is the worst that could happen? I could become Queen! And Father," she added with a sly wink, "if I am Queen, just think of the amazing outfits I shall get to wear. Never again will you feel embarrassed at my garb. I shall be dressed like a queen!" She laughed, and twirled elegantly.

For a moment Sir Balzanno was unable to speak, and his mouth hung slightly agape as he attempted to process what his daughter was trying to help him understand.

Smeraldina concluded her glamorous spin with a flourish, then turned resolutely and resumed walking with brisk purpose forward, while her confused father was left with no choice but to turn as well and hasten to keep pace with her as they proceeded.

"Why," Smeraldina went on robustly, "do I say 'no' to all the young men in the taverna who propose marriage to me? Because I do not love them. There is no point in accepting the proposal of a man whom you do not love. When some of the young men of the *nobility* have proposed to me, however..." She paused for a moment. "I have considered it more carefully, I admit. Though I still have always said 'no'. But if a girl is to marry a young man whom she does not love, there must at least be a compensating benefit to make more bearable a lifetime of not being with the man you love. Nothing could ever possibly take the place of being in love. To be Queen would not be as wonderful as being in love. But being a not-in-love queen would be better than being a not-in-love baroness or a not-in-love duchess. Wealth and status and power cannot bring happiness. But they can help to keep away unhappiness."

With their lively pace, and with Smeraldina striding confidently forward and caught up in the vehemence of her sentiments, and with Sir Balzanno trying his best to keep up and process it all, they both were oblivious and unaware that their progress had brought them right to where Truffaldino and the parrot and Italo were standing at the foot of the drawbridge.

Smeraldina, though propounding adamantly on the topic of where she desired to be going, was however not looking where she actually was going, and at the moment when she and her father arrived at the drawbridge, she unaccountably lost her footing and tripped precipitously forward.

"Watch your step! Watch your step!" the parrot cautioned, but too late. The momentum of Smeraldina's forward motion had colluded by circumstantial conspiracy with her stumble, disrupting the stability of her step and propelling her suddenly headlong. She was saved at the last instant from hitting the hard dusty ground only by the quick reflexes of Truffaldino's unhesitating reaction as he caught her in his arms.

"Oh!" cried out Sir Balzanno as his instantaneous alarm as swiftly became profound relief. "Oh, I say! Thank you, young man!" he exclaimed at Truffaldino. "My daughter Smeraldina is about to have a life-altering audience with the King, and it would never do for her to have a broken bone or a dress soiled with dust from the street! Even," he added under his breath disapprovingly, "if there is but a brazenly meager amount of dress…"

Neither Truffaldino nor Smeraldina had moved since he had caught her. Her momentum had caused him to pivot and lean far to one side as he had cushioned and slowed and safely halted her descent, and now he was bending over her, holding her in his arms as if he had dipped her at a fancy dance, and there in that position they remained, Truffaldino looking down at her, Smeraldina looking up at him.

"Oh!" exclaimed Smeraldina, continuing to lay back nearly horizontal as though she were reclining on a couch. "How unlike me… I've never fallen before…!"

Oh!" Truffaldino exclaimed breathlessly, supporting her with one arm around the back of her waist and the other around her back as he gazed down at her. "It's… It's you…!!"

"Yes, it is me," laughed Smeraldina. "I don't know who else I'd be. Except, maybe, the next Queen of Benebento…!"

Truffaldino could not contain his amazement. "You're the one," he breathed incredulously. "I can't believe it. We've actually found each other…! You're the young lady my master told me about. You're the girl with the red hair that I'm destined to fall in love with…! My master is the enchanter Cagliostro, and he told me it would happen, and I was hoping it would happen, but I don't know if I actually ever really believed—"

Smeraldina put a finger up to Truffaldino's lips to gently but firmly stop him from speaking. "Shhh…." she said affectionately, her red hair draped down and hanging inches from the ground. "You don't need to say everything all at once."

Truffaldino nodded agreeably. "You are the love of my life, Smeraldina," he sighed happily, still holding her.

"Silly boy," said Smeraldina smiling up at him. "We've only just met."

"That's okay," Truffaldino reassured her confidently. "We're destined to be together."

Smeraldina laughed again. "Perhaps…" she said cheerily. "We shall see what Fate has in store for us." She reached up and softly ran her fingers through Truffaldino's wavy brown hair.

Truffaldino smiled with shy happiness.

"What did you say your name was?" asked Smeraldina.

Truffaldino shook his head. "I didn't," he explained simply.

Smeraldina smiled and nodded. "Would you like to tell me now?"

Truffaldino nodded enthusiastically. "Yes," he said, still holding her steadily in his arms. "Yes, I would. That would make me very happy."

Smeraldina looked up at him for a moment then giggled. "In addition to wanting to tell me, perhaps you could also actually tell me?"

Truffaldino nodded again, "Sorry," he said apologetically. "It's so very confusing meeting the love of your life…!"

Still holding Smeraldina in the saved-from-falling position, Truffaldino now tried to get himself and the situation re-oriented, and he carefully raised Smeraldina up, fluidly lifting and re-setting her, back to an upright position where she could stand on her own. Somewhat reluctantly, Smeraldina allowed Truffaldino to take his hands away from holding her, and he nervously and self-consciously tried to re-compose himself by straightening his garb.

Like an inverted plum-bob or a ship's compass gimbaled in a binnacle, the parrot had throughout remained perched on the left shoulder of Truffaldino's jerkin aligned the entire time in true vertical, irrespective of any of Truffaldino's body movements, and the colorful bird continued to remain as discreetly silent as a tactful waiter serving a romantic candle-lit dinner for two, and as unseen as a chameleon.

Smeraldina smiled and raised her arms to put both her hands gently around either side of Truffaldino's face. "And so, will you tell me your name now?" she asked.

"Um…" struggled Truffaldino, increasingly flustered. "Okay, wait. Don't tell me… I know this…!"

In frustration, Truffaldino slapped his hand against his head. "Oh, Truffaldino," he chided himself unhappily. "This is a fine way to present yourself to the love of your life. What a great first impression. You finally meet her, after a lifetime of hoping, and then you can't even remember your own name…!"

"Truffaldino!" repeated Smeraldina with a smile, still affectionately holding his face in her hands.

"Yes?" replied Truffaldino. "Oh! Yes!! That's it! That's me! That's my name. I'm Truffaldino!"

"It's a fun name to say," said Smeraldina. "Truffaldino?"

"Yes, Smeraldina?" said Truffaldino.

"Why is there a colored bird on your shoulder?"

"Being the assistant to an enchanter involves a lot of different kinds of things," explained Truffaldino. "At the moment, it involves having a new friend who says everything twice and also happens to be a hawk. I mean, a parrot."

Smeraldina grinned fondly back at him, her eyes flashing. "Oh, my dear Truffaldino. I know not what I expected, but you are definitely not like anything I ever imagined. How funny. How delightfully unpredictable. I quite adore you, dear Truffaldino. For now, however," she sang animatedly, gently taking her hands from his face and adjusting her dress, "I'm off to convince the King to ask me to marry him. Wish me luck!"

"I'll do nothing of the sort," said Truffaldino matter-of-factly. "And I shall be waiting for you when that game is over," he added amiably.

"Italo!" Sir Balzanno exclaimed with impatient dissatisfaction.

"Right here, Sir!" Italo replied dutifully.

"Italo! Why are you always hiding from me?!" the knight scolded reprovingly.

"I'm sorry, Sir," Italo said with resigned contrition. "It's a bad habit, Sir."

"Well, you're a good squire, Italo," Sir Balzanno consoled magnanimously. "I'll forgive you."

"You're very understanding, Sir," said Italo with patient fortitude.

"Now Italo," Sir Balzanno went on pointedly, "about that broadsword…

"Yes, Sir," Italo acknowledged, nodding with relief. "The sword-smith put a marvelous edge on it, Sir."

"Send it back!" ordered the knight.

"But Sir!" Italo protested. "You gave the armorers exact

specifications! And they crafted the sword precisely as you wished!"

"Italo!" rejoined Sir Balzanno, wagging an emphatic index finger. "Have you any idea how sharp that thing is?!"

"Very sharp, Sir," confirmed Italo. "Just the way you wanted it."

"Oh, do come along, squire!" Sir Balzanno remonstrated. "No one wants a sword THAT sharp! I accidently knocked it off the rack and it nearly cut through two floors down to the basement! That weapon is dangerous! Someone could get hurt!"

"But, Sir," Italo demurred. "You wanted a sharp weapon!"

"A lot of good it will do me if I accidently cut my hands off trying to pick it up!" declared Sir Balzanno, raising his arms with open palms and fingers splayed in expressive emphasis. "It's too sharp, Italo. Send it back!"

Italo's shoulders slumped in defeat. "Yes, Sir…" he said with respectful resignation.

"Smeraldina," instructed Sir Balzanno turning toward his daughter. "Do come along now, my dear. If we are going through with this, we mustn't convey disrespect to His Majesty with a delayed arrival."

"Don't worry, Father," Smeraldina said airily, twirling around and tossing her hair glamorously. "No matter when we arrive, my entrance shall be memorably spectacular."

"Or spectacularly inappropriate," the knight muttered under his breath with deep parental dissatisfaction.

Sir Balzanno turned momentarily toward Truffaldino. "Thank you again for your assistance, young man," he said formally.

"I—" Truffaldino began.

"Italo!!" exclaimed Sir Balzanno.

"Right here, Sir," answered Italo with respectful weary obedience.

"Proceed with us across the drawbridge," instructed Sir Balzanno. "I have some other important chores and errands for you to accomplish that I must explain to you in precise detail."

"Of course, Sir," Italo replied valiantly.

Sir Balzanno and Italo and Smeraldina had started off across the drawbridge toward the grand entrance of the castello, when Smeraldina turned and dashed back for a moment to where Truffaldino still stood with the parrot. Standing on tiptoe, Smeraldina leaned up to Truffaldino and wrapped both arms around his neck. "Thank you for catching me," she said smiling.

"We caught each other," Truffaldino explained happily.

"You're sweet," said Smeraldina. One of her feet lifted of its own accord behind her, causing her leg to bend elegantly upward at the knee as she raised herself on higher tiptoe and kissed him on the cheek.

"Ciao for now, dearest Truffaldino," she sang brightly at him, untangling herself and stepping down and away from him, all the while never fully letting go of him, sliding her hands down the length of his arms, to end up grasping his hands fondly in hers for a last moment.

"I'll wait for you, no matter what," said Truffaldino. "Even if, to make your family happy, you marry a man you don't love. I'll still wait for you. Our hearts belong together, and our hearts will always be together, even if we ourselves are not."

Smeraldina squeezed Truffaldino's hands tighter, then finally forced herself at last to let go, turning and dashing off to rejoin her father and Italo.

Truffaldino watched Smeraldina hastening away toward the drawbridge, moving farther away from him with each lively skipping step. Then he turned his head the other way as far as it would go to the left so that he could clearly look at the parrot.

"You have very good manners, Parrot," Truffaldino said appreciatively.

"Good parrot!" exclaimed the parrot. "Good parrot!"

Truffaldino reached up and gently petted the parrot carefully on top of its head. "That is the truth," agreed Truffaldino. "That is the truth."

The parrot closed its eyes and tilted its head to let itself be petted for a moment, then announced, "Map! Map!"

Truffaldino nodded, reached into his belt-pouch, and withdrew the map.

"Inn next," said Truffaldino, unrolling the map in his hands as they started off in the direction of town. "Inn next."

As Truffaldino and the parrot were heading away from the far side of the drawbridge on one road, via a different path Nicoletta and her father Avogadro were making their way toward the entrance to the drawbridge, arriving just after the departure of Truffaldino and the parrot, but not before Smeraldina, Sir Balzanno, and Italo had finished crossing the drawbridge.

"Father, look…" said Nicoletta as she and her father stepped onto the interlocking massive ancient wooden slabs that made up the weathered formidable bolted surface of the drawbridge.

"Yes?" replied the wise man.

"It's Smeraldina. Up ahead of us. She's with her father and her father's apprentice Italo, and she's already heading into the castle for the interview."

Avogadro placed a hand mystically to his forehead and nodded with deep sagacity. "Yes..." he declared. "Yes, I knew that..."

"Father?" said Nicoletta.

"Yes, my child?" replied Avogadro, lowering his hand and recovering himself after the intensity of his mystical update.

"Father, must I interview with the King?"

"Yes, my dear. I'm afraid it's mandatory."

"But I thought the King's message said it was an *invitation*. Invitations are supposed to be optional."

Avogadro's long whitish hair swept back and forth as he shook his head with worldly regret. "My dear, if there is one thing I have learned as a wise man, it's that an invitation from a king should never be considered optional."

Nicoletta's shoulders drooped in resignation as she and her father continued side-by-side and began to make their way across the drawbridge. "It's no good, Father," she sighed. My heart belongs to another. Even if he doesn't know or care..." she added, almost to herself.

The wise man nodded hastily. "My dear," he said quickly. "There are some things a father is better off not knowing."

"But Father," said Nicoletta. "You know everything."

"Uh… Yes, that's true," agreed Avogadro. "You're right. So, since I know already, you don't have to tell me."

Nicoletta nodded.

The wise man's colorful robes continued to billow like polychromatic clouds, undulating copiously in his wake as he strode alongside his daughter.

"Father," said Nicoletta. "Tell me, will Theramo choose me to be his Queen?"

"Theramo is a good King," the wise man replied without hesitation. "He often has trouble deciding which advice to follow, but he usually bumbles into doing the right thing. And he is seeking a young lady *who loves him*. And that is not you, my dear. No. He will not choose you."

"Oh, Father!" Nicoletta cried joyously, grasping her father's hand as they walked, relief flowing from her voice and washing across her face and uplifting her bearing. "Thank you, Father! No one has a better father than I do!!"

With awkwardness and immense paternal love, Avogadro lightly patted the top of his daughter's head with his free hand as they walked. "You have always brought me great joy, Nicoletta," he said quietly. "I am a lucky man. I have always asserted that I would rather be lucky than wise, yet because of you I am blessed to be both."

Nicoletta smiled shyly, overwhelmed with filial love for her father, as the two of them made their way together toward the vast arched opening in the towering outer gatehouse of the magnificent Castle Delprego.

"Come now," Avogadro proclaimed boisterously, resuming his comfortable idiosyncratic flamboyancy. "Let us now proceed, with our thoughts directed undaunted toward significant matters at hand. You are about to be interviewed by the King!"

Chapter 7

The Prime Minister's Proposal
and
The Confession

As Avogadro and Nicoletta finished crossing the drawbridge and together passed through the great arch of the outer gatehouse into the castello, the Prime Minister and an unhappy-looking young woman walking with him were just arriving at the far side of the drawbridge.

"Odds bodkins!" the Prime Minister exclaimed with irritated displeasure. "Of *course* you must do as I tell you!! Listen to my words carefully, Clarìcé. Surely I need not remind you that as your brother and your elder, since the death of our parents, by lawful precedence I hold full sway over your actions. *All* your actions! And as Prime Minister of the entire Kingdom of Benebento, I possess yet *further* power to ensure that you shall not disobey my will. Do not attempt to argue this point with me any longer. Odds bodkins!"

"But brother—" Clarìcé attempted to begin.

"No!!" bellowed the Prime Minister furiously. "You will address me as 'Your Lordship'! This flagrant disrespect is intolerable!"

Clarìcé nodded with forlorn acquiescence. "Yes, Your Lordship," she said softly.

"Now speak no more to me of evading your interview with the King," commanded Tartaglia. "You *are* going to the interview. By my exercising of *my* royal prerogative, you *will* interview *first*, ahead of the daughters of the King's other advisors. And most crucial of all, Clarìcé, you will ensure that *you are chosen* by Theramo to be his Queen. I have plans, sister. Specific unalterable plans. I will not permit you to ruin them."

"But Your Lordship," Clarìcé said carefully. "I am not in love with King Theramo…"

"Odds bodkins!! That is no concern of mine! Oh, yes, sister, I have heard the ridiculous rumors. I know that you think you are in love with that sniveling palace guard Leandro."

Clarìcé nodded. "It is true, Your Lordship. I am in love with Leandro. And he is in love with me."

"It is an insult!!" raged Tartaglia. "He is but a mere palace guard! You are the sister of the Prime Minister!! He is fit only for bowing to you as you pass! You are to be the queen of all the land! But none of that even matters! I have plans, sister. And no part of my plans involves you being in any way associated with a lowly palace guard! *You will be marrying the King!* You will be solidifying our family connection to the Crown. And you will be making it possible for me to marry a young lady who I have long been patiently planning to have for my own, my very own, to possess in every way as my wife. And I will not allow anyone or any thing to obstruct my path!! If I catch that wretched guard trying to interfere with your interview with the King, you have my promise that I shall make sure he is cast into the Royal Dungeon, never again to see the light of day!"

"Brother, no!!" cried Clarìcé in panicked horror.

Tartaglia pointed a long unkind finger at Clarìcé. "Well, then!

If you wish to keep his worthless soul from being interned for the rest of his insignificant life, then make sure you have no contact or interaction of any kind with him from this moment forward. No words, no looks, no tokens, no messages, nothing! If I so much as catch you making eye contact with him, that will be the end of his freedom forever, and you will certainly never see him again. Do you understand?"

"Yes, Your Lordship…" Clarìcé said, fighting back tears.

"Now stop fretting about a preposterous relationship that of course was never going to happen and *is never going happen*, and start focusing on how you are going to make sure the King chooses *you* to be his Queen. Focus! Focus!! Odds bodkins!"

Two more people now approached together from a different road, heading toward the drawbridge. Chancellor Pantalònè and a young woman at his side were walking with steady purpose, their current path bringing them toward the place where Tartaglia was standing with Clarìcé.

Their approach did not for an instant escape the eye of the Prime Minister. "Behold…!" he exclaimed to his sister in a suddenly pleased voice. "There, Clarìcé! Observe the young woman now coming this way, and learn a lesson in perfection. The daughter of Pantalònè, the exquisite Angiolina…! There she is… That is the epitome of everything a young lady ought to be, everything the wife of the Prime Minister should be…"

"But, brother," Clarìcé began, "Angiolina and I are dear friends. We—"

"Silence!" hissed the Prime Minister in a low tone. "Not another word out of you! I shall first speak with the lady Angiolina and the Chancellor her father, before you and I continue on our way to the King's interview. Do not move from this spot, sister. Do not speak nor gesture. I shall be but a moment…"

Clarìcé stood motionless and said nothing.

Tartaglia moved with quick eager confidence over to Pantalòné and his daughter Angiolina, stepping in front of them and compelling them to halt their forward progress.

"Greetings, Chancellor," Tartaglia began deliberately.

"Prime Minister," Pantalòné acknowledged with polite formality.

Tartaglia allowed his hungry eyes to turn toward the Chancellor's daughter. "And," he continued with honeyed words. "Most felicitous greetings to you, my very dear Angiolina."

"Your Lordship," said Angiolina, tilting her head slightly forward in stiff courtesy.

"I see you are compliantly deferring to the King's perfunctory invitation and are now en route to Theramo's amusing interview," remarked Tartaglia.

"More an honor than a duty, Prime Minister," Pantalòné clarified politely.

"More of a formality, really," said Tartaglia, riposting with a clarification of his own. "Since he will of course be choosing Clarìcé to be his Queen. But I do not begrudge him going through the motions of permitting two or three others to speak their mind. That makes it all seem less pre-determined, don't you agree?"

"Indeed, it certainly does not seem pre-determined," Pantalòné replied diplomatically.

"And yet, *it is!*" Tartaglia laughed heartily at his own comment for a moment.

Tartaglia then became serious and advanced toward Angiolina.

"I have plans for you, my Angiolina," the Prime Minister confided confidently, looking Angiolina steadily in the eye. "Plans for *us*. When all this interview nonsense is over and Theramo has chosen Clarìcé to be his Queen, I shall ask you, Angiolina, to be my bride. You and I shall be married. It will be as it was always meant to be."

Angiolina's expression betrayed no reaction and she did not look away. "Your Lordship is far too kind," she replied with unemotional civility.

Tartaglia smiled widely. "I shall of course first ask from the Chancellor, your father, permission for your hand in marriage," he said matter-of-factly, casually casting a momentary knowing glance toward Pantalòné.

"Of course you will," the Chancellor replied simply. "It would be improper and unlawful otherwise."

Tartaglia's smile widened. "Of course," he said with a dismissive wave of his hand. "A mere formality, but a quaint tradition nonetheless."

"An issue for deliberation at some other time," Pantalòné said evenly. "But for now, Prime Minister, we all serve at the pleasure of the King. The interviews await. It would be dishonorable to keep His Majesty waiting."

"Without question, Chancellor," Tartaglia grinned, turning back to stare at Angiolina. "Very well then, Angiolina. Until later…" he reached to take Angiolina's hand to kiss it, but Angiolina locked the fingers of her hands together.

"Your Lordship," said Angiolina, tilting her head slightly forward again in stiff courtesy with polite finality.

Tartaglia grinned and withdrew his hand, bowing grandly at her, and then turned to stride back over to where he had been talking with Clarìcé.

Immediately Tartaglia realized that Clarìcé had taken crafty advantage of her brother's attention being fully diverted to Angiolina. Clarìcé was gone.

Furious and alert, Tartaglia whirled around first one way then another. "Clarìcé…? Clarìcé!!" he roared, incensed and searching. At last he spotted her, all the way on the opposite side of the drawbridge, the flurried end of her dress visible for a fleeting moment before disappearing through the lofty arch of the great gatehouse that led into the Castle Delprego.

"Odds bodkins!!" howled Tartaglia in rage and frustration. In an instant, he had dashed swiftly past Pantalòné and Angiolina, his long legs propelling his tall frame rapidly forward, the subdued hues of his formal robes trailing darkly behind him, a grim shadowy streak speeding across the immense timber of the drawbridge span. "Clarìcé!" he called angrily out ahead of himself as he ran. "Oh, it shall be the worse for you when I catch up with you, you miserable disrespectful disobedient sibling…!!!"

Pantalòné and Angiolina stood for a moment, still on the far side of the drawbridge.

"Father," said Angiolina. "That man alarms me…"

"Tartaglia is the King's most trusted advisor," said Pantalòné.

Angiolina shook her head. "He's frightening."

"He was not always that way," said Pantalòné. "Some change came over him…"

Angiolina put her arm around her father's arm, and the two of them together proceeded on their way toward the interview, beginning their crossing over the monumental drawbridge, high above the placid surface of the gently moving water far below them, the moat encircling the Castle Delprego, the wide waters of which were of such great length in order to surround the entirety of the magnificent and sprawling castello, that it was nicknamed affectionately as a 'river' by the Benebentoans. And as it was dynamically fed from the tireless outpouring of two different underground fresh water sources whose wellspring force was so potent that a constant current persisted in the moat waters as they perpetually flowed in their unending circuit around the vast distance of the massive hewn stone foundations of the castle, a current which—albeit continuous—nevertheless moved at a rate sufficiently leisurely that one could keep pace with it while walking around the far-side perimeter, the moat had further earned its nickname The 'River' Andante.

"Father," said Angiolina. "There is word going around of an enchanter…"

The Chancellor said nothing in response.

"King Theramo is said to have consulted with an enchanter," Angiolina went on. "And everyone is talking about it…"

Pantalòné nodded. "That sort of talk is to be expected," he replied evenly. "Consulting with an enchanter is highly unusual."

"But why has King Theramo called upon the services of an enchanter? Benebento does not in any way seem to be enduring any manner of crisis." Angiolina looked suddenly alarmed. "Is it the King himself?" she asked quickly. "Is he not well? What is it that troubles him?"

Pantalòné looked curiously at his daughter as she walked at his side. "You seem earnestly concerned on his behalf," remarked the Chancellor.

"I…" Angiolina hesitated. "I just… I simply am concerned—as a subject and a citizen—for the welfare of our King. As would be any subject or citizen of the Kingdom. He… He is our monarch and our ruler, and he reigns over all our land. His welfare necessarily affects the welfare of the entire kingdom, and thereby any individual one of his subjects."

"My dear," said Pantalòné. "You always have patiently and patriotically understood that my position with the King requires me to remain silent on countless issues of state. The job, and the King I gladly serve, demand a confidentiality that is unequivocal, a confidentiality that I wholly believe is appropriate and proper and necessary."

Angiolina nodded. "Yes, Father. Of course. I know. I do understand the necessary constraints on anything you're permitted to say…"

"However," the Chancellor went on. "I will say, that it does seem as though the King's consulting with the enchanter has, directly or indirectly, put wheels of all sorts into motion. It certainly has emboldened the darker more base impulses of the Prime Minister. Tartaglia's distasteful expectation that he would ever be permitted by you or by me to marry you is no surprise, but it is a bit more distasteful that he has actually now spoken his intentions aloud and attempted to presume there is any possibility it might happen, which there of course is not."

Angiolina momentarily smiled a grim and knowing smile of unsurprised acknowledgment, and squeezed her father's arm with nevertheless appreciative gratitude.

The two of them walked on together in silence for a few moments as they neared the castle-side of the drawbridge. As they approached the lofty arched opening of the towering gatehouse, Angiolina stopped their progress and turned to face the Chancellor.

"Father," she began slowly, "I have a confession…"

"My dear…?"

Angiolina looked away for a moment, then took a breath and turned back to face her father. "I am in love with the King," she said. "I am in love with King Theramo…"

The Chancellor looked at her steadily. No trace of either surprise or recognition showed in his expression. "Then you must tell him," Pantalòné said simply. "Today. At your interview."

Angiolina looked down, shaking her head. "No, Father. No, I can't. I could never. It is too embarrassing…"

The Chancellor took both of his daughter's hands in his own and gazed down at her. "King Theramo seeks the Truth, my dear," he said. "The Truth is more precious to him than wealth or power. You need have no fear of telling him the Truth. The Truth is what King Theramo seeks. He has gone to extraordinary lengths to ensure that he can know the Truth. You must tell him the Truth."

"No, Father. I cannot. He would only laugh at me. I couldn't bear it. I would die of shame and sadness. It would break my heart…"

"My child," said Pantalòné. "If your dear mother were still alive, what do you suppose she would say to you at this moment?"

"To… to be true to myself…"

Pantalòné nodded.

"Oh, Father, I'm so scared…"

The Chancellor squeezed his daughter's hands with gentle firm reassurance. "The situation you are about to enter upon is daunting," he said. "But you needn't be afraid of the Truth. And you needn't be afraid of the love in your heart. And you needn't be afraid of our King."

"But he doesn't love me. How could he love me? What am I to do when I hear him utter the words that he doesn't love me? I can't bear to hear him say it…"

"I can support you with what I hope is the benefit of my thoughts and my points-of-view," said Pantalòné. "But I cannot tell you what to do or say. I never have and never will. When the time comes, you will do what is right and best for you, whatever that may be."

Angiolina's face was clouded with uncertainty. "How can you

have such faith in me, Father?" she asked. "I haven't even faith in myself..."

"My child," said Pantalòné. "That is what fathers are for. I do have complete faith in you. Be true to the kingdom, be true to your King, and most important, hold tight to the words of your dear mother who loved you so—be true to yourself."

Angiolina stood immobile for several moments, then nodded an unconvinced but understanding acknowledgment of the view that was being shown to her. "I love you, Father," she said quietly.

"Nothing is more precious to me than your happiness, Angiolina," said Pantalòné. "I am proud to be your father. I love you very much."

Letting go of each other's hands, they turned again toward the castle and proceeded forward, the Chancellor receiving respectful momentary tilt-of-spear-tip salutations from the two stalwart palace guards positioned impassively at either side of the entrance to the outer gatehouse as Pantalòné and his daughter passed through the vaulted archway and into the castle beyond.

Chapter 8

The Witch
and
The Change of Plans

At nearly the same moment as the Chancellor and Angiolina were entering the castle, a tall slender ominous woman in a darkly colored heavily-flowing gown and weighty cape strode forth from a dusty side street, trailed lightheartedly by the two cheery scribes Graphiare and Pentimento. A dimly glimmering necklace with an enigmatic symbol pendant that hung from an eerie chain and draped below her low-cut plunging décolleté neither bounced nor swayed with her grim steps as she appeared to glide along, her unseen feet seemingly never touching the ground. Above the severe features of her blood-red lips and high chiseled cheekbones and arched angular eyebrows, an imposing black Gothic headdress layered in arrayed rows of menacing ornamental finials studded with dusky gems curved in from either side to a downward point below the summit of her high forehead, cutting a sharp helmet-like line of contrast against the ghostly pallid whiteness of her skin, covering nearly all her dark hair pulled tight against her head, accentuating the slight sylph-like points of her ear-tips, and roundly framing her gaunt features and pale complexion and piercing humorless stare.

"You'd better make sure you spell my name right," she admonished the two ascetics in an icy voice. "Or I'll cast a spell on you and turn you both into monkeys."

Graphiare and Pentimento had the caps of their ingenious inkwell rings flipped open and were industriously dipping their quill tips and scribbling text and illustrations on the topmost pages of their hand-held sheaves of vellum.

"Fat Morganna, the witch…" narrated Graphiare as he scratched out precise calligraphic text across the coarse surface of the parchment page.

The witch's gliding came to a halting stop as she turned the penetrating focus of her unforgiving gaze to the two scribes.

"It's not *Fat*! It's *Fatta*! I am the witch Fatta Morganna!" she declared with irritated pride, pronouncing her name as *FAH-tuh mor-GAH-nuh*.

Graphiare nodded agreeably and continued to write without looking up from the parchment page. "Okay, Feta," he replied with simple deference.

The incised details of numerous ornate rings adorning the witch's white wraithlike fingers glinted variously in the light of the afternoon sun as she lifted her hands in annoyance.

"It's *FATTA*. FAH-tuh," she corrected impatiently. "I'm not some sort of sheep's-milk cheese."

"Goat's-milk cheese?" suggested Pentimento helpfully.

Fatta Morganna pointed a long bony finger at the two scribes. "When I get my powers back," she said grimly, "I shall wave my wand and curdle your blood into whey."

Graphiare and Pentimento paused in their scribbling and looked up at the witch. "No whey!" they both protested in unison.

"Whey!" the witch averred categorically.

The two ascetics bent their heads back to their vellum and resumed writing, the feathered ends of their pens once again dancing about in the air as their quill tips scribbled across the parchment pages with diligent purpose.

"Fat Morganna the witch dreamed of making artisanal cheese..." narrated Graphiare as he wrote.

The witch lifted her hands in open-palmed indignation. "Do I look fat to you?" she demanded accusingly.

The two scribes paused in their scribbling again to look up at Fatta Morganna.

"No," said Pentimento impassively. "But you don't look particularly 'Fatta' either."

The witch pointed a threatening ring-laden finger back at the two scribes. "Well, you just make sure I turn out glamorous and elegant in your manuscript paintings. Or it will be the worse for you!"

"No it won't," Pentimento replied simply.

"You said yourself, your powers of magic don't work anymore," said Graphiare.

Fatta Morganna re-aimed her finger speculatively upward. "But they could come back very easily," she asserted with firm confidence. "Especially if my plan works!"

The two ascetics nodded and busily returned to their pen-and-ink depictions.

"Another evil plan…" Graphiare narrated.

"Doomed to failure…" narrated Pentimento.

Fatta Morganna waved her hand dismissively. "Write what you like," she said with cool indifference. "But you'll see!"

"The witch dreamed of the old days…" Graphiare narrated, his quill scratching briskly across the vellum as he wrote.

"When her powers still worked…" narrated Pentimento, his hand energetically steering the delineation of a detailed sketch.

Fatta Morganna smiled. "It was glorious!" she reminisced with poignant pride and a wistful sigh. "Even my wickedest of desires could be accomplished with a mere wave of my wand."

"Compulsively greedy…" Graphiare narrated.

"No impulse control…" narrated Pentimento.

"I did exactly as I pleased," Fatta Morganna declared with satisfaction. "And I did it well. No one was more wicked than I, and no one's magic was more powerful than mine. With one wretched exception. That cursed enchanter Cagliostro. He didn't even know I existed, but I knew about him. Years ago, I came up with a marvelously evil way to spy on him. I was sure he would never suspect the magical trick I was attempting. I was convinced that after spying on him, I would learn some of his deepest secrets, so that I could use them to my advantage and make his magic less powerful, and make my own magic more powerful. But my plan failed. I still don't know what went wrong. It was such a great plan. Somehow it was stopped. But Cagliostro somehow still didn't know I even existed. Even now, he still doesn't know I exist! What a self-centered egotistical fool he is. And I despised all those stories about 'The Great Cagliostro'. All those odious stories of what a great enchanter he was, and how he always used his magic to do good, and how he always worked his magic cleverly so that no one would ever discover how powerful he really was. But I knew how powerful he was. I knew, and I didn't like it!"

"Selfishly resentful…" Graphiare narrated.

"Obsessively competitive…" narrated Pentimento.

"Never satisfied…" the two scribes said in unison, re-dipping their quills into their finger-ring inkwells at the same time.

"Nonsense," Fatta Morganna objected adamantly. "I was perfectly satisfied. I just wanted something more. I just wanted to have the most powerful magic. I just wanted to have better magic than that loathsome goody-good Cagliostro. And I soon found a way to get exactly what I wanted! First, I cast a Finders-Keepers spell so that I would randomly stumble across what I was looking for, even though I didn't know what I was looking for. And then one day while I was walking through the Forest of Aldente, I found it. An ancient tarn with mystical inscriptions carved into the stone.

"A tarn is a mountain lake or pool…" clarified Graphiare.

"It acts like a cistern and collects rainwater…" contributed Pentimento.

"Well, this one had dried up years before," continued Fatta Morganna. "The basin had no water, and the stone was overgrown with weeds and rushes. I couldn't decipher all of the inscriptions, but I understood enough to realize that this was the site of a magical hundred-year spring. The spring has to be summoned, and will only flow if it hasn't been summoned in the past one hundred years. Once the spring flows, it fills the tarn, but the tarn only stays filled for a few moments. But during those few moments, the water has extraordinary powers that can be accessed by whoever has summoned the spring. Magical powers so potent that they will expand and amplify the attributes of whatever is dipped into the water. So I read aloud the incantation carved in the stone to summon the spring. And I was in luck! In the past one hundred years, the spring apparently had not been summoned!

"It surged up from the bottom of the basin and filled the tarn. The water had a sharp lightning-storm smell that, as a witch of remarkable ability, I recognized right away. It was the smell of uncommon magic. Magic so strong that nothing can weaken it or alter its astonishing properties. I had to act fast because no sooner had the tarn filled, then it already had begun to drain away. Thinking quickly and cleverly, I took out my wand and dipped it into the water. The instant my wand touched the water I could feel my powers begin to grow.

"The tarn drained as quickly as it had filled, but I had done what I needed to do. Or so thought. At first I could feel my powers continuing to grow. And with each passing day I felt myself becoming more powerful. But then something happened. Suddenly my powers began to wane, receding just like the water in the tarn, and too late I realized what I done wrong. When I dipped my wand, the places on the wand where I held it had been covered by my hand. And those places, untouched by the waters of the hundred-year spring, had left my powers vulnerable. And now they were leaking away. The very means

I had sought to use as a way to amplify my powers was taking away not only my new amplified powers, but now was sapping my original powers as well."

"Brought down by her own evil..." narrated Graphiare as he scribbled.

"Thwarted by her own greed..." Pentimento narrated.

"But I wasn't thwarted yet!" Fatta Morganna proclaimed defiantly. "With my powers weakening every second, I raced back to the tarn and cleared away more of the weeds and rushes to see if there was more to the inscription than I had first read. There was more. The vulnerability I was experiencing could be reversed. It would not be easy, but it could be reversed. But I had to act quickly, while I still had some of my powers.

"The vulnerability caused by the partially-covered wand could be reversed only by an extraordinary act. And since my powers of magic are evil, the extraordinary act I needed to bring about therefore had to be an act of extraordinary evil. One that affected the entire kingdom. Being as clever as I am, it was not difficult to figure out what that extraordinarily evil act needed to be.

"The epicenter of the goodness of Benebento is King Theramo. His cursed goodness anchors the miserable goodness of the entire kingdom. Even though he is a fool, he is apparently also a paragon of goodness. So I brilliantly realized I needed to destroy his happiness, and destroy him, and thereby destroy the goodness of the entire kingdom.

"And so while I still had a last reservoir of my powers, I came up with a plan. A plan that would use Theramo's own trusted Prime Minister as the instrument of His Majesty's Royal downfall!"

"Has issues with authority figures…" Graphiare read aloud as he wrote.

"Makes bad choices…" narrated Pentimento.

"Makes things needlessly complicated…" narrated Graphiare.

"Rubbish," said Fatta Morganna dismissively. "It's perfectly simple. It's brilliantly simple. I cast a brilliantly evil spell to make Tartaglia fabulously evil! And no one knew! And still no one knows! But because I had lost so much of my powers, Tartaglia's evil could not occur right away. It needed time to grow. And so I have been forced to be patient. For nearly a year I have been biding my time. But now I need wait no longer. Things are beginning to happen! It's very exciting. And everyone is going to live miserably ever after. Everyone, that is, except for that cursed King Theramo. He will not be doing anything ever after, except decomposing. All thanks to the wondrously spectacular evil of Tartaglia!"

"He's the Prime Minister," remarked Graphiare. "He doesn't seem particularly evil."

"He's an irritable fellow," Pentimento commented. "But nothing serious."

"Ah, but just you wait!" gloated Fatta Morganna with a satisfied smile. "He's an evil tree, ready to produce evil fruit!"

"Fruity!" exclaimed Graphiare, scribbling gleefully.

"Juicy!" Pentimento chimed in.

"Magically delicious!" they both sang in delighted unison.

Fatta Morganna waved away their buffoonery with an

uninterested hand. "Tartaglia knows nothing of what I have done to him," she went on. "But within his mind, the evil grows. And once he puts evil action to his evil thoughts, the King's happiness will be stilled, the King will be no more, the goodness of the kingdom will be brought to ruin, and my powers will return!"

"Likes to manipulate others…" Graphiare narrated.

"Enjoys causing trouble…" narrated Pentimento.

"Well!" Fatta Morganna remarked with unimpressed mild surprise. "You finally got something right, you annoying little scribblers. The Witch Fatta Morganna lives to make miserable the lives of others. Her happiness rises from the ashes of other people's misfortune. Especially when their misfortune has been caused by Fatta Morganna!"

"Randomly refers to herself in third person…" Graphiare narrated.

"Well, there's nothing random about my plan," said Fatta Morganna. "And nothing that can go wrong, either."

She turned toward the drawbridge and lifted an arm in the direction of the castello. The long tapered sleeve of her dark gown dripped like a cave of ink from her bone-white arm as she gestured at the soaring stone battlements, one ring-laden finger pointing significantly. "Behold, fools," she said to the two scribes, "the towering Castle Delprego. Here we stand at the crossroads of destinies. All streets and all routes of life converge to meet at this fateful place: the entrance to the drawbridge path into the castle. One day soon this castle will be mine. First the castle, and then the entirety of kingdom of Benebento. My lost powers will be restored, and from the lofty height of my new throne I shall rule over all the land. It will be magnificent. And even at this very moment, within the very walls of the castle, my plan is already in motion. The dark wheels of my evil brilliance have already begun to turn!"

"Occasionally lapses into poetically malevolent prose…" narrated Graphiare.

"Oh," Fatta Morganna retorted derisively, "I know, you conceited little wordsmiths are so sure no one can describe anything as well as you. Well, just make sure your self-satisfied smugness doesn't get in the way of you telling the extraordinary story of my glorious rise to power with all the grandeur it so marvelously deserves. And now, I have work to do…"

"Witch needs to mend broomstick…" narrated Graphiare.

Fatta Morganna rolled her eyes in disdain. "Oh, please. You've been writing too many fairy tales. I don't have a broomstick!"

"Witch's house has dusty floors…" Pentimento narrated.

"Black cat is always sneezing…" narrated Graphiare.

"Stop it!" insisted Fatta Morganna. "I don't have a black cat, either!"

"Doesn't like pets…" Pentimento narrated.

Fatta Morganna shook her head. "Why do I even bother…" she muttered in contemptuous resignation, and with an ethereal billow of her dark gown and weighty cape, she turned and strode back down the dusty side street, gliding grimly away as if her unseen feet were peeved wheels on invisible polished rails.

"And with that, she stormed off in a huff…" Graphiare narrated, his quill scratching busily across the parchment as he wrote.

Graphiare and Pentimento were not archers, however both wore small side-hip-belt quivers that hung from the simple rope belts girding the waists of their monasterial robes. Protruding from these diminutive quivers were not the fletched feather-ends of an archer's sheaf of arrows, but rather the feather-ends of the two scribes' small arsenal of quills. The flights of the feathers had not been entirely removed, but the plumes had been largely cut back to provide a smooth clean central barrel on each shaft for manageable grip and expedient writing and drawing, while still leaving enough feather at the non-writing end to keep the quill ideally weighted as a writing implement, and to provide sufficiently impressive visual spectacle as the feathered-end sprightly waved and swayed whenever the quill was in use.

The only actual weapon of any kind amidst the scribes' equipage was a slim long-handled knife with a short precise curved blade, housed in a dedicated sheath on the outer skin of each scribe's quill-quiver. Far less able than words inked on a page to inflict grievous wounds, this knife was a crucial tool and indispensably relied upon in the regular maintenance of keeping quill nibs sharp and properly shaped, as well as being employed for erasure to scrape away any scribal mistakes by abrading the vellum's surface and scratching off any occurrences of errant ink or other compositional errors.

The dyes used in creating ink were intended to facilitate the leaving of marks that would be durable and permanent, and possessing perpetual ink stains on the thumb and first two fingers of one's writing hand was the telltale sign of a scribe or playwright or ardent writer of any kind. Constant re-dipping of the quill nib into an inkpot and necessarily gripping the pen close to the business-end produced the unavoidable result of continual stain that could not be washed off and was anyway being continually renewed. For many, this perennial blot was a mark of achievement, a badge of honor worn with indelible pride, and that class of proud writers and artists certainly included Graphiare and Pentimento. The first three digits of their writing-hands indeed bore ink-stains as enduring as tattoos, and they duly had no interest in ever attempting or wanting to clean away this emblem of their preferred choice of vocation and its persistent signification of their own markedly surpassing craftsmanship.

However, the two scribes were as fastidious and idiosyncratic as they were flush with self-esteem, and for the sake of neatness both had chosen to keep a fold of linen affixed to the outer rim of their quill-quivers to wipe away excess ink from a nib before returning any recently-used quill to the container-interior of its hip-belt holder.

It was against one of these two densely-ink-streaked pieces of cloth that Pentimento now wiped the end of the quill he had been drawing with, before replacing it into his quill-quiver and taking out a different quill, one which was longer and had a slightly wider-diameter barrel and broader nib which he dipped quickly into his inkwell ring and resumed his depiction.

"Meanwhile," he narrated significantly. "Accompanied by the

strange bird, the young traveling fellow wended his way through the town toward the inn."

Graphiare nodded. "But he won't be getting a room just yet," he explained, scribbling enthusiastically.

"No room at the inn?" Pentimento suggested.

"Plenty of room," clarified Graphiare.

"An unforeseen change of plans?"

"Significant new directions!" confirmed Graphiare, nodding his head excitedly.

"An unexpected indication of what's to come?" proposed Pentimento.

"A portent!" Graphiare exclaimed with gleeful significance.

They paused to look at each other with avid interest.

"Is it important?" Pentimento asked eagerly.

"Aren't all portents important?" Graphiare replied.

"Except those that are unimportant," agreed Pentimento.

The two scribes nodded collaboratively at each other and dived excitedly back into the flow of their writing and drawing.

"This portent," Graphiare narrated, "comes in the form of crucial new instructions!"

"That the young traveling fellow must follow precisely!" illustrated Pentimento.

"Verbatim!"

"Word for word!"

"To the letter!"

"It's a sign!" they both exclaimed together, and burst into a fit of laughter.

"C'mon, let's go write up our notes!" proposed Graphiare breathlessly.

Pentimento nodded his head in vigorous agreement.

They both hastily made a few final jottings before flipping closed the caps of their ingenious inkwell rings with quick successive clinks. Speedily shuffling and straightening their vellum folios, they looked at each other in happy enthusiasm, then turned and scurried off, animatedly narrating in unison, "And so the two scribes headed back to the monastery!"

The center of town bustled with activity. People were everywhere, dressed in colorful garb, carrying goods, selling wares. Gentry strolled the narrow streets in their finery, peasants clustered in lively gatherings laughing, debating, bantering, bartering. Farmers guided wooden-wheeled ox-drawn carts brimming with hay and freshly harvested crops from their fields, and livestock and children of all sizes milled and gamboled in the teeming midst.

Truffaldino and the parrot were not particularly conspicuous within the diverse current of casual commotion as the map guided them toward the inn, but the parrot did periodically enjoy flexing its wings, and with the vibrant hues of its outstretched plumage and slender long graceful tail, it tended to momentarily resemble a living kite perched on Truffaldino's shoulder, eliciting an occasional curious look or appreciative exclamation.

"We're nearly there, Parrot," announced Truffaldino as they

turned a corner and entered a piazza that was even busier with life and activity, and as pleasantly thronging with sounds and smells as it was with people. One whole quarter of this town square was an elaborate shopping plaza that included an open-air market offering myriad sundry food vendibles, and a bazaar with zealous vendors selling all manner of miscellaneous common and exotic merchandise. Of the residences and merchant shops comprised within the four walled-sides bounding the piazza, the most lively and eye-catching frontage was the taverna, which had a sizable multitude of animated patrons at tables outside vast wide-open windows in the shade of a broad veranda, and a steady stream of revelers flowing in and out though its arched front entry.

"According to THE MAP OF HERE," Truffaldino reported encouragingly, "the inn is right next to the taverna, and so we should now be just about right in front of… Hey, wait a minute. What the…? That's odd… The name of the inn just changed on the map. All this time it's been saying 'The Inn Pizzicato', but now it doesn't say that anymore. The name has changed, Parrot. According to the map, now the inn is called…" He held the map closer to see more clearly. "Parrot, the name of the inn is now called 'Message for Truffaldino'. But, *I'm* Truffaldino…. That's a strange name for an inn… And what happened to the inn's other name…?"

"Sign, sign," said the parrot.

Truffaldino shook his head vigorously to clear his thoughts.

"I know, I know," he said, continuing to study the map in search of an answer. "I need to sign us in when we rent our room…"

"Message from Cagliostro, message from Cagliostro," said the parrot.

"Wait," said Truffaldino, looking up alertly. "Wait, what? What? A message from my master? Where? Where?"

Truffaldino slapped himself on the side of his head. "Parrot! You have got to stop making me say everything twice. It's maddening!"

"Sorry, sorry," said the parrot earnestly.

"It's okay, it's okay," said Truffaldino, reaching up and gently petting the colorful tufted top of the parrot's head. "I know you don't do it on purpose."

The parrot closed its eyes for a moment as Truffaldino petted it. "Not on purpose," the parrot agreed emphatically. "Not on purpose."

"But," Truffaldino went on. "But, Parrot… Where's the message?"

The parrot opened its eyes and looked toward the inn. "Sign, sign," it repeated pointedly.

Truffaldino looked around. "Okay, okay," he said slowly. "I can figure this out. Somewhere nearby, there is a sign of a message from my master…"

Focusing on the side of the piazza where they now stood, Truffaldino intently studied the scene in front of them. "So," he reasoned with slow deliberation. "If that's the taverna…" He looked back down at the map in his hands. "Well… If the name of the inn on the map is now 'Message for Truffaldino', then the name on the inn's sign should also now be…"

He looked up again and squinted for a moment, then gave

a happy exclamation of triumph. "Parrot!" he rejoiced. "That's it! The sign! The inn sign! Not the one on the map, but the one in Real Life right there in front of us. There it is! The name on the inn sign reads 'Message for Truffaldino'! That's where the message is! The sign is a message. I mean, the message is a sign!"

The large sign was hanging high above the entrance to the inn, suspended at both ends by chains affixed to the underside of a strong square wooden beam anchored in the wall structure of the building and extending forward several feet into the air of the piazza. The sign did not face out to the front but rather was aimed facing left and right. With the parrot still perched solidly on his shoulder, Truffaldino took several steps to one side to get a more direct line-of-sight and a better view, whereupon he began to laugh with delight and huge relief.

"Parrot!" he exclaimed happily. "Look, the inn really is named 'Message for Truffaldino'! It says so right there on the sign!"

Of the busy multitude currently occupying the populous piazza, only Truffaldino and the parrot at the moment seemed to be showing any interest in the sign above the inn.

Vague wisps of smoky vapor were now emanating from the inn sign like roiling savor exuding from freshly seared mutton. The sign began to sway slightly, and the individual component parts of the blackletter characters composing the words *Message for Truffaldino* now moved as if alive, rearranging themselves into a steadily changing stream of blackletter text that appeared to move across the face of the sign from right to left, creating the effect of a laterally-scrolling procession of words whose component parts disassembled themselves as they reached the extreme left side and flitted in frantic fragments rapidly back to the right where they were quickly re-assembling themselves into the new words being formed as the message was successively displayed.

Truffaldino carefully read aloud each word as it traversed the painted wooden length of the inn-sign surface from right to left.

"*Message for Truffaldino*," he began methodically. "*Truffaldino, before you enter the inn, first return to the castle and arrange for the parrot to be placed in the Palace Gardens. The parrot is to remain there until I give you further instructions. You may then come back here to the inn and get yourself a room and some food and drink and rest. Tomorrow will be a big day.*"

Other than the raptly transfixed Truffaldino, and the parrot, no one else seemed aware of the sign's uncanny temporary transformation, and the change did not last long. Within moments, the small individual component parts of the blackletter characters that had composed the moving message reverted to what apparently was their true form—full-sized rooks. The sudden legion of noisy black birds flocked in their abrupt raucous horde precipitously off the sign and skyward, leaving behind the now fully-restored erstwhile lettering of 'The Inn Pizzicato' appellation, and ascending stridently away as a haughty mob in an exultant cloud of lustrous black flapping wings and boisterous high-pitched cawing.

Chapter 9

The Guard at the Drawbridge
and
The Parrot in the Gardens

"I keep thinking about Smeraldina..." Truffaldino mused aloud as he and the parrot wended their way out of the town and back toward the Castle Delprego. "I know I should be focused on other things, Parrot. But she keeps twirling into my thoughts. I don't know how people in love ever get anything accomplished, or even get through the day, if the person you're in love with keeps dancing through your mind all the time. It's exciting and nice, but it's so distracting..."

"True love! Cagliostro! True Love! Cagliostro!" the parrot squawked sympathetically.

Truffaldino nodded. "You make a good point, Parrot. You make a good point. I do wonder if my master has a true love he doesn't know about. Maybe, like me, he has a true love somewhere that he just hasn't met yet. It's funny how the message he sent to me at the inn was magically made of rooks. It was a sign. I think my master must miss you very much, Parrot. He seems to have birds on his mind..."

Truffaldino stopped for a moment and looked around. "I like Benebento," he said thoughtfully. "But it's awfully confusing to find one's way around. I've been to the castello once already, and

I still have no clue how to get back there. The Castle Delprego is a pretty important place, you'd think they would make it easier to find…"

Failing to identify anything that might have been a familiar visual reference, he resumed walking in the direction they had been heading.

"Though," he continued, "I guess I'm a different Truffaldino now. I used to be Truffaldino who has never met his true love. Now I'm Truffaldino who has met his true love, and who is now madly in love with her. It's all very disorienting…"

"Use the map, use the map," suggested the parrot.

"Of course, of course," Truffaldino agreed contritely. "You see, Parrot? That's just what I mean. My brain is so busy being happy thinking about Smeraldina, it's too busy to let me remember to use the map."

"Busy, busy," repeated the parrot.

"Exactly," agreed Truffaldino. "Exactly. And my master said the map is a tool not a toy, but it's not a particularly helpful tool if I don't actually use it…"

Truffaldino had been holding the map, but had neglected to look at it after they left the piazza. He now unfurled it in his hands and scanned its surface as he continued walking, the parrot cocking its head to peer at the map and looking up to observe their progress in turns.

"THE MAP OF HERE is very clever," remarked Truffaldino appreciatively, perusing the colorful dynamic surface of the parchment. "Everything in view keeps shifting slightly to keep up with where we are as we're walking. This is one very smart map."

"Smart parrot! Smart parrot!" the parrot squawked adamantly, and flexed wide its brightly chromatic wings.

Truffaldino smiled and reached up to gently pet the top of the parrot's head.

The parrot serenely pulled in its wings and closed its eyes as Truffaldino petted it. "Very good parrot, very good parrot," the parrot extolled helpfully.

"Very good parrot," Truffaldino agreed. "Very good parrot."

The parrot opened its eyes and aimed its curved beak into the air, getting some better scents of the surroundings.

"Andante, Andante," the parrot announced informatively.

"Slower?" Truffaldino asked. "Slower, really? We're already taking longer to get there than I'd hoped."

"River, river," said the parrot.

'Oh," said Truffaldino nodding. "Oh, yes. Yes, I see what you mean. The moat. Well, if we're getting near the moat, that means we're getting near the castello…"

He glanced down at the map for a moment while continuing their progress forward.

"I knew we'd get there eventually," Truffaldino went on. "Being in love puts one in a ridiculously good mood, Parrot. I feel really optimistic and positive about absolutely everything. It's a little bit overwhelming. Though, it makes me think about poor beautiful Niccoletta. She's the one who actually taught me how to properly use this map. Why she's in love with that angry snake Tartaglia I will never understand. But that's who she loves, however it turned out that way. But she doesn't seem happy at all. I mean, she's a really good-natured person, but being in love doesn't seem to be making her happy. It only seems to be making her sad. Maybe that's what happens if the love of your life completely isn't even remotely interested in you. It doesn't seem fair. Though, I suppose that sort of thing probably happens a lot. Probably maybe even all the time. Of course, Smeraldina's about to try to see if she can get the King to want to marry her. That really ought to be putting me in a bad mood, but for some reason it isn't. I just feel really happy and positive and sure that somehow everything's all going to turn out perfectly happily ever after. Which at the moment makes absolutely no sense. Oh, Parrot, it's all so confusing!"

"Happily ever after, happily ever after," the parrot repeated quietly.

A moment later, they reached the end of the dusty side street they had been traveling on and found themselves in the broad open space that was the entrance to the drawbridge path into the castle. And making his way with urgent speed across the drawbridge in their direction was a distraught-looking Leandro, the single long half-coil of black hair curling out from beneath the front of his glittering guardsman's helmet and bouncing in the middle of his forehead with agitated vigor as he dashed.

"Truffaldino…" Leandro said with breathless haste as he reached them. "Have you by any chance seen Tartaglia's sister Clarìcé coming this way?"

Truffaldino shook his head. "Sorry, Leandro," he said apologetically, rolling up the map and slipping it back into his belt-pouch. "I've never met her, so I wouldn't know what she looks like. Though, if she's sister to Tartaglia, I feel bad for her. He's extremely surly."

Leandro nodded in hurried rueful acknowledgment, and glanced anxiously over his shoulder toward the castle before turning back to Truffaldino.

"Truffaldino," Leandro said, drawing in a cautious breath and lowering his voice. "Can I trust you?"

"I like you, Leandro," said Truffaldino. "But even if I didn't like you, you could still trust me. I'm very trustworthy. My master, the enchanter Cagliostro, is always telling me how reliable I am. Which is not exactly the same thing as being trustworthy, but my master is always confiding in me, and he is very particular. And he is always giving me special instructions that he trusts me to carry out exactly the way he's asked. He wouldn't tell me half the things he shares with me or give me responsibility for doing so many things that are important to him if he didn't trust me."

Leandro nodded quickly, the dark lock of his hair bouncing. He glanced again for a moment over his shoulder, then turned back to Truffaldino.

"King Theramo is about to interview the sister and daughters of his four most trusted councilors," Leandro began. "He's interviewing to determine if one of them is the person who would best be suited to become his Queen."

Truffaldino thought for a moment and then nodded. "That explains a lot," he said slowly. "Yes, I've heard some things that didn't quite makes sense, but now it's all becoming more clear. Smeraldina's one of the people being interviewed."

"You know Smeraldina?" asked Leandro.

"She's the love of my life," Truffaldino explained. "I mean, we've only just met, but we're destined to be together."

Leandro looked at Truffaldino curiously for a moment, then appeared to have made a decision. "Claricé and I are in love with each other," he said quickly. "And I've got to speak with her alone before she has her interview with the King."

Truffaldino nodded sympathetically. "Well," he said. "Smeraldina and her father already went into the castle for her interview some time ago. I'll bet Claricé is probably already someplace inside. When do the interviews start?"

"Soon," replied Leandro grimly. "Very soon. Which is why I must return to the palace immediately. But I looked around inside the castle, and I couldn't find her anywhere…"

"Looking for Leandro," said the parrot. "Looking for Leandro."

Leandro looked in the direction of the parrot and saw it for the first time.

"Truffaldino," Leandro asked quizzically. "Truffaldino, why is there a colorful talking bird perched on your shoulder?"

"It's a hawk. I mean, it's a parrot," said Truffaldino. "It belongs to my master. It's also very smart and very helpful. And it says everything twice, which can be a bit exasperating at times, but it doesn't do it on purpose, and anyway I suppose if you're always right about things, then probably it's worth saying them twice. For instance, now we know where Claricé is."

"We... We do...?"

Truffaldino nodded. "The really clever helper parrot just told us," he explained matter-of-factly. "Claricé is in the palace, looking for you."

Leandro gazed in growing wonderment from Truffaldino to the parrot and then back to Truffaldino. "That's extraordinary..." he said with perplexed hesitant relief. "Thank you. Thank you both. Really. Alright, then I must get back into the palace right away."

"Leandro, can I trust *you?*" asked Truffaldino.

A brief smile broke through the anxiety of Leandro's face and he looked earnestly back at Truffaldino.

"Truffaldino," said Leandro. "You are a kind and good person, and a fascinating fellow. And I like you, and I give you my word that you can trust me. Is it something to do with Smeraldina?"

"Well," said Truffaldino. "For me, everything has to do with Smeraldina, because now she's all I think about and she is the love of my life. But this has to do with my master. My master trusts me, and nothing is more important to me than my master's trust. I would sooner die than do anything to make my master ever regret how much he trusts me. And this time, he has trusted me to carry out a specific instruction. The hawk—I mean, the parrot is to be brought to the Palace Gardens, and is to remain there until any further instructions from my master. Leandro, may I ask of you this crucial request? That you bring the parrot to the Palace Gardens and make sure it remains there?"

Leandro extended his hand, and Truffaldino extended his in response, and they each grasped each other's forearm in a bond of friendship and loyalty. "I give you my word that I will do as you ask," said Leandro firmly. "The enchanter's well-placed trust in you is safe with me."

The parrot took this opportunity to step off Truffaldino's shoulder and sidle with agile-clawed dexterity across the front of Truffaldino's jerkin and nimbly down his opposite arm, and from there onto Leandro's arm, crossing the momentary bridge of their mutual clasped handhold, then ambling easily up to a new lofty perch on Leandro's shoulder.

Truffaldino and Leandro released their friendly grip of each other's forearm, and Truffaldino reached over to gently pet the tufted top of the parrot's head. The parrot closed its eyes for a moment.

"Very good parrot," said Truffaldino. "Very good parrot.

"Trustworthy Truffaldino," the parrot said emphatically. "Trustworthy Truffaldino."

Truffaldino smiled. "Thank you, Parrot," he said. "Thank you."

"Godspeed, Truffaldino," said Leandro.

Truffaldino nodded appreciatively. "I expect I'll see you on the morrow," said Truffaldino. "The message from my master said it's going to be a big day."

Leandro nodded. "I must first somehow get through this day…" he said anxiously, and the concern and immediacy returned to his face.

Truffaldino and the parrot exchanged a final glance.

"Use the map, use the map," said the parrot.

Truffaldino reached into his belt-pouch and retrieved the map.

"I promise I won't get lost on my way back to the inn," he replied resolutely. "I promise I won't get lost."

Leandro turned, and with the parrot perched securely on his shoulder, he dashed back across the drawbridge, past the ceremonious momentary tilt-of-spear-tip acknowledgement from the two palace guards at the entrance to the towering outer gatehouse, and through the high vaulted archway into the castle.

Leandro was desperate to find Clarìcé, but he honored his pledge to Truffaldino first and raced as stealthily and speedily as he could with the parrot still on his shoulder through the resplendent halls of the palace to the gardens. When he arrived, all preparations ordered by King Theramo and which had been supervised by Leandro himself were entirely in place, and the King was there pacing anxiously.

"Leandro…" said King Theramo in mild surprise as the loyal guard rushed in through the tall trees of the small cypress grove, his boots clattering quietly on the marble walkway of the path from the castle.

"Your Majesty," Leandro said deferentially, coming swiftly to a stop and trying not to sound out of breath. He bowed, then knelt at the King's feet.

King Theramo nodded. "Arise, Leandro," he said. "I was just about to request your presence here in the gardens. And lo, here you are without my even having to ask."

"Your Majesty," Leandro replied, standing up respectfully. "I wanted to make a final observation to confirm that everything here is in complete readiness and fully consistent with your wishes."

"And the individuals to be interviewed?"

"Those who have arrived await Your Majesty's pleasure in the ante-room of the Northwest Great Hall, Sire."

King Theramo nodded and unsuccessfully tried to better adjust his crown. "I wanted to commend you, Leandro, on your consistently reliable excellence," he began. "You are someone I can always count on. Your loyalty and steadfast proficiency are gifts which I value in great measure. Especially at a time such as this. So much seems uncertain, and you are for me an anchor in ever-changing waters. I—"

"Your Majesty?"

"Leandro, there appears to be some sort of bird on your shoulder…"

"It's a parrot, Sire. The enchanter has directed that it be placed in the Palace Gardens and remain here until his further instructions. If it please Your Highness."

King Theramo brightened. "Cagliostro?" he asked enthusiastically. "Why, that is such great good news. Then he hasn't entirely abandoned me after all. Though, it certainly is not a usual sort of instruction. And it's difficult to imagine what the purpose could be. Leandro, did the enchanter speak with you himself?"

"His assistant, Your Majesty."

"Truffaldino? He yet remains in Benebento? That is a profound relief to me, Leandro. Seeing the parrot will now remind me that the enchanter has not really left me to succeed or fail wholly on my own. Perhaps that is why he sent it..."

"I shall arrange an agreeable perch for it over here, Your Majesty," suggested Leandro, taking a few steps to one of the newly-implemented banquet tables.

Amidst the sumptuous panoply of freshly-prepared food and drink were several tall broad candlesticks with squat heavy bases and topped with the wide cylindrical wax of stout candles that flickered calmly in the slight afternoon breeze. Selecting a candlestick situated unobtrusively near the edge of one of the tables, Leandro deftly pinched the flame with his fingers to extinguish it and removed the candle to the surface of the table, leaving the sconce-socket empty and revealing a sturdy thick decoratively-crimped rim, one ideally shaped and textured for easy gripping by parrot claws. He briskly repeated the process with two other candlesticks which he then placed close to the first, pouring a small amount of drinking-water from a ewer into the sconce-socket of one, and depositing a small handful of hulled nuts from a serving bowl into the sconce-socket of the other.

He reached up to his shoulder where the parrot obligingly stepped onto his fingers, and Leandro carefully swung his hand down to the top of the first candlestick, where the parrot stepped adeptly off Leandro's fingers and securely onto the curved rim of the sconce-socket. The candlestick's height was just tall enough to accommodate the downward extended length of the parrot's long graceful tail, and the parrot surveyed the expanse of the banquet table and the vast lush surroundings of the gardens beyond, and blinked its eyes contentedly.

"It seems to be a very well-mannered creature, Your Majesty," said Leandro, returning to where King Theramo was standing. "I do not believe it will be an intrusive presence during your interviews."

"Thank you, Leandro."

King Theramo now looked around at the extensive preparations with some concern. "Leandro, there seems to be rather a lot of food here. It is all appealingly fragrant and appears quite appetizing, but mightn't the formal presentation and ample quantities be perhaps better suited to a royal banquet?"

"The Master of the Kitchen, Your Majesty," said Leandro. "He is keenly supportive of your interviews and wanted the atmosphere to be as festive and bountiful as possible."

King Theramo nodded slowly. "Very thoughtful," he said. "Though possibly a bit overdone. However, very kind of him nevertheless. But Leandro, do you see this enormously tall dome-top cylinder here?"

Leandro nodded respectfully. "It's a cake cover, Your Majesty."

"Yes, I lifted it and looked underneath. There is cake in there. An immensely elaborate cake of excessively great height…"

"Yes, Sire," Leandro replied. "The Master of the Kitchen. He hoped it would bring you luck with finding the right person to marry."

"Very well-intentioned," King Theramo said hesitantly. "If perhaps out of proportion to the circumstances. But unquestionably a kind gesture… Leandro, does the entire palace know that I am interviewing to try to find a queen?"

"News travels fast among the servants, My Lord. It is not malicious. You should know that Your Majesty's happiness is devoutly wished for by everyone in Castle Delprego."

"Thank you, Leandro. Well, I am loathe to get this awkward process started, but more loathe to defer it any longer than necessary. I fear the outcome will be the same as it has ever been. However, the visit from the enchanter has given me new reason for optimism, and so I will cling to that hope for as long as I can."

King Theramo looked up past the tall trees of the gardens, beyond the lofty tops of the cypress grove and the four towering palace walls bounding the gardens piazza, to the sky. "The weather at least is auspicious," he said. "It is a beautiful sun-filled Benebento day…"

After a moment of thought, he brought his attention back to his patiently waiting guard.

"Leandro," the King continued. "I received a confusing message from the Chamberlain of Procedural Formalities about a claim regarding some sort of 'Royal prerogative' that I'm supposed to be complying with. Do you have any idea what that's about?"

Leandro nodded respectfully. "Yes, Your Highness. It regards the sequence of the interview process. Prime Minister Tartaglia has asked to exercise his right of Royal prerogative associated with his position as Prime Minister, whereby you would interview his sister Claricé first, before anyone else."

King Theramo sighed. "Leandro, why must everything be so complicated...?

"There must be many concerns weighing on Your Majesty's mind," Leandro replied with courteous sympathy.

King Theramo nodded slowly and attempted to adjust his crown. "Thank you, Leandro. Well, there is no one I trust or respect more than Tartaglia. I will of course willingly accord him the due privilege he has requested."

"Yes, Your Majesty."

"Leandro, I leave it to you to determine the sequence for the subsequent interviews. It is a detail which I feel unable to properly focus on."

"Of course, Sire."

"Very well. Good Leandro, please make your way to the ante-room and inform me once Prime Minister Tartaglia and his sister have arrived."

"As you wish, Your Majesty." Leandro bowed, then turned and hurriedly made his way back along the marble path into the castle.

Chapter 10

The Tryst
and
The First Interview

"Leandro…!"

Leandro heard his name called out in a frantic whisper from somewhere behind him. He had been taking as indirect a route as possible on his way to the ante-room in a last-minute hope that he might somehow find Clarìcé. He whirled hopefully around at hearing the sound of his name but could not immediately see anyone.

"Clarìcé…?" he whispered back as loudly as he dared.

Out from behind the shadow of a pillar emerged Clarìcé, and after looking furtively in all directions, she ran to Leandro, who was now already running toward her.

"Oh, Leandro…!" she exclaimed softly as they reached each other and desperately took hold of each other's hands. "My dearest Leandro, I've been looking for you everywhere…"

Leandro glanced apprehensively around but saw no one else approaching.

"The parrot was right…" he said in a whisper.

"Parrot… What…?" Clarìcé whispered back.

"Never mind," Leandro whispered hurriedly. "It doesn't matter now. I've found you…"

"Leandro," Clarìcé began anxiously. "The interview with the King—"

"Shhh…" Leandro whispered, and again looked around uneasily. "Not here. Come this way…"

Never letting go of each other's hands, Leandro led them rapidly back down the vault-ceilinged corridor, past the warmth and sunlight streaming in through the numerous open-air arched windows until they arrived at a connection to another passageway. Leandro steered them around the corner and down a darker corridor lit with the patiently-flickering tireless torch-light flames of decorative iron wall-sconces and bounded on all sides by expansive intricate hanging wall tapestries which not only visually beatified the passage but also absorbed so much sound that even Leandro and Clarìcé's quickening footsteps on the polished stone floor were suddenly quieter as they rushed onward and finally came to a stop midway along the length of the long hallway.

They each glanced apprehensively in both directions, but they were alone in the corridor. Leandro backed into the space next to a pillar, and still grasping each other's hands tightly they pulled each other so close that their faces were nearly touching.

"Clarìcé," Leandro began in a quiet whisper. "I wanted to tell you. Whatever happens, I love you. Nothing will change that."

"Oh, Leandro, how I do love you so…"

"My heart is yours, Clarìcé. Forever."

Clarìcé gazed up at him, dancing shadows cast from the torch-light flames accentuating her unhappy expression. "I don't want to do the interview," she whispered miserably. "I never wanted to do it. My brother is forcing me. His cruelty is beyond limits… Oh, Leandro, we are lost. All our dreams are lost. I don't want to marry the King. I don't want to become Queen. I love only you. All I want is to be with you."

"I had hoped you would not have to be interviewed," Leandro whispered grimly. "But when I learned your brother had demanded his Royal prerogative, my heart sank."

Clarìcé shook her head angrily. "Yes," she whispered hoarsely. "Not only am I compelled against my will, but I must also go first…!"

"Your brother is driven by some dark intention…" Leandro whispered.

Clarìcé shook her head again, but her anger had dissolved into sadness. "What has my brother become…?" she whispered plaintively. "He was never like this. He used to be kind. He used to take care of me. He used to protect me. No longer. Now he would destroy me, my happiness, my future, my life, if it served his purpose. I am no longer his sister. I am now just a putlog in the scaffold of his elaborate twisted plan to marry Angiolina…"

Leandro looked anxiously around, but still they were alone in the passageway.

"My beloved Clarìcé," he whispered urgently. "I must go to the ante-room of the Northwest Great Hall where the others to be interviewed await His Majesty's summons. I should have been there by now. And you need to be there as well, but you must go quickly because you have to arrive before me. We must not be seen or perceived as being together…"

Clarìcé looked up at him with renewed apprehension. "But

what if the King chooses me?" she whispered desperately. "What am I to do if he chooses me? I am in terror of my brother's wrath if the King does not choose me. But I cannot let myself be chosen. My life would be broken. Leandro, I don't want to live without you. I will not live without you. I cannot live without you…"

"I don't know what you should or should not do or say at your interview," Leandro whispered uncertainly. "I know only that you must not be disrespectful to our King, and I know that he values the Truth beyond all else. Theramo is a good King. He is a good person. He would never knowingly hurt anyone. He is not simply looking for a queen, he is trying to find someone whom he truly loves who truly loves him. Though he has no knowledge of what you and I share, he seeks his own version of what we have. He wants to find True Love…"

"Leandro, I—"

"Shhh…" Leandro whispered with sudden alarm. "Someone comes this way…!"

They gripped each other's hands even more tightly as they heard a sound that chilled their blood. The voice of Tartaglia furiously calling out Clarìcé's name, getting louder as it came nearer.

"Away, my love…!" Leandro whispered in near silence and rapid urgency. "Make haste! Continue this way. I will go back the other way and interact with him. It will give you the time you need to get to the ante-room ahead of him…!"

Trembling with fear, Clarìcé gave Leandro's hands a last

squeeze, and with a terrified glance in the direction of Tartaglia's voice, turned to run off in the opposite direction.

"Shoes…!" Leandro whispered quickly.

Claricé nodded, slipped off her shoes, and clutching them firmly dashed away in her bare feet at top speed soundlessly down the passageway.

Turning to the opposite direction, Leandro walked briskly back the way they had come until he reached the corner adjoining the first corridor, where he came face to face with Tartaglia.

"Guard!" roared Tartaglia, red with rage. "Have you seen my sister?! Don't dare lie to me! I must have the truth!"

"Your Lordship," Leandro replied steadily. "Your sister is not to be found here. Perhaps you shall find her in the ante-room of the Northwest Great Hall. The King has instructed that all who are to be interviewed and their family escorts await his further instructions there."

"Insolent wretch!" bellowed Tartaglia. "Claricé shall be the first to interview with the King. It is the Royal prerogative entitled to me as Prime Minister!"

Leandro nodded respectfully. "It is of course as you say, Your Lordship. His Majesty is aware of the directive you have claimed in this matter, and he has already made plans to fully honor your wishes."

"Of course he has! He has no choice!! Odds bodkins!"

"I shall go now to inform His Majesty of your presence, Your Lordship. He directed me to do so immediately upon your arrival."

Tartaglia glowered menacingly at Leandro. "Have a care, knave," he snarled. "The slightest insubordination from you will be more than sufficient infraction for me to have you dragged off to the dungeon!"

"I mean you no dishonor, Your Lordship."

"Do you take me for a fool?!" Tartaglia demanded, pointing a long accusatory finger at Leandro. "You cannot deceive me, guard. I know who you are!! Cast your thoughts forever away from my sister! She is not for you! And you most assuredly are not for her! She is to become Queen! Do you understand?! Do not think to try to put yourself in the way of my plans!!"

"I serve the King to the letter, Your Lordship. I mean you no disrespect."

"See to it that you neither transgress nor cross me, varlet!"

"I respectfully now take my leave, Your Lordship, to announce to the King your arrival, per his directive."

"If my sister is not in the ante-room," Tartaglia hissed threateningly, "you shall feel the full weight of my wrath!"

Wheeling around, Tartaglia stalked with swift angry strides back down the corridor in the direction from which he had come, the austere shades of his formal robes billowing like storm clouds behind him, and Leandro turned with agitated relief in the opposite direction and headed hastily back toward the Palace Gardens.

Once again entering through the towering trees of the small cypress grove, Leandro briskly made his way along the marble walkway to where King Theramo was nervously pacing, absently passing the rivet spectacles from one hand to the other.

"Your Majesty," Leandro said, bowing and kneeling before the King.

King Theramo nodded. "Arise, Leandro," he said, coming to a stop and slipping the glasses back into the pocket of his robes.

"The Prime Minister and his sister have arrived, Your Highness," Leandro said, standing up respectfully.

King Theramo nodded again. "Thank you, Leandro."

The King looked around at the gardens for a moment.

"Leandro," he continued. "Forgive me, but I continue to discover curious eccentricities in the preparations… For instance, on that table by the chairs there is a small hand-mirror with rubies on the back…"

Leandro nodded. "Yes, Sire. The Master of the Kitchen—"

King Theramo's shoulders dropped and he sighed audibly.

"The Master of the Kitchen," Leandro resumed cautiously, "felt that making the young women who were being interviewed feel relaxed and comfortable was a priority."

"Good heavens, Leandro. It seems to me a fairly narrow view of things to suppose that all women are so vain that providing them a mirror will put them at ease…" He walked over to the two massive urns with their surfeit of ferns bounding the ornate sides of the large outdoor looking-glass.

"And besides," King Theramo added pointedly. "My parents' mirror is more than sizeable enough to reflect the appearance of anyone. No matter how vain they may or may not be."

Leandro nodded respectfully. "The Master of the Kitchen felt the angle of view would allow you, Sire, to see its reflection as you interviewed, but would not be in the line-of-sight for those who were being interviewed."

"But," King Theramo began precipitously. "No one can see the words of the Mirror of Truth if they're not wearing the—" He stopped himself and glanced over at the parrot, who blinked impassively back at him and said nothing.

"Excuse me, Sire…?" Leandro asked hesitantly.

"Uh…" King Theramo faltered. "Nothing. It's nothing. Forgive me, Leandro. The current arrangements are perfectly satisfactory."

"Yes, Your Majesty," Leandro replied courteously.

"Good Leandro," King Theramo proceeded, gesturing in the direction of the marble path back into the castle. "The solarium is conveniently close to the gardens. After their interview, each individual should be brought there. Please inform everyone that I will formally address them all there, in the solarium, once the final interview is concluded."

"Yes, Your Majesty."

"Very well, Leandro. Please make your way to the ante-room. Be so good as to escort Clarìcé here to the gardens, and direct Prime Minister Tartaglia to wait for her in the solarium."

"Yes, Your Highness," Leandro replied, bowing respectfully. "Thank you, Your Majesty."

Leandro headed out to the ante-room, and King Theramo took the rivet spectacles out of his pocket again. He glanced from the Mirror of Truth, down to the glasses, and back to the mirror.

"Not in line-of-sight…" he repeated dryly, lifting the spectacles and putting them on. His face contorted as he winced in pain from the discomfort, and after unsuccessfully adjusting the glasses, he absently resorted with equal lack of success to amending the fit of his crown.

"Everything is complicated…." he sighed despairingly.

With a distant sound like wind chimes, a nearly invisible swirl of twinkling points of light began to wink and dance across the large surface of the Mirror of Truth, and shimmering instantly into view within the reflection of the looking-glass in large distinct letters were the words: THE TRUTH.

As Leandro escorted Clarìcé along the marble walkway into the gardens, they surreptitiously touched hands for the briefest of instants. It was not noticed or seen by King Theramo, who had returned the spectacles to a robe pocket and was again pacing anxiously.

"Your Majesty," Leandro announced, bowing respectfully. "The young lady Clarìcé is here for her interview."

King Theramo nodded uncertainly. "Thank you, good Leandro. You need not wait in the solarium, but please do remain close by within the castle, that I may recall you easily back here to the gardens."

"Yes, Your Majesty," Leandro replied. Neither he nor Clarìcé let their eyes meet. Leandro bowed and turned, and made his way dutifully out through the cypress grove.

There was an uncomfortable pause as King Theramo stood with his hands nervously buried deep within the pockets of his royal robes, and Claricé stood trembling slightly with hesitancy and apprehension. The simple trickling and gently tumbling water of the great circular marble fountain seemed somehow louder in the awkward sudden absence of voices, and the sprawling geometric hedgerow maze for a moment seemed— rather than whimsically inviting—to close in on the King and Claricé as if trapping them both inside its convoluted paths with no apparent means of escape.

King Theramo at last removed his hands from his pockets and took a polite tentative step toward Claricé, glancing for a moment at the lavish epicurean bounty arrayed across the improbable profusion of banquet tables.

"Would you like something to eat?" he asked tentatively, breaking the awkward silence at last.

Claricé slightly shook her head. "No thank you, Your Highness," she replied with demure politeness.

King Theramo nodded. "Perhaps something to drink?" he offered.

"No," Claricé repeated respectfully. "No thank you, Your Highness."

King Theramo nodded again more hesitantly. "Would you like to use the hand-mirror?" he suggested, gesturing vaguely toward the arrangement of table and chairs so exhaustively contemplated and meticulously positioned by the Master of the Kitchen.

"Uh… No…" Claricé faltered with some confusion. "No,

Your Highness. I... That won't be necessary... Thank you, Your Highness..."

King Theramo again nodded, this time a bit less indecisively. "Clarìcé," he said kindly. "Please. Sit down."

Clarìcé nodded and lowered herself uneasily into the nearest of the several opulent armchairs, not leaning back, and sitting stiffly at the front edge of the plush seat cushion.

"Thank you, Your Highness," she said, clasping her hands together self-consciously in her lap.

King Theramo took a few directionless steps first to one side then the other, and attempted to adjust his crown before finally clearing his throat to speak.

"My dear Clarìcé," he began, continuing to pace as he spoke. "I hold the Truth in the highest veneration. There is perhaps nothing I value more. In that regard, I do not wish to misrepresent myself. This is not my first interview of this kind. Indeed, it is not even my twenty-first. No, I am unhappy and embarrassed to confess that I have previously conducted dozens of such interviews. I will not trouble either of us by recounting any details from those unsuccessful and fruitless undertakings."

He paused for a moment and reached back into the pocket of his robe, where his hand found the rivet spectacles.

"Suffice it to say," he continued, "although today's likewise highly-irregular interview is not my first, my mind is seeing all aspects of this process and these proceedings with such fresh eyes and such awakened enlightened perspective, it is very nearly as if this interview is the first of its kind."

He nodded decisively as if to reassure or possibly convince himself he had indeed said what he wanted to say.

"And I apologize," he concluded diffidently, "if I have been long-winded in conveying this to you."

"I understand," Claricé replied politely. "Thank you, Your Highness."

King Theramo stopped pacing and stood facing Claricé.

"Claricé," he enquired deliberately. "Do you love the kingdom of Benebento?"

"Claricé nodded without hesitation. "With all my heart, Your Highness," she answered simply and emphatically.

King Theramo nodded. "Yes, yes I see."

He thought for a moment.

"Claricé," he asked. "Why have you come to this interview?"

Claricé glanced down at her hands for a moment, then looked up at the King, then back down at her hands.

"Your Majesty…" she began hesitantly. "Your Highness, I… My brother, he…"

"Prime Minister Tartaglia," said King Theramo, "is my most faithful advisor. There is no better man in the kingdom than he. I trust him with my life."

Claricé said nothing.

King Theramo proceeded ahead.

"Claricé," he asked. "What do you feel to be the most important thing about being Queen?"

Claricé thought for a long moment before answering. "I think," she began slowly, "the most important thing is to help the people of the kingdom to believe they can succeed in what they aspire to. To provide them what they need to thrive. To give them hope for an even better future. To look closely and carefully at people to determine what they truly need in order to be happy. Sometimes people are in a difficult situation, and they need the benevolent hand of the monarchy to reach down and help them overcome challenges and obstacles they are unable to or don't know how to overcome on their own."

King Theramo looked at her curiously for a moment.

"Clarìcé," he began carefully, "Are you in love?"

Clarìcé stared down at floor and began trembling. She absently clenched her hands tighter together and her feet shuffled restlessly.

"Clarìcé, I must ask you to be honest with me. I am your King. It is imperative that you tell me the Truth."

Clarìcé nodded miserably. "Y-Your Highness…" she stammered. She paused and then tried again. "Your Highness… Yes. Yes, I am in love… Very deeply, with all my heart…"

She became increasingly agitated and could not look up.

"And your love of this person," King Theramo asked. "It means more to you than the opportunity to become Queen?"

Clarìcé bowed her head in further assent. "It… It means more to me than anything in my life, Your Highness…" she confessed almost inaudibly. "It is my life…"

King Theramo nodded. "I begin to understand…" he said gently.

Clarìcé continued to tremble and was unable to speak.

King Theramo took a step toward her and extended his hand. "Clarìcé, stand up. Please."

She lifted her head to meet the King's gaze, and then rose slowly and obediently up from the armchair.

King Theramo took several decisive steps in the direction of the castle, toward the cypress grove. "Leandro!" he summoned loudly, and then returned to where he had been standing with Clarìcé.

"I am extremely impressed by you, Clarìcé," he said earnestly. "You are a deeply good and decent person. Benebento is a far better place for your presence."

Clarìcé blushed with confusion and humility. "I... Thank you, Your Highness."

"And I want to thank you for having the courage to endure the process of this interview. It has been a valuable and very instructive experience for me. I hope it has not caused you too much distress."

"I... No, I... Thank you. Thank you, Your Highness."

Leandro entered the gardens warily, unable to mask the concern and anxiety on his face.

"Your Majesty," he said bowing and kneeling.

The King nodded. "Arise, good Leandro. My interview with Clarìcé is concluded. Please escort her to the solarium. Upon your return to the ante-room to select the next person to be interviewed, remind Prime Minister Tartaglia that he himself should likewise proceed to the solarium and wait there with his sister until the conclusion of all the interviews."

Leandro nodded respectfully. "Yes, Your Majesty."

King Theramo nodded and turned to Clarìcé. "Thank you, Clarìcé," he said kindly.

"Thank you, Your Majesty," she replied politely.

Leandro gestured courteously for Clarìcé to proceed ahead of him, and then turned and followed her out. As the two of them passed through the cypress grove, their hands could not resist finding each other and grasping each other's fingers tightly for the merest of fleeting moments, but this time King Theramo observed the passion-driven physical interaction. He nodded slightly and smiled to himself.

Turning away, he placed his hands back into the pockets of the robes. His fingers touched the rivet spectacles, and with ironic realization he pulled them out and studied them as he held them in his hands.

"Well, that was certainly absentminded..." he scolded himself aloud, shaking his head incredulously.

He contemplated the glasses for another moment, then looked over at the Mirror of Truth. "Although, apparently," he mused with an ironic slight smile, "there are some things even a myopic king is able to see without any help from magic..."

He glanced over at the parrot, who was contentedly occupied munching nuts from the sconce-socket of one of the candlesticks.

"Oh, Cagliostro," King Theramo lamented. "Is this your plan for me? To have given me the magic I asked for, so I would then prove to myself that—in truth—I have no need of magic...?"

The parrot continued partaking in its share of the Master of the Kitchen's excessive culinary largesse and said nothing.

King Theramo lifted the spectacles and put them on, bracing himself for the intense discomfort which immediately and acutely accompanied the act. Grimacing, he made a half-hearted attempt at adjusting the glasses but it served only to exacerbate the pain, and he abandoned the effort.

"So," he concluded aloud. "It seems Clarîcé and Leandro are deeply and truly in love… They are indeed lucky, and well-deserving. I keenly envy what they have found in each other, but my heart is filled with happiness for them both."

The distant wind-chimes sound resonated faintly, and the nearly invisible swirl of twinkling lights winked and whorled across the surface of the Mirror of Truth. Shimmering into view within the looking-glass reflection in large letters were the words: THE TRUTH.

Chapter II

The Second Interview
and
The Epiphany

It was not long before Leandro returned. King Theramo had once again secreted the rivet spectacles away in his robe pocket, and from a ewer on one of the banquet tables he had poured himself some water which he was sipping contemplatively from a silver goblet as Leandro made his way through the cypress grove and along the marble walkway, escorting Smeraldina into the gardens.

"Your Majesty," Leandro announced, bowing respectfully. "The young lady Smeraldina is here for her interview."

King Theramo nodded. "Thank you, Leandro. Be so good as to remind Sir Balzanno to wait for his daughter in the solarium, and please do remain again close by within the castle, that I may recall you easily back here to the gardens."

"Yes, Your Majesty," Leandro replied. He bowed and turned, and made his way expeditiously out through the cypress grove.

"Good morning, Your Majesty," Smeraldina said genially, taking a step toward the King and bowing low, the divulging front of her dress angled artfully toward his eyes.

King Theramo cast an embarrassed glance in another direction for a brief moment.

"Smeraldina…" he began uncertainly. "There is no need for you to… uh… bow so low. A simple curtsy will suffice…"

Smeraldina stood up respectfully from her deep bow and gave a graceful slight curtsy. "Yes, Your Majesty," she said politely, re-adjusting the strap of her dress which had fallen during her obeisance, and a moment later it again slipped halfway down her upper arm.

King Theramo studied Smeraldina as if trying to acquire a sense of what he was about to get into, and Smeraldina gazed back at him with cool steady calm, her eyes sparkling mischievously.

King Theramo cleared his throat. "Smeraldina," he began, "I would offer you use of the hand mirror, although the large full-length mirror of my parents might perhaps provide you more comprehensive reflection. However, I suspect you attire yourself through deliberate choice and not from a lack of awareness. I laud your self-possessed individuality and your bold confidence to dress as you please, though I wonder if your father is at all troubled by the risqué inappropriateness of your…your lack of fabric…"

"Yes, Your Majesty," Smeraldina replied respectfully. "He is troubled by it. However, I love my father dearly, and he loves me devotedly, and we do not permit differences in points-of-view regarding garb to interfere in our relationship or with the loving harmony of our home."

King Theramo's expression took on a look of mild surprise and earnest curiosity, and he absently attempted without success to better adjust his crown. "Your frankness, Smeraldina," he said thoughtfully, "is, I must confess, somewhat disarming. It is, however, also rather refreshing. I shall endeavor to be more open-minded in our conversation."

"I mean no disrespect, Sire," Smeraldina replied earnestly.

King Theramo nodded. "Yes, I believe that is true. You have not offended me, Smeraldina. You present yourself with straightforward genuineness, even before your King. I do not receive the benefit of that manner of honest candor as often as I wish, and so your truthful directness is in fact very much appreciated."

"Thank you, Your Highness."

Smeraldina turned toward the copious amounts of food and drink arrayed on banquet tables all around them. "Your Highness," she asked politely. "Are we expecting some additional…dozens of people?"

King Theramo sighed. "The Master of the Kitchen," he began. "It turns out he is inclined to rather overzealous enthusiasm in his work… Please, Smeraldina, help yourself to anything you would like. As you intimated, there is an inescapable excess of numerous choices and plentiful amounts…"

Smeraldina smiled. "It seems a kind of mirror for what Your Majesty must have to deal with every day as King. There is always a lot. And even if it is not necessarily a lot of something bad, it still is an overwhelming amount to manage and be responsible for."

King Theramo smiled with appreciative irony. "Your observation is not incorrect," he acknowledged. "And you are perhaps even more perceptively astute than you may realize…"

"Your Majesty is too kind," Smeraldina replied. "Thank you,

Sire. I would, for now, prefer to respectfully decline indulging in any of the feasting delights, if it please Your Highness."

King Theramo nodded. "Of course," he said. "I well understand. Verily, it is so exhaustive a selection to choose from and thus so difficult to know even where to begin, it is perhaps easiest to simply avoid it all altogether."

Smeraldina smiled again. "Your Highness has need of a good Queen to help you better grapple with such formidable and inevitable daily challenges."

King Theramo looked back at her with impressed approval. "You are quick to put your finger on the heart of a matter, Smeraldina," he said. "Would that more of the individuals who advise me were as unflinchingly incisive…"

"Your Majesty is too gracious. Thank you, Sire."

Smeraldina expediently surveyed the interview area of the gardens with a quick pragmatic eye. "Your Highness," she went on. "May I sit down and we can begin?"

King Theramo again seemed taken aback by Smeraldina's assertiveness, and he pondered her with an expression that was a conflicted mix of admiration and disorientation.

"Yes…" he replied, gesturing toward the arrangement of table and chairs. "Yes, please find a seat and make yourself comfortable."

Smeraldina looked at the selection of plush armchairs.

"Even the simplest of things," she remarked, "seems to require making some sort of choice, Your Highness."

King Theramo nodded in agreement. "It is sometimes difficult to discern what is complicated unavoidably, and what is complicated needlessly. Regrettably, much of being King requires me to succeed with imposing order on all manner of complication. It is an art I have yet to master..."

"It is honest of you, Your Highness," said Smeraldina, "to let your prospective candidates for Queen get a fair glimpse of what they will be getting into if they are chosen."

"Thank you, Smeraldina."

Smeraldina briefly considered the selection of chairs, and then sat down in one of them, settling herself and absently tossing her flowing red hair back over one shoulder.

King Theramo took a few steps toward where she now was seated.

"Forgive me, Smeraldina," he said. "But you fascinate me. You have an analytical manner of considering matters, and so you now have piqued my interest in wanting to know why you chose that particular chair."

Smeraldina laughed with polite and humble amusement.

"What a question...! The workings of Your Majesty's mind are themselves intriguing, Sire," she said earnestly.

Smeraldina gazed for a moment at the chairs and table around her, then looked back up at the King.

"Since you have made your enquiry with such candor," she began, "I will answer with complete honesty. There are nine chairs here, which suggests that the Master of the Kitchen truly wishes you to have good fortune in your interview process, since three is a magic number, and three threes therefore are supremely lucky. However, the first three is the most significant, and so my inclination would have been to sit in the third chair. But I can see that that chair has recently been sat in, I presume by one of my dearest friends, Claricé, and I would not want to interfere with her luck if—as she sat there— she hoped she would be chosen, or hoped she would not be chosen. So I wanted to select a different one. The ninth chair, while lucky, is too much on the periphery, and I prefer to be closer to the center. Chair five is of course ideally situated in the center, but chair four is crafted with green fabric, and green is the color of my eyes and my favorite color, so I chose to sit here in the fourth chair."

King Theramo smiled in fascinated interest.

"You are an intriguing individual, Smeraldina," he said. "Thank you for your honesty and your willingness to reveal the path of your thinking. Your ways of seeing are enlightening and distinctive."

"Thank you, Your Highness."

King Theramo cleared his throat as if to focus his thoughts. "Very well," he said decidedly. "Let us please begin. Smeraldina, why have you come to this interview?"

Smeraldina was occupying her chair with innate poise and easy self-possessed confidence as if she were already herself a queen on a throne.

"To rule well," she began, "Your Majesty needs to have a Queen. Your Majesty deserves to have the best Queen. The best Queen for you, Sire. It's possible there is no one who will be that best Queen for you. But that is not a constructive approach. So proceeding on the assumption that, somewhere, there *is* the ideal Queen for you, then with each successive interview you conduct, the closer you theoretically get to finding the one person who is the best Queen for you. I am here because neither you, Sire, nor I, know if I am the that one person, and we both wish to find out whether or not I am. If I *am* the one, it would be egregiously imprudent for me to choose not to be interviewed. If I am *not* the one, then no harm has been done by us being together in this way and talking with each other. So I believe I owe it to both of us to be here, and that is why I have come to this interview."

King Theramo raised an impressed eyebrow.

"You have a keen mind, Smeraldina," he said. "And you are remarkably comfortable in expressing yourself. You articulate your ideas with considerable lucidness, and your reasoning is as compelling as… as you yourself are attractive."

"Thank you," she replied humbly. "You are very candid, Sire. It is an admirable quality, in my opinion. Your Majesty deserves to know," she went on, "that you are a very popular King. The citizens of Benebento are loyal to you and love you. We all wish for you to find the Queen of your dreams, not only to make our splendid kingdom an even better place. But because you deserve it, Sire. Your subjects adamantly believe you deserve to be happy, and we wish for you to succeed in finding that happiness."

King Theramo smiled with humbled surprise. "That… That fills my heart, Smeraldina," he said. "Thank you for so kindly sharing with me that illuminating and gratifying perspective."

He thought for a moment before continuing.

"Smeraldina," he went on. "I would ask you if you love the Kingdom of Benebento, but it is quite readily apparent to me that you—"

He stopped mid-sentence.

"What is it, Sire?"

He shook his head in frustration. "Forgive me... It is my own foolish absentmindedness again plaguing me... It shall not, however, best me this time..."

"I don't understand..."

"It is not you, Smeraldina. It is me, one of my own numerous personal shortcomings... Please, give me a moment..."

Reaching deep into one of the pockets of his robe, King Theramo retrieved the rivet spectacles and, bracing himself for the discomfort, hurriedly put them on.

Smeraldina took one look at him and began to giggle. Her giggles escalated to laughter, and within moments she was fluttering her hand rapidly back and forth to fan her face in a futile effort to stop laughing, and presently she lapsed into a fit of hysterical mirth and hilarity.

King Theramo, already grimacing from the pain of the glasses, wrinkled his forehead quizzically.

"Smeraldina, does something amuse you?"

"No..." she gasped with breathless glee. "No, Your Majesty... It's nothing... It's just... May I please have some water, Sire...?"

Hastening to a banquet table, King Theramo filled a goblet with water and brought it to her. She drank it down, and after successfully composing herself she handed it back to him with grateful appreciation.

"I think I shall be fine now," she breathed with some

relief and residual giggly giddiness. "Truly, Your Highness, I... I believe I have it under control..."

King Theramo nodded with mystified acceptance. After replacing the goblet on the table, he returned to where he could stand before Smeraldina and also have a clear view of the Mirror of Truth.

"Very well," he said resolutely. "Let us attempt to proceed."

Absently flipping her shining hair glamorously over one shoulder, she smiled back at him steadily and nodded.

"Smeraldina," he began again. "Do you love the Kingdom of Benebento?"

"Yes, Sire," she answered. "Benebento is the most wonderful kingdom on earth. I am blessed to live here."

There was a distant sound like wind chimes, and a nearly invisible swirl of twinkling points of light began to wink and dance across the large surface of the Mirror of Truth. Shimmering instantly into view in front of King Theramo within the reflection of the looking-glass in large distinct letters were the words: THE TRUTH.

King Theramo nodded to himself.

"Very well," he continued. "Smeraldina, are you in love with someone?"

Smeraldina shook her head without hesitation. "Oh, my goodness, no! No, Sire, I am not in love with someone."

Shimmering into view within the reflection of the looking-glass in large distinct letters were the words: A LIE.

King Theramo looked pointedly at Smeraldina. "Hmmm…"he remarked. "But, it seems that you are."

Smeraldina lost some of her composure and suddenly looked genuinely surprised. "No," she repeated. "Your Highness, I am not. I am most assuredly not in love with someone."

Seen only by King Theramo, within the reflection of the looking-glass the previous words faded instantly away, and again shimmering into view were the words: A LIE.

King Theramo looked intently at Smeraldina. "I don't believe you are intentionally being untruthful, Smeraldina," he said gently. "But I can assure you, you are in love with someone…"

Smeraldina sat up in her chair, her eyes bright with perplexity.

"But…" she faltered. "But…it's not possible… Why, I've only just met him…"

"Just met who?"

"No… No one, Your Majesty…"

Her face whitened as if her thoughts were racing.

"No…" she repeated faintly. "It's not possible… I couldn't be…"

Again shimmering into view on the looking-glass were the words: A LIE.

King Theramo took off the glasses and rubbed his nose and his ears by his crown in a futile attempt to ease away the discomfort. "In the name of Heaven," he muttered unhappily. "These confounded spectacles are unrelentingly painful… What an excruciating price to pay for clarity…"

Smeraldina was becoming increasingly flustered and her eyes were scanning the ambient gardens in hectic vague desperation as though in search of an anchor to moor herself back to being in control. And then she saw the parrot.

"Oh!" she exclaimed. "Oh, my goodness... It's... It's his parrot..."

King Theramo glanced at the parrot who remained perched atop the candlestick sconce-socket with idle contentedness and was blinking impassively back at them.

King Theramo nodded.

"The parrot..." he began. "The parrot is a... It is a kind of guest. It belongs to—"

"To the enchanter," Smeraldina said quickly. "Yes, I know. But I... I think of it as Truffaldino's, because..."

King Theramo regarded Smeraldina with concern.

"Smeraldina?" he asked. "Are you quite all right?"

"Yes... Yes... I'm fine... I just..."

"My dear... You're crying..."

She was indeed crying. Tears were beginning to cascade down her face.

"I know..." she said, trying to wipe away the flow of wet rivulets that came faster and more profusely with each passing moment. "I know... I... I'm so sorry, Your Highness... I just suddenly..."

She tried unsuccessfully to collect herself.

"I just suddenly miss him... I don't understand... It's so very peculiar... I just want to see his face and hear his voice and... Oh, Your Highness..."

She put her face into her hands and wept.

King Theramo looked around uncomfortably for some indication of what he ought to do next, then awkwardly came over to Smeraldina to try to comfort her while seeming to have no notion of how he might do that.

Smeraldina lifted her face, glistening with the torrent of tears still streaming down, but she was smiling, beaming with happiness.

"You're so kind, Sire…" she said gratefully. "But please, do not be concerned. I'm not sad. I'm happy. I… I'm the happiest I've ever been in my life. It's just really overwhelming… I've never felt anything like this before. Except…"

Her eyes looked upward for a moment as she remembered.

"Except this morning when I met him… Oh, Your Majesty…! You were right. I *am* in love with someone…"

She wiped away more of her tears and tried to compose herself.

"Oh, Your Highness…" she said apologetically. "I am so sorry. This type of behavior before my King is rather inappropriate…"

King Theramo smiled and shook his head.

"No, Smeraldina," he said kindly. "Do not be concerned. Your attire—or risqué lack thereof—is inappropriate perhaps, but not your behavior."

He turned for a moment to collect his own thoughts, then looked back at her.

"I… I find myself profoundly moved by your depth of emotion at realizing that you are in love…" he said intently. "Smeraldina, you… You do me a great honor by freely allowing your feelings to express themselves so openly before me, me whom you do not know… Your King, whom you have no reason to trust as a friend… I confess, I… I am acutely envious of your depth of emotion… But I am not unmindful of the trust you bestow upon me by permitting yourself to bare your honest feelings in my presence…"

Smeraldina nodded tearfully and continued to smile with uncontainable happiness.

"Your passion is so stirring…." King Theramo went on with slow deliberation. "Your humanity is so real… You… You cause me to realize that I have lost my connection to people… I fear that… that I have become too aloof as King, too removed from the subjects over whom I rule. The very subjects whose welfare is, after all, my most important responsibly as King. The subjects who—as their protector—I love. They are the very reason for having a king. They are the reason that I am King…"

He started to pace restlessly, then stopped and stepped closer to Smeraldina.

"I begin to recognize," he said with growing resolve, "that… that I have lost my connection to the most important thing in Benebento, the lives of my own subjects. I will henceforth dedicate myself to finding ways to spend more time among the people, more time in the company of a broader diversity of Benebentoans. The towering fortifications of a castle are not always the best place for a King to be, if he is to be a truly good King."

He paused.

"You have changed me Smeraldina…" he said at last. "You have changed your King for the better. That is no small thing…"

Smeraldina was wiping away tears that still had not stopped flowing.

"Your Majesty is gracious beyond words…" she managed to say. "Thank you, Your Highness…"

She began to laugh again, but it was a very different laugh. It was not a laugh of hilarity or amusement, it was a laugh of joyous exhilaration.

"Oh, Your Majesty…" she exclaimed with relief and amazed elation. "I'm so in love, it hurts…"

Her laughter escalated in a serenely exuberant release of outpouring emotion.

"It's… It's such a wonderful searing pain…" she marveled with quiet excitement. "It's a delicious ache that I don't want to ever stop feeling… Oh, my heart is beating so fast…!"

King Theramo gazed at her in silent wonderment and awe.

Smeraldina fanned her face, fluttering her hands for a moment as if to clear her thoughts, and again wiped away at the tide of tears that appeared to at last be ebbing.

"I mustn't take any more of your time, Sire," she said. "You have a true love to find, and I must go and try to…somehow try to compose myself…"

She stood up unsteadily. King Theramo took a tentative step forward to assist her but seemed to not quite know exactly what to do or how best to help.

Smeraldina smiled at him broadly through her drying tears. The shoulder strap of her dress had long ago slipped again down to one side, and she reflexively pulled it back up. A moment later it slipped back to its previous position halfway down her upper arm as she began to make her way with giddy steps in the direction of the cypress grove.

King Theramo hastened to accompany her, and at the start of the marble walkway she stopped and turned to him.

"Your Majesty," she said, filled with intensity. "This morning, my dear father asked me the same question you asked me, why would I come to this interview. What I answered was…"

She paused for a moment as moist tears again began to well in her sparkling eyes.

"Smeraldina…"

She nodded with rapid smiling reassurance. "Thank you, Sire…" she said quickly. "I apologize, Your Highness… I'm sorry… I shall be quite all right…"

She wiped away fresh tears and tried again to compose herself.

"Your Majesty," she continued resolutely. "The answer I gave to my father was that I believed it was for me better to find a new path, than stand in place or remain on the same path that had not led to where I wanted to go. My current course had not brought me to love, nor had it brought True Love to me. But Your Highness, the path I chose to take—literally the path to Castle Delprego, for the sole purpose of being interviewed here by you yourself, Sire—that is the path that brought me to True Love, that brought True Love to me. Had I not been on that path, I might not have… I might never have met… Oh, Sire, the alternative is too unbearable to even contemplate…! But I *was* on that path. I *did* meet him. We *did* find each other. I credit you entirely for that beautiful gift, Your Highness. It is a gift I shall never be able to adequately thank you for or repay, but it is a gift which has changed my life, a gift for which I shall be always grateful, happily ever after."

Smiling with radiant happiness, she wiped away more tears and looked toward the interior of the castle.

"Leandro, come to the gardens, please," she hailed genially.

"Smeraldina…" King Theramo began.

"Your Majesty," she went on. "One final thing…"

"Yes…?"

"Do not despair, Sire. I have reason to believe that what you seek is soon to be found."

"Smeraldina…?"

"I cannot say more, Sire. It is not my place. But…"

"Yes…?"

"May I… May I respectfully give you an embrace of thanks?"

King Theramo hesitated with awkward discomfort.

"I…" he faltered. "Smeraldina, when I was growing up, my parents… My parents were not always able to express—"

Smeraldina stepped forward and embraced the King in a fond hug.

"You are a wonderful King," she said quietly into his ear. "In your presence, I have discovered that I am the luckiest girl in the world. I shall always treasure this moment, Sire. It will stay with me forever. Thank you, Your Majesty."

She stepped back and tried to adjust his crown for him, but unsuccessfully.

Leandro appeared, making his way with tentative steps in through the small grove of lofty cypress trees.

Smeraldina smiled at him.

"Leandro," she asked politely. "Would you please be so kind as to escort me to the solarium."

Leandro looked with mystified hesitancy toward King Theramo.

King Theramo gave him a reassuring apologetic smile and nodded.

"As Your Majesty wishes," Leandro said respectfully.

Smeraldina turned toward the King and gave a graceful slight curtsy.

"Thank you, Your Majesty," she said, beaming at him with warm intensity.

King Theramo smiled back at her, a muddle of jumbled emotions ranging across his face.

"Your Majesty," Leandro asked respectfully. "Shall I escort the next person to be interviewed here to the gardens?"

"Give me few moments, good Leandro," King Theramo instructed. "And then yes, please do so…"

"Yes, Your Majesty," Leandro replied, bowing. "Thank you, Your Majesty."

Smeraldina and King Theramo smiled at each other a last time, and then Leandro and Smeraldina made their way along the marble path back into the castle.

Chapter 12

The Third Interview
and
The King's Revision

King Theramo was standing in front of the Mirror of Truth lost in thought, absently swiveling the lens frames of the spectacles in his hands by the pivot hinge of the rivet nose bridge, wider then narrower then wider again in slow distracted repetition. He was roused from his contemplations by the sound of footsteps on the marble walkway. Forcibly refocusing his attention and slipping the glasses into a pocket of his robes he made his way toward the entrance to the gardens.

"Your Majesty," said Leandro, bowing. "The young lady Nicoletta is here for her interview."

King Theramo nodded. "Thank you, good Leandro. Please remind Avogadro to wait for his daughter in the solarium, and I ask of you to once again please remain close by within the castle, that I may recall you easily."

"Yes, Your Majesty," Leandro replied. Bowing respectfully, he turned and made his way out of the gardens through the cypress grove.

King Theramo still had not fully brought his mind back from where it had wandered, and only with considerable further effort was he able to muster his thoughts and compel them to focus on the circumstance at hand.

Nicoletta stood motionless, simply-dressed in her unexceptional attire, her forlorn air of melancholy and quiet bleak futility lingering over her with a desolate persistent inevitability.

"Thank you for coming, Nicoletta," King Theramo began. "I must ask your forgiving indulgence… I do not know how I expected these interviews to proceed, but it most certainly is not the way they have unfolded thus far. I find myself filled with thoughts and feelings whose newness holds at present a formidability for which I apparently am quite unprepared, and consequently I—"

King Theramo gazed at Nicoletta as if seeing her for the first time.

"Good heavens, Nicoletta…!"

"Your Majesty…?" she asked with concern.

"Nicoletta… You are extraordinarily beautiful… It's… It's quite remarkable…"

Nicoletta looked down in embarrassment.

"Thank you, Your Majesty…" she said softly.

King Theramo shook his head in slow amazement. "It is yet another of the far too many things I am this day discovering I previously have been lamentably blind to… Your beauty is truly incomparable, Nicoletta. You are without question Benebento's most luminous jewel…"

Nicoletta continued to look down.

"Nicoletta…" King Theramo said hesitantly. "I do not mean to cause you distress… Please look up…"

Nicoletta obediently raised her gaze to the King and met his eyes.

"Nicoletta…" he began again. "I… Oh, what a day this has been…It is so difficult for me to untangle the muddle of thoughts in my mind…"

King Theramo turned in confusion and walked slowly over to the Mirror of Truth. He started to take the glasses from his pocket, then appeared to change his mind. Pushing the rivet spectacles deeply back into his robes, he walked back over to where Nicoletta remained standing and looking at him intently.

"Nicoletta," he said decidedly. "I apologize. I cannot interview you."

Nicoletta continued to look at him and said nothing.

"Nicoletta…" he went on. "I don't know exactly how to articulate this…"

He put his hands into the pockets of his robes, then took them out again and distractedly attempted to adjust the position of his crown.

"Nicoletta, I… I cannot ask you to be my bride… Forgive me…"

A slow wave of cautious relief was beginning to wash across Nicoletta's face.

"That's… That's quite all right, Sire…" she said softly.

"As the daughter of Avogadro, as a citizen of Benebento, as the surpassingly lovely individual standing here now before me, you are dear to me… I care for you very much… And you are very beautiful indeed. Beautiful, in fact, beyond anyone in the kingdom and most probably anyone anywhere. But I find myself thinking of you as a daughter or a sister, and not as my Queen…"

Nicoletta was becoming more relieved and relaxed with each word.

"I understand, Sire," she said kindly.

King Theramo studied her for a moment with renewed apprehensive concern.

"Nicoletta," he asked worriedly. "You don't love me, do you?"

She smiled warmly at him and shook her head slightly.

"No, Your Majesty. I don't. I mean, as my King, of course I do. But not as one who could be your bride."

King Theramo exhaled a sigh of huge relief.

"I am very glad of that, Niccoletta," he said heartily. "Thank you for your honesty, and thank you for your gracious understanding."

"Thank you, Sire," she replied, "for your kindness and your devotion to Truth. Your Majesty's noble resolve to always do only what is right is Benebento's greatest gift. It is exactly as my father says. You are a good King."

King Theramo looked genuinely surprised. "Avogadro said that about me?"

Nicoletta nodded. "My father is eccentric, Sire. But in his own way he respects and admires you more than anyone."

King Theramo shook his head regretfully. "I believe I have been perhaps too impatient with Avogadro at times… Oh, I have so much to do to become a better King…"

Nicoletta smiled at him. "You are already a great King, Your Majesty."

King Theramo smiled back at her with admiring appreciation. "Thank you, Nicoletta. That is very kind…"

He paused for a moment.

"Nicoletta," he went on. "Forgive me, but you have me wondering. I do not intend to pry, and you need not answer. But, since you do not love me as would a bride, and you have no desire to be my Queen, why did you come to this interview?"

Nicoletta glanced down with self-conscious shy embarrassment.

"Your Highness…" she said quietly. "I do not love you as would a bride. But I do love you very much as my King. I felt if I did not come here for an interview that… I feared that you might think… Your Majesty, I felt it would be disrespectful to not…"

"You didn't want to hurt my feelings," said King Theramo.

Nicoletta nodded.

"Nicoletta, you are as divinely beautiful on the inside as you are outwardly exquisitely stunning. As rare as is your beauty, it seems far rarer still that someone so beautiful would as well be so profoundly good a person."

"Thank you, Sire…"

"Nicoletta, it is clear to me you understandably are much relieved I did not mistakenly conclude that you would be ideal for me to choose as my queen. I too am relieved to have not made an error in judgement that would have been so incorrect for each of us. That is a relief we share."

Nicoletta nodded.

"And I begin to fear we share yet another close similarity… Nicoletta, are you in love with someone?"

She hesitated a moment, then nodded silently.

"Does this person love you back?"

She shook her head with slow weary sadness. "He does not love me, Sire," she said nearly inaudibly. "I am invisible to him."

King Theramo nodded with knowing regret.

"As I feared, we each wish to be united with a true love, and for us both that desire seems to be unattainable…"

She nodded a slow melancholy nod.

"Nicoletta, I have learned much already this day. While I have begun to acquire an awareness of the alarming and daunting extent of what I yet do not know how to see, I have as well begun to learn how to see at least some things that before today I would have been oblivious to.

"It is perhaps ironic and deeply unfair that one so beautiful would be so oppressed with such sadness. The weight of your despondency seems cruelly heavy, Nicoletta. Though I know you only as would a King, from a remote distance, it nevertheless grieves my heart as it would a close friend to see you so sad. It further grieves me to recognize that yours is a sadness which you have long become accustomed to. The burden you carry clearly has beleaguered you for some time.

"For myself, I now have inarguable reason to move on from my futile aspirations. This day has opened my eyes. I am astounded and mortified at discovering how much I have for so long been unable to see. I believe that ultimately this new understanding has been the unplanned purpose of these interviews. Unplanned by me perhaps, but perhaps knowingly facilitated by the enchanter…

"But I have realized that what I have been seeking is—in all likelihood—neither what I actually need nor is it even something possible. But I do not believe that is true for you, Nicoletta. What I seek is the idea of a person, one who may not even exist. But what you long for is an actual living person. Your dreams are rooted in reality. Mine are rooted only in yearning…

"Nicoletta, what you long for may yet somehow come to pass. As you bear the dispiriting hardship of your sadness, be thankful that at least your love is associated with a person who actually exists. What is impossible can never happen, but what is possible might happen. It is my opinion that you should not give up hope."

"You are kind, Sire. Your words mean a great deal to me. Thank you, Your Highness."

"It is part of the beauty inside of you," King Theramo went on thoughtfully, "that you both listen and care when I speak my rambling thoughts. I find it passing strange, Nicoletta, that through these interviews I have in fact found what I was seeking, just not in the way I had imagined… I believe this day has taught me how to begin to become a better king. Though I have longed for True Love, a bride, a Queen…there are things that matter more when one is King. I have wanted to be able to rule better, and now I believe I am able to put myself on a new and different and better path. I believe I now know what I must begin to do and how I must begin to conduct myself and my life in order to be a better king, in order to make Benebento a better kingdom, in order to begin to live up to the expectations my parents always had for me. Nicoletta, you are an integral part of that realization. You have been an essential part of my learning what I need to begin to learn, of my finding what in Truth I was actually seeking, what I truly needed to find. Thank you, Nicoletta. The kingdom shall be a better kingdom because of you, and because of you Benebento's king shall be a better king."

Nicoletta hesitated. "Sire…?"

"Please, Nicoletta," King Theramo appealed with earnest invitation. "Speak your thoughts. They are of utmost interest and value to me just now…"

"Sire," Nicoletta went on. "Sire, please… It… It is so romantic that you have until this moment so devotedly sought to find your true love. Please, Sire… Please do not entirely abandon your hope just yet…"

King Theramo smiled a sad appreciative smile.

"I will keep your words in my mind, Nicoletta," he said solemnly. "They are lovely words. I thank you from my heart for giving them to me."

King Theramo stood motionless for a moment, again lost in thought.

"Nicoletta, forgive me…" he at last managed to say. "With your kind consent, I would summon Leandro now to escort you to the solarium. I would much enjoy continuing to converse with you in this way, and if you are not averse, at some time hence we might speak with each other again. However, just now I find my own thoughts demanding and exhausting, and I must comb through in my mind all I have been experiencing this day and attempt to determine how best to make use of all I have learned."

Nicoletta nodded. "Of course, Sire," she replied with

sympathetic compassion. "Please know, Your Majesty. Not only is Benebento supremely blessed to have you as King, but also I am deeply honored to have you as my King."

"Thank you, Nicoletta. Thank you for gracing our kingdom with your matchless beauty, both your outward beauty and your inward beauty. If the day comes when he whom you love at last realizes he loves you as much as you love him, and long-absent happiness becomes a deserved gift you finally enjoy, I believe you will become even more surpassingly lovely as newly-arrived happiness radiates from you, and then we all shall celebrate not that our most beautiful gem has become somehow more beautiful, but we shall celebrate that one who for too long endured sorrow has been given her happiness at last."

Nicoletta smiled faintly, nodding in earnest gratitude and looking down, beset with heavy-hearted doubt and quiet resignation.

The two of them stood together, subdued and silent, sharing their separate sadness, each wrapped in their own thoughts.

A few moments later, King Theramo summoned Leandro, who thereupon escorted Nicoletta out of the gardens, and King Theramo made his way distractedly over to the Mirror of Truth with troubled slow steps, newly burdened with the burgeoning heaviness of beginning to understand the magnitude and complexity of ruling well that weighs down the mind and body and spirit and heart of a good king.

Chapter 13

The Fourth Interview
and
The Aftermath

As he awaited Leandro's return for the final interview, King Theramo had begun to walk back and forth with quickening aimlessness as if trying to keep pace with his racing thoughts while they stumbled through the new labyrinthine twists and turns of his pondering.

"And everyone seems to be in love with someone…" he mused aloud. "Everyone except me. Alas, I feel more alone than ever… And I feel yet more despair to realize that these poor young women—though they have love in their lives—are nevertheless deprived in one way or another of getting to be with their own true love. How has it come about that under my rule, Benebento has become a kingdom where true loves cannot find their way to each other? I am a wretched soul indeed. Forgive me, my parents. I have let you down… I have let down my subjects… I am a miserable king… I am a miserable excuse for a king…

The sound of footsteps on the marble walkway provided him momentary escape from the tortuous maze of his troubled thoughts, and he made his way toward the entrance of the gardens like someone struggling to ascend stairs of wakefulness and climb their way free from the grim confusion of a dark dream.

"Your Majesty," said Leandro, bowing respectfully. "The young lady Angiolina is here for her interview."

King Theramo nodded. "Thank you, good Leandro. Please remind Chancellor Pantalòné to wait for his daughter in the solarium, and do, yourself, please again remain close by within the castle."

"Yes, Your Majesty," Leandro replied bowing, and he turned and made his way back through the cypress grove and out of the gardens.

"Angiolina…" said King Theramo in warm greeting.

"Your Majesty…" Angiolina replied, curtsying. She gazed up at him, then looked down nervously before managing to lift her head and again meet his eyes with hers.

King Theramo found himself standing unintentionally close to her and took a slight polite step back.

"Thank you for coming, Angiolina," King Theramo went on thoughtfully. "You… For no reason I can readily identify, Angiolina, you seem to lift my spirits. You have an unaccountably calming presence that has within moments somehow soothed some of the trouble in my mind and permitted my thoughts to organize themselves with more tranquility. I am deeply grateful."

"Thank you, Your Majesty," Angiolina said with anxious humility, trembling slightly. "You honor me, Your Highness. It is my pleasure to be here with you…"

King Theramo gestured toward the table and chairs. "Please, do put yourself at ease. Find a comfortable seat and make yourself at home…"

"Thank you, Your Majesty," Angiolina said quietly, and carefully made her way toward one of the plush armchairs and prepared to sit down.

"No, wait..." King Theramo said in sudden haste.

Angiolina stopped where she was, her face flush with concern.

"Your Highness...?" she asked hesitantly.

"Do not sit in that particular chair," he requested with vague urgency.

Angiolina nodded in slow uncertainty. She paused for a few deliberative moments, then carefully went to sit down in a different chair.

"No...!" he instructed hurriedly. "Don't sit in that one either...!"

Angiolina froze in baffled perplexity.

"Your Highness...?"

King Theramo exhaled an awkward self-deprecating sigh.

"Forgive me, Angiolina..." he struggled to begin. "I... I'm embarrassed to confess, I am too impressionable... Smeraldina is a very compelling and charismatic individual... I... She..."

He turned away in hesitant frustration.

"Oh, good heavens, man..." he scolded himself. "Out with it...!"

He turned back to face Angiolina. "Smeraldina..." he went on. "She... She seemed to feel a person's luck was affected based on which chair they chose and whether or not someone today had already sat there. And both those chairs have today already been sat in, and so for the sake of luck, I would ask you to please select a different chair..."

Angiolina relaxed slightly and smiled.

"Oh, Your Majesty," she said, brightening. "That is quite

charming. How lovely that you permit yourself to so heartily embrace something so recent and so whimsical. I am very fond of Smeraldina. I am so very fond of all my friends… Sire, you said these two chairs had today been sat in already…?"

King Theramo nodded sheepishly. "Yes… I know, it's ludicrously foolish of me… Forgive me, but please sit in any other chair."

Angiolina nodded. "Yes, I will, of course… But… Have you not today interviewed ahead of me *three* of my friends?"

King Theramo nodded. "Yes, yes, very mathematical and organized of you, Angiolina. In truth, young Nicoletta did not sit in any of them."

"Oh…"

"Yes, you see, Nicoletta and I both realized right away that we were not the right match for each other. In truth, it was quite the same with Smeraldina and Clarìcé. We all easily arrived at the same conclusion, just by different paths. Paths as different, I suppose, as they themselves are each individually and uniquely different."

Angiolina nodded with some understanding, and after measured deliberation carefully sat down in a different chair.

"It seems," she observed, "that the interview process has been illuminating and rewarding for you, Sire. Even if it has not…has not yielded the result you sought…"

King Theramo nodded. "You are sensitive and very perceptive, Angiolina…"

He made his way with slow thoughtfulness to the Mirror of Truth, where he turned and resumed looking intently at Angiolina.

"Smeraldina, too, is very perceptive," he continued. "But you,

Angiolina. Your perceptiveness is somehow... More...more..."

He dropped his hands to his sides in frustrated resignation.

"Oh, bother... Angiolina, I cannot do it! I cannot subject you to this absurd interview process. I have learned so much this day. I have seen what True Love really looks like. My eyes have been opened... Opened to how many of life's most meaningful experiences I have not experienced... Opened to the vast rich treasure that is the population of Benebento, that I have hardly even begun to glimpse... Opened to the bitter realization that here in my palace I have unwittingly isolated myself and deprived myself of truly knowing my own people, and thus of being able to truly know my own self... Opened to the painful realization that I have been unforgivably derelict in my duty of attending to what matters most—being among my subjects, my beloved Benebentoans who trust me to be a good King and to make their lives better...

"Angiolina, I accept failure. And as well I accept that this interview process nonetheless has been worthwhile. What I have learned is invaluable, and I do not believe I could ever have learned it in any other way. Yet, perhaps ironically, I have also learned that interviewing people is not the way to choose a Queen or to find the love of your life. One cannot attain True Love through an interview. Whoever thought this to be a rational approach to problem-solving...?! I cannot possibly—and will no longer preposterously attempt to—find True Love by means of an interview...!

"I am ashamed, but I move forward now as a better person for my heretofore flagrant errors of judgment, and I am resolved to begin by sparing you the needless indignity of being interviewed by me in this way."

Angiolina sat motionless.

King Theramo became unexpectedly uneasy and took a hesitant step toward her in concern.

"Angiolina, are you quite all right…?"

She nodded silently.

"Have… Have I said something to offend you…?

She shook her head no and slowly rose to her feet. "It turns out that chair wasn't lucky for me, Your Highness…"

King Theramo looked at her with mounting apprehension.

Angiolina lowered her head. "If it please Your Highness," she said in respectful quiet calm. "With your permission, Sire, I should go now…"

King Theramo was suddenly panic-stricken. Unaccountably seized with abrupt and inexplicable dread, he thrust out an open hand in the air toward her in a gesture of desperation.

"No…!" he cried out in alarm. "No, it does not please me… Angiolina… Please don't… Please don't go…"

Angiolina looked up, bewildered.

"Sire, I… I don't… Your Majesty wishes me to stay…?"

King Theramo nodded, but seemed unable to speak.

"I…" Angiolina began haltingly. "I…" She took a deep breath. "I don't want to leave you, Your Majesty… I would… I would prefer to stay here with you…"

King Theramo nodded, still unable to speak.

They both stood silent, gazing at each other with anxious probing intensity.

"I thought," said Angiolina, "that Your Majesty had decided you were done with interviewing... And so, since you are not going to be interviewing me, there seems no reason for me any longer to—"

King Theramo took a fretful step toward her, but seemed not to know what to do next.

"Angiolina..." he managed to say at last.

"Your Highness...?"

"I... I... I really would prefer it if you would not leave. I... I cannot explain, but somehow when I think of you leaving, I... Angiolina, please say you will stay here with me. What can I do to induce you to remain...? Will you stay if...if I agree to interview you?"

"Your Highness..." she said. "You are my King, Sire... I would do anything you asked..."

King Theramo shook his head adamantly.

"No," he insisted. "No, that's not right... That's not... Angiolina, I want you to want to stay. But I... I do not want you to stay because your King has asked you to stay. I want you stay because...because you would like to be here with me..."

King Theramo was suddenly overcome and had to make his way with unsteady haste to one of the interview chairs, where he shakily grasped the arms for support and slid in a collapsing descent down to a slouched sitting position.

Angiolina rushed over to him.

"Oh, Sire…! Are you not well…? Should I summon someone to help you…?"

King Theramo forced himself to sit up somewhat and was about to reach for Angiolina's hand, but stopped himself.

"No…" he managed to say. "Summon no one… I… I desire there to be no one here but you…"

Quickly scanning the nearby surroundings of the gardens, Angiolina located the King's goblet, hurriedly filled it with water from a ewer, and rushed it back to him.

"Have some water, Sire…" she said, kneeling alongside the interview chair he had slumped into and urging him with gentle imperative.

King Theramo shook his head.

"No… No, Angiolina… Thank you for your concern… That will not be necessary… I'm fine… Thank you…"

"Please, Sire…" she implored kindly.

King Theramo nodded in reluctant acquiescence, and taking it thankfully from her hands he drank it all down.

"Thank you, thank you Angiolina…" he said.

She continued to lean closely over him for a moment longer, then stood up and took a respectful step back.

Still holding the goblet, King Theramo looked around for a moment, surveying his current circumstance and attempting to recover himself.

"Well," he observed ironically. "It seems I'm here in one of these chairs. I wonder what the Master of the Kitchen would have to say about that… Angiolina, perhaps you would like to interview me…?"

A faint smile made its way cautiously to the surface of Angiolina's face. "If it please your majesty," she said, "I would prefer that you...that *you* would interview *me*..."

King Theramo sat up more alert. "You'll stay then?" he asked with cautious desperate hope. "You'll stay here with me willingly? By your own choice, and not because I am your king?"

Angiolina nodded. "I stay here by my own choice, Your Majesty..."

Putting the goblet down on the nearby table, King Theramo reached into his robe and pulled out the rivet spectacles.

"Angiolina," he said. "I must confess to you—I have a way to know if you truthfully want to be here with me..."

"Sire...?"

King Theramo contemplated the glasses for a moment, then looked up with resolve. "Very well, Angiolina," he announced decidedly. We shall interview..."

Returning the spectacles to a pocket in his robes, King Theramo placed both hands firmly on the arms of the chair to support himself and stood up with renewed life. "Please," he instructed politely, gesturing toward the interview chairs. "Take a seat..."

He began to make his way toward the large mirror but whirled around in sudden alarm as Angiolina was about to sit down.

"No!" he cried out, pointing with urgency. "No, don't sit in a different chair. Sit in the one you first sat in..."

"Your Majesty...?"

"It... It's good luck. For you... For... Please..."

Angiolina nodded with mounting bewilderment.

"Yes… Yes, all right. Of course, Sire… How… How very sweet of you to be thinking… To be wanting…"

Unable to fully articulate what she desired to say, she instead went to the chair in which she originally had first seated herself and once again sat down.

A relieved exhale escaped from King Theramo, and he proceeded to the Mirror of Truth where he turned to face Angiolina from across the short distance that separated them.

"Very well," he said, reaching again into a pocket of his robes. "We begin…"

He retrieved the rivet spectacles and put them painfully on.

The focus of Angiolina's intense attention had been locked searchingly onto King Theramo's every move, and as she beheld his face now adorned with the rivet spectacles, she could not help but start to laugh.

King Theramo stopped and his hands dropped to his sides. "You too..?" he sighed with momentary resigned surprise.

Angiolina was struggling to stifle her laughter and having little success.

"I… I am sorry, Your Highness," she managed to say. "But… Sire, those glasses…"

King Theramo waved a hand dismissively. "Yes, yes," he replied quickly with unconcerned indifference. "I know. Cagliostro told me. I look absurd wearing them. That is nothing compared to the physical discomfort they cause, I can assure you…"

"Cagliostro?" asked Angiolina. "The enchanter?"

"Yes," King Theramo answered. "He gave me two magical gifts.

One of them is this pair of spectacles. They work in partnership with this mirror. Whoever wears the glasses can see what the mirror says."

"And what does the mirror say?"

"It says one thing, and one thing only. Yet, that one thing reveals information which is powerful beyond measure. It says whether or not what has been spoken aloud is a lie or if it is the Truth."

"Your Majesty... That's extraordinary...!"

"It is... And it is unfailing. And so now I ask you, Angiolina. Do you remain here in the gardens with me of your own free will? Because you choose to be here? Because this is truly where you want to be?"

Angiolina nodded. "There is no place I would rather be than here with you..."

There was a distant sound like wind chimes, and a nearly invisible swirl of twinkling points of light began to wink and dance across the large surface of the Mirror of Truth. Shimmering into view in front of King Theramo within the reflection of the looking-glass in large distinct letters were the words: THE TRUTH.

King Theramo took off the glasses with one hand, and with the other rubbed in vain at the places of pain, his face bathed in an expression of confusion and relieved surprise.

He looked intently over at Angiolina and nodded.

"You... You speak the truth, Angiolina," he said with slow bewilderment and hesitant gladness. "I... I do not know why you wish to remain here with me, but it... It fills me with overwhelming gratitude to know that you truly wish to be here... I... I don't know what to say..."

"Perhaps, the next interview question, Sire…?"

King Theramo nodded. "Yes…" he agreed thoughtfully. "Yes. You are a valuable helper, Angiolina. Excellent suggestion. Very well…"

He put the spectacles on, bracing himself for the pain and flinching as the unforgiving sting of soreness again ensued.

"Angiolina," he asked, ignoring the discomfort. "Do you love the kingdom of Benebento?"

Angiolina nodded. "To me, Benebento is the most blessed and wonderful place on earth."

Shimmering into view within the reflection of the looking-glass in large distinct letters were the words: THE TRUTH.

King Theramo nodded. "Yes," he said. "You speak the truth."

He was unable to keep from wincing at the physical ache caused by the rivet spectacles, but he kept them on and proceeded.

"Very well," he said. "Next question…"

He continued to look over at Angiolina. "What do you think," he asked, "is the most important thing about being Queen?"

Angiolina hesitated. "The most important thing about being Queen," she said at last, "is to be fair. To be kind. To bring about goodness. To make the kingdom a better kingdom. To make the King a better king. To… To love the King…"

Seen only by King Theramo, within the reflection of the looking-glass the previous words faded away, and again shimmering into view were the words: THE TRUTH.

"You speak the truth…" he said, nodding. "Very well. Final question…"

He paused and took a deep breath.

"Angiolina," he asked with apprehensive dread. "Are you in love with someone…?"

Angiolina looked down.

"Your Highness, I…" She faltered, trembling, barely able to get the words to come to her lips. "Yes… Yes, Your Majesty… I am in love with someone…"

Shimmering into view within the reflection of the looking-glass in large distinct letters were the words: THE TRUTH.

King Theramo's shoulders dropped and his hands fell limply to his sides in defeat, the weight of weary dispirited hopelessness descending over him.

"Yes…" he nodded with slow heaviness. "Yes, yes of course you are… Everyone except for me apparently has found love… None of the others were in any way distressing to me. I envied them, but I rejoiced for them. I celebrated how lucky and blessed they were to have love pulsing within them, but I was relieved to not be the object of their affection, and I never once wished it to be otherwise…"

Shimmering into view in front of King Theramo within the reflection of the looking-glass were the words: THE TRUTH.

King Theramo had become oblivious to the mirror, and oblivious to the ongoing discomfort of the glasses, pain far eclipsed by the aching despair now closing in around him.

"Yet, somehow…" he struggled to say aloud. "Somehow my heart had begun to believe that you, Angiolina… I… I have never before felt—since you first stepped into these gardens—what I have begun to feel… Angiolina, you have brought to life in my heart something I have never known, something I have never felt, something I did not know I could feel…"

Again shimmering into view on the looking-glass were the words: THE TRUTH.

"It shouldn't matter to me…" he struggled to say, losing strength and will with each word. "None of the others troubled my heart with even the merest flicker of disappointment. But for no reason I understand or recognize, you Angiolina… You are different… I… I am now broken… An enveloping sadness crushes my heart… A wretched unbearable sorrow… My world falls apart… Now I am lost… And—"

"I am in love with you, Your Majesty."

King Theramo froze. He looked over at Angiolina in stunned astonishment.

There was a distant sound like wind chimes. The nearly invisible swirl of twinkling points of light winked and danced across the surface of the Mirror of Truth, and shimmering into view in front of King Theramo within the reflection of the looking-glass in large distinct letters were the words: THE TRUTH.

Angiolina was terrified, her face white with fear. She gripped the arms of the chair and braced herself.

"I… I'm sorry, Your Majesty…" she lamented desperately, looking down in apologetic mortified despair. "I didn't mean to say… I wasn't going to tell you… I wasn't—"

"I'm in love with you, Angiolina," said King Theramo.

Angiolina looked up in incredulous amazement, unable to accept what she was hearing.

"What... What did you say...?"

"Angiolina, I love you," King Theramo repeated, trembling with emotion.

Angiolina shook her head in disbelief. "It can't be... It's a dream... It couldn't possibly be true..."

"Come here," King Theramo beckoned to her, still shaking. "Come here, and I'll prove it you..."

As if in a trance, Angiolina rose from her chair and crossed slowly to where King Theramo stood by the mirror.

King Theramo took off the rivet spectacles and handed them to her.

"Be careful," he warned. "They are extremely painful..."

Angiolina wordlessly put on the glasses and appeared to feel no discomfort of any kind. King Theramo reached for her hand, and she took his hand in hers.

"Go ahead..." she whispered slowly. "Say it... Say it to me again..."

King Theramo pulled her gently closer.

"I am in love with you, Angiolina."

Seen only by Angiolina, shimmering into view within the reflection of the looking-glass were the words: THE TRUTH.

Angiolina slowly took off the glasses and turned to look up at King Theramo.

"Say it again..." she whispered.

"I love you Angiolina."

Angiolina threw her arms around him and they embraced, entwined in an instant and holding each other as if they had been about to drown, clinging to each other with the awed grateful desperation of foundering souls sinking into the maelstrom waters of an unrelenting tempest who have been tossed a sudden lifeline.

"Oh, Theramo," she whispered into his ear. "I have been so terrified of hearing you tell me that you do not love me... It would have torn apart my heart... It would have destroyed me..."

"I love you," he whispered into her ear.

She clung to him more tightly.

"I was terrified..." he breathed into her ear with desperate recollection. "I was terrified you would leave. When you stood up to go...it was the most terrifying cold dread I have ever felt...I suddenly could not bear the thought of... Of you not being here... Of you not wanting to be here..."

"Being with you is all I have ever wanted," she whispered in his ear. "It is all I have ever dreamed of...This is a dream, a beautiful wonderful dream come true..."

"When you said," King Theramo whispered, "that you were in love with someone, my life began to leave my body... I could have withstood you saying you were not in love with anyone, but when you said those words... I was sure, brutally sure, devastatingly sure you must of course be in love with someone else... It never occurred to me that... I never could have imagined that it—"

"It was you," she whispered. "It *is* you. It has *always* been you."

"I love you," he whispered fervently into her ear, exhaling uncontainable relief and exhilaration.

"You love me..." she sighed blissfully, overflowing with rapturous happiness.

They held each other tighter, as if resolved to never let go of each other, as if determined to never relinquish their grasp of this moment that had now changed their lives forever. It was too sudden, too new, too soon for their intertwining hearts to yet know that True Love never lets go. Even when separated by space or place or time, True Love is always devotedly and ardently and everlastingly wrapped in a passionate embrace that cannot be disconnected.

King Theramo at last gently took Angiolina's arms from around his neck, and they stood together with no space between them, clasping each other's hands tightly, before letting go only long enough for Angiolina to reach up and gently wipe away tears from King Theramo's face, and for him to reach down and affectionately wipe tears away from under her eyes.

"I don't want this interview to end," said Angiolina. "Ever."

"If that is your wish," King Theramo said smiling down at her. "Then with indescribable joy and gladness I shall continue to interview you. Forever."

"Do you promise?"

"With all my heart," he said. "Will you honor me by gracing my life with the selfsame promise? Will you interview me, and continue to interview me, and never stop?"

She nodded ardently, beaming at him. "I promise. With all my heart. To interview you and be interviewed by you, happily forever after."

"Angiolina..."

"I love to hear you say my name, Theramo," said Angiolina.

King Theramo smiled and clasped her hands more tightly. "Angiolina… It… It is all such an extraordinary release… So freeing… I have never before felt anything like this. I have never felt such relief. I have never been so filled with excitement. I have never experienced such exultation. It is overpowering…"

Angiolina let her eyes close for a moment, and she smiled and nodded emphatically.

"I believe," said King Theramo, "that I now understand what Smeraldina was experiencing. It is extraordinary. It is exhilarating. It is just as she said, it is overwhelming…"

Still smiling, Angiolina opened her eyes and gazed up at King Theramo.

"Theramo," she said softly. "Am I as attractive as Smeraldina?"

He shook his head and smiled. "No one is."

Angiolina's smile widened and she laughed jubilantly. "That's the Truth!"

"Theramo," she continued. "Am I as beautiful as Nicoletta?"

Still smiling, he shook his head again. "No. No one is."

Angiolina nodded delightedly and laughed. "That's the Truth."

"Am I," Angiolina went on, "as good-hearted as Clarìcé?"

Smiling, King Theramo shook his head. "No. No one is."

She laughed. "Yes, that is the Truth!"

"Angiolina," asked King Theramo. "Are you the love of my life?"

Her smile softened and she looked intently into his eyes. "Yes," she said firmly. "Yes, I am. I am the love of your life."

King Theramo smiled and beamed. "Yes, that is the Truth!"

They both began to laugh and could not take their adoring eyes off each other until King Theramo glanced down to notice the rivet spectacles that Angiolina was somehow still clutching with a single finger wrapped around one of the curved ear-hooks of the straight temple-pieces.

"The glasses," he asked. "They didn't hurt when you put them on?"

Angiolina shook her head. "No. No, not a bit."

King Theramo smiled. "It doesn't seem fair…"

"Perhaps, Your Majesty," suggested Angiolina, "magic just does not suit you."

He nodded. "I think you may be very right about that…!"

Angiolina started giggling.

"And," he asked, smiling. "What is it now that so amuses you?"

Angiolina lifted up one of his hands with hers as she indicated the rivet spectacles. "Theramo, I must show you what you look like wearing these. It is delightful."

"Must you?" he protested, still smiling.

"Yes, I must…!"

"Well," sighed King Theramo. "Here before us is the Mirror of Truth, ready to reflect my embarrassment."

Angiolina shook her head. "No, Your Majesty. There is more than one kind of truth. In this mirror, you see only what is meant. I will show you what is apparent…"

King Theramo smiled at her. "You are now beginning to sound as analytical as Smeraldina."

Angiolina laughed. "That girl's mind," she said with enthusiastic admiration, "is an intricately-beautiful maze of brilliance."

"That," said King Theramo, "is the Truth."

They both laughed, and Angiolina took him by the hand and led him over to the table by the interview chairs. She was about to reach for the ruby-studded hand-held mirror when King Theramo gently stopped her for a moment.

"Angiolina," he asked. "Are you not glad I entreated you to sit in the lucky chair?"

Angiolina nodded fervently, placing a hand lovingly on the side of his face and gazing up at him. "I am glad, Your Majesty. More glad than I will ever be able to properly express…"

King Theramo placed a hand lovingly atop hers for a moment, then glanced down at the hand-mirror on the table.

"Is it not but a smaller looking-glass with little difference from the Mirror of Truth?" he asked.

"Within the Mirror of Truth," said Angiolina, "you see words, or where words once were, but you don't see yourself, My King."

"Angiolina," he replied, gazing at her with adoration. "I am not your *King*. I am *your* King."

"*My* King…" she repeated slowly, letting it sink in.

"Yes," he said, filled with passion. "It is the Truth. I am yours, Angiolina."

"You're mine…" she breathed with incredulous rapture. "My own Theramo…"

They could not resist pulling each other close, until at length King Theramo guiltily re-directed her attention to the hand-mirror.

"I promise," he said with sincerity. "I was not intending to distract you from delivering me my Fate. Proceed with the jest, if you must…"

"Very well," Angiolina said with a playful smile, reaching down to pick up the hand-mirror. "And now, Theramo," she proceeded. "I have a different truth to share with you…"

She pointedly handed him the rivet spectacles and held up the hand-mirror before his face.

King Theramo put the glasses on, wincing in pain.

And then he looked into the mirror and for the first time truly saw his reflection.

He started at first to chuckle, and then to laugh, and then Angiolina began to laugh, and within moments the two of them were lost in an uncontrollable fit of laughter. Years of doubt and pent-up emotion and too-long-stifled yearning now at last found an escape conduit and spilled out of them, a tidal flood of repressed feelings released through a deluge of laughter. Inhibition dissolved in the joyous torrent, the profusion of its surging current flooding out in an ecstasy of exuberance and jubilation. Angiolina and King Theramo laughed and laughed, and held each other, and slid down to the grassy ground in convulsive mirth and giddy hilarity as their laughter welled up from farther and farther inside of them and grew larger and larger and more uncontrollably free.

Soon they both were rapturously laughing with such loudness and elation, it sounded as though two people were in dire crisis and needing some manner of rescue, with noises so resounding and ebullient that all at once the gardens filled with alarmed people fearing a dreadful catastrophe was occurring, hurrying in to protect and defend their King, to save King Theramo and Angiolina from whatever sudden horror was assailing them. Leandro, dozens of formidably-armed palace guards, numerous servants, and everyone from the solarium rushed into the gardens, determined that no matter the nature or magnitude of calamity which had so precipitously befallen, the King and Angiolina would by any means necessary be rescued. What they found were two blissfully happy lovers, rolling together on the greensward turf of the gardens' grass in exultant hysterical laughter amidst the legs and feet of the interview chairs, the King still wearing the rivet spectacles, and both King Theramo and Angiolina euphorically clutching the hand-mirror and each other.

Chapter 14

The Permission
and
The Proclamation

The gardens, expansive as it was, within moments had become crowded with people. Lost in their shared uncontrolled exuberance, King Theramo and Angiolina were not immediately aware of how suddenly surrounded they now were by bewildered onlookers whose eyes were wide and round with amazement. But the clamor and alarm from the increased gathering of concerned people rushing into the gardens at last alerted King Theramo and Angelonia they were no longer alone, and upon realizing they were at the center of a growing throng of perplexed spectators, they began to make earnest efforts to compose and collect themselves. King Theramo managed to take off the glasses and begin helping Angiolina to her feet. Still breathless and teary-eyed and intoxicated with joy and laughter, the two of them continued to clasp one another's hands, and falteringly assisted each other up to less undignified standing positions. King Theramo's crown had somehow never come off during the exhilarated rollicking frolic, and as he placed the rivet spectacles into a pocket of his robes and stood trying to make himself less unpresentable, at the outer edge of his thoughts was a vague awareness that the attempt to straighten his crown was unexpectedly less unsuccessful than usual.

Somewhere in the collective midst, an amazed voice remarked, "I don't think I've ever heard the King laugh before…"

"Nor I…" replied another.

"He looks… He looks positively…happy…!

As King Theramo and Angiolina stood, the raucous din of all who had flooded into the gardens soon hushed to murmurs then fell to complete silence. Thickly encircling the two of them, everyone paused dumbfounded and perplexed and amazed, immobilized with incredulity and bewilderment at this extraordinary private moment which precipitously had become extraordinarily public, and which remained to all but the two of them utterly inexplicable.

King Theramo was in such ascendant high spirits, nothing could perturb him as he looked around at the sudden formidable martial presence—the marksman archers bearing longbows and crossbows, the guards wielding pikes and halberds, the Elite Guard division of the King's musketeer arquebusiers armed with their long-gun harquebuses—and he surveyed the arrayed might with pride and approval.

"Leandro," King Theramo began. "Sir Balzanno. You do your King and your kingdom proud in the speed and resourcefulness with which you have mustered and assembled so swiftly such potent rapid response to a perceived crisis. We have all always felt safe within the protective fortifications of the castello. But we ought to feel manifold further comfort in seeing how alertly capable and disciplined is the readiness of the defenses here within the walls. I very much regret putting anyone ill at ease and giving needless cause for concern, but this response nevertheless is heartening and impressive. Well done. Very well done indeed."

There was a long moment of collective uncertainty.

Sir Balzanno harrumphed, unsure how to react. Lord Pantalòné had his hands on his hips and was shaking his head, but on his face was vast relief and beaming joy for his daughter. Clarìcé and Leandro kept glancing with furtive apprehension at Tartaglia, and separately appeared to have taken great pains to ensure they were not standing anywhere near each other.

Tartaglia had evidently already been in a furious temper, but his ire had turned to bitter horror when he beheld Angiolina with King Theramo. He now was livid, shuddering in rage and disbelief, glowering volcanically as his tormented and wrathful eyes took in the appalling and ruinous spectacle of King Theramo and Angiolina passionately holding hands and unrestrainedly happy together.

Upon recognition that their King's life was in fact not in any jeopardy, the several contingents of palace soldiers stirred restlessly, and slowly began to move as if to leave.

"There is no need to yet disperse," King Theramo directed. "Please, all of you, remain a moment, if you would. I require but a brief consultation with the Chancellor, after which I am hopeful I will have significant news to share with everyone. Please, do stay your departure and for a few minutes have patience. Exchange words amongst yourselves, and I will formally address all of you soon."

Tartaglia was too infuriated even to speak. His fists were clenched, his face red with resentment and fury, his body quaking with anguish and outrage. King Theramo choosing to speak with Chancellor Pantalòné and not him seemed at the moment a slight which could not begin to compare with the conflagration of pain and anger that apparently had been ignited and inflamed within him at the sight of Angiolina with King Theramo.

King Theramo and Angiolina continued holding each other's hands. Even in the face of such mortifying circumstances they seemed to care little for embarrassment, and remained unshakably fixated on each other. They could not help, however, but be aware of the countless eyes now staring at their every move, and they did begin to manage a semblance of propriety more closely appropriate to a King and a future Queen.

King Theramo pulled Angiolina close for a fleeting moment with a measure of Royal decorum, and whispered privately into her ear.

"I must step aside with your father for but the briefest interruption," he said softly. "You and I have been apart for a lifetime, and now we have a lifetime to be together. But it shall nonetheless feel like many lifetimes to be away from you, even for mere minutes, even mere paces away. I am loathe to part from you, but I must speak with your father just now."

"Please don't be long, Theramo," she whispered back discreetly and nearly inaudibly. "I cannot bear to be apart from you. There is unendurable pain in longing for something you believe will never happen. And there is the sweet ache of longing for your True Love who you know will soon be back at your side, soon be back in your arms. The one, I could never have endured or survived. The other,

I can abide. Each painful moment you are away from me will just make all the sweeter my joy at your return. I wish to never be apart from you, my King. But I shall bear it bravely and make you proud to have chosen me to be your Queen."

"Angiolina, I did not choose you," he whispered. "We have been blessed by Fate to have had a dark veil of my own making lifted away from my eyes. I did not choose you. We chose each other, and through no intended action on my part. I now know what it means to be lucky. We are blessed. I am blessed. I love you, Angiolina. With all my heart."

"Hurry back to me soon, Your Majesty," she whispered. "I wish to continue being interviewed by you…"

King Theramo smiled happily. "We have much interviewing to do," he whispered passionately. "My heart craves to be near you. It will not let me be apart from you for long…"

Reluctantly they relinquished each other's hands.

King Theramo made his way with purposeful directness toward Lord Pantalòné who stepped forward to meet him. Putting a guiding hand on the Chancellor's shoulder, King Theramo briskly led the two of them several paces away and out of earshot to anyone but each other.

"My Chancellor," King Theramo begin in a soft confidential tone. "Lord Pantalòné. I beg your forgiveness and kind indulgence. I am newly more impetuous than I have ever been. I am swept away on a wave of impulsiveness and unrestrained joyous immediacy. I wish to request from you your permission for me to marry your daughter, Angiolina. If this is acceptable to you."

Lord Pantalòné beamed, and replied with respect and an equally quiet voice. "Sire, Your Highness does not need my permission to marry my daughter."

King Theramo nodded with solemn gravity. "Perhaps not legally," he admitted. "But I absolutely do, by all that I hold dear. I would not marry your daughter without her consent and her desire, and I would not marry her without both your permission and your blessing."

Lord Pantalòné smiled. "My beloved King. I am honored beyond words. If my daughter Angiolina truly desires it, then you have my permission, my blessing, my congratulations, and my most heartfelt thanks. The magnitude of her deeply-rooted love for you, Sire, is equaled by the fearful conviction that has possessed her for as long as she has loved you—that no circumstance of Fate could possibly have brought about her King loving her as she loved him. Though I would never have confessed it to her, her heartbreak would have been something I could not have endured… She is too precious to me. Her happiness is my very life."

King Theramo nodded with kind understanding. "Her happiness is now my very life as well, Chancellor. I once longed for what I thought was Truth. But the True Love she has blessed me with is a Truth far beyond anything I have ever before this day dreamt of. A Truth that I could never before this day have imagined or recognized or understood. There are few experiences or sensations as freeing, as uplifting, as exalting, as life-altering, as the abrupt removal of pain. Even more so with pain that has resided within oneself for so long that it has become an unrecognized source of continual affliction. Angiolina has taken away my pain, and in its place engendered an exhilarating joy that continues to overwhelm me. She has rescued me from an abyss that likely few but you yourself and Prime Minister Tartaglia understand."

"Your Highness," Lord Pantalòné said in an even more hushed tone. "About Prime Minister Tartaglia, I begin to grow concerned that—"

"Chancellor," King Theramo interrupted gently. "Forgive me. We shall speak of this, if you wish. But I ask your kind indulgence—not at this moment, not in this place. Not while I am still blissfully reeling with the euphoria of experiencing what it feels like to truly be in love. Not while I am still thankfully beginning to process the benevolent reality that I, with my wondrous new Queen by my side, am on the threshold of elevating Benebento upward toward the greatness to which my parents always envisioned I would shepherd the kingdom."

Lord Pantalòné nodded respectfully. "Of course, Your Majesty. This is a glorious moment, a glorious day. We should give thanks, and rejoice, and celebrate."

King Theramo smiled and nodded, placing his hands on both of Lord Pantalòné's shoulders. "Beyond even your friendship," he said. "Beyond your guidance, beyond your noble goodness—you give me your daughter. I am humbled. And I am blessed beyond any reckoning. Many, many thanks, Pantalòné."

"Sire," replied Lord Pantalòné, "I am moved and honored, and I too am immeasurably blessed."

They smiled at each other with great warmth and mutual

respect, then turned and made their way back, Lord Pantalòné to the encircling throng, King Theramo toward the center of the spectacle, where Angiolina was at the moment closely surrounded by Smeraldina and Clarìcé, all three bubbling with thrilled effervescent happiness, hands clasped, heads together, beaming with smiles, all three laughing quietly and animatedly talking over each other in covert low excited voices.

Notwithstanding the conspicuously tall height of his stature and the darkness of his garb, Tartaglia had left the scene unnoticed by the eyes of anyone save for the mournful longing gaze of Nicoletta. The Prime Minister had stalked unseen to someplace farther within the foliate depths of the gardens, consumed with bitterness and enmity while the gathered throng buzzed with chattering, conversing among themselves at the momentous unfolding events they were in the midst of witnessing and the historic unprecedented developments proceeding before them.

Smeraldina and Clarìcé released Angiolina's hands and scurried with haste and happy giggling back to the density of encircling spectators who circumstantially composed such a broad diversity of kingdom subjects and castle personages and palace personnel, as King Theramo arrived back at Angiolina's side. The two of them came together like lodestones, their hands finding each other, their fingers interlocking as discreetly as they could manage given the desperation of their need to be holding each other after having been separated.

Taking advantage of the talk and rising murmurs ensuing all around them, King Theramo leaned close to Angiolina's ear.

"Angiolina," he whispered. "You are the love of my life. I have secured your father's permission, as is right and proper, although what I am about to ask you is perhaps not as proper to the current peculiar scene we find ourselves in the midst of. But I cannot stop myself, and I beg your forgiveness for these awkward unprecedented circumstances. I cannot defer another moment what I am desperate to ask you. Angiolina, will you be my Queen? Will you marry me?"

She squeezed his hand more tightly and looked up at him, beaming and on the verge of tears. Trembling with emotion and the euphoric pleasure of sweet discomfort and agitation, she closed her eyes for a moment and nodded emphatically, before standing higher on her toes to whisper into his ear.

"Yes. Yes. Yes," she breathed. "Oh, Theramo, sometime very soon I shall better express to you how happy you make me. Yes, I will marry you. Yes. Can we get married today? Right here? Right now? I don't want to wait. I don't think I *can* wait…"

She stepped slightly away from him and opened her eyes, and they gazed lovingly and longingly into each other.

King Theramo clasped her hand tighter and smiled at her. "I feel just as you do," he whispered. "However, we have so confounded our beloved friends and family, and our loyal subjects… But I too do not want to wait, not another moment…"

Angiolina sighed in realization and smiled. "For the sake of our kingdom," she whispered. "And out of consideration for your subjects who will want to prepare and celebrate, we should wait. My heart and my body do not want to wait, but my better judgement knows we should."

King Theramo smiled at her. "You are already a Queen," he whispered with adulation and admiration. "I thank the heavens that you are my Queen. Yes, I believe we do owe to our subjects and our kingdom the modest concession of allowing adequate time to enjoy the planning and preparation of the most glorious wedding in the history of Benebento."

Angiolina smiled up at him and nodded. "You are wise, and you are right, my King. We now have everything we have ever wanted. We have no right to be selfish. How strange that in this context, being generous to the people means giving them time to prepare for *our* wedding. Yet, that is precisely what we should do. Their loyalty and their devotion to the happiness of their King are treasures which should be respected and honored."

King Theramo's smile widened. "All is just as you say, my Queen," he said glowingly. "And when the people realize the great goodness of their new Queen, they will further realize that their loyalty and devotion are even more richly rewarded."

Angiolina smiled up at him. "I will be the best Queen I can possibly be," she whispered. "To my people, to my kingdom, to my King… Although I cannot bear to wait another minute for us to be married, I will find a way to somehow endure the delay of weeks or months, or whatever span of time Your Majesty believes best serves the good of the kingdom."

King Theramo pulled her slightly closer. "So," he whispered. "Tell me if this would please you. A Royal feast tonight, a Royal hunt tomorrow, and a Royal wedding the following day."

Angiolina's eyes became bright with eagerness and adoration. "Yes, Theramo," she whispered. "That would please me. That would please me very much…"

King Theramo seemed to be fighting the urge to take her into his arms. "Very well," he at last managed to say, and glanced toward the crowd. "We have kept them in abeyance longer than they deserve." And still tightly grasping her hand, he turned to face the faces gathered all around them.

In an instant, all talking ceased and everyone looked expectantly toward King Theramo and Angiolina.

But it was Avogadro who spoke first, his eyes closed and one of his hands placed significantly to his own forehead.

"I'm getting something…" he announced, his brow furrowed with concentration. "Something that starts with an 'H'… Avogadro opened his eyes and looked directly at King Theramo.

"I sense Your Majesty is happy about something…"

King Theramo directed his focus toward the wise man.

"You are quite correct, my good, good friend!" King Theramo pronounced with earnest enthusiasm and a wide genuine smile. "Dear Avogadro, you lift my already elevated spirits. I am glad to have you as my wise man, and I thank you from my heart for all your counsel."

This magnanimous response raised more than a few eyebrows in the gathered multitude.

Avogadro looked a mixture of perplexity and flustered appreciation.

"Uh…" he faltered for a moment. "Thank you, Your Highness… Thank you for your kind and gracious words…"

Nicoletta looked from her father to King Theramo, and a smile of pride and gratitude momentarily brightened her face. Putting her hand to her heart in gratefulness, she silently mouthed 'thank you' to King Theramo, who in turn glanced a warm smile in her direction with inconspicuous discretion and nodded nearly imperceptibly back at her in equally appreciative acknowledgment.

This silent exchanged went unnoticed, as did Smeraldina and Clarìcé's taking subtle and stealthy opportunity of the moment to locate Nicoletta within the throng and make their way unobtrusively to her side, putting their arms companionably and warmly around her shoulders.

"My gathered friends," King Theramo said with more volume, addressing the entirety of the crowd. "My dependable military, my most trusted advisors and your families, my faithful servants, and all my loyal subjects. You are assembled here for the sole reason that, out of loving concern for your King, you rushed toward what you perceived as danger, that you might put yourselves protectively between the threat and your King. I do not believe there is a king in any kingdom anywhere who is as fortunate as I am to have such extraordinarily devoted subjects. I am humbled, I am honored, I am grateful. I have always sought to be worthy of your devotion, though I believe before today I have not lived up to what you deserve from your King…"

At this there was a general outcry of disagreement, and countless voices were raised in spontaneous praise of the King.

King Theramo smiled in apologetic gratitude and had to let go his grasp of Angiolina's hand in order to raise both of his arms to silence the demonstrative gathering.

"Peace," he requested steadily, lowering his arms as the throng civilly brought themselves to silence. "You do me immeasurable kindness. However, I have expectations for myself, for how I ideally ought to rule over our blessed Benebento, and until today I have fallen grievously short of those expectations."

The adamant vocal protestations again began to rise, and King Theramo again had to lift both hands high to quiet them.

"Forbear," he asked of them, and all immediately complied.

"You must trust me," he continued. "As your King, I know only too well of what I speak. But I do not now address you to lament my shortcomings of the past. Of all things in our lives we struggle to be master over, one of the hardest to control is our own thoughts. It is a deeply lamentable and inescapable Truth of human nature that too often we ruthlessly inventory in our minds what we have lost, where instead we should gratefully rejoice in the catalog of what we have. We darkly dwell on what is gone forever, or what we do not have, what we never can possess or attain, or what can never be, where instead we should joyously celebrate blessings we have had, goodness we do possess, joys that yet might be, progress which yet may come, triumphs within our power to achieve yet ahead. We let ourselves founder in the punishing squall of what Fate has taken, where instead we should let fill our sails the favorable winds of appreciative recognition for gifts given us by Destiny. We taunt and torment ourselves with what has gone wrong, when we should buoy and bolster ourselves with what has gone right. Too often we allow ourselves to be haunted and brutally consumed by the tyranny of our own cruel broodings, re-living over and over in our minds distress and regret and pain from our past. Too often, from founded or unfounded fright or anxiety, we persecute ourselves with bleak expectations and presentiments of failure, reflexive imaginings of impending rejections and pitiless vivid projections of disappointment or calamity that freeze us in place too apprehensive to act, that blight our present with an unending procession of fears about our future. Too often our aspirations and initiative are stricken with doubt, reduced to the paralysis of immobilized indecision and ruinous inaction, a discouraged resignation that cripples our will and crushes our motivation to look up, or look ahead, or move ourselves onward. Too often we cannot disperse inward poison clouds of bitterness and bygone suffering and grievous woe from loss that suffocate breaths we've yet to take, and loom as intruding shadows obscuring our view of the paths before us, misleading us to self-destructive meanderings of pessimistic dread, smothering our hopes, stifling idealistic imagination of what might be, choking off what should have been the fresh sweet air of forward-gazing dreams.

"I instead address you now and here to announce the end of the era of my inadequacies, and the beginning of a glorious new reign. Ofttimes, it is better not to start at the top, to not begin one's path at the pinnacle of accomplishment and excellence, where everything thereafter is some manner of descent or comparative failing. Ofttimes, it is better rather to begin with a more humble, more modest, more flawed standing, a position from which we can aspire and rise. The profound growth and exhilaration of betterment and ascent are rewards whose propitious magnitude is too vast even to be measured, whose roots extend infinitely deep into what is best within ourselves, what is most essential in our desire to thrive, what is so fundamental to keeping free and unfettered the treasured ability to enrich our days with experiences that are fulfilling, what is so vital to the quality of our cherished enjoyment of precious life.

"A good king ensures the safety of his kingdom. A good king rules well. A good king is a reliable leader for his subjects. But a great king inspires his people. And that is what I aspire to. I expect nothing less of myself, and you deserve to expect nothing less of your King. While I have a long way yet to go to attain that greatness and be wholly worthy of your loyalty, I have today—for the first time in my kingship or my life—begun at last to truly be on the right path to achieve that greatness.

"And no leader can be great alone. It requires help. It requires having the guidance of wise and insightful advisors who are unafraid to speak their mind with forthright candor and untempered counsel. It requires the willingness to listen and the open-mindedness to be available to the thoughts and feelings and experiences of individuals whose interaction with you is unplanned and unforeseen, individuals who have been placed by Fate beneficently and unexpectedly in your path. And above all, it requires a partner who is best suited more than any other to make that leader a better leader, and who—by being an indispensable other half to that partnership—creates and complements and completes a pairing which elevates both partners to heights of success that soar far above anything either could have achieved without the other or on their own.

"In the past few hours, my eyes have been opened, my mind has begun to learn how to see. These marvelous gardens all around us, as richly diverse in arboreal and botanical splendor as Benebento is richly diverse in the beauty of its myriad populous… These splendid gardens, thriving with growth and reaching ever upwards to the light of the sun that smiles down its luminous resplendence upon our great kingdom… Into these gardens you all rushed to put yourselves in jeopardy that you might save your King. With Heaven's mercy, your extraordinary willingness to sacrifice was unrequired, and no injury was suffered.

"However, your King did need to be saved. And I am happy beyond words to tell you that your King *has* been saved. I have been saved by someone who is the reason Benebento now embarks upon its glorious new reign. My dear friends, my loyal subjects, please extend your kindest felicitations to she who is the savior of the King, she who embodies the wings which will lift Benebento to higher goodness and a more lofty greatness… I would like to formally present to you my fiancé, the person who two days hence shall become… Queen Angiolina of Benebento…!"

The gardens erupted in thunderous applause, celebratory ovation and approval that echoed across the banquet tables, around the fountain, through the cypress grove, across the intricate expanse of the hedgerow maze, deep into the farther depths of the gardens, and up through the splayed striated radiance of afternoon sunbeams and toward the overhead sky. Caps and hats and all manner of headwear were tossed jubilantly into the air, and hearty cheering resounded everywhere.

King Theramo and Angiolina had once again tightly grasped each other's hands, their fingers interlocked in loving desperation, and they stole a moment to gaze at one another as their eyes tried to express to each other all the different exaltations of love coursing through their bodies.

Presently, King Theramo turned back toward the encircling throng, and everyone brought themselves with great effort once again to respectful silence.

"The following three decrees," King Theramo announced, "that I will now present to you shall—shorty—be made duly and appropriately formal with the imminent issuance of an official Royal Proclamation. First," he went on. "From here, from within these magnificent gardens, let us now together proceed to the Southeast Great Hall, where all of us—and many others who will join us— shall celebrate with a Royal Feast!"

Another joyful cheer ensued, and at length settled back to quiet in deference to the King.

"On the morrow," King Theramo continued. "To further our rejoicing, we shall celebrate with the event of a Royal Hunt!"

More boisterous approval resonated, and again—though with greater difficulty—then settled itself to respectful quiet.

"And most momentously," King Theramo went on, beaming with pride and happiness. "Two days hence, on the sprawling verdant beauty of The North Great Lawn, there shall be a ceremony to join in marriage your King and your Queen Angiolina... A Royal Wedding!"

The crowd erupted in applause and cheers that nothing now would or could silence, and all at once everything was a noisy sea of activity and commotion moving in all directions. With chaotic joyfulness, the celebratory tumult started to undulate unhurriedly in the general direction of the marble walkway, gradually beginning to wend its way toward the interior of the castle and ultimately the Southeast Great Hall, the languorously-migrating swell of animated happy humanity proceeding with slow boisterous leisure, taking its time to exit, lingering, and savoring the vibrant new excitement still freshly pulsing the air of the Palace Gardens.

Chapter 15

The King's Directive
and
The Prime Minister's Resolve

King Theramo and Angiolina were quickly surrounded by the King's inner circle of advisors and Smeraldina and Clarìcé. People still were everywhere, milling about, taking their time with making their way toward the cypress grove and back into the castle, and the gardens continued to reverberate with more celebration and joyful conversation than ever they had contained since first they were conceived and constructed and landscaped by King Theramo's parents, King Bernini and Queen Donatella.

Still the locus of energy and attention, King Theramo and Angiolina stood where they had been, and within moments—while each still held the hand of the other—they had shifted from being side-by-side to standing back-to-back as King Theramo became engaged with the advisors of his inner circle, and Angiolina again was encompassed by the affectionate and enthusiastic celebratory zeal of Smeraldina and Clarìcé. Nicoletta was nowhere to be seen, having slipped away and out of the gardens once the King had finished speaking.

Joined by their hands and their love, Angiolina and King Theramo were bound to each other in their private world of mutual devotion while also at the same time each occupying a different world, Angiolina inhabiting a realm of companionship with her friends, and King Theramo inhabiting a world of eminence and governance with his trusted advisors.

"My Liege," Sir Balzanno was suggesting. "Why not have the feast here in the gardens? There is already all around us food and drink enough for several banquets!"

King Theramo nodded, laughing. "You are of course unerring in that observation," he admitted cheerily. "However, I believe the vast and unencumbered floorplan of the Southeast Great Hall will better accommodate the even larger numbers of guests I am with hopeful anticipation expecting to attend. And I have the greatest confidence in the Master of the Kitchen, that he shall be able to work his characteristic wonders and whimsy there on short notice, as well as dispatch his capable legion of assistants to transfer to there all the savory culinary excess currently residing here. None of this lavish abundance shall go to waste. It is a moveable feast and shall follow us thither!"

All surrounding the King nodded and laughed in accord and amusement at the diverting jest of this pronouncement.

"Sire," interjected Leandro, smiling with happiness for his King. "I should remind Your Highness, the instructions of the enchanter were that the parrot remain here in the gardens."

King Theramo nodded. "Very scrupulous of you, good Leandro," he said with appreciation. "As always. We of course shall follow the enchanter's directions to the letter. The parrot shall remain. Please do yourself personally take charge of ensuring that the over-eager Master of the Kitchen and his zealot minions clearly understand that by direct order of the King, they are to leave the parrot and its current perch-arrangement untouched and utterly undisturbed as they go about perpetrating their various catering and décor-installation eccentricities."

"Yes, Your Majesty," Leandro replied respectfully.

"But Leandro," King Theramo went on. "The chairs…"

"Yes, Your Majesty?"

With his free hand, King Theramo indicated the ninefold assemblage of plushly-upholstered interview armchairs.

"I have imperative need," he continued, "of your steadfast dedication to detail…"

With an unseen quick loving squeeze of his other hand, King Theramo signaled a silent request to Angiolina who instantly seemed to grasp the intent, and without their turning or otherwise acknowledging each other, she quickly squeezed his hand in reply and they reluctantly released the interlocking of their fingers, while all the while continuing to outwardly maintain their focus on the interactions they each were separately in the midst of.

King Theramo put a hand on Leandro's shoulder and steered him over to the array of seating.

"Leandro," he went on, now placing a hand firmly on the high decorative back of one specific seat. "This chair is the Lucky Chair. It is the chair Angiolina sat in. It is to be moved to the throne room to become her throne."

"Yes, Your Majesty," Leandro replied.

"And," King Theramo continued, placing his other hand on the back of the chair next to it. "This is the chair *I* sat in."

"Sire…?"

King Theramo smiled. "It is a long story, Leandro. I shall happily share it with you. But for now, this chair is to become my throne. It is to be moved to the Throne Room where it will replace my current throne. Both these two chairs will be set side-by-side, as the new thrones for the new King and new Queen. I say 'new' King because I am a very different King than I was when this day began. And in addition to the supreme inner significance they hold personally for me and Angiolina, I hope as well these outwardly less-extraordinary chairs will serve as palpable reminders of the inestimable value of Good Luck and the crucial importance of maintaining a humble seat when trying to rule well…"

Leandro nodded, smiling with understanding and admiration. "All will be as you have said, Your Majesty," he replied with great respect.

King Theramo smiled appreciatively at his loyal and dependable most-trusted of guards, and led himself and Leandro back to the inner circle of advisors and the innermost circle of the sublime sphere of Angiolina's presence.

Returning to his former stance, King Theramo discreetly reached behind himself until his hand found Angiolina's and their fingers tightened together in gladness and relieved reunion as the two of them continued their separate conversations.

"Lord Pantalòné," King Theramo resumed. "I…"

He paused for a moment and looked around.

"Where is Prime Minister Tartaglia?" King Theramo asked with sudden surprise and mild concern.

Avogadro took a deep mystical breath and touched a hand to his forehead. "Your Highness," Avogadro began, gesturing with an open palm. "I sense he is not here with us…"

King Theramo placed a kind hand for a moment on the shoulder of his wise man's vibrantly-colorful exotic raiment.

"Avogadro," said King Theramo earnestly. "As you are dependably wont, you have once again reliably revealed a relevant insight whose import is considerable. Thank you, my good friend."

More eyebrows were raised at this compliment, but Avogadro seemed cautiously relieved and pleased, and visibly appreciative of the newly magnanimous praise from his King. Without a word of response he simply nodded a grateful acknowledgement toward King Theramo.

"Does anyone know where he is?" King Theramo went on.

"I have not seen him since first we all entered the gardens, My Liege," reported Sir Balzanno.

"Nor I, Your Highness," said Leandro.

Lord Pantalòné shook his head in accord with the others.

"Regrettable, and oddly inexplicable…" King Theramo said thoughtfully. "Very well. We must nevertheless proceed. Lord Pantalòné?"

"Your Highness?"

"In future, Royal Proclamations are to be issued jointly, in shared authorship and authority by both the King and the Queen, beginning with the official Royal Proclamation I spoke publicly of moments ago. I desire that Proclamation to be issued not by me, but rather by me and Angiolina together.

Notwithstanding that she has yet to be formally installed on her throne as Queen, by my Royal directive she has the authority—for this proclamation—to act as fully empowered Queen. I shall invoke the *Grandmother Clause.*"

Pantalòné looked quizzically at King Theramo.

"Sire…? he asked with some hesitation. "*Grandmother Clause*…?"

King Theramo nodded matter-of-factly. "Is it not a legitimately legally binding instrument?"

"Sire…?"

"Come along, Chancellor. The *Grandfather Clause* exempts from new regulation certain circumstances based on their status in the past. Does not the *Grandmother Clause* exempt from current regulation certain circumstances based on their status in the future?"

Chancellor Pantalòné's brow wrinkled as he struggled to interpret what he was being directed to implement.

"Your Majesty, I…" he began. "Yes. Yes, of course, Sire. It shall be as you deem. For this proclamation, Angiolina shall be… er… *Grandmothered*-in to act as Queen in a way that is legally binding throughout all the land."

King Theramo nodded and smiled broadly. "Good man, Pantalòné," he extolled with appreciation. "Thank you indeed."

"Thank you, Your Majesty," Lord Pantalòné replied with polite respect.

And now the inner-circle group-clusters all found themselves finally ready to make their way out of the gardens. King Theramo and Angiolina silently and unwillingly recognized the inconvenient and inevitable necessity of again letting go of each other's hand. In a brief span of time they had become wholly accustomed to indulging in the luxury of uninterrupted physical contact with each other, a luxury which but a short time earlier had been entirely outside the realm of possible reality for either of them, and a luxury that in turn they would now have to learn how to periodically endure being without.

Lord Pantalòné found his way at last to his daughter and embraced her, and Angiolina put her head on her father's shoulder and for a moment wept private silent tears of relief and happiness.

King Theramo removed from a pocket of his robes the rivet spectacles that had—in no way he could precisely identify—nevertheless somehow indispensably assisted him in finding what he had sought. But however it had come about, they had indeed served their purpose and should be returned with boundless gratitude to Cagliostro. King Theramo handed the glasses to Leandro and asked him to place them on the banquet table by the candlestick where the parrot remained contentedly perched. Two things together that would be returned gratefully to the enchanter.

And then amidst unending high-spirited laughter and conversation, they proceeded all together as a group out of the gardens, heading toward the joyous celebration awaiting them in the Southeast Great Hall, the history-making Royal Banquet to honor the imminent marriage of King Theramo and Queen Angiolina.

Presently the gardens was returned to its former tranquility, and the only sounds now were the faint stirring of leaves in the highest trees moved by the gentle gusts of a warm breeze, and the cheering chirping of birds, and the hushed endless cascade of placidly spilling waters trickling and slowly-overflowing from tier to tier in the ornately sculpted circular vasques of the great marble fountain.

The afternoon had slipped inexorably into late afternoon, and as the shadows had lengthened, the brightness of the gardens had gradually dimmed, and the flickering glow of always-lit pole-torches arrayed like faithful sentries all throughout the gardens began to more visibly glimmer amidst the darkening foliage of the vast greenery.

Into this peaceful solitude, Tartaglia emerged from where he had taken refuge with his fury in a remote corner of the verdant piazza. He now stalked in smoldering rage back to the scene of the awfulness he had escaped from, awfulness he could not bear to witness, though the too-clear sounds of the appalling proceedings had not spared his ears, or ceased to inflict cruel pain upon his heart, or slowed the terrible wrath seething in his veins.

With only mild interest he surveyed the nearby gardens to confirm he was indeed alone as he began to pace back and forth before several of the banquet tables in nearly uncontainable anguish and anger.

"I assuredly shall NOT subject myself to the humiliation of that absurd feast," he muttered furiously. "I have nothing to celebrate... And I refuse to have my eyes tormented by having to see that incompetent fool Theramo with *my* Angiolina... And I most assuredly will NOT allow *my* Angiolina to ever become married to that thieving imbecile Theramo...!! Odds bodkins...!!!"

From overwrought outrage, Tartaglia's voice had surged to a thundercloud yell, and at length he paused to look furtively around, ensuring there still remained no one to observe or hear him in his blistering throes of hurt and hatred.

"It boils my blood…" he lamented viciously. "I must figure out a way to right this horrific turn of events… I have two days in which to resolve this problem… Think, Tartaglia… Think…"

He clenched his fists and pressed his knuckles against the temples of his head as though to further punish his mind, or by force and might somehow compel an idea to formulate itself within his desperate thoughts.

And then it came to him.

"Of course," he said aloud with chilling calm and sinister realization. "The simplest answer is always the best solution. Theramo must die. And I shall be the one who puts him out of my misery. I shall be the one who kills the King…

"By sovereign edict and Royal protocol, the line of succession to the crown is well-established and unchallengeable. Theramo has no living relative or next-of-kin. When he dies, he will not yet have married, so there will be no queen. Therefore, by statute and long-standing decree, the next in line to the throne is the Prime Minister. So once the King is dead, Tartaglia shall by law ascend to the throne, and then I shall be the King of Benebento…!

"No one must know it was I who ended his worthless life. Nothing must interfere with my at last being able to hold my Angiolina in my arms…

"Oh, the image of Angiolina clutching him with love burns

my mind and scalds my heart… Odds bodkins! The unfairness of it all…!!

"It is the magic of that accursed enchanter… That is what Theramo wanted magic for… That is why he insisted on speaking to the enchanter alone… That is why he arranged the sham pretext of those fraudulent interviews… He used the enchanter's magic to make Angiolina falsely think she is in love with him…

"That power could be very useful for me… It would be a shame for that knowledge to die with the King when I kill him… I shall be vigilant for an opportunity to force him to confess to me how it was done, to force him to give that power to me. If I cannot extract the information and ability from him in one way or another, then I shall simply proceed with killing him. But if I can get the knowledge, acquire the power, and THEN kill him, that would be fitting retribution and sweet vengeance for all he has forced me to suffer…

"I shall not long have to endure the agony of this punishment. The Hunt is tomorrow. I shall insist that Theramo and I hunt together alone. Two shall go out, but only one will return. A terrible hunting accident. So tragic. I will ascend to the throne, and console Angiolina with the assurance of a marriage to ME…

"And if the enchanter's magic ceases to affect her once Theramo is dead, it will all be so much easier.

"But if the enchanter's magic persists, then I must be sure to possess the same power myself, that I can forcibly shift her affections of love onto me. Oh, Theramo. What a shame that from your grave you will not be able to see how I shall undo the wrong you have done to me. All I ever wanted was Angiolina for myself. But you and your enchanter had to take her from me!! Odds bodkins…! Well, Theramo, I shall take back from you three times what you have stolen from me. You took from me my Angiolina. I shall take from you Angiolina, AND your throne, AND your life…!"

The rage and pain portrayed so grimly across the gaunt features of Tartaglia's face were now complicated by evident determination settling with resolute antipathy into his expression. And where his body had been bent with defeat and despair, his frame now had straightened and strengthened, reinvigorated with the dark energy of his newly-crafted scheme. Minutes earlier he had skulked away with vanquished spirit, recoiling in covert retreat to agonized isolation deep within the outer gardens; now animated with sinister purpose and fortified with menacing intent, he stalked tall and daunting in long decisive strides along the marble walkway and through the cypress grove, making his way ominously out of the gardens, the swelling billows of his dusky robes swirling around him like new smoke from a rekindled fire.

Chapter 16

The Witch's Expectation
and
The Squire's Allegiance

Emerging from unseen concealment behind one of the cypress trees, Fatta Morganna came forth onto the marble walkway and made her way into the heart of the gardens, seeming to glide along as if invisibly suspended just above the surface of the grounds, coasting with fluid strides and deliberate purpose to one of the banquet tables.

"Italo!" the witch summoned imperiously, glancing back in the direction of the entrance to the gardens. "Come here to me, boy!"

Reluctantly compliant, Italo came with unwilling steps in through the cypress grove and along the marble walkway until he arrived where Fatta Morganna stood with poised expectance.

"What do you want from me, witch?" Italo demanded with dislike and disinclination.

"Silence!" Fatta Morganna commanded, and pointed a long pale ring-laden finger at the parrot. "The enchanter can see all the bird sees and hear all that it hears. I shall soon put a stop to that."

"But," protested Italo. "You have no magical powers…"

"Fool," Fatta Morganna retorted with impatient derision. "Most things that need accomplishing can be done without the need for magic. Observe…"

As the parrot blinked impassively and watched with its head tilted to one side, Fatta Morganna reached for the polished knob atop the gleaming metal dome of the enormously tall cylindrical cake-cover. With a single smooth motion she lifted the cover off and away from the suddenly visible vivid colors and ornate elaborateness of the towering multi-tiered cake, then lowered the huge covering over the parrot, effectively enclosing the candlestick perch, the parrot, and the full length of the parrot's lengthy colorful tail completely within the shiny silo, dropping the cover all the way down until the bottom rim settled flatly and securely onto the surface of the banquet table, sealing off the parrot's ability to see or hear anything outside the high domed-top containment.

"Miserable bird," Fatta Morganna groused. "I once arranged for Cagliostro to receive as an anonymous gift that winged wretch. And I had put onto it a very special spell, that I might peer through its eyes and ears to spy on the enchanter. But that odious Cagliostro detected my spell and negated it so I could neither see nor hear through the detestable parrot! Loathsome sorcerer! And then he had the gall to steal my idea and make it so that HE could now use the eyes and ears of the idiotic bird to spy on others. Well, he won't succeed with using my idea against me. Not now, not here."

Fatta Morganna glanced for a disdainful moment at the towering superfluity of the now fully-revealed cake. "Wasteful and idiotic," she remarked with contempt. "It's an embarrassment. So typical. A garish glut of confection. A sickly-sweet oversized monument to all their misplaced priorities and wasteful extravagance…"

Swiping a finger across one of the tier-tops, she scooped a dollop of icing and ornately festooned confectionary decoration, closing her mouth over the sugary haul and the end of her finger, licking off the frosting.

"Hmm…" she mused. "Tasty. But stupid. Who makes a cake this big? It's absurd. Only that ridiculous Master of the Kitchen could cook up a half-baked idea this disproportionately stupid."

Italo was outraged. "This is the Palace Gardens!" he protested. "We're not permitted here without the express invitation of the King! How did you even get into the castle?"

"I'm a witch," Fatta Morganna said simply.

"But, you've lost all your powers…"

"Not my powers of cleverness, idiot," she replied disdainfully.

Italo stood firm. "Why have you compelled me to follow you here?" he demanded.

"I have need of you, Italo," she explained calmly. "I intend to put you to good use. Your squandered skills and blind devotion will at last be put to work on something worthwhile instead of on scampering frantically around like a servile child attending to all the ridiculous whims and nonsense of that fool knight Balzanno."

"I faithfully serve Sir Balzanno as his loyal squire," Italo stated with pride. "I help to make him a better knight. And one day he will reward me by elevating me to knighthood, making me a knight myself."

Fatta Morganna shook her head in contempt. "Such touching devotion. And such stupidly blind trust. He will never knight you. He wishes only to keep you at his beck and call. He has no view of your future beyond your ability to serve his own selfish needs and wants."

"You do not speak the truth, witch."

"Silence, idiot. You're too young and stupid to know what you're talking about or to understand the bitter realities of the harsh world. And besides, becoming a knight is an idiotic ambition. What a waste of life."

Italo remained proudly protective and tenaciously steadfast. "No matter what you think, witch, becoming a knight is the noblest of aspirations. I desire and intend nothing more nor less than to one day become a knight, and I know Sir Balzanno will help me to achieve that ambition, just as he has always promised me."

"You're pathetic," remarked Fatta Morganna dismissively. "Regardless, we have work to do. YOU have work to do. For ME. Did you see Tartaglia leaving just now?"

"I did," replied Italo. "What of it?"

Fatta Morganna licked cake-frosting residue off the end of her finger. Against the pale complexion of her face, the deep crimson of her lips stood out starkly as they thinned and spread into an eagerly sinister smile. "Tartaglia has a fabulously evil plan in his mind," she said with wicked enthusiasm. "Tomorrow, in the Forest of Aldente, he shall kill King Theramo."

Italo looked stunned. "Kill the King?" he exclaimed, appalled and incredulous. "We must stop him!"

"Stop him?" grinned Fatta Morganna. "We are going to help him!"

Italo shook his head adamantly. "Not I, witch!" he declared.

"If it costs me my own life, I shall thwart Tartaglia's evil plans! No one shall take the life of my King!"

Fatta Morganna scoffed with offhand scorn. "Oh, don't be so sentimental. No one will miss Theramo. Besides, the King's death is the centerpiece of Tartaglia's plan, and Tartaglia is the centerpiece of my plan!"

His face tense with alarm and his fists clenched in righteous resolve, Italo turned to leave. "I'm going to tell Sir Balzanno...!"

Fatta Morganna pointed a long ring-adorned finger at him. "Not so fast, tattletale. You wish to become a knight, Italo, do you not?"

Italo paused. "I do," he replied defiantly. "What of it?"

"Balzanno will never allow that to happen. He will keep you serving him as his squire until you are an old man."

"Then I shall die as a loyal squire!"

"You shall die as a loyal idiot. Listen to me, Italo. Tomorrow is very important. Once Tartaglia has killed the King, I shall then regain my powers as soon as the sun sets. If you help Tartaglia complete his evil plan, I will reward you. By making you a knight. But it is imperative that Tartaglia not know it was I who first planted the seeds of evil in his mind. So when you assist him with accomplishing his plan, you must help him secretly."

Italo stared at Fatta Morganna in disbelief. "Not only have you lost your powers, witch, but you have lost your wits. Did you really think I would ever help you? For any price? I answer only to the Code of Chivalry!"

Fatta Morganna scowled with annoyed resignation. "Fie on you and your chivalry…!"

With the speed of a swordstroke, one of her hands had reached into a fold of her cloak and withdrawn a dark glass vile whose stopper she now flipped off and away with a flick of her thumb, and in an instant she had poured the contents onto Italo's head. The thick inky fluid spread like spilled mead and dripped downward, coating the entirety of Italo's body from top to bottom in a heavy viscous flow that burbled like swamp water in a bog and pulsed with iridescent blackness as it tumbled down and dissolved into evaporated dissipation.

Fatta Morganna shook her head in reproof. "I may have lost my powers, but I still have my potions. You will remember nothing of what has just happened here!"

Italo had become docile and motionless, now in the throes of an indolent trance and murmuring with mindless obedience. "I… will…remember…nothing…"

"Curses!" Fatta Morganna fumed with annoyed disappointment. "Now I shall have to trust that Tartaglia will succeed on his own. If he fails, I will be powerless forever…! Oh, Cagliostro! I'll get the better of you yet…!"

She gazed with vexed displeasure at Italo.

"Go to bed, useless oaf!" she commanded irritably.

"I…was…a…useless…oaf…" Italo summarized in trance-induced self-recrimination. "So…I'm…going…to…bed…"

Italo turned dreamily around and began walking as if already asleep.

"If any of the guards wants to know what's wrong with you," Fatta Morganna said to his back as he shuffled away, "just say you made a poor career choice…"

Moving with vague slow half-steps, Italo proceeded in torpid reverie the way he had come, along the marble walkway and languidly back toward the interior of the castle.

"Idiot…" muttered Fatta Morganna.

She turned her stern gaze to the banquet table and contemplated the high shining domed-cylinder of the cake-cover with contempt.

"It seems my unwitting protégé Tartaglia was so intent on his own fabulously evil scheming, he completely neglected to detect that stupid bird. Hard not to notice with the gaudy obvious colors of those obnoxious feathers and that idiotic *who, me?* look of pretend-innocence on its stupid bird face. I hope Tartaglia is better at killing kings than he is at spotting eavesdroppers…"

She looked for a moment back toward the cypress grove.

"I have some bad news for you, Tartaglia," Fatta Morganna said to the empty air. "Your amusing tale of killing Theramo and becoming king is charming. But once you have done my bidding, once you have served my purpose, once Theramo is dead, you, Tartaglia, will be disposed of. You will never be king. Once Theramo is dead, my powers will return, and your usefulness, Tartaglia, will be at an end. So many surprises I have in store for Benebento!"

She laughed and turned back to the domed cake-cover.

"And you, odious parrot," she went on. "Repeat words all you like. You shall never be returned to your former self, never restored to your original form in which I first found you and compelled you to do my bidding. A parrot you've become, a parrot you'll remain. Let that be a lesson to you for failing to do the one thing I spelled you to do…"

She reached forward and grasped the polished knob which clanked with muffled clangs from the many rings adorning the long clutching fingers of her pale hand. Lifting the large covering up and off of the parrot, Fatta Morganna swiped a final fingerful of frosting and consumed it before replacing the gleaming cylinder back over the towering cake.

Licking the last of the cake residue from her finger, she aimed the displeasure of her stern focus at the parrot.

"You failed," she berated it. "Miserably! Miserable bird-brain. When my powers return, I shall transform you one final time, and make you into parrot-cake. You shall be served your just desserts, and you shall be served *for* dessert, at the banquet feast to celebrate MY becoming queen."

The parrot blinked back at her. "Cagliostro," it squawked. "Cagliostro."

Fatta Morganna let go a haughty laugh. "In your dreams, bird-brain. In your dreams. It's too late. It's too late. The wheels of my evil plan turn now in irreversible motion. Your wretched enchanter can do nothing to alter what now will be. Oh, I know he can hear me. Finally, he shall know of Fatta Morganna. Cagliostro cannot ignore me any longer. Finally, he has to listen me. But it will change nothing.

"I'm glad he picked Benebento to meddle with, because it gives me a chance to finally teach him a lesson. Meddlesome meddler.

He's always meddling! The great goody-good Cagliostro, reaching down with his meddlesome magic into other people's troubles to bring order to chaos and save the day, and never taking credit, always meddling in ways where no one ever realizes it was his meddlesome meddling all along that solved all their problems for them, the helpless sheep. What an annoyance. What a waste of power. What an idiot! It's revolting. I ALWAYS take credit."

The parrot tilted its head to one side and blinked innocently.

Fatta Morganna glanced now with more attention in the direction of the cypress grove.

"And now," she stated quickly, "I must away. I hear the fool underlings of the Master of the Kitchen coming to fetch all this ridiculous extravagance and cart it off to the slovenly gluttons stuffing themselves at that stupid feast. Disgusting."

With surprising speed, she moved from the parrot and the banquet table to the marble walkway and toward the entrance to the interior of the castle, gliding away like a newly-christened sailing-ship slipping along greased beams into a harbor, heavy with portent and freighted with portentous possibility.

But it was not yet the minions of the Master of the Kitchen who were making their way into the gardens. Moments after Fatta Morganna had made good her escape, the two scribes Graphiare and Pentimento scurried with enthusiastic zeal in through the cypress grove and bustled with rapid efficiency to the very spot where Fatta Morganna had been standing before the parrot's banquet table.

Graphiare drew a quill pointedly out of his quiver and aimed it with significance at the ninefold array of interview chairs.

"Well," he said cheerily. "This is all turning out well!"

"For some people…!" observed Pentimento.

"For now…!" Graphiare agreed.

"And tomorrow," narrated Pentimento, pulling a quill from his own quiver and pointing it meaningfully into the air, "there's going to be a hunt! Why go on a hunt when you've just found what you've been looking for?"

"There's always a hunt," Graphiare explained. "The hapless animals of the forest always get the short end of it when the people celebrate."

"Bad things happen on hunts," said Pentimento with a cheerful gleam in his eye.

"Is something bad going to happen on this one?"

"What do you think?"

"Of course!!" they both exclaimed together in unison and delight.

"We're going to need more ink," observed Graphiare.

"I'm going to need more red ink," Pentimento remarked enthusiastically. "Will the parrot go on the hunt?"

"Parrots don't go on hunts," said Graphiare. "Only Hawks."

"Truffaldino!" they said at the same time, and burst into laughter.

"Tomorrow's going to be an exciting day," Graphiare said as the two scribes recovered themselves from their hilarity-interlude.

Pentimento nodded. "The witch was right about one thing," he said. "There are going to be a lot of surprises…!"

All at once, their four eyes moved as one and glanced alertly toward the cypress grove.

"The minions of the Master of the Kitchen approach!" reported Graphiare with excitement.

"Culinary heroes coming to rescue banquet-loads of food and drink from the threat of neglect!" Pentimento described.

"Courageous kitchen staff who will bravely save these abandoned meals."

"It's a deeply moving story."

"All the way to the Southeast Great Hall."

"To a previously unscheduled banquet, already in progress."

"Because you can never have too much banquet food at a Royal Feast," supplied Graphiare.

"The royal guests will be served enough food and drink for palatial indigestion!"

"It will serve them right!" Graphiare contributed.

"It will be good for what ales them!" Pentimento said merrily.

"Time for us to leave so that we can remain unmoved by the heroics of the kitchen-brigade champions," noted Graphiare.

"Time for us to head to the scriptorium to prepare for tomorrow's hunt!"

"It will serve us write!"

Again lost in laughter, the two scribes sheathed their quills and scurried back along the marble walkway, through the cypress grove and out of the gardens.

Chapter 17

The Dissemination
and
The Wise Man's Tale

The day of the Royal Hunt dawned warm and clear, and bright with promise. The King and future Queen's joint-proclamation had been posted before sunrise, and word of the previous day's extraordinary happenings and all the auspicious significance they portended for the land of Benebento and its citizens had traveled speedily and spread throughout the kingdom. Like the purity of mountain water coming down through tributary streams and brooks, branching diversely into swift rivers and rushing to the sea, the news flowed through the realm. From elaborate mansion estates, to the white wattle-and-daub and dark wooden-frame geometry of half-timbered houses, through low-roofed homes nestled astride wide cobblestoned avenues, to the angular narrow canyons of densely packed stacks of residences closely flanking intricate dusty streets, along the unpaved packed dirt of roads and paths leading to the pastures and arable land of the vast fabric of countryside landscape, across stables and paddocks and white rail fences, over patchworks of wondrously varying green bounded by sprawling networks of hedgerows and hand-piled field-stone walls, to the well-tilled terrain and patterned ridge-and-furrow fields and farmland stretching broadly in long swathes of lushly flourishing acreage, and reaching across the furthest expanses of forests and fens and grassland toward the outermost bounds of Benebento. It all looked the same as it had the previous day, but everything now felt different and enhanced. The world this day was somehow a better place than it had been the day before. From the most menial farmhands, to the humblest peasants, to the most industrious artisans, to the noblest elite of the aristocracy—the historic events unfolding at the palace were on everyone's lips and foremost in everyone's mind. The morning was brimming with eager happy chatter about the life-altering transformation of the King by the imminent new Queen. The new day overflowed with jubilant expectation of how beneficially she and her partnership with the King would transform the realm, and the very air seemed nearly lightning-strike-electric with excitement at the prospect of the forthcoming Royal Wedding.

A planned post-marriage-ceremony parade and procession of unprecedented proportion though the streets of the kingdom would ensure that all who wished to in some way enjoy closer celebratory proximity to history would be well-satisfied. And reliable rumors were rampant that the choice of the outdoor-cathedral-esque stadium-sized majesty of the North Great Lawn had been selected as venue for the momentous nuptials, in large part to accommodate an audience comprising not just upper-echelon nobility, but also hundreds of citizens from all walks of life—from every class, from every tier of Benebentoan society—that the kingdom would be truly represented in all the great depth and breadth of its myriad diversity.

It was, however, primarily those from within the higher ranks of nobility who had been invited to participate in the current day's main event: the Royal Hunt. Proceeding in parallel with the frantic massively-elaborate preparations for the wedding, were the hurriedly-assembled arrangements for the hunt—an event whose formidability stemmed not from how complicated it would be to properly orchestrate, but rather from the immediacy of how soon it was scheduled to take place.

Among the privileged few selected to receive an invitation to the hunt and now duly heading toward the palace for the commencement of the event was Avogadro, who was walking side-by-side with his daughter as the two of them made their way along a cobblestoned street that would eventually bring them to the entrance of the castle drawbridge.

"My dear," Avogadro was saying, the florid colors of his exotic raiment catching moments of sunlight as his robes billowed and his long whitish hair bounced with his steps as he walked. "Did you enjoy yourself at last night's feast? I myself found it disproportionately excessive. But the food was good."

"I did not see Prime Minister Tartaglia there…" Nicoletta replied quietly as she walked closely next to her father.

"No," agreed Avogadro. "He was unaccountably absent. But, celebrating is not for everyone. I, of course, knew he wouldn't be there. Not everyone likes the same things. For instance, I shall not be going on today's hunt."

Nicoletta looked over at Avogadro.

"Father, what will you do instead?"

"What I do every day, my dear," Avogadro explained with pragmatic solemnity. "Proceed to my atelier sanctum and work on finding ways to advise the King. Will you be meeting up with your young friends?"

Nicoletta nodded. "Yes. I'm not part of Angiolina's formal wedding party. But she has asked all of us to help her plan details of the wedding."

"Which will take place in two days…!" Avogadro exclaimed with critical disapproval. "It seems needlessly precipitous."

"Angiolina and King Theramo are very much in love," Nicoletta said with wistful admiration. "They just want to be married to each other right away. I think it's romantic."

Avogadro's long hair swayed as he shook his head skeptically. "It doesn't leave much time for planning."

"Planning it will be hectic," agreed Nicoletta. "I think that makes it more exciting and fun…"

Avogadro glanced at his daughter's face.

"My dear," he said kindly. "I sense you are despondent about something…"

Nicoletta smiled a small sad smile for a moment. "You always see everything, Father," she said. "But… No, it's nothing…"

"Are you not relieved to have not been chosen to be Queen?" her father asked.

Nicoletta nodded. "I am relieved beyond words. King Theramo was very kind. You were right, Father. I had no need to worry he might choose me."

"He made the right choice," Avogadro observed with deep sagacity. "I knew he would."

They walked on for a few minutes is silence.

"Father," Nicoletta said at last. "Is it always a good thing to know what's going to happen?"

Avogadro lifted his hands with both palms opened upward toward the wide sky. "What is going to happen is going to happen," he pronounced with vast significance. "Sometimes, when people know, and they want it to happen, they end up actually causing it to happen. And sometimes when they know, and they try to stop it from happening, that is what makes it happen. In both situations, it is their actions that cause what happens to happen. Anticipating something good can make life more enjoyable. Dreading something bad can make life dark. Sometimes people want to know ahead because they don't want to endure the suspense beforehand without foreknowledge of the outcome. Some people don't want to know ahead because they prefer to continue to believe all possibilities are available."

Avogadro lowered his hands and looked over at his daughter.

"My dear," he asked. "Is there an outcome you desire to know?"

Nicoletta shook her head. "No," she said. "I don't want to know for certain that what I want will not happen…"

Avogadro nodded. "You are your father's daughter," he said. "You are wise. To know what inevitable difficulty and grief and pain lie waiting in the future robs one of hope. And hope is what allows us to live our lives forward rather than giving up."

"I have little hope, Father," said Nicoletta. "But it still is better than knowing for certain it will never happen."

"My dear," Avogadro replied with energy and conviction. "Keep in mind that strange and often unforeseen combinations of cause-and-effect events can surprisingly bring about something that had seemed unlikely. Do not give up your hope. Hope is precious."

Nicoletta looked thoughtful. "It's funny thing, Father. At my interview, King Theramo said to me something very similar to what you have just said."

Avogadro was encouraged. "The young monarch may be beginning to learn something from me after all," he remarked with sanguine optimism. "I have long hoped that would one day begin to happen. It is a good sign, my dear. You should hold it in your heart as a portent that your faith in hope should not be abandoned."

Nicoletta nodded, now even more thoughtful.

"I wonder," she said, "what my sister would have to say about such things if she were here. I often wonder, Father, about the kinds of thoughts my sister would have, and the kinds of things she would say if she were still with us. How strange that the aching seems the same—missing something you've had that is now gone, and missing something you've never had... There is something I yearn for that I don't believe can ever happen, but I miss it terribly. It is with that same kind of regretful longing that I wish my sister were here with us. And it's a strange sorrow that I miss mother, since I was so young and don't remember her. I miss my sister in the same way, but I remember her very well. I wish my sister were here. I wish she could be with us and talk with us, the way you and I always talk together..."

Avogadro smiled, but with a trace of concealed sadness. "My dear," he said kindly. "You are the light of my life. But like you,

I, too, feel the emptiness of where your dear sister should be…"

"Father, tell me again the story of the prophecy."

"It is a painful tale for a father to recount, my child."

"I'm sorry, Father. Let us talk of other things."

Avogadro shook his head resolutely. "No," he said. "You are wise, my dear. And you are right. We still have hope. Sometimes talking about things makes pain more deep, but often talking about things makes hope more strong."

They continued walking, and Avogadro drew into his lungs a deep breath and steeled himself before he began.

"The day your sister was taken," he recounted, "I found all that was left: her empty clothes lying heaped in the middle of a lonely grass field, as if they had fallen from the sky. Possessed with despair, I took up her garments with my hands and in senseless anguish threw them upward. In the air they transformed suddenly into a glowing scroll that tumbled earthward back into my miserable hands. With trembling fingers, I unfurled the strange parchment that already was disappearing even as I read the luminous letters of its prophetic message.

"*Ripples*, it declared, *from the dark disturbance of her own grim design will one day reverse the witch's evil. Behold this prophecy which will inevitably come to pass: New wings shall bring the gift of flight, an old man shall become young, a bird shall disappear, a daughter shall return.*

"And with a last luminous flash so bright I was forced to cover my eyes, the parchment vanished as if it had never been. I thank the forces of the Universe only that your blessed mother was not alive to endure the terrible pain of this unspeakable loss of her only other daughter, your dear sister."

"Who is the witch, Father?" Nicoletta asked.

A shadow of dismay crossed Avogadro's face. "A nefarious scourge of evil named Fatta Morganna," he said. "A bitter villainous blight who revels in the disruption of order and goodness, and thrives on afflicting the lives of others with the self-serving malevolence of her vile machinations…"

They walked on together in thoughtful silence for a few moments.

"Will the prophecy come true, Father?" Nicoletta asked at last.

"Prophecies always come true," Avogadro pronounced with simple unequivocal certainty. "But the true meaning of a prophecy's words is not always direct or clear. I have no confidence the true meaning of this prophecy literally foretells that for which we desperately wish. I hold but the merest sliver of hope that we shall ever truly be restored and reunited as a family."

Nicoletta nodded. "You were right, Father. It is a painful story, but it may also perhaps be a hopeful one. I will try to do a better job of hoping for what I wish…"

"Sometimes, my dear," Avogadro explained, "the only way to bring about a desired outcome is to take action and do something to make it happen. But sometimes there are things genuinely beyond our ability to influence. And for those things, we must hope. Even if that hope on its own cannot possibly help the outcome to happen, that hope can keep us alive and strong and moving forward with our lives."

"You are so wise, Father," Nicoletta said with admiration and ardent fond affection. "I'm so glad you are my father…"

Two citizens traveling along the same street walking in the opposite direction tipped their heads in cordial greeting as they passed, and Avogadro and Nicoletta responded courteously in kind as they went by. A few moments later, the citizens' voices—though apparently intended to be politely discreet—nevertheless made their way back to the ears of Nicoletta and her father.

"Merciful Heaven," one voice exclaimed in hushed awe. "That young lady is beautiful…! Never before have my eyes beheld anything like such beauty…!"

"It is extraordinary to the utmost…!" the other voice responded. "Beyond one's ability to comprehend…!"

Whereupon their continued progress on their way carried them out of the range of hearing.

Nicoletta recoiled slightly in embarrassment and lowered her eyes to focus on her steps as her feet continued alternately to move her forward along the well-maintained pavement of the street's innumerable interlocked cobbles.

Avogadro awkwardly placed a comforting hand for a fleeting moment on his daughter's shoulder.

"My dear," he said kindly. "Your outward appearance beautifies the world, but it is your inward beauty which is the sole source of all the radiance that illuminates my being. You are the light of my life, my precious child. There is no luckier father in Benebento or anywhere else. But, come along now. You must shift your thoughts to the happiness of young Angiolina's wedding. And I must shift mine toward advising our well-intentioned but perilously impressionable and impulsive young King, and how best to help him—in his current euphoric state of ecstatic bliss—to not make any decisions that are too foolhardy."

Nicoletta nodded and at last looked up, forward in the direction they were walking, before turning a moment to look at Avogadro.

"Thank you for always cheering me up, Father," she said with intense quiet gratitude and loving appreciation.

"Take heart, my dear child," said Avogadro confidently. "Your sadness will one day leave you in peace. The sadness which has cruelly held you in its dark grip for so long will one day be driven from you by a happiness it cannot withstand."

"Truly, Father?"

Avogadro nodded. "A father knows these things," he said.

Chapter 18

The Wedding Preparations
and
The Wedding Eve Plans

After being escorted by two palace guards through more than a dozen of the splendid and splendidly diverse labyrinthine halls and passageways and corridors of the castello, Claricé and Smeraldina at last stepped out into the sunny radiance and sprawling grassy splendor of the Southwest Courtyard, where they found Angiolina seated at a large decorative table whose polished marble surface was covered with parchment and vellum scrolls of various sizes and shapes and colors. She was surrounded by a large contingent of colorfully-attired and fastidiously-groomed men of varying ages, all exuding perfectionism and innate expertise and proud efficiency, and all of whom were busily conferring with Angiolina and each other, exchanging discussion with animated adamance, and making copious hasty notes on the various parchment pages with rapidly-dipped and purposefully-waving quill pens. The air nearly crackled with time-sensitive urgency and deadline-stress imperative.

Angiolina was not lavishly or ostentatiously dressed, but in place of her own customary unassuming clothing she now was attired in palace casual finery that manifestly was garb more opulent than anything she previously had ever donned.

She leapt to her feet with joy as she spotted Claricé and

Smeraldina, and eagerly dashed over to embrace them as they raced toward her and threw their arms happily around her in joyful greeting.

"Oh, I am *so* glad you two are here!" Angiolina gushed with gratitude and intense relief.

"Angiolina!" Claricé said with lively enthusiasm. "It's real! It's really happening!"

"Look at you!" said Smeraldina energetically. "You're planning your wedding!

"My wedding," agreed Angiolina, laughing. "That's going to happen in just a few short months from now... I mean, TOMORROW...!"

"Angiolina, you're going to be Queen," Claricé said in thrilled happy amazement. "You're going to be *the* Queen...!"

"It's so exciting!" Smeraldina exclaimed passionately.

It's like magic!" declared Claricé dreamily. "Like a Real-Life fairy tale!"

"And," Angiolina lamented with cheery pragmatism, "with more Real-Life details which have to be attended to than you can imagine...! Come, let me introduce you to the tirelessly supportive regiment of extraordinarily capable helpers in charge of making sure I don't ruin anything. They are wonderfully tolerant, and so accommodatingly patient in the face of my considerable and challenging ignorance and inexperience...!"

She ushered her two friends with giddy enthusiasm to the busy site of the planning-table.

"This," she said to them politely, indicating the tallest and best-dressed of the well-attired team, "is Lord Vellutzio, the Royal Event Planner. And these other lovely gentlemen are his assistants. They all are doing a wonderful job of helping me plan the wedding. But honestly, there are so many details to attend to, it makes my head swim. And it's up to me to make all the final decisions for everything…!"

"Ladies…" Lord Vellutzio acknowledged with brisk courtesy and a slight bow. Prim and courtly as he was, he could not conceal the arduous effort he was exerting to suppress impatience at the interruption, but he did successfully manage a quick and momentarily genuine smile of greeting.

"Lord Vellutzio," Angiolina went on. "These are my two bridesmaids, Clarìcé and Smeraldina. Fortunately for me, they are here to help me navigate my way through all these decisions…!"

Angiolina turned to her friends and boasted with affable earnest esteem. "As you can see," she asserted proudly, "Lord Vellutzio is the best-dressed gentleman in the palace, although he is too modest and professional to admit it, and his marvelous helpers obviously follow his fine example. And they are all, all of them, supremely helpful and patient. I am quite confident their great good taste and skilled proficiency will overcome my many deficiencies, and lead to the most successful preparations for tomorrow…"

"Your Ladyship," Lord Vellutzio said with terse expedience. "The ladies must with all haste make their way directly to the Mistress of Costume and Habiliment to begin getting fitted for their wedding attire."

"Yes, of course, Lord Vellutzio," Angiolina replied courteously.

Lord Vellutzio nodded with respectful brevity and immediately returned his focus to the flurry of work at hand and the busy locus of the planning-table, around which his several assistants were efficiently crowded amidst the orderly commotion of multiple discussions transpiring simultaneously, non-stop conferring, animated gesticulation, and well-mannered vehement interjections.

Angiolina turned to Clarìcé and Smeraldina and smiled apologetically.

"I'm so sorry...!" she said with rueful commiseration. "I can truly empathize with the ordeal you two will painstakingly be subjected to. I myself already spent much of this early morning being measured at great length within an inch of my life, and barely after the sun had come up...!"

"Angiolina," said Clarìcé. "There is so no need for you to apologize. It's hardly an imposition. Being fussed over for new clothes! Fancy clothes! Royal clothes...!"

"So that we can be in a Royal Wedding...!" said Smeraldina. "So that we can be in *your* wedding! This is all so glorious, and such extraordinary fun!"

"You two are wonderful," Angiolina said, smiling broadly and full of happy gratitude. "Thank you! Truly, I don't know how I would get through all of this without you both by my side!"

"Do you think," Clarìcé asked mischievously, "they'll let Smeraldina 'modify' her Royal dress so that it won't hinder her style with too much fabric?"

This launched the three of them into laughter, and for a moment they were a storybook picture of close friends reveling in friendship and mutual love and respect, sharing in wordless exuberance feelings and thoughts common to just the three of them.

Angiolina recovered herself first, and turned courteously to the busy bevy of Royal-Event planners.

"Lord Vellutzio," she said politely. "Claricé and Smeraldina shortly will make their way with all directness to be fitted for their outfit…"

Lord Vellutzio turned to her and nodded with concerned acknowledgement. "Your Ladyship will please remember: it is not merely a single outfit, but several outfits they each must be fitted for. The events of the day on the morrow will proceed in three discrete segments, and there is a different style and color-theme for each. Your Ladyship herself may remember being this morning fitted for each of those different segments, as well as for the final culminating Royal dress Your Ladyship will change into for the final post-vows ceremony prior to the reception."

Angiolina nodded. "Of course, Lord Vellutzio. But first, I would kindly ask you to please give me a few minutes alone with my friends, so that we can discuss some of the oh-so-very-many things I need to discuss with them privately."

Consternation clouded Lord Vellutzio's face. "I must remind your Ladyship," he said with restraint. "The wedding is early tomorrow morning. There remains precious little time for you to make the remainder of your final decisions, and yet less time than that for me and my team to make ready the necessary arrangements to properly implement all the many details which must be precisely attended to and properly prepared."

Angiolina nodded. "Yes, of course," she said. "I completely understand. We won't squander too much time, I promise. I just would like to please have a few minutes."

Lord Vellutzio attempted to stifle a sigh of resigned frustration.

"Very well, Your Ladyship," he said with respectful reluctance. "We shall adjourn for the nonce, and return here to you in ten minutes time, if it please Your Ladyship."

"That would be lovely," replied Angiolina. "I very much appreciate your understanding, Lord Vellutzio. Thank you."

"Thank you, Your Ladyship," Lord Vellutzio said, bowing with stiff deference and turning to make a quick signaling gesture to his assistants, who—after a moment of perplexed incredulity—hastily gathered up all their planning materials and dutifully followed Lord Vellutzio off across the grass in the direction of the entrance to the castle.

"Angiolina!" Claricé exclaimed with admiration and awe once the planning-team was out of hearing-range. "You're so good at being in charge and managing people!"

Smeraldina smiled and nodded in accord. "Authority looks good on you, Angiolina!" she agreed, laughing.

"It's a good thing I shall have a lifetime to adjust to it," said Angiolina. "Because I'm going to need that long to get used to it…!"

The three of them laughed again, and Angiolina led them to the planning-table where they all sat down together.

"It's too much…!" said Angiolina, smiling with overwhelmed

happiness. "It's all too much. I wish Theramo and I could just quietly and privately ride off into the sunset for a few days, or a few weeks… Or a few months…!"

Clarìcé smiled and shook her head. "No more quietly privately anything for you, young lady!"

"Speaking of King Theramo," said Smeraldina. "Angiolina, aren't you going to watch the commencement of The Hunt?"

Clarìcé nodded in agreement. "After all," she added. "It is in your honor!"

Angiolina smiled and shook her head. "I originally was going to attend," she explained. "But there's so very much to do before tomorrow…! And Theramo and I seem to just distract each other… I thought it might be better for us both if he is able to simply focus on The Hunt and not have to worry about the two of us trying to regulate our public behavior. We're the center of attention whenever we're together, and it's a bit overwhelming for me. I'll have to get used to it, obviously…! But I'm not used to it yet… And presentation and decorum apparently are very important when you're about to become royalty…! So instead, Theramo and I are going to meet each other in the Palace Gardens later this afternoon when he returns after The Hunt."

"Uh-oh…" Smeraldina said suddenly.

"What…?" asked Clarìcé.

With her head and her eyes, Smeraldina indicated the direction of the entrance of the castle, where at the moment the two scribes Graphiare and Pentimento were scurrying with rapid cheery eagerness toward the planning table.

"Oh, no…" echoed Clarìcé. "It's *those* two…"

"They're infuriating," agreed Smeraldina.

"I think they're just trying to do their job," Angiolina said diplomatically.

"I think they just enjoy bothering people," said Clarìcé.

"Well, they're very good at that…" said Smeraldina.

Graphiare and Pentimento had the caps of their ingenious finger-ring inkwells flipped open as they hurried to a stop in front of where Angiolina and Clarìcé and Smeraldina were sitting, and immediately withdrew from their quivers their sharpened quills and began dipping the tips and scribbling text and illustrations on the topmost pages of their hand-held sheaves of vellum.

"What's all the excitement?" asked Graphiare.

"The Royal Wedding is tomorrow," Angiolina said patiently.

"Yes," said Pentimento, nodding vigorously. "That is correct!"

"If you already knew," said Clarìcé with less patience than Angiolina, "then why did you ask?"

"We want to be sure we're not missing anything!" said Graphiare excitedly.

"We serve an invaluably important function within the kingdom," Pentimento explained with great importance.

"Your function seems to be to annoy people," said Smeraldina.

Graphiare nodded with enthusiasm. "Chronicling all the doings of Benebento requires constant investigative vigilance."

"And scrupulous comprehensive diligence," added Pentimento.

"Well," said Clarìcé "You just seem like busy-bodies."

Graphiare nodded. "Yes," he confirmed proudly. "That is correct!"

"Busy, busy, busy!" agreed Pentimento.

"Tireless dedication to finding facts!" explained Graphiare.

"Undeterred devotion to transcribing Truth!" Pentimento added.

"We are not unreliable narrators."

"Our chronicles are unbiased."

"They are completely impartial."

"But never partially complete."

"We get every side of the story."

"So, what's today's big occasion?" asked Pentimento.

"Don't you know already?" Clarìcé said with irritation.

"Of course we do!" Graphiare agreed with delight.

"It's a celebration!" said Pentimento excitedly.

"Yes," said Smeraldina. "It's a hunt, to celebrate the Wedding of King Theramo and Angiolina."

"Killing helpless woodland creatures to honor the new Queen..." narrated Graphiare, scribbling busily. "Excellent!"

"Well..." Angiolina said hesitantly. "That's not exactly—"

"And will you ALL be doing the killing?" said Pentimento. "Or just some of you?"

"Look here," said Clarìcé, beginning to lose what was left of her patience. "You've got this all wrong. It's not really killing. It's a sport."

"Yes," confirmed Smeraldina, tossing her flowing red hair back over one shoulder. "And it's *a man's sport*. We ladies shall not be participating."

"Ladies no good at hunting…" narrated Graphiare. "Marvelous!"

"No!" said Clarìcé with mounting annoyance. "It has nothing to do with that!"

"Their eyes flame with passion as they await the heroic killing of innocent animals…" Pentimento said, nodding with delight and drawing industriously. "What a compelling scene!"

"Ohh!" muttered Clarìcé in frustration. "You two are *so* aggravating!"

"Angiolina," said Smeraldina. "You're the Queen. Or, at least you soon will be. Can't you do something?"

Angiolina looked politely at the two scribes.

"King Theramo told me," she began pointedly, "that because this is such an *important* hunt, everything they kill will be skinned and prepared *by the palace scribes*. Because they're so good with their hands, you know…"

Graphiare and Pentimento paused and turned to look at each other.

"Eeewwwww!" they exclaimed in unison and revulsion.

They sheathed their quills in their quivers and flipped closed the caps of their ingenious inkwell rings.

"Good-bye!" said Graphiare.

"Good-bye!" agreed Pentimento.

They turned and scampered off across the grass toward the entrance to the castle, and within moments were nowhere to be seen.

Smeraldina laughed. "Thank you, Angiolina!" she said smiling.

Clarìcé nodded. "Those two are such pests…!"

Although Smeraldina was wearing a different dress than the day before, it nevertheless was an unmistakably Smeraldina-outfit, and consequently one of the shoulder straps persistently refused to stay in place.

"Angiolina," Smeraldina said enthusiastically, reflexively re-adjusting the errant strap, which promptly slipped back halfway down her upper arm. "I believe you are going to make an *excellent* Queen!"

The three of them clasped hands, and for a moment were lost again in laughter.

"Angiolina," Clarìcé said at last. "You should see yourself. You look so happy."

"Oh, I *am* happy," Angiolina agreed emphatically. "So indescribably happy...!"

"Has either of you seen the enchanter's assistant?" asked Smeraldina.

"Truffaldino?" said Angiolina.

Smeraldina nodded. "Yes..."

"No," Clarìcé began. "I— Smeraldina!"

"What?"

"Smeraldina!!" Angiolina and Clarìcé said together.

"What?!" said Smeraldina. "I can't help it. Young men are always chasing after me. I've never known what it feels like to desire someone myself. It's exciting. I want more."

"Smeraldina!"

"I can't stop thinking about him," said Smeraldina. "I miss him so much. I don't know what to do with myself..."

"Angiolina," said Clarìcé. "Do you think the parrot is still in the gardens?"

Angiolina nodded tentatively. "It was when we left the palace this morning…"

Clarìcé looked at Angiolina in scandalous delight. "You spent the night in the palace…?! Angiolina!"

Angiolina shook her head and smiled. "Hush!" she chided. "My father and I were invited by special order of the King to overnight in a suite in the northwest wing. At the *opposite* end of the castle from King Theramo…!"

"A Royal suite!" Smeraldina remarked with appreciation. "Sweet!!"

"Looks like you didn't waste any time starting to live the fancy life!" said Clarìcé, and again the three of them lost themselves in laughter.

"Well," Angiolina said at last. "You two had better get used to it. You're going to be spending *a lot* of time with me in the palace!"

"Smeraldina," Clarìcé said encouragingly. "I'm sure the enchanter will be back at some point to collect his parrot. And when he shows up, I'm sure Truffaldino will be with him."

Smeraldina squeezed Clarìcé's hand in appreciative gratitude.

"Angiolina," said Smeraldina. "Do you think there's any way King Theramo might be willing to influence Prime Minister Tartaglia in giving Leandro permission to ask to marry Clarìcé?"

Now it was Clarìcé's turn to squeeze Smeraldina's hand. "Smeraldina," she said. "How extraordinarily thoughtful and kind of you to think to ask such a thing…"

Angiolina looked down. "The situation with Prime Minister Tartaglia is a bit complicated…" she said thoughtfully.

"We know…!" Claricé and Smeraldina said together.

Angiolina looked up apologetically. "I don't think the subject of Leandro should be brought to King Theramo's attention too soon," she said with regret. "Tartaglia's going to be in an evil mood for awhile, until he has time to get used to and accept the fact that I would never ever have married him, and that I'm now happily married to the King…"

"And you'll be Queen," said Smeraldina. "Which means he'll have to obey you."

Angiolina shook her head. "That technically is true…" she said uncertainly. "Though I'm not looking forward to the day when I'll have to put it to the test…"

Claricé took Angiolina's hand and smiled at her. "Something will work out," she said, trying to sound hopeful. "Leandro and I love each other, and we'll wait for each other no matter what, for as long as it takes until we can at last be together."

Angiolina nodded.

"Oh, look," said Smeraldina brightly, looking in the direction of the entrance to the castle.

Angiolina and Claricé followed her gaze.

"Oh!" Claricé exclaimed happily. "Here comes Nicoletta."

Angiolina sighed with relief. "I'm so glad she's here. I was afraid she might not come."

Claricé was in awe. "I always forget how beautiful she really is…"

Angiolina nodded emphatically. "She's so incredibly beautiful. It's breathtaking..."

"But she always looks so sad..." said Smeraldina. "It breaks my heart..."

Nicoletta was making her way toward them across the grass, but was not yet close enough to hear them speaking.

"Angiolina," Smeraldina said quickly. "It's not my place to suggest, of course... But do you think... Would it be possible to..."

Angiolina immediately nodded. "Yes. Yes, of course. Of course it's possible. I'll make it possible. They can't limit me to only two bridesmaids. I'm going to be Queen. I get to make the decisions that affect my wedding. I don't care how inconvenient it is for the wedding-team."

Clarìcé reached up a hand and smoothed it affectionately for a moment down the back of Angiolina's hair. "You are a lovely and wonderful person, Angiolina," she said. "I'm so glad you are going to be the Queen of Benebento."

As Nicoletta arrived at the planning-table, Angiolina and Clarìcé and Smeraldina stood up and threw their arms fondly around her in warm greeting.

"Congratulations, Angiolina," said Nicoletta.

"Thank you so much, Niccoletta," said Angiolina. "And thank you for coming. I'm so glad you're here. There's so much to do...!"

"And," said Smeraldina slyly. "You, Nicoletta need to steel yourself for when you come with us to be fitted...!"

Nicoletta looked at Angiolina in confusion. "I..." she began. "I don't understand..."

"It's all about the Mistress of Costume and Habiliment," said Claricé enticingly.

Nicoletta looked from Angiolina, to Claricé and Smeraldina, and then back to Angiolina.

"Angiolina…?" she asked quietly.

"Nicoletta," said Angiolina. "You don't have to be like us. We love you. I love you. You *are* one of us. Just the way you are. You think in your own way, you live your life in your own way. But Nicoletta, you are one of us. We four are a kind of family. A kind of lovely weird dysfunctional family. Whenever you can, whenever you want, we always want you with us. And that includes my wedding. Not just helping me plan my wedding. Being part of my wedding. Being *in* my wedding, as one of my three bridesmaids, where you belong."

Nicoletta looked down, filled with emotion.

The four of them all came closer together with their arms around each other.

"You don't have to," Smeraldina said soothingly, "if it's going to make you uncomfortable to be in front of so many people. But Nicoletta, we four are sisters. We four are best friends. We love you, and we want you to be with us, where you belong."

Nicoletta nodded. "I do want to be there," she said. "Thank you… Thank you for being my sisters…"

From somewhere in the near distance, the unmistakable two-note sonorous call of a hunting horn sounded.

The four best friends tightened themselves together for a last embrace, and then separated.

"The Hunt will be starting soon," said Angiolina.

"We three should go to be fitted, Angiolina," said Claricé. "Before the planning-team returns and has a fit of their own…!"

The four of them laughed cheerily at this.

Angiolina smiled and nodded. "Any of the guards just inside the castle from here will be able to bring you to the Mistress of Costume and Habiliment. And then, if the three of you are willing, I would ask you to please return home and collect whatever you need to spend a night away, and then please come back to the castle. If you're all three willing, I would like for us all to be together for a slumber party tonight in the palace. Just us. Just the four of us. For my last night being single. For my last night being not a Queen."

This proposal was immediately and enthusiastically agreed to by one and all, and instantly elicited a great deal of animated enthusiasm, and suddenly there was even more to plan, and more to look forward to, and more to be excited about. But the celebratory exuberant anticipation was temporarily curtailed as the planning-team appeared making their way purposefully across the grass. Claricé and Smeraldina and Nicoletta hastily said their thanks, and congratulations, and ciao-for-now *a bientôt*s, and then hurried back across the courtyard, steering clear of the returning planning-team, and making their way back to the palace.

And a few furlongs away, outside at another part of the castle grounds, the Royal Hunt was about to begin.

Chapter 19

The Stranger
and
The Enchanter's 2nd Message

Truffaldino came out of the Pizzicato Inn and looked around.

"I'm sure I should be doing something for my master," he said aloud to himself. "But since I don't have any instructions, I don't know what I should do… Though, my master did say I should take responsible initiative and be sensibly independent. But that's not so easy if you don't know what you're supposed to be trying to do…"

It was still early morning, but already the piazza was wide awake and alive with activity. The merchant shops all were open and doing business, and the shopping plaza already bustled. Garrulous bazaar vendors volubly touted their myriad wares, and dozens of keen customers eagerly engaged in energetic transactional haggling up and down the colorful rows of spices, herbs, grains, nuts, dried drupes, newly-picked berries, freshly-gathered fruits and vegetables, and sundry other food goods appetizingly displayed amidst the arrayed booths and stands and stalls of the open-air market.

In contrast to the several patrons enjoying their daybreak repast and morning sunlight at the unexceptional tables in front of the inn, at this early hour the more-ornate outside tables of the taverna were as yet unoccupied, but lively fraternizing inside was well underway and supplementing the general steady flow of sociable chatter suffusing the town square. Genial talkative discourse and sporadic bursts of convivial exclamation and spirited laughter spilled freely through the high-arched wide-open window fenestration of the inveigling taverna frontage along with the steady aromatic waft of beer and ale, all collectively carrying like an ocean breeze and abundantly occupying the circumambient air. The aggregate textured jumble of smells and noise and voices seemed utterly normal, but an ineffable pervasive sensation nevertheless made it all seem somehow different. The first breaths of this particular new day seemed charged with elated energy and eager anticipation.

All roads of thought now led ultimately to the palace. Kingdoms love Royal weddings, and the ambient avid fascination was vibrant with the thrill and celebratory hopeful expectation for how the realm would be transformed. The devoted citizens of Benebento already loved their King and their kingdom, and prospects of the realm's goodness blossoming into somehow even greater goodness filled everyone with excitement and joy and pride.

Truffaldino contemplatively eyed the hearty breakfast consumptions in progress at the inn's outside tables, which were near enough that he could smell the food's savor while he remained a distance away sufficient that no patron would mistakenly think Truffaldino might be addressing them as he mused aloud to himself.

"And also," Truffaldino went on, "my master always says you should never attempt anything important when you're tired or hungry or both. Well, I had a good night's sleep. The beds at the inn are very comfortable. Although, I dreamt about Smeraldina all night, which was wonderful, but also really distracting. But I don't feel tired. I just feel full of energy and excited. I'll bet that's from being in love. Being in love certainly changes you. I feel so different. About everything. I don't think I'll be the same ever again. And that's probably not a bad thing, because I like this Truffaldino even better than the Truffaldino who hadn't yet ever met Smeraldina. Although, I suppose no one's ever the same again all the time. Just being alive means you're always changing. So, I suppose I've never been the same anyway. Being in love makes you think confusing thoughts…! But I've not yet had breakfast, so I think I should have some delicious food. Maybe then I'll have a better idea of what I should be being sensibly independent about taking responsible initiative for doing…"

"Hey there," a friendly voice said suddenly next to him.

Truffaldino turned to see a young lady about the age of Smeraldina and similarly attired standing next to him and smiling with warm greeting.

"Hi…" Truffaldino replied.

"You're not from around here," the young lady observed. "I can tell by the way you're dressed."

Truffaldino nodded. "I'm just visiting," he explained. "But I'm having a wonderful time. Coming to Benebento is probably the best thing I've ever done in my life."

The attractive young lady's smile widened. "You're cute," she said with earnest affable candor. "Why are you standing around talking to yourself?"

"I get confused really easily," said Truffaldino. "And saying all my thoughts out loud sometimes helps me feel less confused. But also, my master says everything's harder when you're hungry, so I think I really need to eat breakfast."

"Your 'master'?"

"The enchanter Cagliostro," Truffaldino said with forthright modest pride. "I'm his assistant."

"You really aren't from around here," the young lady said. "But you seem nice, and you're very friendly. And you're easy to talk to."

"Thank you," said Truffaldino. "Would you like to join me for breakfast? I was just going to order something to eat from the innkeeper and then sit down at one of these tables."

The young lady shook her head. "The food is better next door at the taverna," she said. "I should know, because I work there serving at tables. My turno-di-lavoro starts soon, and I was going to first have breakfast with some of my friends inside before our work starts. But I eat with them all time. Why don't you come over, and you and I can have breakfast together at a table outside in front of the taverna."

"Okay," agreed Truffaldino. "Thanks."

"What's your name?" the young lady asked.

"I'm Truffaldino."

"Hi, Truffaldino. I'm Bèllabrèzza," she said, still smiling and pronouncing her name as *BELL-ah-BRET-zah*. "I know everyone who works at the taverna, and I'll make sure they give us extra-large portions and a lower price for whatever we eat and drink."

"Thanks, Bèllabrèzza," said Truffaldino. "That's very friendly. You have a really nice smile. It's the nicest smile I've ever seen. It makes everything seem like the world is a wonderful place and everyone is going to live happily ever after."

Bèllabrèzza laughed softly with surprised pleasure and modest graciousness. "That's a lovely thing to say, Truffaldino. No one has ever said that to me quite like that. Thank you."

Bèllabrèzza took hold of Truffaldino's hand and they walked together as she led them the several steps to the taverna, where they separated while Bèllabrèzza briefly stepped inside through the arched front entry to order their breakfasts. Within moments she had come back out, and she and Truffaldino sat down opposite each other at one of the outside tables under the broad boldly-colored veranda of the taverna's overhead frontage portico.

"You remind me of Smeraldina," said Truffaldino. "But please don't be offended. Everything makes me think of Smeraldina. Even eating breakfast makes me think of Smeraldina."

"Smeraldina?" asked Bèllabrèzza. "Sir Balzanno's daughter? I know who she is. She comes in here all the time. Although, I don't think her father's too happy about that. But I like her. She's got a lot of personality. How do you know her?"

"We met yesterday," Truffaldino explained. "She's the love of my life."

"Seriously...?"

"Smeraldina and I are destined to be together," Truffaldino said happily. "My master told me so. Only, I didn't know she was the one he was talking about until yesterday when I met her."

"Oh, Truffaldino," Bèllabrèzza said smiling warmly. "You're

adorable. It's hard to imagine Smeraldina settling down with one person, though."

Truffaldino nodded. "She was skeptical about it, too. But that's okay. The right person for you is the right person for you. Smeraldina and I are going to live happily ever after. Unless of course she got chosen by the King to be the new Queen. Then she'll marry him. But it still won't change the fact that she and I are meant to be together."

Bèllabrèzza laughed a friendly laugh. "Truffaldino, you are quite an unusual person. I really like you. If Smeraldina doesn't want to marry you, I would enjoy spending more time with you to see if possibly you and I are meant to be together."

"That's really nice of you, Bèllabrèzza," Truffaldino replied. "I like you too. But I'm in love with Smeraldina. And also, you don't have red hair."

Bèllabrèzza laughed again. "Okay, Truffaldino. I would color my hair red if you wanted to give things a try. But I don't think you have to worry about Smeraldina marrying King Theramo. Haven't you heard?"

"Heard what?" Truffaldino asked.

Another young lady now emerged from the taverna carrying a well-weathered wooden serving tray laden with generous amounts of breakfast foods and drinks which were greeted and welcomed with a polite and heartfelt thank-you from Truffaldino, and which she carefully and courteously offloaded and arranged on the equally well-weathered wood of the ornate table in front of Bèllabrèzza and Truffaldino with experienced speed, professional agility, and discreet tactful wordlessness before turning and heading back into the taverna, though not without sneaking a subtle conspiratorial teasing wink at her friend Bèllabrèzza.

Bèllabrèzza rolled her eyes in friendly admonishing reply, and waited until her friend had fully disappeared back inside the taverna before resuming her conversation with Truffaldino.

"Truffaldino," Bèllabrèzza went on. "What time yesterday did you meet Smeraldina?"

"Yesterday afternoon," said Truffaldino, beginning to eat his breakfast. "When she was on her way to the palace to be interviewed for the job of becoming the King's wife."

"Well," Bèllabrèzza began. "A lot's happened since then…"

Their conversation paused while Bèllabrèzza also began eating her breakfast, and for a few moments neither of them spoke as they sat and ate together, silently enjoying the food and each other's company. The rise and fall of ambient noise and collective voices of the piazza alternately swelled and momentarily lowered then rose again like the irregular soothing sound of waves breaking on sand at a shoreline. In a mechanical-arts farrier shop not far off, the repeating solid clinking clank of metal hammered on a blacksmith's anvil was halted and replaced by the sizzle and hiss of hot iron being quenched in water, before the rhythmic measured hammering clanks resumed. A nearby horse gave a short genial snort and nickered good-naturedly, giving momentary articulation to a fleeting equine musing with idle untroubled patience.

Presently, Bèllabrèzza reached a comfortably-sated stopping-place in her meal and resumed her thought. "A Royal Proclamation was posted early this morning, Truffaldino," she went on. "Like you, King Theramo has found the love of his life. And it's not Smeraldina. He's going to marry the Chancellor's daughter, Angiolina."

Truffaldino was now beaming.

"There apparently was a Royal Feast of historic proportions at the castello last night to celebrate," Bèllabrèzza continued. "And this morning there's going to be a Royal Hunt in the Forest of Aldente to continue the celebrating. And then tomorrow, there's going to be a Royal Wedding. The King and Angiolina are going to be married, and then a Royal procession and parade like nothing Benebento has ever seen is going to take place, and the route extends throughout the kingdom so that all of us humble subjects will get to celebrate right along with them. Personally, I think it's romantic, and I think it's really good news for the whole kingdom. It's very exciting, and it's all everyone's talking about."

"Bèllabrèzza," Truffaldino said, radiant with gladness. "You've made me very happy. I never wanted to believe that Smeraldina would be chosen to marry the King. And in my heart, I really didn't believe she would be. Thank you, Bèllabrèzza."

"Dear Truffaldino," Bèllabrèzza said kindly. "You must keep in mind that just because she's not going to marry the King, it doesn't necessarily mean you and Smeraldina are going to end up being together. Life is not always as simple as that."

Truffaldino nodded in acknowledgment. "Well," he said, "I'm in a really happy mood anyway. I think being in love makes you feel happy about everything. I'm really happy for King Theramo, and I'm really happy for Angiolina, too. And I'm the happiest I've ever been every time I think about Smeraldina, which lately seems to be all the time."

Bèllabrèzza smiled at him. "Truffaldino," she said. "You are such a sweet goodhearted person. If things don't work out with Smeraldina, I hope you will seriously consider spending some romantic time with me to see if possibly things could work out for the two of us. And if you and Smeraldina really are right for each other, I hope you will invite me to your wedding. You have a lovely energy that I would very much enjoy continuing to be around, even if we're just friends."

"Thank you, Bèllabrèzza," Truffaldino replied with honest enthusiasm. "I would like that. Your nice smile would brighten everything more than sunshine. And also, Bèllabrèzza, you remind me of Nicoletta. She didn't know me at all, but when we first met, all she did was help me out of trouble I was having, and she taught me how to use THE MAP OF HERE, for no reason other than she's a nice person. You're like that, Bèllabrèzza. You're a really nice helper person. I should introduce you to Nicoletta. I think you would both like each other very much."

"Nicoletta the wise man's daughter?" asked Bèllabrèzza. "Truffaldino. You certainly travel in important circles. And you even work for an enchanter. What an exciting life...! And forgive me, but I have no idea what a 'Map of Here' is or what it does. Although, it certainly does sound intriguing."

"THE MAP OF HERE is a really remarkable feat of enchantment," said Truffaldino. "I would show it to you, but my master says it's a tool not a toy, so I must be sure to only take it out when I really need to use it."

"Of course," she said kindly. "I understand. You're very responsible."

They both had resumed eating when Bèllabrèzza looked skyward as a large gang of arrogant rooks flew raucously past just overhead in the direction of the inn. She followed them with her gaze for a moment, and then her eyes widened in fascination.

"Speaking of enchantment…" she said, her observation now directed above and behind Truffaldino. "Truffaldino, take a look at the sign over the inn. There seems to be something crazy going on with the lettering…"

Truffaldino turned for a moment to look, then turned energetically back to Bèllabrèzza.

"Oh! Bèllabrèzza!" he exclaimed, brimming with appreciation and excitement. "You really are like Nicoletta. You're helping me to not get in trouble and to not disappoint my master. That's about to be a message for me. It would be absolutely awful if I didn't see it. Nothing is more important to me than making sure I don't disappoint my master. Bèllabrèzza, thank you for alerting me. Thank you!"

"Truffaldino, that's so exciting. You're about to get a magical message from an enchanter! That is so wonderfully extraordinary! And I wonder why no one else has noticed all the strange smoke and jumbled letters happening on that sign…"

"That's because at the moment it happens to be enchanted," Truffaldino explained. "Anyone who bothered to look could see it, but no one's interested in looking because of the enchantment. My master is very good at what he does, Bèllabrèzza. There is no one better. He does big important things, but using specific small-sized steps, and in ways that no one ever realizes he's been helping them. It's a real talent…"

Above the entrance to the inn and extending forward into the air of the piazza, one side of the left-and-right-facing inn sign was in Bèllabrèzza's direct line-of-sight upward from where she sat. Truffaldino had been sitting with his back to that direction, and as he now turned in his seat again and looked up behind him, he too was able to see it plainly.

Wisps of vapor were once again roiling vaguely from the sign, and as it had the previous day, the suspended sign now swayed slightly on its chains, seemingly from activity transpiring across its surface. The original inn-name letters were nowhere to be seen. Small dark disconnected pieces of something else now ranged for a moment over the light-color paint of the sign's background before organizing themselves into the individual component parts of discernable blackletter characters, ultimately arranging themselves into recognizable text which appeared to scroll from right to left, disassembling in manic fragments at one side and dashing back to re-assemble differently on the opposite side to successfully display the effect of procession in a moving lucid message.

As he had done the day before, Truffaldino again carefully read aloud each word that materialized and traveled the horizontal distance across the painted wooden length of the inn-sign surface.

"*2nd Message for Truffaldino,*" he began methodically.

"Truffaldino, the parrot has flown away from the Palace Gardens and is now somewhere in the Forest of Aldente. Use THE MAP OF HERE to find the parrot, and bring the parrot back to the Palace Gardens."

Truffaldino's forehead wrinkled in momentary confusion. "Parrots can fly…?" he said with perplexed surprise.

"What color head?" asked Bèllabrèzza.

"Blue and gold," said Truffaldino, turning back around to face Bèllabrèzza. "And green on the top."

"And then some more green? And the rest all beautiful hues of all different blues? And a really long tail?"

Truffaldino nodded.

"Yes, they can fly," said Bèllabrèzza. "When they're soaring, they look like angels."

On the inn sign, the change had not lasted long. The small component parts of the message's characters once again reverted to full-sized rooks, rising off the sign like black champagne bubbles and bursting back to their true form with slapping flaps of ink-dark glossy wings that caught the sunlight like obsidian. The mob re-assembled, no longer as letters but now once again as an unruly triumphant airborne throng cawing with clamorous arrogance, as though irritated at having been temporarily re-purposed but smugly self-satisfied at the successful mastery of their performance, and defiantly daring anyone or anything to challenge them in any context. Leaving behind the now once again fully-restored sign, they made their way with unapologetic stridence and aerial commotion back the way they had come.

Truffaldino stood up, and across the table from him Bèllabrèzza stood up as well.

"Bèllabrèzza," Truffaldino said hurriedly. "I have to go. Right now. I have to find the hawk... I mean, parrot."

Bèllabrèzza came around the table and wrapped one of Truffaldino's arms with both her hands. "Truffaldino," she said with concern. "The Royal Hunt is about to start, and it's taking place in the Forest of Aldente. Please do be careful..."

Truffaldino nodded quickly. "Thank you, Bèllabrèzza. You're very kind. I promise to be careful. My master would not send me into a situation that was too dangerous for me to handle. He trusts me, and I trust him with my life."

Bèllabrèzza smiled. "I really admire you, Truffaldino. And I envy the remarkable relationship you obviously have with your enchanter. You lead quite an amazing life."

"Thank you, Bèllabrèzza," Truffaldino said, reaching into his belt-pouch and withdrawing the map and some of the money given to him by Cagliostro. He gently took one of Bèllabrèzza's hands from around his arm and carefully placed the money into her palm.

"Here are some silver coins to pay for breakfast," he said. "You are a great friend, Bèllabrèzza. I'm really glad we met, and I'm really glad you decided to come over and talk with me, even though you didn't know me. My master says the course of the Universe is always changing, and it usually changes because of something very small, and something very unplanned, and something that seems unimportant. Your coming over to talk with me changed the course of my universe. Thank you, Bèllabrèzza!"

"This is way too much money, Truffaldino," she said, shaking her head. "And anyhow, I shall myself gladly pay for both of us. You should take these coins back."

"Please keep them anyway, Bèllabrèzza," said Truffaldino. "Then I can at least repay you a little for being so kind and so helpful."

"I would have helped you no matter what, Truffaldino."

"I know," Truffaldino said, nodding. "That's because you're so good and so nice."

Bèllabrèzza stood on her toes for a moment, and leaning over toward Truffaldino's face she kissed him lightly on the cheek.

"You are sweet beyond words, Truffaldino," she said. "I hope for Smeraldina's sake she's smart enough to not let you get away, and I hope for my sake she isn't! Don't forget me, Truffaldino. If you remember, send a missive to me here at the taverna so that you don't leave my life as suddenly as you came into it."

Truffaldino nodded earnestly. "Thank you, Bèllabrèzza," he said.

Bèllabrèzza reluctantly let go of Truffaldino's arm, and Truffaldino turned and headed out of the piazza, unfurling THE MAP OF HERE as he walked, beginning to avidly scan the ever-changing image of its uncanny surface for any sign of the parrot and for the quickest route to get himself to the Forest of Aldente.

Chapter 20

The Hanging Gardens
and
The Commencing of The Hunt

The towering outer-curtain gatehouse of the Castle Delprego was known as the Solian Gate, and it was the primary portal of ingress and egress to and from the castello. At the front-facing entrance on the castle-side of the drawbridge, it was duly and effectively designed and built to withstand and repel any incursive aggression or siege. With the formidable iron-fortified grating of its massive portcullis and the immense paired wood-and-iron doors of its colossal arched opening, it was virtually impenetrable. But it was only the second-most secure entry into the castle.

There was an access-point more sturdy and imposing even than the Solian Gate, and that was the Vitaian Gate—the castle-side gateway to the Hanging Gardens. This gatehouse was larger, and its towers and battlements rose higher. Instead of one portcullis it had two, both with latticed grilles formed entirely from steel, and it had paired doors of wood and steel that were twice as thick as those of the Solian gatehouse.

The authors and architects of the Hanging Gardens were the same two people who had designed and created the Palace Gardens—King Bernini and Queen Donatella. The Hanging Gardens were an architectural marvel. Built as a broad skybridge spanning the vast empty air over the moat, the foundation of the Hanging Gardens was made from stone excavated at the same quarry where all stone used in the original construction of the castle had once been hewn, generations before even the reign of King Theramo's illustrious parents. Massive oblique bulwarks supported the extraordinary weight of the Hanging Gardens, reinforcing the load-bearing strength of the skybridge footing with the expedient function and divine form of cathedral buttressing, and the stonework alone had elegance and engineering complexity surpassing any structure ever built anywhere in Benebento.

The span of the skybridge bowed upward in a slight curve, its midpoint more than a dozen meters in the air above the surface of the moat where the water was deepest. The stone sidewalls of the span were nearly four meters high to contain the soil and stone root-bed of the gardens, while still leaving a meter-height of ornamental baluster parapet over which the deliberately-excessive lush and luxurious perimeter floral growth spilled and dangled.

True to its name, the cascading stems and fronds and vines at the outer edges of the Hanging Gardens trailed and draped over and through the parapet barrier so thickly that the balustrade stonework was nearly indiscernible. Myriad overgrowth hung in countlessly varying lengths toward the water below, the longest tendrils ending still a half-dozen meters above the surface of the water.

The skybridge, and the ground and growth it supported, were nearly twenty-five meters wide from balustrade to balustrade, an extensive breadth that was uniform across the entire length of the span over the moat. Surpassing even the Palace Gardens, the botanic diversity of the Hanging Gardens was as remarkable as the architecture and engineering of the skybridge was extraordinary. Flora and horticultural vegetation of countless varieties and species populated the expanse. From the appealing bitter zest of the flourishing long-ago-planted olive grove, to the woody pungency of ferns and mosses, to the piquant tang of herbs and spices, to the leafy redolence of plants and shrubs and bushes, to the sweet fragrance from the arboreal splendor of fruit tree blossoms, to the nectarous scents from the luxuriant profusion of wildflowers— the biotic smells were an exquisite blend of natural perfumes as aromatically diverse as the colors were chromatically assorted. The physical foliate-proportions were as sundry in the height of their growth upward toward the sky as they were varied in the trailing lengths of their dangling from the parapets down toward the water.

The gardens were a pathway link between the innermost grounds of the castle and the forest. Across the moat on the far side of the skybridge, the Hanging Gardens progressively became more wild and overgrown as they merged with the Forest of Aldente. Apart from the sheer artistry and celebratory hybrid beauty of their amalgamated mingling of structure with nature, this was the intent of the original design: to create and maintain a bridge-access of gradual transition from the untempered wilderness and woodland canopy habitat of the forest, to the fashioned-by-the-hand-of-man societal domestication and open air spaces of the castle grounds.

The unsurpassed defenses of the Vitaian Gate had never been used. The portcullises had never needed to be lowered, the doors had never needed to be closed. The Hanging Gardens had been completed during a time of peace, when there was no perceived threat of invasion or attack upon the castle by way of the Forest of Aldente. Consequently, the gates remained perpetually open, permitting creatures of the wood to freely come and go to and from the wide-ranging verdant terrain of the grounds inside the castle. The likes of exotic deer and wild goats and foxes and hares were often appreciatively observed by people residing in or visiting the palace, as the untamed animals foraged and browsed and wandered the castle grounds unaccosted and unconcerned. The open connection of this deliberately-devised linkage between civilization and wilderness had been highly prized by King Bernini and Queen Donatella. While they recognized the necessity of a protective fortress, so long as there was no perceived belligerent martial threat or hostile incursion danger of any imminence, they preferred that the fortified enclosure of the castle would preserve and retain this organic element of access to natural life.

Numerous informal earthen footpaths meandered throughout the Hanging Gardens, but the paved thoroughfare of transit for people and animals was an intricate-mosaic walkway depicting Benebentoan idylls and moments of glory from kingdom's storied history. Assembled with tiles of vivid hues which both rivaled and echoed the color-gamut of the flowers and blossoms of the gardens, the pointillistic walkway composed a pictorial variegated linear esplanade from the boundary of the forest, over the length of the skybridge to the opposite end of the gardens, and on to the manicured grounds inside the castle. The sturdy inlaid stone of the marble mosaic-tiles had remained resilient and unmarred and unworn. Their smooth durable surfaces had withstood undamaged, even after countless seasonal cycles of weather and after decades of traverse by claws and paws and hooves, by the supple undersides of bare feet, by the leather soles of long-pointed tapering-toed poulaines, by the dense cork foot-elevations of chopines, by the hard-wood shoe-platforms of pattens, by the reinforced tread of armored boots, by the trotting and cantering and galloping impact of roughshod horses.

The battlements of the Vitaian Gate connected to the wall-walks of the abutting castle fortifications. The Castle Delprego had been built on the highest elevation in all of Benebento, and the ramparts surrounding and protecting the castello were more than thirty meters in height. With massive round towers anchoring each angular junction of the sprawling perimeter footprint, the nearly two miles of wall-walk atop the battlements of the contiguous outer-curtain walls afforded spectacular panoramas and unequalled sweeping views of the entire kingdom. In peacetime, with increasing interest and frequency, non-military citizens had sought and been granted the opportunity to stroll for leisure atop the walls, to behold the extraordinary vistas once enjoyed only by lookout guards on routine vigilant patrol.

The Hanging Gardens did not terminate at the Vitaian Gate. Their growth persisted and continued all the way to the inner-curtain wall, on through that rampart by way of a towering arched opening in the fortification, all the way to the inside castle grounds. There they thinned and ultimately petered out altogether with the end of the mosaic-tile footpath, merging at last into the vast grassy-field undulations of the South Great Lawn, which received the best of sun's resplendence in the late light of sunset at twilight and in the early light of dawn at sunrise.

On this morning, the South Great Lawn was a tableau of picturesque pomp and aristocratic pageantry and festive royal opulence, as the traditional open-air meal of the ceremonial lavish breakfast before The Royal Hunt neared its conclusion.

The scene was a tapestry of activity and color. Festooned decorative fabric, banners bearing heraldic insignias, broad-vertical-stripe pavilion tents flying bright triangular flags, and courser horses decked-out in blazoned caparison cloths all flaunted chromatic brilliance from every direction. Exotically-outfitted minstrels meandered rhythmically as they played wandering melodies on their eclectic diversity of string and wind and percussive instruments, while formally-attired heralds and pages dashed about with urgent purpose, and noblemen and ladies of the aristocracy promenaded and conversed, garbed in their brightest finery.

Profusely interspersed everywhere was the delectable spectacle of the meal itself. While no doubt saving his best for the morrow's wedding reception, the Master of the Kitchen had nevertheless once again worked his savory wonders across a fleet of banquet tables, all bountifully and appetizingly spread with copious quantities and enticing varieties of sumptuous food and hearty drink.

Those who would participate in the Hunt were dressed in a celebratory elegance which necessarily had been moderated by the forthcoming need to be easily-active and unencumbered for the happy vigorous sporting rigors of the day's main event. All other guests had actively sought to outdo each other in apparel and presentation, and the arrayed extravagant garb and ornate footwear and fanciful decorative headdress were suitably opulent and appropriately ostentatious.

Although they too would be hunting, Leandro nonetheless was handsomely dressed in his best palace-guard finery, and Sir Balzanno gleamed in the burnished brightness of armor freshly polished for the occasion, likely by Italo's capable hands.

The air comprised an energetic atmosphere of excitement and celebration, deliciously laden with rich aromas of luxurious refreshment, and garnished with lively voices cheerily swept up in eager discussion and elated chatting and the jubilation of the day. Talk was of change, the future, the extraordinary good fortune for the kingdom, and the much deserved greatly-wonderful turn of events for their King.

King Theramo seemed unable to stop smiling. He was clearly present, but at times his thoughts seem to have happily escaped to another place.

The very heavens initially had seemed to be smiling down upon the day and kingdom and the festivities. But although the morning had started with Spring warmth and brilliant sunrise radiance, now in the distance dark clouds had begun to gather.

Upon conclusion of the breakfast, all eyes turned to the Master of the Hunt, an imposing figure of tall stature and rugged features whose bearing exuded a square-jawed pragmatic efficiency and the easy confidence of unambiguous expertise, standing in proper seriousness with his half-dozen huntsmen. On the ground behind them and their ornately-caparisoned courser steeds, seven well-groomed and robust scenthound lymer dogs lounged alertly as a pack, muscles resting but ears twitching attentively at the sound of any voice belonging to one of the huntsmen.

King Theramo now raised the ceremonial goblet of wine, first toward the noble guests, then toward the noble men who would participate in the hunt, and at last to the Master of the Hunt himself.

"On this glorious occasion," King Theramo announced in a stentorian voice to the wide audience populating the Great South Lawn, "and in glorious anticipation of the morrow's great occasion which this day's events so gloriously celebrate, I do hereby give my Royal blessing to the conclusion of this great breakfast feast, and to The Hunt which is about to commence."

He paused to lift his goblet higher, before proudly pronouncing the traditional Benebento benediction.

"Good luck to all, good will to all, good life to all!"

Everyone raised high their own goblet, and all as one responded in a unison of great pride with the traditional reply.

"Benebento, să-lū-té!"

All present took a sip or more of their wine, and King Theramo took a brief ceremonial drink from his own goblet before placing the vessel down on a banquet-breakfast table and turning to the Master of the Hunt.

"Lord Mirino," said King Theramo. "I now leave it to you to proceed with the formal directives of The Hunt."

"Thank you, Sire," replied Lord Mirino with a respectful bow, before turning to address everyone collectively. "Your Majesty, noble lords and ladies, fellow honored Benebentoans. I now formally welcome you all to The Royal Hunt to commemorate the morrow's historic wedding of King Theramo and Queen Angiolina."

This preamble salutation was greeted with a momentary chorus of hearty cheers and widespread applause.

"Participants of The Hunt," Lord Mirino continued, addressing them directly. "By tradition and Royal custom, you shall proceed to divide yourselves into hunting parties of small groups. At the conclusion of The Hunt, awards to the victors shall be bestowed in one third portion to the party killing the most game, and two thirds portion to the party felling the largest game. All awards shall go to a single party should that hunting group triumph in both measures, and that party thence shall be considered undisputed victors of The Hunt. A *geras*-and-*kudos* prize of gold treasure and acclaim shall be awarded to those who triumph, and their victory will be memorialized in a Royal Proclamation, if it please Your Majesty."

King Theramo smiled and nodded his assent.

Lord Mirino nodded back in respectful acknowledgment before resuming his address.

"Prior to this ceremonial Morning of the Hunt Breakfast Feast we have been enjoying," he continued, "all heard the ceremonial call of the horn to signify readiness. The next call of the horn will formally signal the start of The Hunt, and the third and final call will signify that The Hunt is concluded.

"In a few short moments from now I will sound the horn, after which I shall ride ahead with my huntsmen and our dogs to flush out game. The hunting parties will proceed on foot after us through the Hanging Gardens and into the Forest of Aldente. As neutral and impartial participants, my huntsmen and I shall endeavor not to in any preferential way drive game toward a particular party, but rather merely compel as much game as possible out of safe hiding and into motion back toward the general direction of the castello, and thus into the paths of the approaching parties.

"Pursuant to the agreed-upon conditions, all participants will hunt with long-gun matchlock harquebuses. No other weapons are to be used. Slowmatch cord-fuses will be lit upon the formal commencing of The Hunt, and are to be doused and extinguished upon the sounding of the third and final horn. If these instructions all be clear and agreeable, please signal your assent."

Apart from the crowd of invited spectators, the participants in the hunt as one all replied with a hearty 'Aye'.

Lord Mirino nodded. "Very well. Gentlemen, form your parties."

While Lord Mirino had been making his address, Tartaglia had surreptitiously been making his way closer to King Theramo until he was successfully positioned to be at the King's side with few steps, steps which he now took.

"Your Majesty," Tartaglia said confidentially as he reached King Theramo. "I should like to hunt alone with you, as a pairing of the two highest in Royal rank... In honor of the greatness of this occasion."

Tartaglia's demeanor was one of eerie calm and uncharacteristically good spirits. If any present were aware of or concerned by this, it was not apparent in the look or words or actions of any of them.

King Theramo smiled at Tartaglia and nodded. "I should like that very much, Prime Minister," he said happily. "It would give me great pleasure, and I look forward to sharing your company and conversation as we strive to best our noble companions in the competition."

Tartaglia smiled broadly. "We shall bring about a kill of historic proportion, Your Majesty. I am committed to it."

"Auspicious and excellent," King Theramo proclaimed enthusiastically.

Lord Pantalòné, Sir Balzanno, and Leandro agreed to hunt together, and the several other noble personages who had been invited to participate in the hunt accordingly grouped themselves into amicable parties of two or three or four. Lord Mirino mounted his regally-caparisoned steed, and the dogs immediately reacted, springing to their feet, looking eager and expectant.

One of the lymerer doghandlers brought a leashed hound to Lord Mirino, who fastened the long leather tether of his dog to the decorative saddle of his horse, while other lymerers fetched the remaining hounds and brought them by leash to the six huntsmen now mounting their own steeds.

Lord Mirino reached with a leather-armor-gauntleted hand for the hunting horn at his side that hung around his neck and shoulder by a long golden chain, lifted it to his mouth, and blew into it with strong expert breath. The two-note call echoed portentously off the nearest of the castle walls and resounded out across the surrounding land.

The Master of the Hunt now spurred his horse and galloped off, his exactingly well-trained lymer dog easily keeping pace and obediently neither pulling ahead or lagging behind the pace. The six huntsmen and their hounds set off close behind, the dogs now all taking advantage of the implicit freedom to bark and bay, all of them riding out onto the mosaic walkway, into the Hanging Gardens, and onward toward the Forest of Aldente.

In the wake of departing huntsmen and horses and hounds, the hunting parties took up their harquebuses, lit their slowmatch cord-fuses, and proceeded on foot along the same path—to the mosaic walkway, into the Hanging Gardens, and toward whatever lay ahead before them in the Forest of Aldente.

The Hunt had begun.

Chapter 21

The Tracks of the Stag
and
The Hermit

The Hunt had been underway for some time. Beneath the verdant density of the overhead canopy within the Forest of Aldente, amidst the woody scents of moss and leafy foliage and tangled underbrush, the distinctive smell in the air before a storm was not present, so there currently seemed no immediate threat of rain. But the light in the forest had inexorably diminished as somewhere high above the newer and ancient tree growth the late morning had steadily continued to darken, and an ominous foreboding seemed to be borne on the gathering clouds and looming within the lowering sky.

The sounds of the hounds continued to rise and fall as their boisterous baying regularly revealed either how near they were or what current direction the shifting traces of wind happened to be gusting in.

Just as the eager purposeful noises of the lymer dogs divulged the general momentary location of the huntsmen at their business of flushing out game, so too the unmistakable smell of slowly-burning saltpeter from the harquebus match-cords continued to disclose the momentary whereabouts of participants in the Hunt.

Into a wide clearing bounded by a towering aged oak and several large boulders, the hunting party of Leandro and Sir Balzanno and

Chancellor Pantalòné made their way, looking about attentively and grasping their firearm weapons with firm readiness as they came. As lightly as they were attempting to tread, their arrival at the glade nevertheless disturbed into flight a coterie of sparrows who fluttered with startled throaty chirping and sudden fast flapping out of a bush and hurriedly off through the easily-bird-navigable obstacles of closely clustered trunks and branches and leaves, away toward some less-trafficked part of the woods.

Unruffled and unseen on a branch of the oak tree just slightly higher than eye-level, the parrot sat silently perched, calmly composed and casually preening, blinking with mild interest as it eyed the newly-arrived hunting party.

"The weather was so nice earlier this morning..." Sir Balzanno remarked with disappointment, glancing upward at where the sky would have been if the forest canopy had not been obscuring the view.

"No matter," said Lord Pantalòné buoyantly. "We shall continue to brighten the day with our high spirits and good cheer."

"And not so much as a quail or partridge or pheasant," Sir Balzanno went on. "It's almost as if the animals are hiding from us."

"That would seem a sensible tactic..." replied Lord Pantalòné.

"Well," observed Leandro, inspecting the ground for any vestigial telltale animal signs, the single long half-coil of black hair curling across his forehead from beneath his guardsman's helmet. "Something large came this way. We passed no boot tracks leading to this spot, but branches along the way have been recently broken. Possibly by red deer, and maybe even a buck..."

"I've heard no shots fired as yet," said Sir Balzanno.

"Nor I," agreed Lord Pantalòné. "From the sounds of it, Lord Mirino and his team have been making industrious effort, but if they have been successful in goading forth game, they seem to have not succeeded thus far in driving any quarry profitably to any of the parties."

Sir Balzanno nodded. "It bodes well for our party. No shots fired means no other party has yet bested us. The contest remains ours for the winning. We'll show them what hunting is all about!"

"What *is* hunting all about...?" Lord Pantalòné mused rhetorically.

"At the moment," replied Sir Balzanno," I believe it is about time to take a brief rest. This armor gets heavier with every step. I shall have to again speak with young Italo about that..."

Lowering his harquebus and leaning it against the broad trunk of the oak with the barrel aimed vaguely upward and the stock down amidst the venerably gnarled tangle of protruding roots at the base of the tree, Sir Balzanno sat himself with heavy relief down on a shelf-like irregularity of one of the boulders.

"Although," the knight continued, "it seems to me it would not in any way diminish the glory of the King's celebration if no party were able to claim the awards. After all, the glory of the day requires not the attainment of any palpable result, and in the end resides simply within the very occasion of The Hunt itself, does it not?"

After glancing at Leandro who was searching with assiduous diligence for animal tracks, Lord Pantalòné scanned the uneventful surrounding woods before stepping over to the oak and leaning his own harquebus stock-down against the thick bark of the wide trunk next to the long-gun of Sir Balzanno. Lifting the leather strap of his costrel flask pouch off one shoulder, the Chancellor pulled the turned-wood stopper from the neck of the bottell and took a sip of wine-water before proffering the costrel with an extended hand to Sir Balzanno. The knight nodded gratefully and accepted the offer, taking the pouch into his appreciative hand and tilting it with his head back for a moment to take a drink, while the strap hung down in a loosely curved catenary.

"Balzanno," Lord Pantalòné began, seating himself on the flat of a boulder next to where Sir Balzanno was sitting. "Have you ever killed an animal?"

Sir Balzanno finished taking his drink but continued to grasp the costrel pouch as he looked at Lord Pantalòné in guarded surprise.

"Chancellor," the knight protested defensively. "What a question. As if I, leader of all the armies of the Kingdom of Benebento, would never have killed an animal."

Several paces away, Leandro seemed to have noticed something on the ground and was inspecting it more closely.

"You've never killed a person either, have you, Balzanno?" Lord Pantalòné went on, his question delivered not as an inquiry but as a statement.

"Surely," the knight responded with adamant pride, "you don't think I've led men into battle and never killed anyone?"

"You've never been in battle, Balzanno," replied Lord Pantalòné.

Sir Balzanno looked back at the Chancellor intently. "Now see here, Pantalòné," he began. "What's this all about? What are you implying?"

"That I believe," Lord Pantalòné said solemnly, "that one of the reasons Benebento is such a peaceful kingdom is because we don't have a bloodthirsty war-monger as our commander."

"Well!" Sir Balzanno began, preparing to become indignant. "That is the most outrageous... That is to say... I never... Er... Thank you, Chancellor."

Lord Pantalòné smiled sincerely at the knight and placed a kind hand for a moment with companionable appreciation on the brightly burnished armor of Sir Balzanno's shoulder.

"It is an honor to serve with you, Sir," the Chancellor said with earnest admiration.

Sir Balzanno nodded back in mutual respect. "The peace enjoyed by Benebento owes much as well to your expertise, Chancellor," said the knight. "It is not only the unused sword, it is also the well-used word that staves off war and conflict, and keeps our kingdom at peace. I am honored to serve with *you*, Pantalòné."

The Chancellor smiled. "Thank you, Balzanno."

From the matchlock mechanisms of the harquebuses leaning against the massive oak, the cord-fuses slowly and silently smoldered, the thin diaphanous coils of saltpeter smoke drifting lazily upward.

Sir Balzanno took another draught of wine-water and handed the costrel back to Lord Pantalòné. "I want to assure you, however," the knight added, "that although I'm loathe to take a life—any life—when no true necessity exists, should a dark need ever arise I would not hesitate. Our King, our kingdom, their safety and security—there is no higher priority. None."

Lord Pantalòné replaced the stopper back into the neck of the bottell. "Of that I have no doubt," he said, nodding gravely. "It is not only the King's trust in you that is well-placed, Balzanno. I and all of Benebento rest at all times secure in knowing that as your hand rests upon the hilt of your sword, it is at all times also ready to raise that selfsame sword and lead our military might to prevail by any means necessary."

Sir Balzanno nodded appreciatively. "And speaking of necessity," he noted. "I cannot grasp the necessity of The Hunt. It is a peculiar celebration indeed that glorifies and prizes death as a means to celebrate newfound happiness..."

"I cannot disagree," said Lord Pantalòné. "The slaying of a noble beast whose head will hang in dubious decoration as a trophy of senseless killing seems unfitting commemoration for an historic and joyful event."

"Young Leandro, however," said Sir Balzanno, "would have us nevertheless present at least the appearance of a good-faith effort in the enterprise, to properly honor the King and the occasion."

"He would not be wrong," the Chancellor said, nodding in agreement and re-hanging the leather strap of his costrel flask pouch back over one shoulder. "Let us demonstrate our earnest commitment in that regard."

Lord Pantalòné and Sir Balzanno stood up and retrieved their firearms before turning toward Leandro, who was looking back at them and pointing to the ground in excitement.

"Excuse me, Sirs!" he said eagerly. "But... Tracks! A stag! A big one, too, by the looks of it! He came through here not too long ago...!"

Sir Balzanno suddenly looked off toward a direction in the wood beyond the glade.

"Something comes this way..." he warned.

The three men as one raised their harquebus long-guns and pivoted to face the approaching sound, aiming together at whatever was about to enter the clearing.

Into the glade came an old man stooped with age, hobbling with difficulty and a cane fashioned from the knobbed length of a sturdy tree bough. He was clothed in ragged but not unclean tatters, and his wizened face was ruddy and tanned from untold time in the outside sun and framed with long hair and a beard of nearly the same length, both comprising dense straggly textures of white and grey.

"Good-day, gentlemen..." the old man said with cordial greeting, looking pointedly at the barrels of the three harquebuses aimed directly at him. "I don't think all that firepower will be necessary," he went on. "I promise to behave."

Leandro, Sir Balzanno, and Lord Pantalòné lowered the ends of their long-guns and looked with curiosity at the old man.

"Many apologies, old sir..." Leandro said with polite haste.

"Old fellow," said Lord Pantalòné. "Tell us who you are, and how you happen to be wandering here in the forest."

"You have strayed right into the middle of the King's Royal Hunt," said Sir Balzanno.

"I am Cigolotti," explained the old man, pronouncing his name as *Chih-goh-LOT-tee.* "I am a hermit. I live here in these woods. My life is near its end, but…"

Cigolotti paused and again eyed the harquebus weapons warily.

"…it's not ready to be over just yet," he finished.

In more unequivocal amity, Leandro and Sir Balzanno and Lord Pantalòné shouldered their guns, the long barrels now aimed behind them toward the sky with the matchlock firing mechanisms unthreateningly settled near their waists, as the barely-perceptible slow smoke of the match-cord fuses wafted with vague continuous indolence.

"My dear old sir," said Lord Pantalòné. "Do you earnestly mean to say you make your home here in the Forest of Aldente?"

"Why do you not live in a dwelling sheltered within the protective shadow of the castle?" inquired Sir Balzanno.

Cigolotti smiled and shook his head. "Too many walls," he explained with good-natured candor. "I far prefer the open vastness of the woods. Here, all is beautiful and peaceful and—"

Cigolotti's body went limp and collapsed in a heap to the ground. His cane fell next to him. His eyes had closed, and his greyly-bearded face had taken on a sudden vacant stillness.

"My word…!" Lord Pantalòné exclaimed with quiet astonishment.

"I… I do believe the poor old fellow is dead…!" remarked Sir Balzanno.

Lord Pantalòné shook his head with slow incredulity. "Well, that certainly was most unexpected…"

"He must have been closer to death than he realized…" said Leandro.

An instant later, Cigolotti had opened his eyes and was back up on his feet with uncanny agility and his cane solidly back in his grasp. He seemed in all ways completely recovered, and as if nothing had happened he continued his thought from where he had left off.

"…and I am quite fond of the animals," Cigolotti went on. "And I love the smell of the trees." He paused to take in a deep luxurious breath and smiled with contented satisfaction.

"Just smell that!" he extolled emphatically. "Isn't it marvelous?"

The three members of the hunting party stared at him in puzzled bewilderment.

"I say, Cigolotti…" said Lord Pantalòné. "Are you quite all right?"

Cigolotti smiled knowingly and nodded.

"Oh," he began with affable patient understanding. "I know it's not a commonly accepted lifestyle, living in the woods. But I—"

"No," Sir Balzanno interrupted him. "No, not that. Just a moment ago. When you—"

Cigolotti's body again abruptly crumpled and dropped to the ground with his cane next to him and eyes again lifelessly closed.

Leandro and Sir Balzanno and Lord Pantalòné stared, their mouths open in befuddled wonderment.

"Good heavens…" said Lord Pantalòné.

"Surely," observed Sir Balzanno with perplexity, "this time he now truly is dead…"

Lord Pantalòné shook his head in sympathy. "What an odd unfortunate fellow…" he said with mystified compassion.

Leandro bent down over the inert Cigolotti and carefully inspected the condition of his motionless body.

"Rest in peace, old sir…" said Sir Balzanno with kind respect.

Leandro turned and looked up at the other two members of the hunting party.

"He's asleep," Leandro reported simply.

"What…?!" exclaimed Sir Balzanno.

"It's true," Leandro said, nodding with certainty. "He's not dead. He's just sleeping. See for yourselves…"

Sir Balzanno and Lord Pantalòné joined Leandro bending down over Cigolotti.

Sir Balzanno shook his head in amazement.

"What do you know…" the knight remarked incredulously. "He is asleep!"

"It came on rather suddenly, did it not…?" said Lord Pantalòné.

At that instant, Cigolotti awoke and sat up, grasping one end of his cane for support and staring back in confused indignation at the three faces looming over him.

"Hey!" Cigolotti exclaimed with perturbed vexation. "What's the idea?"

"You fell asleep," said Lord Pantalòné.

"I was never asleep," asserted Cigolotti, shaking his head adamantly.

"Yes you were," said Sir Balzanno.

"No I wasn't!" insisted Cigolotti.

"Come along," said Sir Balzanno. "We all saw you. You just keeled over like you were dead."

"It's not true!" Cigolotti contended.

Cigolotti's eyes closed, and he slumped and fell back from sitting to wholly collapsed unmoving repose as his cane again toppled to the ground next to him.

The three members of the hunting party looked on in bewilderment.

"What's wrong with him?" asked the Chancellor.

"He must have the sleeping fits…" Leandro surmised.

"What's that?" asked Sir Balzanno.

"That…" explained Leandro with a simple finger extended, pointing to the slumbering Cigolotti.

"Do you mean to say," inquired Lord Pantalòné, "he just randomly falls asleep for no reason?"

Leandro nodded hesitantly. "Apparently…" he concluded with some skepticism.

"How inconvenient," Sir Balzanno observed, shaking his head.

"Should we wake him up?" suggested Lord Pantalòné.

"No," said Leandro. "Let him rest in peace."

"But he's not dead," countered Sir Balzanno.

"For how long will he sleep…? the Chancellor asked.

"I know of no way to ascertain the length of his fits," replied Leandro. "The previous three have been brief, but any one of them might last for any amount of time…"

"What should we do?" asked Sir Balzanno.

"I see no need to disturb him further," Leandro offered.

"Do we just leave him here…?" questioned Lord Pantalòné.

"Well," said Sir Balzanno. "He does seem to have thus far survived quite well enough on his own…"

Leandro nodded in accord. "I do think we ought to resume The Hunt. Out of respect for the King."

"Verily, that is spoken in truth," agreed the knight. "Irrespective of this singularly curious encounter, we should not permit even such an oddity as this to hinder our honoring the King's wishes on this festive occasion."

"Indeed," Lord Pantalòné concurred. "Very well…"

The three of them rose to their feet and took a last look at the sleeping body of Cigolotti, which by all outward appearance seemed a lifeless corpse.

"He slumbers as soundly as he does suddenly," marveled Sir Balzanno.

The Chancellor nodded that the time had come to move on. "Come, young Leandro," he said decisively. "Lead the way and guide us forward on the path toward apprehending your mighty stag."

The parrot watched them leave. In the skies above the forest canopy, more clouds were gathering. The light in the clearing had continued to darken, and even through the arboreal thickness of the wood a wind was beginning to stir, bringing with it a cooling chill and the first mists of fog. The baying of the lymer hounds had become more distant and infrequent, and within minutes of Leandro and Sir Balzanno and Lord Pantalòné departing out of the glade, approaching from the opposite direction came new sounds—the muted crunching of leaves crushed, and the muffled cracks of twigs snapping underfoot, as differently treading steps could now be heard on the verge of entering the clearing.

Chapter 22

The Estrangement
and
The Reconciliation

The parrot watched in silence from the branch of the ancient oak, gazing down and observing impassively as the hunting party of King Theramo and Tartaglia made their way into the glade, looking about and grasping their firearm weapons. As unseen as the parrot, the sleeping figure of Cigolotti remained inconspicuous where it lay thin with age and flat on the forest floor, partially concealed within clustered tufts of weedy ground growth which by happenstance thickly surrounded the area where the hermit had last collapsed, circumstantially shielding his prone profile from easily apparent view. Neither King Theramo nor Tartaglia noticed the slumbering body, the King likely preoccupied with seeking game of more upright quadrupedal stature, the Prime Minister likely focused on dark contemplations of how best to execute his deadly mission of retribution against the unsuspecting monarch.

The fog was thickening with each passing minute, and ground-mist was swirling in slow eddies low to the forest floor, further obscuring the inert hermit.

"The weather has turned as quickly and capriciously as men's fortunes," remarked Tartaglia, stopping in the middle of the clearing and looking around thoughtfully.

King Theramo nodded as he came to a stop next to his trusted Prime Minister. "It is of no matter, dear Tartaglia," he said cheerfully. "My mood cannot be darkened or dampened. My spirits soar to such great heights, nothing can bring them to earth."

"As your advisor," Tartaglia admonished, "I would council you not to bait Fate, Sire. The heavens visit vengeful reprisal upon those who fly too high."

"Well-thought and well-spoken, as always, dear Tartaglia," King Theramo agreed appreciatively. "I shall endeavor to heed your wisdom and keep its light shining in my thoughts."

"Sire," Tartaglia began carefully. "That puts me in mind of something troubling, about which I have been meaning to speak with you…"

"My dear Tartaglia," replied King Theramo, lowering his harquebus and holding it by the barrel with its stock resting on the ground near his feet. "Please. Speak frankly, and hold nothing back."

"Sire," Tartaglia went on, lowering his own weapon and forcing a regretful expression to his face. "I must resign my position as your Prime Minister."

King Theramo stared aghast at Tartaglia.

"What…?!" he exclaimed with alarmed incredulity. "But… My most trusted Tartaglia… Why…?"

Tartaglia nodded with slow contrived dejection.

"That," he replied, "is precisely the difficulty, Your Majesty. I am NOT your most trusted."

"Tartaglia…!" King Theramo responded in perplexed concern. "What are you saying? Why, I confide everything to you. Without your counsel, I could not rule. I could not effectively or successfully run the Kingdom of Benebento!"

Tartaglia shook his head with convincing plaintive sorrow.

"No, Sire," he said. "You do not confide everything to me. The secrets given to you by the enchanter Cagliostro. Those you have chosen to keep to yourself."

"Cagliostro instructed me to tell no one," said King Theramo.

"Exactly, Your Majesty," Tartaglia replied. "Keeping these secrets from all others, I understand. But to keep the secrets from me, your own beloved most trusted Tartaglia… Surely this means I do not have your full trust. And without your full trust, I can no longer continue to be your Prime Minister. And in truth, Sire, I cannot go on with the charade of this pretense of friendship. I have come to the unhappy realization that I have been deluding myself in so long believing you and I shared a transcendent bond of kinship. These undisclosed secrets constitute a bleak barrier between us, but more sorrowfully they represent the extent to which we have grown apart. This selfishly withheld and hidden information, by its very secrecy and concealment, has revealed the obstructed distance which has interposed and separated us, dividing the deep closeness that once with intimate confidence and unconditional trust bound us to each other."

King Theramo shook his head unhappily. "Dear Tartaglia," he said. "It crushes my heart to learn that because of me, our friendship has apparently become so grievously fractured. I beseech you, tell me what I might do to make things right between us…"

"Your Majesty," replied Tartaglia. "I have always only wanted to serve you to the best of my capacity as we shared together a private closeness unique to the two of us alone. I would ask only that that special relationship be continued, that we keep no secrets from each other, that you share with me knowledge of the magic given to you by the enchanter."

"My dearest Tartaglia," King Theramo exclaimed emphatically. "I shall not lose you! You, the guardian of my life. My faithful Prime Minister and my closest friend. We will share the secrets together. I shall confide in you, that you will know of my trust. But you must give me your word of honor, Tartaglia. That you will stay on and continue to serve as my beloved Prime Minister if in this way I restore your faith in my trust."

"I give you my word, Your Majesty."

"Very well," King Theramo began. "Tartaglia. My own dearest Tartaglia, I was given by Cagliostro two extraordinary gifts of enchantment. The first was a pair of magic spectacles that—by a working of Cagliostro's power—could be used in partnership with the Great Mirror in the Palace Gardens, making the looking-glass into a mirror of Truth. Whosoever wears the glasses while watching the mirror's reflection can know without doubt whether words spoken aloud are a lie or the Truth."

Varied confusion ranged across Tartaglia's face. "Magical glasses...?" he demurred. "Truth mirror...? But... But that can't have been what you used to compel her to... I mean... That's extraordinary... Of course. But, what power did you use to... I mean... You said there were two gifts given. What was the second?"

King Theramo nodded, smiling with keen eagerness. "The

second is yet more wondrous enchantment than the first, Tartaglia. It is so marvelous a work of magic, that I have myself never even tried it…"

King Theramo stepped quickly over the base of the oak tree and leaned his harquebus against the trunk before returning to Tartaglia in the middle of the glade. Reaching then into a pocket of his robes, King Theramo took out the Bi-Scepter, whose two conjoined ornate lengths of decorative gold and silver gleamed with glittering clarity even in the murk of diminishing light and increasing fog.

"Behold this wondrous Bi-Scepter, Tartaglia," said King Theramo, grasping a shaft of the device in each of his hands and swiveling it apart at the pivot-hinge so each end aimed in a different direction.

"Direct the two pointing-rods," King Theramo explained excitedly, "press this emerald, and you can *switch bodies* with any person or animal!"

Tartaglia momentarily was genuinely impressed.

"Odds bodkins…" he said in soft amazement. "It is not possible…"

"Ah, but it is!" King Theramo reassured him with avid conviction. "An extraordinary work of enchantment, is it not?"

"But I don't believe it…" said Tartaglia.

"But," replied King Theramo confidently, "it is true!"

"But you yourself just said you never have tested it," said Tartaglia. "How do you know?"

King Theramo paused for moment and thought.

"Well…" he said at last. "Well, the glasses and the mirror

worked perfectly. I have no reason to doubt that this Bi-Scepter will also perform precisely as Cagliostro told me it would."

Tartaglia nodded, suddenly distracted as his eyes revealed rapid thoughts racing through his mind.

"And…" Tartaglia began hesitantly. "That is all…? That is the only enchantment he provided…? Only those two gifts…? But… But there has to have been also another magical power he gave you…"

"Is that not enough?" asked King Theramo. "It is a trove of enchantment! What more magic would a king need?"

Tartaglia turned away from King Theramo, his face contorted in bitterness and confusion.

"But…" Tartaglia said to himself in inaudible private distress. "That would mean that she… No… It can't be… It's not possible… This is all far worse than I first thought…"

"What are you musing, my dearest Tartaglia?" said King Theramo.

Tartaglia turned slowly back toward the King.

"Are you," King Theramo pursued, "as awed as I at this extraordinary mechanism of enchantment?"

"I…" Tartaglia faltered. "What… What will you do with the device…?"

"I'm going to return it to Cagliostro."

"Why would you do such a thing?"

"I have no use for it," King Theramo said simply. "It was not needed for me to find the Truth I was seeking."

For a moment, Tartaglia was lost in troubled thought.

And then a realization appeared to have occurred to him.

"Sire," Tartaglia began. "As your advisor and your friend, I must counsel you to not relinquish this remarkable power."

"But," said King Theramo, "why would I not give it up and give it back? What would I ever use it for?"

"That is exactly why you should keep it," said Tartaglia. "You do not know if you might one day require it."

King Theramo shook his head. "No, my need for enchantment has ended. I am grateful to Cagliostro for how he has enabled me to discover and embark upon a new and better path in my life and in the life of the kingdom. I am resolved to give Cagliostro my boundless thanks, and to return to him all the gifts he—with such incomparable and miraculous generosity and kindness—has given to me."

"But Sire," said Tartaglia with compelling sorrow. "You used to listen to me. You used to value what I had to say above the words of all others. It seems after all that we irretrievably are finished, Your Majesty. Apparently, it is as I first feared. I am no longer suitable to be your closest friend, your most trusted advisor, your Prime Minister. With deep regret I recognize now that I must proceed and submit to you my request to be discharged from my responsibilities and duties as your Prime Minister. Grant me, if nothing else, this: my unwilling wish to step down and step away, officially, from what is now apparently lost, what we once had—true trust."

"No, no, dear Tartaglia," King Theramo protested with hasty urgency. "I cannot endure losing you. Even amidst the elation of my newfound happiness and joy, I cannot bear the terrible thought of you leaving me. The two of us being together matters more to me than any resolve I may have about returning the enchanter's gifts. Very well. If I promise to keep this Bi-Scepter device, will you remain true to your honored word and stay on with me as my Prime Minister and my dearest friend? Will you at last let go all your ambivalence and allow us to proceed forward without any further backward-facing looks at your leaving me?"

"Yes, Your Majesty," said Tartaglia firmly. "I do promise. I want only for things between us to remain as they have always been. And you now give me unshakable foundation for knowing that what I feared we had lost is—after all—not lost, and is in fact fully and soundly intact."

"Thank you, Tartaglia," said King Theramo, exhaling with relief. "This is comfort and mitigation for me of a magnitude beyond my words to properly articulate. Thank you, Tartaglia. Thank you."

King Theramo pivoted the two cylindrical shaft-halves of the Bi-Scepter back together. "At your advice and council," he said, "I will accept that the device may yet in some unknown way on some unknown day prove to be a gift I shall yet celebrate having not given up."

Tartaglia extended a purposeful hand toward the Bi-Scepter. "Hold a moment, Sire," he said deliberately. "Do not just yet put the enchanted object away. Does not Your Majesty think it best to now put the device to a test? Your Highness no doubt would not wish to be in need of its powers, only to discover too late it does not actually work. You should try it. Now. At this moment, while you are not in need of its power. So that if it fails to work, you lose nothing."

King Theramo hesitated. "I suppose it could be given a trial usage..." he said uncertainly. "Though I confess, I am troubled at the notion of employing the enchanter's magic when there is no genuine need to avail ourselves of its power..."

"But there is nothing to stop us, Your Majesty," Tartaglia persisted. "It can be easily accomplished now and here, without qualm."

King Theramo nodded slowly in unconvinced apprehension.

"Just because a thing is able to be done," said the King, "it perhaps does not necessarily follow that the thing ought to be done..."

Tartaglia chuckled in mildly derisive rebuke. "Come now, Your Majesty," he admonished with thinly-guised condescension. "You are starting to sound as though your thinking has been corrupted by the enchanter."

King Theramo shook his head in disagreement.

"Or, perhaps," King Theramo rejoined thoughtfully, "finding my true Queen simply has begun to lift a life-long veil from my ability to see..."

Tartaglia had to again turn away to mask his infuriation at this allusion to Angiolina.

"She is not yours!" Tartaglia muttered inaudibly under his breath to himself. "She is mine...! You stole her away from me...! But that will soon be remedied... Just you wait..."

"What thoughts do you privately ruminate, my dearest Tartaglia?" inquired King Theramo.

Tartaglia re-collected his composure and turned back toward the King.

"It is of no great consequence, Your Majesty. I did—after all—give you my honored word. It... It is only that I feel as though—apart from the unsurpassed intimacy of our unwavering friendship—the kingdom, its continued success, and your success as its sovereign are foremost in the focus of my interest and concern. My most valuable gift to give, my greatest contribution that I can proffer toward those paramount priorities, is the benefit of my insight and my ability to recognize all aspects of a situation. My urging for you to test the power of this device arises solely from my desire to ensure that any potential benefits will inure to you and to the kingdom with nothing less than success, and that all avenues of possibility are explored only under circumstances of controlled safety."

King Theramo now nodded in agreement. "You are right, dear Tartaglia," he concurred. "The device, if it is ever to be used at all, should first be tested in a situation free of immediacy and in a setting where any failure will be of no consequence."

"No consequence indeed," Tartaglia agreed readily.

"That is wise council," said King Theramo appreciatively. "Oh, this is precisely why I cannot rule without you at my side, why I cannot thrive without your friendship in my aspirations toward betterment."

"Your words move me, Sire." said Tartaglia. "And together, Your Majesty, let us now test the enchanter's magic."

King Theramo nodded. "Together, my beloved Tartaglia, we shall test the powers of the Bi-Scepter!"

Chapter 23

The Stag
and
The Betrayal

King Theramo looked around, surveying the clearing vaguely in search of any creature that might be suitable for a test of the Bi-Scepter. With the inexorably gathering daytime darkness and steady amassing of fog, the likelihood of the parrot being noticed where it had thus far remained undiscovered was increasingly diminished, but the colorful bird nevertheless seemed to be making a purposeful effort to somehow be even more motionless and to blink with even less frequency.

"The fog around us continues to thicken, Tartaglia," King Theramo remarked. "And the heavy mist below collects so heavily that I am nearly unable to see even our very feet...!"

"The weather is of no concern, Sire," Tartaglia replied dismissively. "It changes, as all things change, and I expect that very soon now the winds will shift and bring about significantly different conditions."

King Theramo nodded. "Although," the King continued, "even with the noble efforts of Lord Mirino and his huntsmen, game has been singularly scarce this day, and I have no confidence that should any animal of consequence arrive in our path, we would be able to even discern its presence with our eyes. All of which taken together would appear to formidably challenge our resolve to test the enchanter's device…"

"Your Majesty…" Tartaglia proposed carefully. "Might I suggest a simple obvious solution? Why do we not test it on ourselves? You and I could switch bodies."

King Theramo looked at Tartaglia with surprise. "What a thought…!" he said, gazing wonderingly at his Prime Minister with contemplative reflection.

Thin coils of saltpeter smoke curled nearly invisible off the slowly smoldering cord-fuse of the harquebus still held firmly in Tartaglia's grasp as the Prime Minister looked back at the King with calm assured resolve. "It would serve our purpose to perfection, Sire," he said. "Would it not?"

King Theramo hesitated.

"I suppose it would…" King Theramo said at last. "However…"

The sound of something large approaching the glade could now be heard with distinct clarity. King Theramo turned his eyes from his Prime Minister and looked past Tartaglia's shoulder to something just at the edge of the clearing.

"Look where it comes!" King Theramo exclaimed suddenly, raising his arm and extending an excited indicating finger. "A stag…!"

Tartaglia turned to follow the direction of the King's pointing.

Even in the fading light of the overcast day and the drifting shroud of increased fog, the great animal could be seen unmistakably. A large male red deer with a distinctive white spot on its forehead stood without fear just inside the perimeter of the clearing, intently eyeing King Theramo and Tartaglia.

"Its size is extraordinary…!" King Theramo breathed in awed appreciation. "What a masterpiece of Nature. What a bold and beautiful animal…!"

Tartaglia silently raised his long-gun with steady capable hands and aimed the end of the barrel at the white spot on the stag's forehead.

King Theramo placed one hand on Tartaglia's arm and the other on the harquebus, pressing downward and compelling the Prime Minister to lower the weapon.

"Hold, Tartaglia…" commanded the King quietly.

The stag did not move.

Neither King Theramo nor Tartaglia took their eyes from the stag.

"Perhaps Your Highness wishes to have the glory of the kill for himself?" suggested Tartaglia, trying to mask his irritation at the interruption.

"This animal is too majestic to be brought down by the likes of us," said King Theramo.

"With due respect, Sire," Tartaglia replied with mounting frustration. "That is absurd. Has Your Highness forgotten this is a hunt? Your Majesty's own Royal Hunt? Here before us, sauntering in to deliver itself to slaughter is quarry which is the very object of the day's endeavor. There is no sensible reason to not deliver the beast to its fate and bring to fruition the ambition of Your Majesty's grand event."

King Theramo shook his head. "The life of this great stag is not ours to take," he said.

"Sire, I must protest—"

"My own Tartaglia," said King Theramo quietly. "Though we thus shall not be victorious in The Hunt, we may yet be successful in accomplishing the test we both seek to undertake."

Tartaglia shook his head in annoyance. "Your Majesty, I do not—"

"The Bi-Scepter," said King Theramo. "Is this unanticipated opportunity not ideal to try the power of the enchanter's magic?"

"What do you mean, Sire?"

"Cagliostro said the device would work with animals as well as people. Why not try it out on this glorious stag?"

Tartaglia shook his head dubiously. "I don't know, Your Majesty… I think it would be better if—"

"Come along, Tartaglia," King Theramo said with quiet enthusiasm. "Do not be concerned. I shall perform the test myself, now and here."

Tartaglia thought for a moment, then seemed to find a path to what he wanted to attain.

"Very well," Tartaglia said, setting down his harquebus and leaning it against the edge of a boulder. "I came to The Hunt prepared for a diversity of possible necessities, Your Highness…"

Tartaglia opened the front of his robe revealing a long length of rope wrapped in repeating winds around his waist as though it were a kind of belt. He quickly untied the simple knot that held it in place and began to uncoil the quantity of line into his hands.

The stag continued to stand where it stood, without moving or taking its eyes from the King and the Prime Minister. The temperature of the air had continued to drop as the darkness of the day's overcast had descended and the fog had amplified, and strong steady puffs of vapor from the stag's calm even breathing could be seen coming from its nostrils.

"The animal seems at the moment senselessly uninterested in fleeing," said Tartaglia. "But that foolhardy stance may change abruptly, so I propose we first secure the brute to a tree before we begin the test, Sire, so the beast doesn't run off with you inside of it…"

"No, no, Tartaglia," King Theramo said, laughing quietly without taking his gaze from the gaze of the stag. "My dearest Tartaglia. If the test is a success, then *I* will be in the body of the stag, and the stag will be in *my* body. And I assure you, I shall not run off. Even within the body of a stag!"

Tartaglia had become too restless to consider this deeply or further debate the situation, and he tossed the long coil of rope impatiently onto the boulder near his long-gun.

"Very well, Your Majesty," he said with some irritation. "Let us put the magic to the test…"

The stag remained proud and unmoving, his magnificent antlers towering above his head from their sturdy iron-strong bone shafts, their armature of graceful bone-branch curves lifting like the outstretched arms of a triumphant athlete or a sorcerer summoning a storm, their bone-tines pointing like elegant ivory flames poised in place or ethereal fingers reaching up to touch sublimity.

"Why does the infernal beast simply stand there?" complained Tartaglia in mounting annoyance. "Why does it not either charge or run off? What does it want?"

"Irrespective of its intention," said King Theramo, swiveling apart the two shafts of the Bi-Scepter, "its inaction serves to suit our purpose…"

A strong wind began to stir the leaves of the glade as King Theramo aimed the two Bi-Scepter shafts, one at himself, the other toward the stag, and positioned his thumb over the emerald button. High above the clearing, the forest canopy had begun to sway from the sudden force of gusting air agitating the density of the lofty treetops with a sound like a downpour. But there was no rain, only the now urgently swirling fog and ground-mist that now churned like rapid river water. The rising wind lifted the stag's fur in tufting hackles and billowed Tartaglia's robes. The smoke of the matchlock-fuses was blown into invisibility and the slow burn of the saltpeter cords glowed in bright amber pinpoints as the wind charged the wicks like bellows pumping air across forge coals.

If King Theramo was going to hesitate, he had missed his chance because the downward pressure of his thumb against the emerald was already underway. He pressed the lustrously-faceted surface of the deep-green gemstone, and whatever was going to happen was now going to happen.

There was a distant sound like chimes that was immediately lost in the rising rush of wind and replaced with a new sound like faraway thunder rolling and rumbling like an approaching avalanche. Around the Bi-Scepter, jagged tendrils of tiny lightning crackled and danced up and down the lengths of the shafts amidst nearly invisible swirls of twinkling motes of illumination. The ends of the pointing rods for an instant glowed blue-white as bright as sunlight. The entire glade then seemed to flash, but there was no true flash—it was an inversion of light and color. Everything dark for an instant became light, everything green became red. All light values flipped and all color hues reversed, and in an instant reversed back, then flashed negative again, then reversed back, in turns, four times in fast succession.

And then the wind stopped and the noises ceased, and everything was abruptly still and quiet. The fog hung motionless in the air, the ground-mist blanketed the forest floor in heavy stillness.

Nothing stirred and no one moved.

At the outskirt of the glade, the stag faltered, then again stood steady.

Next to Tartaglia, the King's eyes closed, then opened.

For a moment it seemed as though everything was just the same as it had been. A moment later it was clear something had changed.

"Tartaglia!" said a voice from the mouth of the stag. "My dearest Tartaglia, I am here! Here in the body of the stag…!"

Tartaglia stared at the stag in amazement.

Next to him, the mouth of the King moved and spoke.

"I am the great stag," said the voice of King Theramo. "But I find myself now in the body of the King…"

Tartaglia whirled to look at the body of the King standing next to him.

"It worked!" exclaimed an excited voice that came from the

mouth of the stag. "Tartaglia! The enchanter's magic worked! What an extraordinary sensation…!"

Tartaglia turned back again toward the stag.

"Your… Your Majesty…?" he said in astonishment. "Sire, is that truly you…?"

At the edge of the clearing, the stag's head nodded, its mighty antlers sweeping up and down through the fog-laden air.

"Yes!" said the King from the body of the stag. "Tartaglia, I truly am here!"

There was no outward evidence of change, but careful inspection might have revealed a subtle essential change in the facial features of the stag, or the mien and posture of the body of the King. It was a difference, but it was only slight. In all other respects, no outward physical change was obvious or evident.

"But Sire…" said Tartaglia. "How is it you are able to speak? Without you inside it, the beast had no voice. How is it that the creature's mouth is now able to give forth words?"

The stag took a step forward, as if testing its legs.

"It must be part of the Bi-Scepter's enchantment…" said King Theramo from the body of the stag.

The words spoken may have been the words of the King, but the voice was not King Theramo's voice. It was unlike the voice of any person, and it was rich and resonant, and deep with strength and power.

Tartaglia turned back toward the body of King Theramo. The King's eyes were quickly flicking back and forth, looking around rapidly as if trying to process overwhelming new information.

"And…" Tartaglia said hesitantly to the body of the King. "And you are truly the stag…?"

King Theramo's head nodded slowly. "Yes," it said in the King's voice. "I am the stag. I am truly here within the body of your King…"

"Odds bodkins…" Tartaglia breathed in wonderment, looking back and forth between the body of the king and the body of the stag. "It is utterly fantastic… This… This may turn out even better than I planned…"

"Tartaglia," said King Theramo from the body of the stag. "I believe we have successfully completed our test of the enchanter's magic. Perhaps you should use the Bi-Scepter and switch me back now…"

Tartaglia hesitated again, then cautiously reached for the Bi-Scepter still grasped in the hands of King Theramo's body. The body of the King seemed unsure of itself, and made no resistance as the Prime Minister took hold of the magical device and separated it from the hands of the King's body.

"Uh… Just one moment, Your Majesty…" said Tartaglia.

Tartaglia swiveled the two shafts back together. Placing the Bi-Scepter down on the boulder next to him, he picked up the rope and swiftly wrapped it around the body of King Theramo, pinning the arms tightly so they could not move. The King's body with the stag inside it started to struggle, but Tartaglia had acted with surprise and speed and strategy, giving him complete advantage over his new prisoner. He dragged King Theramo's body to a wide tree and used the remainder of the rope to bind the body of the King by the waist to the trunk with repeated wrapping winds and finally tying the ends together in front with a thick knot.

"Tartaglia...!" cried King Theramo from the mouth of the stag. "What is going on...?!"

Tartaglia exhaled a slow victorious sigh and walked calmly over the boulder, retrieving his harquebus before returning to the tree where the body of the King with the stag inside was fighting for freedom against the restraint of the rope.

Tartaglia observed the futility for a moment as King Theramo's body struggled in vain. The Prime Minister then turned his back on the body of the King to look toward where the stag with King Theramo inside still stood near the edge of the glade.

"But, Tartaglia...!" exclaimed King Theramo through the mouth of the stag. "What... What are you doing...?!"

"I'm going to kill a stag," Tartaglia said, smiling. "And then I am going to become King!"

"What are you talking about?" said the King in the stag's body. "Tartaglia... Perhaps it would now be best for you to use the Bi-Scepter and switch things back to the way they are supposed to be..."

Tartaglia laughed. "Oh, I intend to use the Bi-Scepter, all right. And I will indeed be switching things to the way they are supposed to be. But I will not be switching you back."

"What..." the King said from the stag's body. "What are you saying...?"

"I am saying that no one will question the killing of a stag on

The Hunt. And after I kill you, I shall switch into your body, and then at last I shall be King!"

"But... Tartaglia!" said the King in the stag. "My dearest friend! My most trusted Prime Minister...! Why would you do such a thing?"

"Because I hate you!" Tartaglia raged in sudden fury. "Odds bodkins! Everything you have, I want! It was not enough for you to be King of Benebento! You had to take from me my beloved Angiolina! Well, now I shall possess the kingdom I have always wanted. And I shall have Angiolina for my own at last!"

"Tar... Tartaglia...!" lamented King Theramo in appalled bewilderment from the body of the stag. "I... I cannot believe what I am hearing..."

Tartaglia smiled in contempt and resolve as he raised the harquebus and pointed the end of the barrel at the body of the stag. "In a moment, Your Majesty," he said with calm disdain, "what you can or cannot believe will not matter..."

A single thin coil of saltpeter smoke was rising from the steady slow burn of the cord-fuse as Tartaglia's finger curled into the trigger of the long-gun's matchlock firing mechanism.

"Long live the King..." said Tartaglia with smug wry finality as he took careful aim at the white spot on the forehead of the body of the stag.

Behind Tartaglia, because the body of King Theramo was bound to the tree by its waist so securely, the stag was able to lift both of the King's legs off the ground, pulling the King's knees up to the King's chest. In a single powerful motion, it then sent a thrusting kick with full force and both feet at once into the back of the Prime Minister.

The long-gun flew unfired from Tartaglia's surprised hands as the Prime Minister reeled from the sudden impact of the unseen kick, and Tartaglia in an instant was sent flailing and sprawling headlong to the ground.

"Run, King!" the stag called from the mouth of King Theramo's body. "My legs are swift! You'll not be killed if you run! RUN!"

Without a word or hesitation, the body of the stag with King Theramo inside turned from the edge of the clearing and ran off at great speed.

The stunned and winded Tartaglia lifted his head from the misty ground and struggled unsteadily to his feet in time to see the last of the fleeing stag's body disappearing into the woods.

"Go ahead, Theramo!" Tartaglia called after it angrily. "Run! You'll not escape death at the hands of your own hunters!!"

The last of the sounds of quickly snapped twigs and momentarily crushed leaves from the pounding hooves of the stag's running legs faded and were gone.

Tartaglia brushed off his robes and composed himself, picking up the harquebus from the ground and confirming that the cord-fuse was still smoldering and ready to fire the weapon. Shaking with anger, he took several steps toward where the body of the King was bound to the tree. Raising the weapon, he aimed the end of the barrel at the face of King Theramo and placed his finger on the trigger of the matchlock mechanism.

"And you, stag!" he bellowed. "You shall now pay for your treachery…!!"

Through the face of King Theramo, the great stag smiled back at the Prime Minister.

"Think for a moment, Tartaglia," the stag said with King Theramo's voice. "Does not your plan to take over the life of Theramo need the BODY of Theramo in order to succeed?"

Tartaglia froze.

The stag stared with calm steadiness through the King's eyes at the Prime Minister. "You shall find it difficult, Tartaglia," the stag continued, "to steal a kingdom and a Queen from within a DEAD body."

Tartaglia slowly lowered the long-gun. "Odds bodkins...!" he muttered. "The beast speaks the truth..."

Tartaglia thought for a moment, then turned and went over to the boulder where he retrieved the Bi-Scepter before striding back, his long steps leaving whorled eddies of ground-mist in their wake as he made his way again to the tree where the King's body remained bound securely to the trunk.

"You are indeed clever, stag," said Tartaglia, still holding his harquebus but now spreading apart the pivoting shafts of the Bi-Scepter. "And for that, I thank you. You shall not long profit from your cleverness, however. Once I am in Theramo's body, your life will be ended. I shall kill the body of Tartaglia, with you inside it. The murder of the Prime Minister shall be blamed on the King's jealous advisors. Oh, how I have longed to be rid of them! Once I have killed you, their deaths for treason shall soon follow. As King, I shall see to it!"

Tartaglia aimed the Bi-Scepter, one pointing rod toward himself, the other toward the stag in the body of the King.

A strong wind again began to stir the fog and leaves and ground-mist of the glade as Tartaglia positioned his thumb over the emerald button. High above the clearing, the forest canopy again began to sway from the force of gusting air moving the lofty treetops.

As Tartaglia pressed the emerald button, there was a distant sound like chimes that was lost in the rushing wind and replaced with a rumbling sound like faraway rolling thunder. Jagged tendrils of tiny lightning danced and crackled around the Bi-Scepter shafts amidst nearly invisible swirls of twinkling motes of illumination. The ends of the pointing rods for an instant glowed with a brilliantly bright blue-white light, and then the entire glade again flashed with inversion as all light values flipped and all color hues reversed, and in an instant reversed back, then flashed negative again, then reversed back, in turns, three times in fast succession.

And then the wind stopped and the noises ceased, and everything was abruptly still and quiet. The fog once again hung motionless in the air, the ground-mist blanketing the forest floor again settled back to heavy idle stillness.

The body of Tartaglia faltered for a moment, then stood strong.

The eyes of King Theramo closed briefly, then re-opened.

"At last!" exclaimed the mouth of King Theramo's body. "I, Tartaglia, am now inside the body of the King! I am King! I am the King!!"

The head of Tartaglia nodded in agreement. "You are also tied up," said the great stag in Tartaglia's voice from the body of the Prime Minister.

King Theramo's eyes looked down at where his body's arms were with winding coils of rope securely bound to his sides and the tree trunk. His face contorted with horrified regretful anguish as awful recognition of the predicament dawned.

"Oh, no…" Tartaglia lamented ruefully from the mouth of the King. "No…! Odds bodkins… NO…!!!"

"And I," the stag went on, "am now here inside the body of you, Tartaglia. Also, please notice that I am now holding the weapon."

In the body of the Prime Minister, the stag let the Bi-Scepter drop to the ground where it disappeared into the ground-mist, and with both of Tartaglia's hands the stag raised the long-gun and aimed it with calm precision at the forehead of King Theramo with Tartaglia inside.

The eyes of King Theramo stared defiantly back at the eyes of Tartaglia. "You won't kill me, stag," declared Tartaglia with the King's voice. "For the same reason I wouldn't shoot YOU. You would kill the body of the King!"

Inside Tartaglia's body, the stag slipped one of Tartaglia's fingers steadily into the trigger of the matchlock mechanism that held the still smoldering cord-fuse, ready to fire.

"Don't kid yourself," the stag said through Tartaglia's mouth. "You. The King. All of you. You have been hunting and killing my kin for years. The least I can do is avenge their deaths by taking your life and the life of your King's body. Besides. The enchantment of this magic is powerful. When you spared my life, you did not realize what your King already knows—that a dead body can be brought back to life if a living being is switched into it. Once you are dead, the King can easily switch back into his own body, and thereby bring it back to life. Only YOU will then be dead, Tartaglia. Only you will forever be gone from this earth, and the earth will be well rid of you."

From inside the body of King Theramo, Tartaglia was unperturbed. "But you would never stoop to that same low level of killing, stag," the Prime Minister said in the King's voice. "It would make you as distasteful to yourself as we hunters are to you."

The body of Tartaglia with the stag inside paused for a moment, then lowered the long-gun. "That is true…" the stag said with the Prime Minister's voice. "You are a remarkable individual, Tartaglia. Through all your evil, your wits are as keen as a carving blade. What a waste…"

Tartaglia's body turned, and the great stag strode with Tartaglia's long legs to the oak tree where it retrieved King Theramo's harquebus before returning with both long-guns back to where the body of the King with Tartaglia inside was bound.

"I will go now," said the stag from Tartaglia's mouth. "I leave you here with your thoughts, evil man. When I return, it shall be with your King, and all this shall be put aright."

Carrying the two weapons, the stag in the body of Tartaglia turned and strode off through the fog, the Prime Minister's dark robes billowing out behind its body as it made its way out of the clearing and into the woods, proceeding in the same direction that the body of the stag with the King inside had been running.

From its unseen perch on the branch of the oak, the parrot silently observed as the body of King Theramo desperately struggled to free itself. But the rope had been secured too well, and Tartaglia inside the bound body of the King was left furious and thwarted, with no immediately available option other than to wait for whoever might next make their way into the glade.

He did not have to wait long. Only minutes after the stag in the body of Tartaglia had left the glade, the body of the stag with King Theramo inside returned to the foggy clearing. The stag's head thrust tentatively into the open space through a closely clustered stand of thick foliage and looked around with furtive caution, its large array of exquisite antlers turning first one way then the other as the stag's alert keen eyes surveyed the glade, taking in details of the scene, and apparently detecting no presence other than the body of the King still bound to the tree. The absence of Tartaglia seemed sufficiently reassuring, and King Theramo in the body of the stag emerged from the leafy periphery and came with guardedly emboldened confidence fully into the space.

Stepping with care as the placement of each hoof on the forest floor was lost in the murk of ground-mist, the body of the stag made its way with massive grace across the glade until it came to a stop before the immobilized body of the King.

"You saved my life, great stag," said King Theramo from the mouth of the stag. "I shall be forever in your debt... But... What has become of the treacherous villain I once called friend? Where is Prime Minister Tartaglia…?"

"King Theramo!" exclaimed the deceitful words of Tartaglia from the mouth of the King. "Tartaglia ran off to shoot you!"

The body of the stag shook its mighty head in disappointed incredulity. "Is there no end to that man's evil?" said the King in the stag. "How and when he came to be so bitter and cruel is an utter mystery…"

"King Theramo," entreated the false words of Tartaglia from the King's mouth. "Untie me! Please! Quickly!"

"Yes," King Theramo replied sympathetically from the mouth of the stag. "Yes, of course. I will untie you post-haste. Only… How shall I go about it…? Were you here in our own body, great stag, how would you go about undoing the confinement of the rope…?"

"Is it not obvious?" said the words of Tartaglia from the mouth of King Theramo's body. "I thought Kings were supposed to be smart. Use your stag teeth to chew through the knot!"

"Yes," said the King from within the body of the stag. "Yes, of course! That is clever and swift thinking, great stag…"

The body of the stag took a step closer to the body of King Theramo and lowered its great head to begin to chew through the rope.

"Careful, imbecile…!" complained the words of Tartaglia from the mouth of the King. "Turn your head to the side, or you'll gouge my eyes out with those confounded antlers…!"

"Yes, yes…" King Theramo said apologetically within the body of the stag. "Please forgive my clumsy thoughtlessness…"

"Enough talk!" the words of Tartaglia inside the body of the King carped impatiently. "Just do it already!"

The head of the stag turned to one side so the network of reticulated bone curves and formidable points comprising its splendid antlers were steered safely away from the face of the King's body, and the teeth of the stag went to work biting and chewing at the rope's thick protruding knot.

"Mrrrghh trrtll errgght srhttr..." said King Theramo unintelligibly, trying to talk through the mouth of the stag whilst striving to sever the entwined bond.

"Odds bodkins!" complained the irritated words of Tartaglia from the mouth of the King. "I can't make out a word you're saying! Just untie me, and be quick about it!"

At last the teeth of the stag attained success, and the knot was successfully broken through. The coils of rope loosened and unwound from their own weight, spilling in a haphazard spiral to the ground, and the body of the King was freed.

The body of the stag with King Theramo inside took a few hoofsteps back to better view the fruitful release, as the body of the King took a relieved step forward and pointed a victorious finger at the face of the stag.

"Theramo!" exclaimed the triumphant scornful words of Tartaglia with the King's voice from within the body of King Theramo. "It is I! Tartaglia! Your gullibility is astonishing! How did I ever endure the endless years as your Prime Minister?!"

The body of the stag took several more steps backward in

regretful horror. "Tartaglia…?" lamented King Theramo from the mouth of the stag. "Oh, no… What have I done…?!"

"You have freed me, fool!" crowed the cruelly laughing words of Tartaglia from the body of the King. "And now, I bid you adieu. When next we meet, you will be dead, carried on the shoulders of your own hunters. And I shall be preparing to marry the bride you stole from me, my beloved Angiolina!"

"Tartaglia! No! NO!!" King Theramo cried out from within the body of the stag. "What has become of you? How is it that the great man and treasured friend you once were could have been so bitterly consumed and so brutally transformed by such depraved unspeakable darkness? What has happened to you, Tartaglia? What has become of your wisdom and goodness? How did you come to lose your true self to such monstrous spiteful evil…?"

In the body of the King, Tartaglia took an enraged furious step toward the stag. "What do you know of truth!?" the Prime Minister's words demanded in the King's voice. "You asked the enchanter for the ability to *know* the truth, but he gave you the power to *change* the truth. But you were too much of a fool to understand what you held in your hands. And now that power has become mine. And now you see the truth of what I say and what I have done. You were blinded by needing to see the truth. What is the truth that will be seen now? This is now the truth: I am King. When I stand before Angiolina, will she be in love with you, or with me? When I take my beloved Angiolina in my arms on our wedding night, will she desire you, or will she desire me? When I stand before your magical mirror, and put on your magical spectacles, and speak the words *I am King*, what do you think the looking-glass will say? What is the truth? Tell me, Theramo. What is the Truth? Are you king? Or am I?! This is the truth: I am King, as I was always meant to be. The power. The kingdom. The love of Angiolina. They are now mine. All mine. That is the truth now. And you, Theramo? What is your truth? You are now an animal, and this is a hunt, and before the sun at last sets on this day, you will be a dead trophy for your own people. You will be a departed relic. Your head will hang on a wall. People will look at what is left of you, then pass you by. Just as your wasted life has passed you by. You will not be missed, Theramo. Because the King will still be there. Because I will be there. Because *I am the King*. Farewell, simpleton!"

Tartaglia, in the body of King Theramo, turned and left the clearing, walking off through the woods back the way he had first come, along the same route, but along a very different path.

In the fog of the glade, the stag's forelegs legs buckled in despair and the front of the stag's body dropped to the ground in defeat. Its great head fell forward, and its mighty antlers sank hopelessly down into the cold mist.

Chapter 24

The Parrot
and
The Gunshots

On the branch of the ancient oak, the parrot spread its wings, revealing even in the failing light and thickening fog the resplendence of its vividly colored plumage as it pushed off from the tree bough and took flight in a swift descending dive to alight on one of the curved bone-branches of the stag's magnificent antlers.

"You're the King, you're the King," the parrot squawked emphatically.

"I'm the King..." repeated King Theramo's words, empty of any meaning as they came laden heavily with only doleful defeat out of the mouth of the stag. "I'm the King..."

"Can't give up," the parrot insisted. "Can't give up."

"I can't give up..." the King said despondently from the body of the stag.

The wind was now gusting slightly. The fog of the glade was beginning to drift with more motion, and the low mist which had been suspended inertly just above the level of the ground was starting to shift with movement.

The mighty head of the great stag lifted from where it had dropped in abject hopeless resignation and came up through the mist and fog, elevating with it the parrot perched on its antlers.

"I can't give up…" King Theramo said through the mouth of the stag with a voice that sounded less lost and possessed perhaps a glimmer of conviction.

"Be strong, be strong," said the parrot.

"I have to be strong…" said the King from the body of the stag, the voice seeming to regain some energy with each spoken word. "I have to be strong…"

"A leader leads," said the parrot. "A leader leads."

The body of the stag raised its head higher, unfolding its collapsed forelegs and forcing itself up to standing. "I am the leader of my kingdom…" said King Theramo in the stag. "I am the leader of my kingdom, the leader of the people… I have an obligation to find a way to prevail… For my realm… For the memory and honor of my parents… For myself… For Angiolina… For the Truth…"

The parrot again spread its vibrantly-hued wings and lowered itself slightly before pushing off into flight from the rising antlers of the great stag and descending again in a short flying dive, to alight on a shaft of the Bi-Scepter as it lay still-shrouded in mist on the forest floor of the clearing where it had fallen after being dropped by the hand of Tartaglia while the stag was in the Prime Minister's body.

The eyes of the stag were continuing to lose more of their look of defeat, and through them King Theramo observed with slowly awakening interest the parrot in the mist at the ground below.

"You… You're Cagliostro's parrot…" said the King in the stag. "Is… Is Cagliostro coming to save me…?"

"Not a chance," the parrot said definitely. "Not a chance. Save yourself, save yourself. Be the King. Be the King."

"Yes…" agreed King Theramo from within the stag. "Yes, a King should not need help…"

"Everyone needs help," scolded the parrot. "Everyone needs help."

The mighty head of the stag nodded. "You are right…" said King Theramo through the stag's mouth. "You are right, everyone needs help. Even a king. Especially a king… Parrot, are you here to help me…?"

"Good parrot! Good parrot!" the parrot exclaimed enthusiastically.

"Yes," agreed King Theramo in the stag. "Yes, you are indeed a good parrot. You are helping me reclaim my will to prevail…"

"Switch," instructed the parrot. "Switch." The parrot spread its wings and flapped several wide outstretched flaps, disturbing the ground-mist and revealing the glittering shafts of the Bi-Scepter, one of which was currently in its dexterous claws, adeptly grasped as a perch.

"Switch…?" wondered the King from the stag's mouth. "Switch into whom…? I know not how the enchanted device came to be left carelessly there on the ground, and I thank you greatly for showing me its presence, but…"

The parrot again spread its wings and lowered itself, then pushed off from the Bi-Scepter shaft and took to the air, flying across the glade and alighting on the fallen cane of Cigolotti, whose sleeping body still was nearly impossible to discern. The parrot flapped its wings vigorously with excited animation as it landed, deliberately disturbing enough ground-mist to reveal some of the tattered rags of the hermit's garb.

In the body of the stag, King Theramo had followed the flight of the parrot with the stag's head, and now fully turned to walk with cautious hoofsteps through the mist over to the part of the clearing where the parrot had landed.

"Why, it's a poor dead elderly peasant…" the King exclaimed from the mouth of the stag. "But how will this…"

In the body of the stag, King Theramo paused for a moment, and then a moment later appeared to remember.

"Cagliostro…" the King began through the mouth of the stag. "He told me… He said… He said if you used the Bi-Scepter to switch into a body which was dead, that body would then come to life with you inside it… And the body you switched out of then would have inside it the deadness from the body you now occupy… I begin to understand, parrot… In the body of a peasant, I might escape the unknowing aim of my own hunters and the all too knowing aim of Tartaglia…"

The body of the stag with King Theramo inside turned and made its way again with careful hoofsteps through the fog and mist back to where the Bi-Scepter lay on the ground.

"Parrot…" said the King through the mouth of the stag. "How will I—"

"Hooves and nose! Hooves and nose!" said the parrot, taking off from Cigolotti's cane and flying back to the safety of its perch on the bough of the oak tree.

The stag's head nodded in realization and understanding. "Yes," said King Theramo in the stag. "Yes, of course... I... I have not yet become accustomed to the body of this great animal, though I expect that will soon be of little consequence..."

"Praise the parrot!" said the parrot. "Praise the parrot!"

A grateful sigh of genuine appreciation issued from the nostrils of the stag in the form of diverging puffs of vapor, condensing in the steadily cooling ambient air, visible even amidst the still-growing density of the fog.

"You are a very helpful parrot," said the King though the stag's mouth. "You are a very helpful parrot. You have in kindness goaded me away from despair and defeat, and you have enabled me to recover a semblance of strength and resolve, and you have shown me the way to save myself. I am truly thankful, parrot. Thank you."

"Theramo is the King," said the parrot encouragingly. "Theramo is the King."

King Theramo mustered a not-fully-convinced nod with the stag's head in nevertheless appreciative acknowledgement. With awkward but ultimately successful effort, he used the stag's nose and the hooves of the stag's forelegs to spread apart the Bi-Scepter so that one hinged shaft pointed in the direction of the prone Cigolotti, and the other was directed upward toward himself, canted and braced in place against a fetlock.

"Forgive me," said the King in the stag. "Forgive me, old man, for borrowing your lifeless body. But I am desperate! And wherever you are, great stag, forgive me for leaving your body here and no life left within its noble shell..."

A rising wind stirred the glade as King Theramo in the body of the stag positioned the stag's nose against the emerald button of the Bi-Scepter. High above the clearing, the forest canopy swayed from the sudden force of strong air moving the lofty treetops.

With the nose of the stag, King Theramo pressed the lustrously-faceted surface of the deep-green gemstone.

A distant sound like chimes was lost in the rushing wind and replaced with a deep rumbling like faraway thunder. Jagged tendrils of tiny lightning danced and crackled around the Bi-Scepter shafts amidst indistinct swirls of twinkling motes of illumination. The ends of the pointing rods for an instant glowed brilliantly blue-white, and then the entire glade flashed with inversion as all light values flipped and all color hues reversed, and in an instant reversed back, two times in fast succession.

And then the wind stopped and the noises ceased, and everything was abruptly still and quiet. The fog once again hung motionless in the air, the cool ground-mist blanketing the forest floor again settled back to idle stillness.

With a weighty thud the body of the great stag collapsed and dropped ponderously to the forest floor, momentarily agitating displaced mist in heavily roiling cloudy whorls.

The body of Cigolotti sat up with a start, muscle memory causing it to reflexively and immediately find and grasp with one of its hands the knobbed shaft of the tree-bough cane from where it had lain close-by on the ground.

In the body of Cigolotti, King Theramo leaned on the cane and used its leverage to elevate the body of the hermit up from sitting and the clustered tufts of weedy ground growth, and the low-lying gathered mist which had heretofore obscured its presence from easily apparent view.

"Oh, old man...!" said the troubled words of the King in Cigolotti's voice as he worked to raise the hermit's body unsteadily to its feet. "This body of yours is feeble indeed! But it is my only hope..."

From the woods beyond the clearing, voices could now be faintly heard but distinctly growing nearer as they approached.

The eyes of Cigolotti filled with alarm as King Theramo appeared to recognize the voices. In the body of Cigolotti, the King cast a quick final glance over toward the fallen body of the great stag.

"My heart breaks for you, noble beast," said King Theramo in Cigolotti's voice. "Rest in peace..."

The body of Cigolotti turned, and with labored effort and hurried immediacy, the King hobbled out of the glade and into the forest in the opposite direction from the approaching voices as quickly as Cigolotti's frail aged legs would carry him.

"But Sire..." said one of the voices as it came steadily closer. "Where is the Prime Minister...?"

"Imbecile!" exclaimed another of the voices. "I'm right h— I mean... My faithful Prime Minister must have headed in a different direction. I... We... There was a lot of confusion when we suddenly saw the stag..."

In the glade, the antlers of the great stag began to move as the mighty head suddenly lifted. Inside the body of the stag,

Cigolotti was again fully awake, and as if nothing had happened he continued his thought from where he had left off.

"It's not true, I say!" protested Cigolotti through the mouth of the stag. "I never fall asleep except in my own bed in my own cottage. And furthermore…"

In the body of the stag, Cigolotti paused in bewilderment.

"Where did they all go?" he said from the mouth of the stag. "Where are the gentlemen with the guns…?"

The head of the stag turned quickly, looking first to one side then the other.

"And whose words are saying my thoughts…?" Cigolotti demanded in the stag's voice, rich and resonant and deep with strength and power.

The body of the stag leapt to its feet and looked rapidly around at itself, inspecting every inch it could manage to see, its magnificent antlers slicing through the air and disturbing the fog in severed swathes with quick cleaving sweeps as the mighty head swung about.

"What manner of strange dream is this?" Cigolotti wondered aloud in the voice of the stag. "Perhaps I am asleep after all…"

The body of the stag with Cigolotti inside continued to explore itself, testing its legs, lifting and lowering each hoof up and down from the mist-hidden ground.

"And what a marvelous dream…!" Cigolotti exclaimed with delight though the mouth of the stag. "How youthful and strong I feel inside the body of this powerful animal! When is the last time

I was able to run? So long ago, it is not within my memory... I want to run! I want to run...!"

In sudden joyous giant strides, the body of the stag took off at a gallop, as Cigolotti bolted from the clearing and dashed off into the forest, hurdling with high effortless bounding jumps over ground obstructions, slaloming through the labyrinthine density of trees, bypassing obstacle trunks on alternating sides with easy sidelong leaps, gathering speed and jubilance as he ran.

"There he goes, fools!" called an outraged voice from the nearby woods. "The stag! With the white mark on his head! After him!"

"Your Majesty? Are you quite all right?" questioned another voice.

"You seem...different..." said another.

"It's just a stag, Sire. There are other—"

"SILENCE! Enough of your gibbering! All of you!! Kill the stag! Kill the stag!"

"Yes, Your Majesty..."

"Let's go! Let's go!! Now! MOVE!!!"

The voices moved off and faded away at nearly the same moment that Truffaldino made his way into the glade, in turns studying the map in his hands, and looking around at the surrounding forest, and trying to watch his steps amidst the deceptive mist.

"According to the map," Truffaldino said aloud to himself, "the parrot is here in this clearing..."

Stopping near the tree where the body of the King had been bound, Truffaldino looked more closely at the map, which was giving off a slight radiant light and casting a vague colorful glow into the fog-filled air, faintly lighting Truffaldino's face from below.

"It's a good thing my master enchanted THE MAP OF HERE to send light up from inside itself," he mused gratefully. "Because the farther I go into this forest, the darker everything around here gets…"

Ground-mist still swirled around his motionless turnshoes from the last steps he had taken as Truffaldino continued to inspect the surface of the luminous map.

"It says…"

Truffaldino's feet disturbed the mist again as he rotated his position and took several steps toward the ancient oak tree.

"It says," he went on, "that the parrot is on a branch of *this* tree…"

He glanced up, then looked down to check the map again.

"…and is sitting on a branch right…up…"

He looked away from the map and tilted his head upward.

"…there!"

"Truffaldino!" squawked the parrot. "Truffaldino!"

"Parrot!" exclaimed Truffaldino. "Parrot!!"

"Pick it up! Pick it up!"

"What?" said Truffaldino. "What do you want? I'm already talking as fast as I can…!"

"On the ground! On the ground!"

"Wait. Wait, what are you even talking about…? What's on what ground where…?"

The parrot took off from the oak branch and flew down through the foggy air to land once again on the Bi-Scepter, which now lay where King Theramo in the body of the stag had left it after switching into Cigolotti's body. With its long tail extended out behind it to account for the lack of clearance from being so close to the forest floor, the parrot flapped its colorful wings with animated purpose, disturbing the ground-mist sufficiently to reveal the glittering gold and silver presence of the enchanted device.

Truffaldino furled the map and tucked it into his belt-pouch before stepping across the glade through the mist until he arrived at the Bi-Scepter. The parrot took off and flew up to alight atop the left shoulder of Truffaldino's jerkin as Truffaldino reached into the swirls of mist and picked the device up from the ground.

"This belongs to my master," said Truffaldino turning the Bi-Scepter in his hands. "But I thought he was going to give it to the King. What's it doing out here in the middle of the forest…?"

"Palace Gardens!" said the parrot. "Palace Gardens."

"I know, I know," said Truffaldino. "I'm supposed to bring you back there. I'm not even going to bother asking you what you're doing here, or why you left in the first place…"

"Hurry! Hurry!" squawked the parrot, lowering itself for a moment before spreading its wide colorful wings and taking off from Truffaldino's shoulder to fly from the glade, through the foggy air, and out of sight into the forest.

"Seriously…?" said Truffaldino incredulously.

Pivoting the two pointing rods, he swiveled the hinged shafts back together. They interlocked side-by-side with a soft precise metallic click, and Truffaldino tried to then put the device into his belt-pouch. But the Bi-Scepter was too long to fit properly, and he had to resort instead to tucking it like a small double-sword into the side of his belt.

Staring with brief exasperation into the part of the forest where the parrot had disappeared, Truffaldino again reached into his belt-pouch and took out THE MAP OF HERE with a resigned impatient sigh. Unfurling the map, he studied the glowing surface for a moment, before proceeding to make his way out of the clearing in the same direction the parrot had flown, back toward the Hanging Gardens and the palace.

"I see it!" exclaimed a sudden voice close by.

"Something's moving! There! There!! It must be the stag! Shoot! Shoot! Imbeciles! Why do you hesitate?! I am the King! You have to do as I say! Kill! Kill!! Kill!!!"

Three shots were fired, nearly at the same time, the reports of the nearby blasts echoing portentously through the forest. The sounds of the lymer dogs baying could suddenly be heard, and a moment later came the two-note sonorous call of the horn, resounding through the wood, its fading echo lost in the amplifying energetic barking of the dogs.

The Hunt had ended.

Chapter 25

The Cartography Library
and
The Guard's Report

The Royal Cartography Library housed all the maps in the palace. Outside its high arched windows, the gloom and clouded heaviness of the lowered rainless sky loomed with the growing darkness of the fading day. But inside, the library was brightly illuminated. Cheering firelight radiated in warm flickering splendor from every direction—from the steadily-rippling collective torch-light flame-glow of plentiful elegant gold wall-sconces, and from the calmly-continuous quietly-crackling voluminous blaze within the robust brick, polished tile, and carved marble of the palatial fireplace. And suffusing the space in lambent brilliance with wide enlightenment from above was the vast elaborate brass and glass chandelier, hanging massive and motionless, alive with moving light, suspended in the middle of the large room on a stout chain anchored at the center of the overhead domed ceiling, whose lofty concave surface was frescoed with a vibrantly-colored and precisely-detailed map of Benebento.

The room was a resplendent place, its long ranges of multi-level shelf-storage cases and cabinetry crafted from diverse light-colored hardwood species like white oak, beech, ash, and maple. Maps were everywhere—mounted in frames along the walls, and rolled in scrolls held closed with ribbons and stacked like hollow logs by the dozens in deep decorative shelf cubbies or individually stored in scores of horizontal curved-slot racks like bottomless wine bottles, all with a small round catalog identifier tag dangling from a leather thong tied at the protruding exposed end of each scroll. Banks of shelves lining the walls brimmed with map folios, quires of maps bound in codices, and atlases of map collections bound as gilt-edged books with finely-tooled textured leather spines labeled in embossed and incised gold lettering.

In open-closeted alcoves and bays, racks of hanging maps were suspended on curtain rails like hangered-garments in vertically sandwiched profusion. Maps enclosed in leather document-tubes were arranged in orderly upright cylinder clusters in every corner of the room. Moveable-cabinet banks of wide low-height lateral drawers—which could be pulled out like deep sliding trays by far-apart pairs of small brass handles—stood high on the unseen rollers of their slightly-elevated bases, and jutted out from the library's several wall niches. Covering the numerous broad-surfaced tables of the room, recently-viewed land maps and Portolan navigational charts were spread out and held down at their edges with lead chart-weights shaped as three-masted carrack sailing ships, and littered across the cartographic expanses were a diversity of tools and instruments—map divider calipers, straight rulers, parallel rulers, rolling parallel rules, directional compasses, mechanical protractors, triangular scales, navigational quadrants, and brass nocturnals.

The floor of the library was an immense marble-tiled inlay image of an ornately-colored and detailed compass rose, properly oriented relative to the corresponding Real-World directions beyond the walls of the castello. The circular hub of the compass rose lay positioned directly beneath the center of the chandelier in the middle of the library, and it was there that one mapping table had been cleared for the occasion to provide a surface where the Royal Event Planners could pursue and complete with Angiolina all the unfinished work which required attending to, while there still remained some time left in the day to implement whatever arrangements had yet to be made final.

Appearing wearied from continual planning, but still fresh with energized excitement at all the momentous events suddenly composing her new life, Angiolina was dutifully studying every document placed before her by Lord Vellutzio, and thoughtfully and decidedly making selections and choices from all options proffered and delineated by the entirety of the nattily-attired and rigorously-meticulous event-planning team.

The busy tedium was interrupted as two palace guards arrived at the main doorway escorting Clarìcé and Smeraldina, ushering them courteously into the Cartography Library and carrying the young ladies' overnight bags which were stuffed to capacity, the tapestry-like embroidered linen of each valise's textile fabric bulging from the quantity of contents—one travel bag whose exterior was floral patterns of foliate design reminiscent of manuscript illumination borders and seemed to belong to Clarìcé, the other covered with boldly woven images of forest animals and fantastic mythical creatures in rampant poses, and seemed to be the travel bag of Smeraldina.

At the sound of their entrance, Angiolina turned from her work with the event-planning team and exhaled a joyous sigh of relief as she beheld her friends.

"Oh, you've come to rescue me at last!" she exclaimed happily. Claricé and Smeraldina hastened across the library expanse, over the polished surface of an outer point of the compass rose, navigating their way through the map-covered tables, the wooden soles of their footwear energetically clattering with softly clacking taps on the inlay marble floor as the two young ladies arrived at their destination and gently threw themselves into the welcoming arms of Angiolina.

"I am so glad you're here!" Angiolina said with deeply appreciative happiness.

"How is the planning going?" Claricé asked eagerly as the three friends stepped out of their embrace but continued to clasp one another's hands for a few moments longer.

"I can't believe you're still working," said Smeraldina. "Have you been having to do this all day? On the day before your wedding? It doesn't seem fair…!"

Angiolina nodded. "I really have been at it nearly all day," she said. "There just are so many decisions that have to be made. The details of all these preparations seem to never end…!"

"Well," said Claricé with a smile. "I guess you do only get married to a King once in your life, so you might as well have as many things as possible arranged the way you want them."

"And," Smeraldina added. "It must be fun and exciting that every decision you make is a wonderful reminder that you actually are about to be married, and about to become Queen of the realm, and about to start the beginning of your happily-ever-after with the love of your life!"

"Who just happens to be The King…!" agreed Angiolina, and the three of them laughed with each other together.

"How has your day been going?" asked Angiolina. "I want to hear all about how things went with the Mistress of Habiliments."

"Oh, Angiolina," said Clarìcé. "The dresses are gorgeous!"

"They're amazing!" said Smeraldina. "We felt like fairy tale princesses!"

"And looked like them, too!" said Clarìcé.

"I wish Truffaldino could have seen me…" Smeraldina said with wistfully longing, absently flipping her shining red hair over one shoulder.

"I wish Leandro could have seen me…" agreed Clarìcé.

Angiolina smiled happily and nodded. "Well, be patient," she said. "They will get to see you tomorrow, and with all your hair and makeup as well. The alchemists in the Royal Apothecary have formulated a selection of makeup which is lead-free, so we can safely apply as much as we'd like. I've arranged that the Royal Corps for Coiffure, Headdress, and Cosmetology will work their magic on the four of us all together tomorrow morning, although that beauty marathon starts before the sun comes up, so we can't stay up *too* late tonight…!"

This set the three of them laughing again with mirthful excitement.

Oh, I'm so excited!" exclaimed Clarìcé. "It's all going to be so amazing…!"

"But Truffaldino won't be at the wedding…" lamented Smeraldina sadly.

"Well," said Angiolina. "Earlier today I directed a contingent of the Royal Reconnaissance Squadron to see if they could find him…"

"But wouldn't he have left Benebento with the enchanter?" asked Clarìcé with sympathetic unhappiness and pragmatic skepticism.

"He said he would wait for me…" said Smeraldina. "Though, people do often simply say things they don't truly mean. But Truffaldino's so straightforward. He wouldn't have said it if he didn't mean it… And I could tell by the look in his eyes he meant it. His eyes are green. Like mine, only greener. I wish I could be looking into them right now…"

"Well," Angiolina went on. "Reconnaissance reported to me a while ago that they found out Truffaldino spent last night at the Inn Pizzicato, so it seems he did not leave with the enchanter."

Smeraldina seemed to come back to vibrant life, and she excitedly grasped Angiolina's hands. "Oh, Angiolina!" she breathed happily. "You are so wonderful…! Thank you…!!"

"He did not check out this morning," Angiolina went on, smiling back at Smeraldina. "And they are to report to me immediately as soon as they learn more. They're going to keep looking for him, and when they find him, they have Royal instructions to officially inform him he is invited to the wedding, and that he is politely and strongly urged to attend under any circumstances."

Smeraldina threw her arms around Angiolina and hugged her affectionately, and Clarìcé stepped forward and threw her arms around them both.

"Oh, Angiolina," Smeraldina said suddenly, stepping back from their group embrace. "You should have seen Nicoletta at her fitting… She always dresses so plainly, and yet her beauty still is so breathtaking—"

Clarìcé too stepped back from their embrace. "But Angiolina," she added, nodding in emphatic agreement. "When Nicoletta first put on her dress for the wedding—"

"Everyone in the Hall of Habiliments stopped what they were doing," recounted Smeraldina. "She looked like a goddess… No one could move. We were all in awe—"

"It was as though we all had been transformed just by seeing her," said Clarìcé.

"It was life-changing to behold her like that," Smeraldina agreed. "My heart still races when I think about it…"

"Poor Nicoletta," said Clarìcé. "She *hates* to be looked at or to be the center of attention. Her dress of course fit her perfectly, but she couldn't get out of it fast enough."

"Will she be all right during the wedding ceremony events tomorrow…?" Angiolina asked with concern.

"I think so," said Smeraldina. "But we must have the event planners find ways to—as much as possible—have her not in the main view…"

Angiolina nodded. "I'll tell them to adjust the staging and choreography with that in mind, as much as they possibly can…"

"Is she already in the suite?" asked Smeraldina. "Did she get here ahead of us?"

Angiolina shook her head. "She's not here yet."

Claricé nodded. "She doesn't do it deliberately or disruptively, but she does seem to just need to do things in her own way. And she just needs to be on her own clock."

"She'll be here," agreed Smeraldina. "It's just that even something as seemingly unthreatening as arriving at the same time as other people makes her feel like everyone is looking at her."

Claricé nodded. "She seems to feel as though she's less likely to be noticed if she just slips into a scene or situation when no one is expecting her, as if that way she might be treated as a kind of afterthought that people won't really pay attention to."

"You know Nicoletta," said Smeraldina. "She just prefers her own way of going about things…"

"Yes," said Angiolina. "Well, I've left instructions with the guards to escort her to the suite whenever she arrives. I agree, I'm sure she'll be here. She'll arrive when she feels ready and comfortable to come."

"Sometimes," said Smeraldina, "I just want to put my arms around her and protect her and shield her from the eyes of the world that make her so uncomfortable…"

Angiolina nodded. "I know just what you mean…"

"My brother made me promise I would report to him before the start of our slumber party," said Claricé with resigned dissatisfaction.

Smeraldina nodded. "And my father," she said. "He wants me to find him in the Royal Banquet Hall after the end of The Hunt to discuss our schedule for the various ceremony events of the wedding."

"Yes," said Angiolina. "Of course. My father, too, wants to see me briefly after The Hunt before the four of us disappear into the happy private seclusion of the suite for our slumber party. I have asked for and received permission for accommodations to be arranged for him in one of the guest suites in the southwest wing, and additional rooms are being readied for Sir Balzanno and Avogadro and Prime Minister Tartaglia, should they wish to overnight in the palace."

From the library table that had been temporarily re-purposed as a planning surface, Lord Vellutzio cleared his throat with a there-is-still-a-lot-of-work-to-do sound which unmistakably was directed at Angiolina.

Angiolina glanced obligingly at the planners, then turned back to Claricé and Smeraldina. "Okay," she said. "You two should go on ahead to the suite. The guards will take you there. I just want to wait until Theramo is back from The Hunt. I'll keep at it here with the planners until then, and then I'll meet him, as he and I planned, at the Palace Gardens. Then I'll come join you. The Master of the Kitchen, even with all he has on his plate, has quite graciously somehow spared a strand of his attention to focus on our slumber party. He has with very generous adamance insisted on diverting a capable handful of his minions to set up a festive spread for us in the Royal Suite in the northwest wing. I'm told that quite a lavishly prepared bounty of food and drink now awaits us in the suite, so please do feel free to indulge to your hearts' content while waiting for Nicoletta and for me to join you there."

The two guards who had escorted Clarìcé and Smeraldina were waiting patiently at the pointed-arch main entrance to the Cartography Library with the young ladies' travel bags, but they were suddenly joined by another guard who was just arriving, and who proceeded with swift purpose across the reflective marble floor to where Angiolina stood with her two friends.

Attired in Royal martial garb whose quality and presentation seemed to suggest a rank higher than the two guards with whom he had just briefly conferred but lower than that of Leandro, this guard delivered a quick perfunctory respectful bow to Angiolina before addressing her. "Your Ladyship requested to be informed upon conclusion of The Hunt," he said with succinct courtesy.

"Has it ended?" asked Angiolina.

"It has, Your Ladyship."

"And have all returned safely?"

The guard hesitated.

"Good sir, do you have some news...?" she asked with sudden anxiousness.

The guard glanced at Clarìcé and Smeraldina.

"Your Ladyship," he said. "May I speak freely?"

Angiolina nodded hastily.

"These are my two closest friends, good sir," she said quickly. "You may speak freely in their presence. But... What has happened...?"

"Prime Minister Tartaglia has gone missing, Your Ladyship,"

replied the guard. "There was no accident that any are aware of. However, his…his disappearance is at present unexplained and…and is of some concern…"

"That is indeed of concern…" said Angiolina. "Have all the others returned?"

"The assistant to the enchanter—"

"Truffaldino!" Smeraldina exclaimed. "He was there? What was he doing on The Hunt? Is he somewhere in the palace? Is he all right?"

"The enchanter's assistant," the guard reported, "is at present not in the palace. A battlement guard on patrol at the wall-walk of the Vitaian Gate, routinely overseeing proceedings of The Hunt, witnessed through a spyglass at a great distance the assistant to the enchanter entering the Forest of Aldente some time ago as the darkness of the day was descending. The young man was not seen exiting the forest, either on the town-side of the moat or on the Hanging Gardens side."

Smeraldina covered her mouth with her hand, filled with emotion.

"Good sir," said Angiolina. "Where is everyone else?"

"The only quarry felled in the hunt, a great stag, has been brought back on a litter by Lord Mirino and his huntsmen, and they themselves have since retired to the stables and kennels for post-hunt routines. The body of the stag lies undisturbed on display within the Royal Trophy Hall for viewing until the close of day. Participants of The Hunt have adjourned to the Royal Banquet Hall for food and libation refreshment."

"And His Majesty…?"

"His Royal Highness returned with the others," reported the guard, "but did not join them in the Royal Banquet Hall."

"Is that usual…?"

"It… It is not, Your Ladyship."

"Good sir," Angiolina went on. "What is your measure of the mood of the hunting parties on their return?"

"Your Ladyship…" the guard said hesitantly.

"I beseech you, please speak with frankness and candor."

"The noblemen are in high spirits, Your Ladyship, as are the many invited guests who have now joined them in the Royal Banquet Hall. His Majesty's advisors, however, are… They are of a more reserved mood, Your Ladyship."

"Likely due to the concerning disappearance of the Prime Minister, I imagine," suggested Angiolina. "Is there now a search underway to seek his whereabouts?"

The guard again hesitated.

"Good, sir, I entreat you, do not withhold information…"

"Your Ladyship… A search party was assembled, however His Majesty ordered they not be sent forth…"

"The King told them not to look for the Prime Minister…?"

"Yes, Your Ladyship. That is correct…"

"That seems odd to me…"

The guard did not offer a response.

"Has a search party been dispatched to seek the whereabouts of Truffaldino?" Angiolina asked. "That is, to seek the whereabouts of the enchanter's assistant?"

"His Majesty was explicit that no search parties be sent forth for any reason, Your Ladyship…"

"Good sir, is the King suffering any manner of ill effect as a result of The Hunt…?"

Once again, the guard again hesitated.

"Good sir…!"

"His Highness has… There have been—as all know, as you yourself know, Your Ladyship—many changes in His Majesty within a very short period of time. It would not be inconsistent with such recent and momentous changes that His Highness would be…not entirely Himself…"

"Your words trouble me, good sir, but I thank you for them, and I thank you for your candor…"

"Yes, Your Ladyship…"

Smeraldina took hold of Angiolina's hand. "Angiolina," she said. "What's going on? What's happening…?"

Angiolina clasped Smeraldina's hand. "I… I don't know… But something doesn't feel right…"

"Will there be anything else you require of me, Your Ladyship?" the guard inquired respectfully.

"Yes," said Angiolina. "Please, if you would, find Chancellor Pantalòné, my father, and tell him I wish to see him at his earliest convenience. Please tell him he may find me in the Palace Gardens, if he is available to come there."

"Yes, Your Ladyship," the guard replied, delivering a brief perfunctory courteous bow before turning and making his way briskly back across the inlay compass rose of the marble floor, past the two waiting guards at the pointed-arch main entrance, and out of the Cartography Library.

"Angiolina," said Clarìcé with apprehension. "What should we do…?"

"Theramo said he would meet me in the Palace Gardens after The Hunt," Angiolina said quickly. "I'm going to go there now and make sure he is all right, and see what is happening with the disappearances of Prime Minister Tartaglia and Truffaldino…"

"Angiolina, I'm so worried…!" said Smeraldina.

"We'll figure out and find out what's going on…" said Angiolina. "You two should go along with the guards to the suite. Unpack your things and get settled in, and then wait for Nicoletta. But don't wait too long. And then come and find me in the Palace Gardens…"

The three of them hastily embraced, and Clarìcé and Smeraldina turned to make their way toward the two guards waiting at the library entrance. Angiolina turned and stepped hurriedly toward the event planners, where Lord Vellutzio seemed already anticipating imminent news of her impending exit, his comely facial features arranging themselves impeccably into an expression of peeved dismay.

Chapter 26

The Hunting Party
and
The Squire's Report

In one of the passageways just outside the Royal Banquet Hall, Pantalòné and Sir Balzanno and Leandro stood close together speaking in low tones so as not to be overheard. The noise of festive celebration spilling out of the nearby hall effectively composed sufficient background sound that their conversation was likely to be as private as they required. The mood within the banquet hall was a mixture of celebration at the conclusion of the Hunt, glad rejoicing at the overall greater goodness perceived as having so beneficially affected the realm in so short a period of time, excited expectation about the morrow's momentous wedding event, all complicated with a disconcerting ineffable sense that since the commencement of the Hunt, something now somehow was not quite right.

"I do not understand it..." Sir Balzanno was saying, trouble furrowing his brow. "Chancellor, you are his closest comrade and have known him the longest. Have you ever before observed the King to behave in this way?"

Lord Pantalòné shook his head. "I have not..."

"Never before," Leandro said carefully, "have I ever heard His Majesty speak to anyone in this way..."

"It is as if he is no longer himself..." said Sir Balzanno.

"Something happened in the forest…" said the Chancellor.

"The disappearances of the Prime Minister and the enchanter's assistant are as concerning as they are impossible to explain…" said Leandro.

"His Majesty's aberrant reaction to your concerned questions, Chancellor…" said Sir Balzanno. "I found it to be singularly disconcerting…"

Pantalòné nodded uneasily. "The reaction of His Majesty was uncharacteristic, and peculiarly defensive and antagonistic…"

"He seemed to imply," said Sir Balzanno, "that the three of us somehow posed to him a threat of some kind…"

"Lord Pantalòné," said Leandro. "It was my observation, as well, that your benign inquiries into his welfare did indeed trigger in His Highness an alarming and rash reaction. It was as though he suddenly perceived us as adversaries…"

"Or, perhaps," the Chancellor agreed darkly, "as though he suddenly perceived us even as enemies…"

"Hold…" said Sir Balzanno. "Young Italo approaches. I would advise that no overt indication is given by us of this matter we currently discuss."

"Agreed," said Pantalòné quickly. "His young mind need not be perturbed by misgivings until such time as there exists more information to better account for what we as yet are so unsure of…"

"With respect, good sirs," Leandro said hurriedly. "It seemeth me we ought nevertheless to pursue our dialogue post haste to determine what next measures, if any, are incumbent upon us to undertake…"

"Verily, I am in completely agreement…" said the Chancellor.

Sir Balzanno nodded quickly. "As am I," he concurred hastily. "Forebear but a few moments…"

Italo had been making his way with rushed light-footed steps along the polished stone floor of the vault-ceilinged corridor, and now arrived at where the hunting party stood closely clustered in the quickly-flickering glow of torch-light flames from one of the passageway's abundantly recurrent decorative iron wall-sconces.

Further down the corridor, from an archway opening into the banquet hall, the noises of revelry and celebration mixed with the sounds of food and drink being heartily enjoyed continued to spill in rising and falling waves into the passageway, along with rich savors of delectable cuisine expertly prepared, and the thick redolence of beer and mead and ale and wine.

"Good afternoon, sirs," said Italo, breathless from the haste of his approach and bowing respectfully to the three members of the hunting party.

"A good late afternoon to you, Italo," said Leandro courteously.

"Italo," acknowledged the Chancellor, inclining his head for a moment in polite response.

Italo directed his attention to Sir Balzanno. "Might I have a word with you, Sir?"

Sir Balzanno nodded. "You may speak your mind freely in the presence of these good men, Italo."

Italo nodded in polite response. "I have been looking for you, Sir," said the squire.

"Yes," said Sir Balzanno. "It is your charge to look and as well know how to find. Someday when you are a knight, you will thank me."

"Yes, Sir," said Italo contritely. "Of course, Sir. I am glad to see you safely returned from The Hunt, Sir. All of you, good sirs."

"We all stand in appreciation of your kind thoughts, squire," said Sir Balzanno. "Italo," the knight went on. "You appeared unwell this morning when you helped me into my armor. I am unhappy to see you now looking none the better."

Italo seemed unprepared for the kindness of this concern. "Th… Thank you, Sir," he managed to say. "You are not wont to notice such things…"

"That," said Sir Balzanno, "is an unacceptable lapse on my part which I shall in future make a point of remedying."

"Th… Thank you, Sir," Italo said, a bit flustered. "I… I slept not well last night, Sir. I was troubled by dark dreams that…that upon my waking left my head filled with foreboding and confusion…"

"It may be small comfort, Italo," said Sir Balzanno, "but like vague misgivings are borne as well by others this day, and as inexplicably."

Italo appeared more perplexed. "Forgive me, Sir," he replied. "But you seem…changed from The Hunt…"

Sir Balzanno nodded. "We found no success in the endeavor, but I believe that I myself may have instead found some crucial clearer paths of thought…"

"But," said Italo. "I understood that it was you and your party here who triumphed in The Hunt with the felling of the great stag now on display in the trophy hall…"

"Indeed, that is what is being put forth," said Sir Balzanno. "However, that account may not prove entirely factual."

"I... I don't understand, Sir," said Italo with increased confusion.

"These are matters," said the knight, "which will in good time and with good luck become less enigmatic. For the nonce, cast your thoughts aside from such concerns and explain why you sought me here. Though, I need you to do so with all possible brevity, squire, as there are pressing matters at hand which immediately require my attention."

"Yes, Sir," replied Italo. "Of course, Sir. It...it is only that I wanted to inform you of progress in the several areas you charged me with attending to. The sword has been returned to the armorer and will have its point and edges ground to be made less sharp. The addition of a glass panel for the eye-portal of your helmet visor was deemed unadvisable, due to the likely and undesirable consequences of shards from inevitable shattering as a result of impacts. But I found an artisan metal-smith in town who will craft a fine-mesh grille from steel which will give you the eye-protection you requested with minimal compromise in your ability to see through it clearly. This same smith not only is a proficient craftsman, but also is skilled in metallurgy. He is in possession of ingots imported from the Near East of a rare crucible alloy known in some regions as Damascus steel, and the metal-worker believes he can—from those ingots— create for you armor which is both stronger and lighter than that which you currently wear."

Sir Balzanno could not stop himself from smiling in pride. "You are a diligent and resourceful squire, Italo," said the knight.

"You have dispatched your charges admirably. You now should proceed to the armory, where you will find the matchlocks used in today's hunting endeavor. Locate my harquebus, clean and inspect it thoroughly, and then report back to me."

"Yes, Sir," Italo replied with dutiful obedience. "Where shall I find you, Sir?"

"Wherever I am, young Italo, that is where you shall find me," said Sir Balzanno.

"Yes, Sir," said Italo, turning to leave.

"Italo," said the knight, stopping the squire's departure with the tone of his voice.

Italo paused and turned back to Sir Balzanno. "Sir?" he asked cautiously.

"Italo," the knight went on. "These details of which you have spoken... The particulars are unnecessary—and verily too abstruse—for me to understand. But they are details whose importance I nevertheless recognize and acknowledge. They all are details I depend upon you to attend to, details which entail arcane and expert knowledge that I depend upon you to acquire and apply as necessary. You take seriously your apprenticeship responsibilities, Italo. Your dedicated devotion to the chivalric code and the knightly arts is commendable. Do proceed with following to fruition all you have described regarding armaments. And keep in your mind this other thing that I tell you—I spoke earlier this morning with Her Ladyship Angiolina, and secured from her a willing promise to arrange for you to be formally invited to the morrow's wedding event. You are a good apprentice, Italo. And one day, you will be a good knight. It is appropriate that you are present and welcome at such a momentous and historic event."

Italo was nearly unable to speak. "Thank you, Sir Balzanno…" he said with deep humility and appreciation.

The knight nodded. "Very well, squire," said Sir Balzanno. "Tarry no longer here, and get thee to the armory."

"Yes, Sir," Italo said obediently, bowing to the hunting party, and turning to hurry back down the passageway the way he had come, and with the same brisk alacrity.

"That was uncharacteristically gracious of you, Balzanno," observed Lord Pantalòné as Italo disappeared from view.

"He is a good lad…" the knight said thoughtfully. "The events of the past two days have caused me to realize I do not properly appreciate his loyalty and dedication."

"Indeed," replied the Chancellor. "And the events of past two hours have caused me to realize we are not properly fulfilling our obligations to the kingdom. I have been ruminating on our dilemma as you exchanged words with young Italo. It occurs to me we must needs formally confront His Majesty."

"To what end?" asked the knight.

"To honestly and officially convey to him with specificity our misgivings, and request from him some manner of explanation, if an explanation is possible to be given…"

"I am in agreement," said Leandro. "However, another concern as well causes me to misgive…"

"Speak your thoughts, Leandro," said Pantalòné.

"I believe we were perhaps distressed most by the King's behavior with regards to felling the stag…"

"Agreed," said Pantalòné, nodding.

"Aye," Sir Balzanno concurred, nodding as well.

"We none of us were of a mind to comply with His Majesty's singularly peculiar insistence," Leandro went on. "But out of proper respect for His Highness we all nevertheless fired our weapons."

"I aimed at the trees," said Pantalòné. "As high as I could without revealing to His Majesty that I was intending to shoot at nothing whatsoever."

"We were of like minds, Chancellor," said Sir Balzanno. "I likewise directed my weapon such that nothing anywhere near the ground would be struck by my shot."

Leandro nodded. "As did I. Unless the stag was in winged flight through the height of the wood, the animal was not felled by the shot from my weapon."

"I take your point, young Leandro," said Sir Balzanno. "How is it the great stag was killed when only we three fired weapons, and we all of us aimed deliberately too high…?"

"Leandro," said Pantalòné with concern. "Is it your thinking that the assistant to the enchanter may have for some unknown reason been aloft in one of the trees, and that in our efforts to not kill the stag, we by some terrible chance killed the poor lad…?"

Leandro shook his head. "The effective range of the matchlocks is limited. Had a round from one of our harquebuses strayed to hit a person who may have climbed into one of the trees, we would necessarily have been therefore close enough to hear the sound of his body fall to the forest floor."

"Unless," Sir Balzanno said with uneasiness, "the unfortunate lad was struck and died where he was perched, and the tree limbs around him simply stayed his fall…"

Pantalòné gave a grim nod. "His body could have slumped over and remained held in place by boughs of the tree…" the Chancellor agreed unhappily.

"How is it that this day of such joy has descended into such consequence and dark confusion…" Sir Balzanno mused aloud, his face clouded with disquiet.

"Leandro," said Pantalòné. "Do you have thoughts that one of our three errant shots may have in some unknown way struck Prime Minister Tartaglia?"

Leandro again shook his head. "No, Your Lordship. We know not for what reason the enchanter's assistant so ill-advisedly entered the forest during The Hunt, and we thus cannot know if he had some reason to climb into one of the trees, whether for concealment or to gain a better vantage point or from some other unknown motivation. But possibilities that the Prime Minister would have been aloft are even less reasonable. Therefore, the likelihood of any of us having unwittingly harmed him is even more improbable than as regards the assistant to the enchanter."

"I heard no shots fired either in the morning or the afternoon other than our own," said Sir Balzanno. "Leandro, did any member of another party fire a shot?"

Leandro once again shook his head. "None. I inquired with

the other hunting parties, and as well conferred with Lord Mirino. Some game was stirred forth variously throughout the day by the huntsmen on horseback, yet inexplicably none of the creatures was ever encountered by any of the parties hunting on foot. No shots were fired at any time other than our three at the conclusion of The Hunt."

"Young Leandro," said Pantalòné. "Do please connect these troubling questions you so astutely bring to the surface of our concerns."

"To my mind," said Leandro, "these paths lead only toward a greater confusion. The unattributable felling of the great stag, the disappearance of the enchanter's assistant, the disappearance of Prime Minister Tartaglia, and the extraordinary dark change which has taken hold of the King all seem to have befallen within a short frame of time. I therefore feel that—though there is no comprehensible way to explain any of it—these events nevertheless all are in some unknown way connected to each other…"

"A dilemma," said Pantalòné, "further knotted by His Majesty's extraordinary and utterly unaccountable adamance that no search team be allowed to set out toward finding either Tartaglia or the enchanter's young assistant."

"We must meet with the King at once," said Sir Balzanno. "Too much of this is unexplained and of grave immediate concern."

"Yes," said Pantalòné.

Leandro nodded. "From my guards, I know that His Majesty has been trying to locate Her Ladyship Angiolina since his return from The Hunt. I have good reason to believe she may at this moment be awaiting him in the Palace Gardens, per a previously-agreed-upon arrangement between the two of them."

"Were that so," said Pantalòné, "why then would His Highness not simply proceed directly there upon his return…?"

"That is another irregularity without any understandable explanation," said Leandro.

"Balzanno," said Pantalòné with sudden concern. "Is my daughter safe to be alone with the King in his present uncharacteristic state of mind?"

"Chancellor," replied the knight quickly. "Instead of blindly contemplating that dire question, let us rather proceed directly to her side at once."

Lord Pantalòné nodded hurriedly. "Leandro," he said. "Please get a discreet and reliable contingent of your men assembled immediately and meet us in the gardens."

Leandro bowed with respectful swiftness before turning and speeding off down the passageway.

Chancellor Pantalòné and Sir Balzanno turned toward the other direction, and began moving with urgent rapid strides in the direction of the Palace Gardens.

Chapter 27

The Faux King
and
The Former King

The slow inundation of fog had gradually swirled and engulfed its way with roiling inexorability like a leisurely writhing leviathan to the palace, and its unrelenting reach now stretched down into the Palace Gardens. Fingers of fog had become more like tentacles, probing with slow coiling inevitability down through the lofty opening above the vast quadrangle of the inner-palace piazza and descending with imperceptible sinking heaviness onto the expansive courtyard. In the thickening moist murkiness and the fading light of the darkly grey day, the colors of the gardens' spectacular diversity of floral species were becoming muted and swallowed. The uppermost peaks of the cypress trees and the verdant tops of their abundant arboreal companions were increasingly shrouded in the languorously drifting pall, and the geometry of the low-grown hedgerow maze was beginning to become indistinguishable amidst the unhurried tumbling and creeping agglomeration of the fog's nebulous eddying vapor.

Still clearly visible at the lowest level of the ground was the complete absence of all furnishings which had been there the day before. Only the parrot's banquet table remained. Everything else not ordinarily a part of the gardens' lush and ornate presentation—

the fleet of feast-food surfaces, the ninefold array of interview chairs, the hand-mirror table—all had been removed. Left in their stead was an area of trampled grass, a large almost circular range of trodden compression, wide and still-flattened in a verdurous vestige of foot-traffic from all the populace and activity of the previous day. Like a kind of turf palimpsest, the round swath of tromped grass both showed where hours earlier so much had occurred, and as well now seemed blank and ready to be the site of some yet-to-transpire new momentousness.

The only thing more omnipresent at the moment than the languidly descending fog was the hushed utter quiet of the gardens. No wind stirred leaves, no sounds of natural-life-in-progress from insects or birds disturbed the noiselessness of the unmoving air. Apart from the simple trickling and gradual flow of the fountain's gently tumbling water as it cascaded and spilled with endless aqueous aural softness, the only sound was the quiet wooden clack of the soles of Angiolina's shoes on the marble walkway as she made her way through the cypress grove into the gardens.

Walking with slow anxious steps, she seemed apprehensive and lost in thought. Had the parrot not been there, Angiolina might have noticed its absence. But it was there, on its candlestick perch as it had been in the morning earlier that day, and so it did not attract her attention. More attentive eyes might have observed that the colorful bird was lifting first one claw then the other, adjusting its footing, preening traces of woods-debris from its plumage, smoothing its feathers, eating hungrily from the sconce-socket of one candlestick, drinking thirstily from the sconce-socket of the other, and in many unsubtle ways revealing that it was re-settling itself after having recently landed from a flight of some kind. But Angiolina's mind appeared to be very much uneasy and elsewhere.

The tireless and tirelessly attentive Master of the Kitchen had apparently ensured the gardens would not become entirely lost in the flurry of focus and preparations for the morrow's wedding event, and evidently had diverted and dispatched some of his minions to maintain the refreshment status of the lone remaining feast surface. The parrot's banquet table had, earlier that morning, been replenished—albeit in more sensibly smaller-proportioned quantities—with a characteristically appealing spread of breakfast-food fare, and the table now was laden with an equally presentationally-meticulous array of ewered-drinkables and pre-dinner gustatory delights, expertly and pleasingly arranged without encroaching on the parrot's candlestick perch or candlestick snack and water reservoirs, and without disturbing the small hand-mirror with rubies on the back or the rivet spectacles.

Angiolina drifted vaguely through slowly growing traces of the falling fog, which was just beginning to sink its way with more visible density down to the ground level of the gardens. Wandering past the parrot's banquet table and out into the heart of the flattened-grass area, she lingered for several long moments as if remembering and re-living in her mind all that had happened there, before continuing her uneasy meander and making her way with troubled aimless steps distractedly over to the Mirror of Truth. She paused again between the two massive urns whose exotic ferns spilled over the classical-stonework brims, absently lifting a hand to let it rest atop the back of the decorative frame of the full-length looking-glass.

So lost in her thoughts was she that Angiolina did not notice the hurried purposeful arrival behind her of the body of King Theramo, as Tartaglia strode with the King's legs in through the cypress grove and along the marble walkway, heading with deliberate haste toward Angiolina.

"Ah! There you are my beauty!" Tartaglia exclaimed hungrily with King Theramo's voice. "I've been searching everywhere for you. One of those imbecile guards finally told me you were here. I don't know why you're here, but it gives me a chance to be alone with you at last!"

Snapping with alarm out of her troubled reverie, Angiolina whirled around in a fearful panic.

The body of King Theramo did not slow its approach as Tartaglia loomed toward her, reaching eagerly and expectantly out to her with the King's hands.

"Now you're mine!" said Tartaglia through the mouth of King Theramo. "All mine!"

Angiolina recoiled in terror.

"Get away from me!" she cried out.

In the body of the King, Tartaglia halted to an abrupt stop in front of her, hesitantly lowering King Theramo's arms halfway, momentarily as stunned and disconcerted as if he had been slapped.

"But…" he stammered with the King's voice. "Angiolina… You… You look as if you don't recognize me…!"

Angiolina took a step back and moved to stand behind the

frame of the looking-glass, putting the Mirror of Truth between her and the King's body.

"Yes…" she faltered, her eyes desperately scrutinizing the body of King Theramo as if urgently searching for a sign of anomaly in the King's face and outward appearance. "Yes, it… It looks like it's you… But something's wrong… I don't know what it is…"

In the body of the King, Tartaglia resumed his forward motion and again stepped toward Angiolina. "Let me take you in my arms!" he said with King Theramo's voice. "Then all will be well!"

Angiolina reached up both her hands and tightly gripped the top of the mirror's decorative frame in reflexive defensive protection.

"Stay back!" she demanded in fear.

In the body of the King, Tartaglia paused again.

"But…" he protested with the King's voice. "Angiolina, darling… I am your King Theramo!"

"No!" insisted Angiolina, shaking her head adamantly. "I don't understand how… But… You are not my Theramo!"

The face of the King contorted with Tartaglia's frustration.

"But, my love…" he said. "What can you mean?"

Heavy metallic clanking from the reinforced tread of several armored boots came suddenly from the direction of the marble walkway as a small retinue of four palace guards marched in to the gardens bearing a large ceremonial litter which held the body of the stag. The male red-deer with a white spot on its forehead was large, but the ornate gilded litter was larger, and from the considerable effort being obviously exerted by the guards, the animal and the litter together were also extremely heavy.

Tartaglia in the body of the King turned toward their precipitous arrival as the retinue marched in shouldering their unwieldy burden and marched to a halt near the parrot's banquet table.

"Your Majesty," they all said together in virile martial unison.

Angiolina looked desperately at the guards as if she were about to call out to them for some manner of assistance, but she seemed overwhelmed with confusion and paralyzed with indecision, hesitancy which likely was compounded by how matter-of-factly the guards accepted that the man before them was King Theramo. With no reason for any doubt to occur to them, their reverence and respect and loyalty to the body of the King appeared to be as unmitigated and absolute as it would be to the King himself. It was not a matter of being convinced. One does not need to be convinced of what one already believes. There was nothing dreamt of in their philosophy about the present situation or the current scene or the known nature of existence that would possibly cause them to question that the body of King Theramo was anyone other than King Theramo.

"Yes, yes," Tartaglia said impatiently with the mouth of the King. "Just put it down!"

"Yes, Your Majesty," the guards replied in respectful unison, and began to simultaneously go through the synchronized steps of systematically lowering the heavy load.

"No, imbeciles!" shouted Tartaglia with King Theramo's voice. "Not there!"

With the King's hand, Tartaglia pointed irritably toward

the middle of the flattened-grass area. "There! Just put it down somewhere there. And be quick about it!"

"Yes, Your Majesty," replied the guards.

"Curse this bothersome crown..." Tartaglia muttered with the voice of the King as the ornate and weighty Royal headpiece slipped slightly to one side. "Why can't it ever fit properly..."

The four guards turned as one and marched to the center of the flattened grass where they proceeded to shift the weight of the litter from their shoulders to their hands and then with bended knees to the ground. Heavy as their burden was, with practiced collaborative effort they nevertheless completed the maneuver with skill and fluidly smooth success.

"Now get out!" Tartaglia demanded from the King's mouth. "Go into the castle and don't come back!"

"Yes, Your Majesty," the guards replied in respectful and apparently unconcerned unison. Turning at the same time, the four of them marched the way they had come, back to the marble walkway, through the cypress grove, and away toward the interior of the castle.

In the body of King Theramo, Tartaglia turned back toward Angiolina.

"I hope you are impressed, my love," he said with the King's voice.

"It's... It's a dead stag..." said Angiolina.

"Yes!" Tartaglia crowed proudly from King Theramo's mouth. "It's dead!! It was killed in The Hunt! And it is a gift to you, my dear. It is a wedding gift. A gift from me to you, to celebrate our wedding to each other. It has special significance. It embodies the end of the past and signifies the beginning of our lives together. Just you and me, my darling Angiolina. Oh, how I have longed for the time we will be spending together!"

Angiolina was slowly shaking her head. "It's awful…" she said quietly. "The poor creature…"

"Good riddance!" Tartaglia said triumphantly with the King's voice. "His death ensures that no one will take you from me ever again!"

Angiolina was looking increasingly distressed. "That makes no sense…" she said slowly. "Something is terribly wrong… Where is Prime Minster Tartaglia?"

"Dead," said Tartaglia through King Theramo's mouth.

"What… What do you mean…? What happened…?"

"He was killed during The Hunt. By my own advisors! On purpose!!"

"Why would they do that…?"

"They were jealous!" Tartaglia said with the King's voice. "Tartaglia was always the K— I mean, Tartaglia was always MY favorite! So they killed him! And now they shall be executed for treason. All of them! Especially Pantalòné!!"

Angiolina's fear began to be replaced with incredulous anger. "You would kill your own advisors?" she demanded. "And my father? My Theramo would never be so cruel or so barbaric or so swift to judgment!"

"I am Theramo!" Tartaglia insisted from the mouth of King, his outrage and frustration begin to seethe. "I am your King Theramo! I am the King!! I am YOUR King!! Angiolina! You WILL marry me! You and I are going to be married tomorrow as planned! Nothing will prevent that! Do you understand?!!"

"I will never marry you! Do you hear me?!"

"We shall see, Angiolina my darling… Tomorrow morning, we shall see…!!"

In the body of King Theramo, Tartaglia turned in frustration and furious determination, and stormed off past the body of the stag to the cypress grove and out of the Palace Gardens.

Angiolina watched until she was sure he was gone. Then her knees buckled and she slid slowly to the ground, closing her eyes and leaning against the looking-glass in crumpled despair. Tears began to run silently down her anguished face, and from somewhere high above, the fog continued to slowly pour down and amorphously gather closer and closer to the grass-level of the gardens.

Only a few minutes had passed, when King Theramo in the body of Cigolotti hobbled with the help of Cigolotti's tree-bough cane into the Palace Gardens. He did not enter through the cypress grove, but instead had come from somewhere else in the vast courtyard piazza. Moving with slow cautious steps and periodically glancing around with furtive apprehension, he made his way at last to the parrot's banquet table where he stopped and leaned heavily on the table's edge, Cigolotti's frail body gasping for breath and shaking from exertion.

What little grey light had remained from the darkness of

the day was now gone, and evening twilight had taken its place. Battling valiantly against the gathering fog, the innumerable pinpoints of firelight from the flickering glow of the gardens' widely-dispersed legion of always-lit pole-torches pushed back against the eventide gloaming and the cloudy vapor with moderate success and glimmering halos, one of which was caught in reflection by the hand-held mirror on the banquet table and drew the weary disheartened attention of King Theramo's gaze through the eyes of Cigolotti.

With the hermit's hand, King Theramo warily reached down and picked up the small ruby-studded looking-glass, bringing it up to the face of Cigolotti. He took one look at the reflection, and for the first time saw the ancient decrepit face that was now his own. His defeat was complete. Cigolotti's hand fell limply back to the banquet table. The aged wrinkled hand released the mirror, and the hermit's eyes filled with tears as King Theramo began to weep.

"Who's there...?" said Angiolina in a small voice brimming with sadness. "Who is that weeping, even as I weep...?"

"Angiolina..." King Theramo said softly, his misery undisguised in the aged voice of Cigolotti. "My Angiolina..."

"Theramo...?" said Angiolina, bringing herself to her feet and wiping her eyes. "Theramo, is that you...?

"Alas..." King Theramo said with the hermit's voice. "It is but a shadow of Theramo that I have now become..."

Angiolina looked desperately around until she spotted the body of Cigolotti, wretched and miserable, and leaning weakly against the parrot's banquet table. Coming out from behind the Mirror of Truth, she made her way slowly toward the hermit's body.

"Who..." she began. "Who are you, old sir...?"

In the body of Cigolotti, King Theramo could not bring himself to raise the hermit's head and look upon Angiolina.

"Through enchantment," he said with the hermit's voice, "and my own ruinous carelessness, I am your Theramo..."

Angiolina continued to approach until she was right in front of him.

"Please..." she said gently. "Please lift your head and look at me..."

King Theramo forced himself to lift the straggly white-and-grey-haired bearded head of the hermit. Through Cigolotti's eyes he beheld the love of his life, and from those same aged eyes poured a flood of new tears.

"It..." Angiolina struggled to say. "It seems impossible... And yet..."

"I promised..." King Theramo said through tears with the voice of Cigolotti. "I promised I would meet you here after The Hunt... I... I never in my darkest nightmares could ever have imagined I would meet you here like this..."

Angiolina began to tremble as realization started to dawn upon her.

"Theramo..." she whispered.

With a withered hand, King Theramo reached back to the table, and the feeble fingers of the hermit found the rivet spectacles. He picked them up, and with Cigolotti's arm he wordlessly moved them through the air and held them out to Angiolina.

Angiolina took them cautiously from the old hand and put them on.

"They still cause you no discomfort…?" King Theramo asked through the mouth of Cigolotti.

Angiolina now herself began to cry again. She shook her head, and through her tears a sad unhappy smile broke for a moment to the surface of her face.

"No, my love…" she said quietly. "No, they… They still don't hurt… But I… I am in terrible pain to see you like this…"

"Go to the mirror…" said King Theramo in the hermit's voice.

"But, I…" Angiolina faltered.

"Please…" King Theramo said through Cigolotti's mouth.

Angiolina nodded, and made her way back to the Mirror of Truth.

"Go ahead…" King Theramo said with Cigolotti's voice, the tears from the eyes of the hermit at last beginning to ebb. "Say it…"

Angiolina looked ahead into the mirror's reflection for a moment, then looked up and over at the body of Cigolotti.

"You are King Theramo," she said. "You are my Theramo…"

There was a distant sound like wind chimes. A nearly invisible swirl of twinkling points of light winked and danced across the surface of the Mirror of Truth, and shimmering into view in front of Angiolina within the reflection of the looking-glass in large distinct letters were the words: THE TRUTH.

Angiolina slowly took the glasses from her face. Stepping

around the mirror, she made her way back to the body of Cigolotti and gently placed the rivet spectacles down on the surface of banquet table.

"Theramo…" she said, her voice tremulous with emotion. "Theramo, what… What happened…?"

"Tartaglia," said King Theramo with the voice of Cigolotti. "He is evil. Evil beyond words…"

"Oh, Theramo…" Angiolina said miserably. "My Theramo…"

"The glasses and the mirror…" King Theramo began from the hermit's mouth. "That is not the only magic given to me by Cagliostro. There was another enchanted means he gave me the power to use. He warned me to tell no one, but I did not heed his warning…"

"What kind of gift causes this terribleness to happen…?" said Angiolina.

"The fault lies not with the enchanter. The fault is entirely my own… I… I told Tartaglia of the magic Bi-Scepter…"

"The… The what…?"

"It is a device… An extraordinary device, with extraordinary power…"

"But…" said Angiolina. "What kind of power could cause… What kind of power could do this…?"

"The Bi-Scepter gives the power to switch bodies. Whosoever holds the Bi-Scepter has the power to switch into the body of another…"

"But…" Angiolina stammered. "But that's impossible…!"

The ancient head of the hermit nodded ruefully. "But it is

possible…" said King Theramo with Cigolotti's voice. "I am wretched proof that such extraordinary power is possible…"

"I…" Angiolina began. "I don't understand… How… How did you get into the castle…? How did you get here into the Palace Gardens…?"

"The fog has been a strange friend. It helped keep me hidden from easily-noticed view as these old tired legs struggled to carry this weary aged body through the forest and across the span of the Hanging Gardens skybridge…"

"But…" said Angiolina. "But how did you get past the guards….?"

"My dearest Angiolina…" King Theramo said from the thickly bearded mouth of the hermit. "There are— There were many secrets I once hoped to share with you… I grew up in this palace. What I did not discover on my own, my father the King shared with me when I was old enough to apprehend and understand the responsibilities I would one day shoulder when I took his place on the throne… There are secret entrances and exits which connect to secret passages and pathways hidden throughout the architecture of the castle. They were built with secrecy into the fortress framework as a last-resort means for the Royal family to escape the castello under the most dire of circumstances, should such terrible need ever manifest. These hidden paths of ingress and egress are the product of a different time, a different age. Once, the monarchy of Benebento feared—as with so many other neighboring and distant realms— that the possibility, however remote, had to be accepted as always existing that there might one day be a revolt or uprising against the

Royal family. The kingdom has been blessed over the years with a goodness which has rendered the likelihood of ever needing such contingencies increasingly improbable.

"The concealed passageways of these secret arteries permeate nearly every wall of the castle, and in my youth I explored and played within them with a lighthearted enjoyment their builders never planned or imagined would be the energy of the souls passing through them. This day, as I made my way through them in hopes of finding you here, my heart was filled only with the fear of discovery and the cold dread of capture by my own guards. And layered onto my newfound wretchedness and misery was the realization that the fright and terror coursing through this frail body was precisely the kind of energy the builders of those narrow winding passages must have once imagined would fill the souls of those needing to make grim use of their secret paths of safety and pathways to refuge and escape."

"Theramo…" said Angiolina. "What happened in the forest…?"

"Tartaglia. I… I thought I knew him… But the Tartaglia I thought I knew does not exist… He may have existed once, but no longer… The Tartaglia who was with me in the forest is evil… He covets the throne… And worse, far worse, he covets my bride, my True Love, the love of my life… He covets my Queen to be his own… He used my affection for him against me… He used my trust in him to deceive me… He used the Bi-Scepter to steal my body from me, to attain all he desires…"

"Oh, my poor Theramo…" Angiolina said, her voice filled with compassion and remorse. "Only you, with your pure heart, would never believe a friend could be capable of evil. The Tartaglia you once knew ceased to be himself long ago... Only your guileless eyes could not see how he was changing. He was once a deeply good man, but long ago some shadow took hold of him. His soul has been growing darker and darker... It was so plain to so many..."

"But not to me..." King Theramo said with the hermit's voice. "In my own words, I spoke of how blind I have been for so long... I now have learned that I have been blind even to the extent of my blindness... I knew not how much I was unable to see... I have always only seen the Tartaglia who once was, who I loved, who I expected and hoped he would always be... I was blind to who he was becoming, to who he had become, to who he is now... I have lost my best friend... And I have lost more... I have lost my very self..."

Even with her love for Theramo, Angiolina seemed unable to bring herself to embrace the King to comfort him. It apparently was too much for her, to see her own true love now in the body of an old man.

"Theramo," she said, her voice heavy with guilt and self-recrimination. "It is as you and I once laughed about. It breaks my heart and fills me with bitterness at myself, but I am not as good a person as Smeraldina, or Clarìcé, or Nicoletta. I... I don't know how to love you in this form you now are so unfairly punished to be within... My heart aches for you, and longs for you, and loves you so. But... But I cannot even bring myself to put my arms around you... I loathe myself for it..."

She put her head into her hands and began to weep, and cool

damp fog drifted purposelessly and formlessly around her and what had become of her King.

"No, my dearest Angiolina…" King Theramo said with deep sadness from the mouth of Cigolotti. "Do not loathe yourself. Loathe me… I am not worthy of your love… One worthy of your love would not have ever allowed this to happen to himself…"

"Oh, Theramo…" Angiolina said quietly through her tears, lost in a misery the two of them both shared, a misery that separated them both from each other.

And from the direction of the cypress grove came the sound of running as the footsteps of several people could now be heard hurrying along the marble walkway into the Palace Gardens.

Chapter 28

The Deliberations
and
The Confrontation

The hunting party of Pantalòné, Sir Balzanno, and Leandro rushed into the Palace Gardens. As Angiolina saw them, she turned and ran to her father's arms.

"Oh, Father…!" she said, weeping anew into the shoulder of the Chancellor as he tenderly and protectively embraced his daughter.

"My dear…" he said with rising concern. "What has happened…?"

"Theramo…" Angiolina managed to say.

"Has he been here?" Pantalòné said with apprehension verging on anger. "Did he harm you in any way?"

"Oh, Father…" said Angiolina miserably, pointing toward the parrot's banquet table. "Father, he is there…"

"But…" Pantalòné started to say.

"But that is the hermit!" exclaimed Sir Balzanno.

"That is Cigolotti…!" said Leandro.

"What… What is he doing here…?" said Sir Balzanno.

Angiolina shook her head with sad adamance. "No. It is Theramo…"

Pantalòné extricated himself gently from the arms of Angiolina and began striding toward the body of the hermit. "Cigolotti," he said accusingly. "What have you been saying to my daughter?"

Angiolina hastily caught up to the Chancellor and stopped him with a hand on his shoulder. "Father, no!" she said desperately. "Do not be cruel to him. He already suffers a wretched circumstance…!"

Pantalòné let himself be stopped and he turned again to his daughter. "My dear…" he said to her with confusion. "What are you saying…?"

"Tartaglia…" Angiolina replied unhappily. "It is by Prime Minister Tartaglia's devious commandeering of the enchanter's magic that Theramo now is trapped within the body of an old man… And it is by my own use of the enchanter's magic that I know it to be so…"

"But…" Pantalòné began. "But that is too extraordinary…"

"The enchanter's magic gives the power to put a person into the body of another…?" said Leandro incredulously.

"It… It is impossible…!" declared Sir Balzanno.

Angiolina shook her head. "It is possible," she asserted with quiet certitude. "There is a magic device. It's called the Bi-Scepter. It gives the power to switch bodies. Whoever holds the Bi-Scepter possesses the power to switch into the body of another…"

"But," Leandro said sensibly. "If His Majesty has been switched by the device into the body of Cigolotti, does that not mean Cigolotti is now in the body of the King?"

"What a peculiar plot for the Prime Minister to enact…" said Sir Balzanno.

Everyone present turned toward the body of Cigolotti and

slowly and respectfully approached the parrot's banquet table where the body of the hermit—though still upright—was leaning unsteadily on the edge of the table and the tree-bough cane, heavy with the weight of sorrow and circumstance, and without the physical strength to endure the ordeal it had been—and was currently—undergoing.

"Your Highness," Angiolina said gently. "Who is it that now is in your body?"

King Theramo slowly shook the aged weary head of the hermit. "I... I cannot now know with certainty..." he said weakly. "There... There has been more than one switching of bodies... When last I saw... When last I saw my own body, inside of it was Prime Minister Tartaglia..."

For a moment, no one spoke.

Leandro turned toward Pantalòné. "My Lord," he said steadily. "These circumstances are beyond extraordinary. However, you and Sir Balzanno and I all are aware of a very recent and very troubling inexplicable change that has come over His Majesty. Whether or not this incredible tale of magic and deception is in fact true, it would seem that in your role as Chancellor, under such circumstances Your Lordship is both authorized and compelled to step in and assume command leadership of the Royal military forces and the kingdom itself."

All focus now was on the Chancellor.

"Pantalòné..." King Theramo said with the voice of the hermit. "You know that good Leandro speaks the truth in what he says..."

Sir Balzanno looked in perplexity from Pantalòné, to the body of the hermit, and back to Pantalòné. "Merciful heavens…" the knight said in awed confusion. "Chancellor, it seems… Chancellor, I am inclined to concur that Leandro has indeed formulated the current situation as best as it can be assessed at this difficult moment. The Royal forces stand ready to accept without condition or hesitation your assumption of command, should you do so. Which, with unease but complete resolve, I would recommend you choose to do."

Pantalòné had opened his mouth to respond when the sounds of numerous footsteps came from the direction of the cypress grove, and within moments a half-dozen palace guards appeared escorting Clarìcé and Smeraldina and Nicoletta along the marble walkway and into the gardens.

Upon seeing one another, Clarìcé and Nicoletta rushed to Angiolina, and the three of them immediately embraced and started hastily talking with each other in anxious low tones.

Smeraldina had run to her father and now was embracing the knight who awkwardly did his best to reciprocate.

"Father!" Smeraldina said hurriedly. "I am so glad to see you back safely from The Hunt!"

"Thank you, my daughter," said Sir Balzanno as the two of them ended their embrace and stood back to look at each other. "Is all well and good with you, my dear?"

"Yes, Father," Smeraldina replied, nodding and then looking around to take in details of the scene she suddenly found herself in the midst of. "Father…" she went on with some confusion. "Father, what is happening…?"

Sir Balzanno nodded gravely. "Our kingdom is suddenly in

crisis..." he began. "That old fellow there is the hermit Cigolotti whom we met in the wood on The Hunt. How he has come to be here in the palace is a mystery. But of greater concern is that he insists he is King Theramo, somehow trapped in a body that is not his own, and Her Ladyship Angiolina vouches without hesitation that he is speaking the truth. Of equal concern, the King is not himself. Some terrible dark change has come over him. The only challenge greater than determining what grim force underlies all this madness is the challenge of how we shall set all this aright..."

Smeraldina nodded, not in understanding, but in acknowledgment that she had heard and taken into her mind all that her father had just conveyed to her.

"Father," Smeraldina said quickly, "I must go and be with Angiolina..."

Sir Balzanno nodded. "Of course," he replied. "Go to her. She is in need of any possible support and succor from one and all, just now."

Leandro had meanwhile made his way to the six guards who had escorted the young ladies from their guest suite to the gardens, and he appeared to be conferring with them and giving them instructions. As Smeraldina was joining the intimate companion circle of Angiolina, Claricé, and Nicoletta, the half-dozen palace guards were nodding with formal assent to whatever Leandro was directing them to do. As one, the guards all gave a solemn bent-head acknowledgment, and two of them turned to make their way back along the marble walkway toward the cypress grove and the interior of the castle.

As they left, they passed Avogadro who was just entering the gardens, and who made his way to the end of the marble walkway where he stopped to look around and address everyone present.

"I got here as quickly as I could," he announced, taking a deep mystical breath and putting one hand significantly to his forehead. "I sensed a strange disturbance..."

At the sight of her father, Nicoletta hastily took leave of her friends and hurried toward the entrance of the gardens to embrace her father.

"Oh, Father," she said quietly. "I am so glad you've come. Angiolina has just been giving us terrible and extraordinary information. Father, the Prime Minister has used some of the enchanter's magic against the King. There is a device called a Bi-Scepter, and it has been used to switch King Theramo into the body of a hermit named Cigolotti. And Prime Minister Tartaglia is now in the body of King Theramo, trying to take over the kingdom and to force Angiolina to be his bride..."

"Yes..." said Avogadro, nodding with troubled sagacity. "Yes, I knew that..."

Nicoletta smiled lovingly at her father. "I know you did, Father," she said with pride. "You know everything."

"The enchanter's magic is powerful," Avogadro said contemplatively. "It brought with it great disruption to our peaceful kingdom..."

Nicoletta nodded. "You warned King Theramo not to meet with the enchanter, Father," she said. "You knew it would be too hazardous."

Avogadro looked meaningfully at his daughter. "Knowing is not necessarily the same thing as being right, my child," he replied. "Theramo sought to better himself, and thereby to better the kingdom. It was a bold aspiration, and he sought bold means to accomplish it. Great change cannot come about without great disruption. The current dire circumstance may yet resolve ultimately for the better…"

Nicoletta nodded again. "You make everything better, Father," she said quietly. "You have always made everything in my life better."

"My child," he said. "You are a blessing to me every moment of my life. Go now, and return to your friends. Lady Angiolina will need you by her side as she endures this ordeal. And I must confer with the other advisors."

"Yes, Father," Nicoletta said. "Thank you, Father. I love you very much."

"I love you, my child," said Avogadro. "Your heart is beautiful."

Nicoletta smiled and hugged her father before hurrying back to Angiolina.

Avogadro made his way importantly over to the parrot's banquet table, where he was greeted with solemn gravity by Pantalòné and Sir Balzanno, and by Leandro who had just returned to where they all stood together with the body of the hermit.

"Your Majesty," said Avogadro, bowing respectfully to the body of Cigolotti.

"My good friend…" replied King Theramo with the voice of the hermit. "Your kindness at this moment fills the broken aged heart that struggles to beat within this ancient body… I am overwhelmed with gratitude…"

"Avogadro—" Pantalòné began.

The wise man held up an open-palmed hand in mystical protestation. "There is no need, Chancellor," he said respectfully. "I understand there is no certainty about this peculiar circumstance. However, I can assure you the King does indeed reside within the body of this hermit."

"Avogadro—" said Sir Balzanno.

"Good sir knight," Leandro interjected respectfully. "With all deference, Sir Balzanno. If we are to assemble a plan to attempt to resolve a crisis whose true nature or scope we yet do not comprehend, would not the thoughts of every member of His Majesty's inner circle be of worthwhile consideration?"

It was the Chancellor who responded to this notion. "Young Leandro," said Pantalòné. "You are wise beyond your station. Yes, I am in accord with your stance here."

Sir Balzanno thought a moment longer, and then nodded. "As am I," the knight concurred.

Avogadro had closed his eyes and put one of his hands significantly to his own forehead. "I'm getting something…" he announced, his brow furrowed with concentration. "Something that starts with a 'T'… Is it… Thirst?" Avogadro opened his eyes and looked directly at the body of Cigolotti. "Does Your Majesty need some water?"

King Theramo wordlessly nodded with the head of the hermit.

"That is hardly perspective to inform a plan of action," Sir Balzanno said with disappointment.

Pantalòné nodded. "But it is a necessity," he said definitely. "The old body of this man clearly has this day been pushed beyond its limits. Replenishing water is vital."

"When addressing a complex situation," said Avogadro, "not all steps need to be complicated. Some are simple."

Leandro had already moved to the banquet table and located a ewer and goblet. He quickly poured water for the body of Cigolotti and helped to place the silver drinking vessel into the tremulous grasp of the old man's hand.

Through the mouth of the hermit, the King drank the water thirstily. The eyes of Cigolotti momentarily closed with relief, the head of the hermit nodding slightly in gratitude and deep appreciation.

At the marble walkway, Italo was now entering the gardens. He swiftly visually located Sir Balzanno and proceeded quickly to where the knight was standing with the Chancellor and Leandro and Avogadro by a frail old man who was leaning weakly on a cane against a banquet table and clutching a goblet of water.

"Sir," Italo began breathlessly from the haste of his transit to the gardens. "I am glad indeed to find you here…"

Sir Balzanno nodded. "You always find me, Italo," he said. "That is part of your duty, and you consistently fulfill my expectations of you in that regard."

"Thank you, sir," Italo replied appreciatively. "Sir," he went on.

"I have completed the work with your matchlock as you instructed me."

"Very prompt," commended Sir Balzanno. "I expect nothing less of you."

Italo nodded and looked around again. "What… Sir, what is transpiring here…?" he said with confusion and concern.

"The brightness of our realm," said Sir Balzanno, "has been suddenly plunged into darkness, squire. I know not what to make of it, or what next steps we must needs take, or even what strange event may happen next…"

At that moment, in the middle of the flattened-grass area, the body of the stag suddenly moved and stood up on the top surface of the litter.

Everyone in the gardens gasped.

"But… But it was dead…!" one of the four remaining palace guards exclaimed.

"How can it have come back to life…?!" exclaimed another of the guards.

"Maybe it was just asleep…?" proposed another guard dubiously.

"I wasn't!" insisted Cigolotti from the mouth of the stag. "I was NOT asleep! Why is everyone always saying that?"

"Cigolotti…?" said Leandro with incredulous amazement.

"Yes?" replied Cigolotti with the stag's voice. "What is it? What do you want?"

"The beast speaks!" exclaimed one of the guards.

"The animal is talking!!" exclaimed another.

The head of the stag turned from side to side as Cigolotti

looked around. "What is everyone staring at?" he demanded from the mouth of the stag. "Who are all you people? Where is this place? How did I get here?"

Through the eyes of the stag, Cigolotti suddenly identified Pantalòné and Sir Balzanno and Leandro.

"Oh," Cigolotti said with the stag's voice. "It's you. The gentlemen with the guns."

The stag's eyes looked more closely and suddenly identified the body of the hermit.

"What..." Cigolotti said through the mouth of the stag in perplexed confusion. "Wait a minute... What's going on...? What am I doing over there? I thought I was here..."

"Cigolotti," said Sir Balzanno. "What are you doing inside the body of the stag...?"

"Oh, yes," said Cigolotti with the stag's voice. "That's right. I forgot, I'm having a dream. I love this dream. This animal's body is young and powerful, and its legs are nimble and strong. I feel better than I have in years. In fact, I don't think I ever felt this good, even when I was young. This is a good dream."

"It is a nightmare..." countered Sir Balzanno.

"What strange enchantment has overcome our kingdom...?!" one of the guards exclaimed in bewildered alarm.

The legs of the stag buckled and folded, and the body of the stag collapsed with thudding heaviness to an inert heap back onto the surface of the litter.

"It's alright..." said Pantalòné.

"He's fine..." Leandro concurred with confident reassurance.

"He's just sleeping," said Sir Balzanno. "He does that all the time…"

The four escort guards who had remained in the gardens suddenly stood at attention and stepped aside as Tartaglia in the body of King Theramo stormed in through the cypress grove and along the marble walkway trailed closely by a contingent of twelve elite palace guards, all fully armed and bearing matchlock harquebus long-guns.

"Your Majesty…!" exclaimed Pantalòné.

"No!" Angiolina cried out. "No, he is not the King!"

In the body of King Theramo, Tartaglia strode to the middle of the flattened-grass area near the litter and the collapsed stag, and the elite guards took positions flanking him, six on each side.

With the head and eyes of the King, Tartaglia looked around furiously for a moment before pointing with the King's hand an accusing finger at the group surrounding the body of the hermit.

"You three!" Tartaglia said angrily from the mouth of King Theramo. "The sniveling low-life Leandro! The has-been cowardly knight Balzanno! The inept wind-bag Chancellor Pantalòné! Always together! Always plotting! Plotting against ME! Pouring lies into my bride! Turning my own beloved Angiolina against me!!"

The twelve elite guards raised their long-guns and directed them authoritatively in the direction of the group around the body of Cigolotti.

"You three will rue the day you ever dared to conspire against your own King!" Tartaglia declared angrily with King Theramo's voice. "You are now under arrest! All three of you! For murder!

For the jealous murder of the K— I mean, of MY favorite advisor, Prime Minister Tartaglia! You will now be taken away and placed in locked confinement, and tomorrow morning you three shall all be executed for treason!"

There were neither protestations nor horrified gasps. There was only paralyzed utterly stunned silence. No one could have believed what they were hearing or what seemed to be happening.

The twelve elite guards stood implacably still, their guns aimed, the matchlock cord-fuses of their harquebuses slowly smoldering in readiness, the twelve lazily-rising coils of saltpeter smoke drifting upward and disappearing in the gathering fog.

A sound came from the direction of the cypress grove as footsteps could now be heard approaching along the marble walkway, and the body of Tartaglia entered the Palace Gardens.

Chapter 29

The Standoff
and
The Indecision

"Who's been murdered?" the stag asked through the mouth of Tartaglia, walking into the gardens with confidence but still with a measure of unsteadiness, as if walking on only two legs was a trick of coordination he still had not yet fully mastered.

"Prime Minister Tartaglia…!!" several voices exclaimed in startled amazement.

In the body of the King, Tartaglia was aghast. He stared with the horrified eyes of King Theramo at his own body as it strode unevenly forward into the area of flattened-grass, making its way toward where the body of the stag lay in a motionless pile atop the litter.

"You…!" Tartaglia managed to say with King Theramo's voice. "But… I thought you…"

"I told you I'd be back," the stag said with the voice of Tartaglia.

The elite guards flanking the body of the King seemed suddenly confused, and partially lowered their weapons.

In the body of Tartaglia, the stag gazed with the Prime Minister's eyes down at the body of the stag. "Though, perhaps I am too late…" the stag said through the mouth of Tartaglia. "It seems my body—my former body—has been felled…"

Leandro began to step forward, but the elite guards on either side of the body of the King overcame their momentary bewilderment and swung their long-guns into action, back up and pointing directly at Leandro.

Seeing the half-dozen weapons now suddenly aimed in his direction, Leandro sensibly chose to stop moving, coming to an immediate stop where he was, standing just slightly apart from the group surrounding the body of Cigolotti.

He looked away from the barrels of the harquebus guns and directed his focus to the body of the Prime Minister. "May I assume you are the great stag?" Leandro asked him.

In the body of Tartaglia, the stag turned and looked for a moment at Leandro with the eyes of the Prime Minister. "I am the great stag," confirmed the stag with the voice of Tartaglia, before turning back to gaze down again on the body of the collapsed stag.

Leandro nodded. "Although it appears otherwise," he said to the body of the Prime Minister, "your body—your former body—is not dead, great stag. It is only sleeping."

"I am at loss to understand how that is possible," the stag said skeptically with the voice of Tartaglia.

Leandro nodded. "You see before you there on the ground the hermit Cigolotti, who has the sleeping fits, and apparently brought them with him when he was switched into your body."

In the body of Tartaglia, the stag contemplated this information for a moment. "And to think," he at last said from the mouth of the Prime Minister, "that I thought this day could not get more peculiar…"

"It's a trick!" exclaimed Tartaglia with the voice of King Theramo. "Tartaglia is part of the conspiracy! He has schemed with the others! It is all a plot to steal my kingdom! They are all in it together! They are trying to steal away from me my beloved Angiolina!!"

More sounds came from the direction of the cypress grove as many fast-moving footsteps could now be heard approaching heavily along the marble walkway, and into the gardens rushed a contingent of twenty-four palace guards—two units of marksman archers bearing longbows and crossbows, a unit of guards wielding pikes and halberds, and a unit of musketeer arquebusiers armed with long-gun harquebuses.

The entire contingent streamed in, now joined by the four escort guards who had remained in the gardens, and they all took positions at the opposite side of the flattened-grass area from where Tartaglia in the body of the King stood amidst the protection of his twelve elite palace guards.

Leandro turned from the stag in the body of Tartaglia, to face Tartaglia in the body of King Theramo. "These guards are not loyal to the body of the King," Leandro informed him. "They are loyal not to a monarch's shell, but to the kingdom of Benebento."

The twelve elite palace guards swung the aim of their weapons from Leandro to the contingent of palace guards now opposite them, who now had their weapons raised and aimed back at the twelve elite palace guards.

"Imbeciles!" declared Tartaglia from the mouth of King

Theramo. "You cannot prove I am not the King. I am King Theramo! Look at me! I am the King! I am the King!!"

The stag, in the body of Tartaglia, turned toward the body of King Theramo. "You," the stag said with Tartaglia's voice, "are behaving neither like a king, nor like King Theramo."

Several guards on both sides of the standoff indecisively exchanged hesitant glances, both within their ranks and as well with their currently opposing counterparts across the flattened-grass.

"Silence!" demanded Tartaglia from the mouth of the King, pointing with the hand of King Theramo an accusing finger at the stag in the body of Tartaglia. "You are just another conspirator! Go to the feast table and join the others! Go stand where you belong, with the others who have been plotting against me! Move!!"

The six guards flanking the body of the King mustered their resolve and re-aimed their weapons, now pointing the barrels of their long-guns at the stag in the body of the Prime Minister.

In the body of Tartaglia, the stag looked with the eyes of the Prime Minister away from the elite guards and their weapons, and directed his focus to Leandro.

"Would your guards truly fire upon me?" the stag asked Leandro from the mouth of the Prime Minister.

"I should like to think they would not," replied Leandro. "But at the moment it may be best not to test them…"

"Understood…" the stag said with the voice of Tartaglia, nodding assent with the head of the Prime Minister. He slowly turned and walked with Tartaglia's legs over toward the banquet table, stopping when he reached where Leandro was standing.

"Well, this is awkward…" the stag remarked with Tartaglia's voice.

Leandro looked from the body of Tartaglia standing next to him, to the body of the King, then back to the body of Tartaglia.

In the body of the Prime Minister, the stag attempted to quickly communicate with Leandro without attracting attention. "Is there a plan…?" the stag asked from the mouth of Tartaglia in a nearly inaudible whisper and trying to not obviously move the lips of the Prime Minister as he stealthily uttered the question.

Leandro glanced about with swift furtiveness and was about to whisper an answer when his expression became suddenly alarmed, and he made quick eye contact with Pantalòné.

"Chancellor…" Leandro whispered. "Where is the body of Cigolotti…?!"

Everyone's attention had been focused on the escalating tension in the center of the flattened-grass area, and no one had noticed the body of the hermit slip away. It had hobbled unseen and unnoticed to behind the twenty-eight loyalist guards. The body of Cigolotti now emerged, coming out from amidst the contingent, first directly in front of them, then proceeding with weak steps and the tree-bough cane to stand ahead of them, alone on that side of the flattened-grass and opposite Tartaglia in the body of the King, the two of them facing each other in the middle of the area and with mere meters of separation in between.

The six elite guards swung the aim of their long-guns around and aimed the matchlock barrels at the body of Cigolotti.

"It is no trick," King Theramo said with the voice of the hermit. "The body of the stag only sleeps. And I am no longer inside."

In the body of King Theramo, the eyes of the King were filling with Tartaglia's rage as the Prime Minister stared out from the King's face in fury back at the body of the hermit.

"I used the Bi-Scepter," King Theramo went on with the voice of Cigolotti, speaking directly to the Prime Minister in the King's body. "The hermit is now in the body of the stag. And here in the hermit's body am I. I am Theramo. Your evil plan has not succeeded, Tartaglia. I yet live."

"You shall be executed with the others, old man!" declared Tartaglia from the mouth of King Theramo. "But first, you will see me married to Angiolina! Our wedding will be the last thing you see before you die!!"

Three of the half-dozen elite guards suddenly swung their weapons around and aimed toward the direction of the cypress grove at the same time as six of the loyalist-contingent guards swung their matchlocks around and aimed in the same direction, toward the entrance of the gardens.

Truffaldino was being escorted in along the length of the marble walkway, and although his two guard escorts halted at the point where the marble path ended, Truffaldino simply kept on walking, making his way into the gardens and continuing toward the body of King Theramo.

"Truffaldino!!" Smeraldina exclaimed excitedly, her voice full of emotion.

"Hi, Smeraldina!" Truffaldino said happily and giving her a cheerful wave with a carefree hand.

Standing with her friends apart from the hunting party and the rest of the group still clustered by the banquet table, Smeraldina had immediately started to move toward Truffaldino, but she had been wisely prevented from doing so by the alert initiative of Angiolina and Clarìcé who with gentle but unequivocal firmness hastily grasped her arms to keep her where she was.

Guns from both sides of the standoff followed Truffaldino's progress as he proceeded over toward where Tartaglia stood in the body of King Theramo.

"Your Royal Majesty's Highness," Truffaldino said politely as he approached.

"Stop where you are, imbecile!" the Prime Minister commanded from the mouth of the King.

Truffaldino obediently and immediately stopped, near the body of the stag, in between the body of the hermit with King Theramo inside and the body of King Theramo with Tartaglia inside, and slightly nearer to the body of the King, toward which he had been deliberately heading.

"Guards!" shouted Tartaglia with the King's voice. "What is the meaning of this?!"

"The enchanter's assistant has come in through the Vitaian Gate of the Hanging Gardens, Your Majesty," one of the two escort guards replied respectfully and with courteously appropriate loudness to clearly carry across the gardens' distance to the body of the King. "Your Majesty left a standing order that the enchanter or his assistant were to be granted full access to the castle and the palace as they pleased. The enchanter's assistant has requested admission to the Palace Gardens. Something about a parrot, Your Majesty…"

"Well, I rescind my standing order!" Tartaglia said impatiently from the King's mouth. "He is part of the conspiracy! Arrest him and take him away to locked confinement!"

"But Your Highness's Royalness," Truffaldino said politely, taking the Bi-Scepter from his belt and holding it out toward the body of King Theramo. "This was left in the woods, and I'm pretty sure my master wanted you to always have it with you."

"The Bi-Scepter…!" gasped King Theramo with the voice of the hermit.

The reaction of Tartaglia in the body of the King was instantaneous.

"Give that to me!!" the Prime Minister demanded with the voice of King Theramo, extending one of the king's hands forward with swift open-palmed insistence.

"Truffaldino, no!" exclaimed Smeraldina from where she was still being restrained in place by her friends. "That's not King Theramo! Don't give it to him!"

"Do not give him the device!" shouted Leandro emphatically.

"What's going on?" said the voice of one of the guards. "What are they talking about?!"

"What is that thing…?" said the voice of one of the other guards.

"What's a Bi-Scepter…?!" said another.

On the other side of Truffaldino, King Theramo now spoke to him with the voice of Cigolotti. "Truffaldino," the King said with the hermit's voice. "I am King Theramo. Cagliostro did give the Bi-Scepter to me. Amidst overwhelming confusion, and blinding despair, and terrified haste, it was unintentionally left in the forest by mistake. Please hand it me…"

"No!" commanded Tartaglia from the mouth of the King. "Nobody move!! Except you, boy! Bring that device to me this instant!"

All the guards in the gardens except the two escorts re-directed the aim of their weapons, and in seconds there were harquebus barrels aimed at Truffaldino by the elite guards, at the body of the hermit by the elite guards and the loyalist guards, and at the elite guards by the loyalist guards.

Truffaldino looked around for a moment and seemed to notice for the first time the guards and their weaponry.

"That's really a lot of guns," Truffaldino said, impressed though perhaps not properly concerned.

"Truffaldino…" said King Theramo through the mouth of the hermit. "Please… Give me the Bi-Scepter…"

"No!" Tartaglia exclaimed in a mounting rage with the voice of the King. "Give it to me! Give it to me right now!!"

From its perch atop the candlestick on the banquet table, the parrot squawked loudly. "Truffaldino! Truffaldino!"

All heads turned in surprise toward the direction of the parrot.

"Parrot!" exclaimed Truffaldino with a mixture of relief and annoyance, looking around and trying to visually identify the location of the colorful bird. "Parrot, where are you? What's going on…?"

"Boy!" Tartaglia shouted in seething vehemence with the voice of the King. "Give that device to me now! Or I will have you shot this instant and I will take it from your dead body!!"

Truffaldino looked at the Bi-Scepter in his hand. He then looked around at the crowd of personages and guards, and at the barrels of the long-guns arrayed around him pointing at his head. He looked from the body of the King, to the body of the hermit, and back to the body of the King whose face was contorted with anger and adamance and determination. And from the look on Truffaldino's face, he seemed thoroughly confused and hopelessly indecisive as to what he was supposed to do next.

Chapter 30

The Return
and
The Revelation

"**N**o!" Pantalòné warned with decisive insistence. "Truffaldino, that man is not King Theramo! Do not give it to him!"

Upon hearing the voice of the Chancellor, all the guards in the gardens appeared to falter with confused indecision, and all weapons were hesitantly lowered part way.

"Truffaldino…" said King Theramo from the mouth of the hermit. "Please hand me the Bi-Scepter…"

"Use the map!" squawked the parrot from atop its candlestick perch. "Use the map!"

"The map…?" Truffaldino repeated, mystified. He reached into his belt-pouch with the hand that was not holding the Bi-Scepter and pulled out THE MAP OF HERE.

"The map…" Truffaldino said again, trying to understand.

He held the map out in front of himself and let it roll open, the scroll unfurling downward as he raised it up while grasping an edge at the top of one end. The uncurled light emanating from the map was more distinct in the murk of ambient fog. It illuminated Truffaldino's face from below, and some of its multicolored glow was caught and reflected back by the drifting vapor around Truffaldino's head in a misty nimbus.

"The map!" Truffaldino exclaimed in sudden understanding, his eyes now rapidly scanning the map's surface in racing perusal.

"There are a lot of people around here…" he remarked as he looked hurriedly over all the map was showing him.

He extended his other hand up into the air and began to wave the Bi-Scepter widely back and forth through the gathering fog leaving ghostly eddying swirls in the vacillating wake of his motion.

"Okay…" Truffaldino said carefully. "There I am… That's me… I'm the one waving… Nicoletta taught me how to do that… And… Hmm… That's weird… *That*—" he said, now pointing with the Bi-Scepter toward the body of Cigolotti. "*That* is King Theramo…"

The gardens suddenly hushed to utter silence.

"And *that*—" he said, now pointing with the Bi-Scepter toward the body of the King. "*That* is Prime Minister Tartaglia."

The terror and anguish and rage of Tartaglia filled the face of the King. "No!!" he demanded furiously with King Theramo's voice. "No, no, NO!!! Don't give it to him! Don't let him have it back!! I am the King! I am the King!! I am the King!!! Give it to me now! Do you hear?! Odds bodkins!!!"

Nearly everyone in the gardens gasped.

"Tartaglia…!!!" exclaimed innumerable voices.

"But… It's impossible…!" a voice cried out.

"It cannot be…!" cried out another.

Truffaldino nodded, still observing the map. "But it can be, and it is. THE MAP OF HERE says so. It doesn't always show everything, but what it does show is always true…"

Still looking at the map, Truffaldino turned toward the body of Cigolotti.

"You," said Truffaldino, "look like an old man, but you are actually King Theramo. So this Bi-Scepter should be returned to you..."

"NO!!!"Tartaglia cried from the mouth of the King and started violently toward Truffaldino with both of the King's outstretched arms reaching in desperation for the Bi-Scepter.

Two of the elite guards who had been flanking the body of the King now stepped decisively in front of the King's body, blocking Tartaglia from approaching Truffaldino.

"Imbeciles!!" the Prime Minister cried out. "What are you doing!!?"

Truffaldino stepped over to where the body of the hermit was unsteadily standing. Arriving in front of Cigolotti's body, Truffaldino at last looked up from the map and extended the hand that held the Bi-Scepter toward the body of the hermit.

"My master Cagliostro wanted you to have this, Your Highest Royal Excellency..." Truffaldino said respectfully, handing the Bi-Scepter to the hand of Cigolotti that was not clutching the tree-bough cane.

The wrinkled ancient hand of the hermit took trembling possession of the Bi-Scepter, and the aged head gratefully nodded, moving the long grey and white beard and hair slightly against the top of the tattered rags that were Cigolotti's clothing.

"Thank you, Truffaldino..." the King said quietly with the

hermit's voice. "And now please, step away to the side, for your own safety…"

"Stop…!!" Tartaglia bellowed frantically with the King's voice from where the body of King Theramo was still being blocked by elite guards. "He must be stopped…!!!"

With difficulty, holding the Bi-Scepter with one of the hermit's hands while also clutching the top knob of tree-bough cane to keep from falling over from weakness and exertion, King Theramo in the body of Cigolotti maneuvered apart the two pointing rods of the device.

In the group clustered by the parrot's banquet table, Avogadro had closed his eyes and put one of his hands significantly to his own forehead. "Chancellor Pantalòné…" the wise man announced in a low voice, his brow furrowed with concentration. "I'm getting something… Something that starts with an 'R'… And it's… Release." Avogadro opened his eyes and looked directly at Pantalòné. "Chancellor," he continued quietly. "The guards should release the body of the King…"

"Step aside from the body of the King!" Pantalòné commanded loudly with firm authority.

The two elite guards hindering the forward progress of King Theramo's body together looked over toward the Chancellor, then at each other. And then at the same time they both stepped back, allowing Tartaglia in the body of the King to resume his urgent motion forward toward the body of the hermit.

But the body of King Theramo had taken merely two steps when he stopped abruptly, frozen in place with horror as he beheld one end of the Bi-Scepter pointing directly at him. The other end of the Bi-Scepter was pointing at the body of Cigolotti with the King inside. Every part of the hermit's body was shaking with frailty, except for the hand that held the Bi-Scepter, which somehow King Theramo was managing to grip with whatever strength was left in the body of the hermit, and with all the will that remained within the mind of the King.

In the body of King Theramo, Tartaglia threw one hand protectively forward, the King's fingers spread helplessly wide, the King's arm protectively outstretched, as if desperation at a distance might stop what could not be stopped. The mouth of the King gaped wordlessly, filled with Tartaglia's speechless abject horror at what was about to happen.

"I want my body, back, Tartaglia," said King Theramo from the mouth of Cigolotti.

A strong wind began to stir the fog and everything else within the Palace Gardens as King Theramo positioned Cigolotti's trembling thumb over the emerald button. All the foliage throughout the gardens—the high tops of the trees, the bushes and shrubs and hedgerows, the flowers and plants and vines, even the grass at the level of the ground—all was suddenly and powerfully stirred and moved and pushed about by the force of gusting air whose turbulent power surged in the span of a moment.

As the King pressed the emerald button with the hermit's thumb, there was a distant sound like chimes that was lost in the rushing wind and replaced with a rumbling sound like faraway rolling thunder. Jagged tendrils of tiny lightning danced and crackled around the Bi-Scepter shafts amidst nearly invisible swirls of twinkling motes of illumination. The ends of the pointing rods for an instant glowed with a brilliantly bright blue-white light, and then the entirety of the Palace Gardens flashed with inversion as all light values flipped and all color hues reversed, and in an instant reversed back.

And then the wind stopped and the noises ceased, and everything was abruptly still and quiet, the still-gathering fog once again hanging motionless in the air.

The body of King Theramo faltered for a moment, then stood strong.

The eyes of Cigolotti closed briefly, then re-opened.

"Oh, merciful heavens…!" exclaimed King Theramo, exhaling with emotion and relief. "Back in my own body… At last…!!"

"Odds bodkins…" Tartaglia despaired miserably with the frail voice of the hermit. "This wretched body is so feeble and old…"

Everyone in the gardens looked on in silent open-mouthed astonishment at the extraordinary occurrence unfolding before their eyes.

"No one could endure the odious prison of this crumbling useless body…" Tartaglia lamented through the mouth of Cigolotti. Shaking with weakness and leaning heavily on the tree-bough cane, Tartaglia looked over at King Theramo and glared hatred and determination though the eyes of the hermit.

"Theramo!" Tartaglia taunted with the voice of Cigolotti. "You fool! Look! It is I who now holds the Bi-Scepter!! And now, it shall be a simple matter for me to switch back into your body!!"

In the hand of the hermit, the Bi-Scepter remained positioned as it had been, one pointing rod aimed at King Theramo, the other back at the body of Cigolotti. And now it was the King's turn to throw out a desperate outreaching hand toward the body of the hermit. "No!" cried King Theramo. "Tartaglia! No! Please!!"

"Too late, Theramo!" Tartaglia cried with victorious vengeful viciousness in the voice of the hermit. "You cannot stop me!"

Tartaglia positioned Cigolotti's trembling thumb over the emerald button and pressed it down.

Nothing happened.

"I… I don't understand…" Tartaglia muttered with the voice of Cigolotti.

With the hermit's weak age-wrinkled thumb, Tartaglia pressed the button again. And again. And then again. And still nothing happened.

"Odds bodkins…! Why won't this thing work…?!!"

"Cagliostro!" squawked the parrot. "Cagliostro!"

"The enchanter…!" someone gasped.

"The enchanter!" exclaimed someone else.

Guards and personages alike stepped apprehensively aside, creating a clear path for the enchanter as he strode over the marble paving stones of the walkway and into the gardens. Cagliostro's layered robe shimmered with shifting ripples of iridescent black and indigo as he walked. Even through the growing fog, thin nearly imperceptible wisps of smoky vapor could be seen wafting off the enchanter's every movement as though he were a recently materialized apparition.

"What number is showing?" said Cagliostro as he approached the place in the flattened-grass where the body of the hermit stood frantically pressing and re-pressing the emerald button of the Bi-Scepter.

"Read the number!" squawked the parrot from its candlestick perch on the banquet table. "Read the number!"

"What…?" said Tartaglia, confusion and fear infusing the voice of the hermit. "What…?"

"On the handle, Tartaglia," the enchanter said with quiet power in his deep, calm, commanding voice that always seemed to be coming from somewhere else. "What number is showing?"

"I… I didn't know there was a number…" Tartaglia murmured with dread in the dwindling voice of the hermit.

"The number tells how many more times the Bi-Scepter will work," said Cagliostro. "What is the number?"

The aged head of the hermit bent forward as Tartaglia lifted the Bi-Scepter with Cigolotti's hand and strained to see clearly enough through the hermit's old eyes to resolve the number on the small mechanical turn-drum counter recessed within the glittering surface of one of the Bi-Scepter shafts.

"Zero…" uttered Tartaglia in ruinous defeat from the heavily-bearded mouth of the hermit. "The number it says is zero…"

"Well, then," said Cagliostro. "There can be no more switching. Everyone is where they will be."

"No…" Tartaglia wailed faintly and pitifully with the voice of Cigolotti. "Please… No…"

With the hand of the hermit, Tartaglia pressed the emerald

button with Cigolotti's old wrinkled thumb, then pressed it again, and again, over and over without end.

"Please…" Tartaglia begged with quiet plaintive despair in the failing voice of the aged hermit. "Please… Angiolina… Save me…"

A short distance away, the body of the stag suddenly moved and stood up on the top surface of the litter. "In fact," said Cigolotti with the stag's voice, and continuing his thought from where he had left off, "it's such a good dream, I'm not sure I ever want to wake up. And that should make all you people happy, because you all seem to think I'm always asleep anyway. Even though I'm NOT ASLEEP!"

The legs of the stag buckled and folded, and the body of the stag once again collapsed with thudding heaviness to an inert heap back onto the surface of the litter.

All the guards in the gardens now lowered their weapons and stood at ease, all martial alertness relaxed, and all of them standing as they were, in an ever-thickening cloud of growing fog and covered with confusion and amazement.

Personages throughout the gardens in an instant became filled with life and motion, and as if on cue shot like billiard balls forward and straight toward specific other people in the midst. Angiolina ran to the arms of King Theramo. Clarìcé ran to the arms of Leandro. Smeraldina ran to Truffaldino and threw her arms around him as though she would never let him go ever. Pantalòné and Sir Balzanno along with the stag in the body of Tartaglia began to make their way to where Cagliostro was standing. Nicoletta embraced her father, and then turned to head with timorous uneasy steps over toward Tartaglia in the body of Cigolotti.

"Please… Please…"Tartaglia was repeating faintly in the voice of the hermit, staring miserably though the eyes of the hermit at the Bi-Scepter he still gripped in the hermit's shaking hand as he pressed with the hermit's thumb the emerald button over and over.

Nicoletta took a deep breath, and then reached out a kind hand and placed it gently on top of the hermit's, stopping Tartaglia from continuing to press the Bi-Scepter button.

"Tartaglia…" she said softly.

Through the tangle of wispy ancient hair, Tartaglia slowly shifted the focus of the hermit's eyes from the Bi-Scepter to the smooth compassionate lovely hand that now rested atop his own. As if starting to awaken from a mercilessly recurring nightmare, Tartaglia let the gaze of the hermit's eyes follow the hand to the exquisite wrist, along up the slender impossibly perfect arm, all the way to the miraculously impossible beauty of the face of Nicoletta.

"Nic… Nicoletta…"Tartaglia stammered in bewilderment with the tremulous voice of the hermit. "Nicoletta… I… I don't think I've ever noticed before… You… You're beautiful…"

Nicoletta looked down shyly at her own hand and slightly tightened her hold of Tartaglia's hand in the body of the hermit. "I don't think you have ever even noticed me at all…" she said cautiously. "But…"

She paused and took another deep brave breath. "I have always loved you, Tartaglia," she said to him at last.

Nicoletta seemed nearly overwhelmed with the emotion of finally being able to tell him. Tears now began to spill in glistening bittersweet relief from her beautiful eyes. "And…" she went on, stepping even closer to him, "I shall always love you, Tartaglia. No matter what you look like…"

Still leaning for support on the tree-bough cane with one hand, with the other hand of the hermit Tartaglia let go of the Bi-Scepter. The device fell soundlessly into the flattened-grass, and Tartaglia turned the hand of hermit over to gently take hold of Nicoletta's hand as their fingers softly interlocked.

"Oh, Niccoletta…" Tartaglia began haltingly, slow tears beginning to form in the unhappy eyes of the hermit. "Dear sweet Niccoletta… I have been so blind to so many things… And now it is too late for me… Alas, in this body, I am far too old…"

"I don't care what body you are imprisoned within…" said Nicoletta, her voice filled with emotion. "I love you. I want to be with you. I want us to be together. And… And I have wanted to tell you that for so long… For so very long…"

Nicoletta's tears now began to flow more intensely with the relief and release of at last being able to tell her true feelings to her true love.

"Sweet Nicoletta…" Tartaglia struggled to say in the voice of the hermit. "My soul has been filling with darkness for so long, that I do not even remember when it started… Even through my downward spiral into evil, you yet love me… It breaks my heart… Your love… Your love for me, Nicoletta… It is the most beautiful thing on earth or in Heaven…"

Nicoletta pulled herself closer to Tartaglia in the body of the hermit and let her head rest on the clean ragged tatters that clothed his shoulder, and she continued to quietly cry.

Unnoticed for a moment by anyone, a faintly glowing blue-green light began to emanate from every part of the hermit's body.

Chapter 31

The Transformations
and
The Prophecy

"Enchanter," the stag was saying to Cagliostro from the mouth of Tartaglia as he stood next to Sir Balzanno and Chancellor Pantalòné. "I am the great stag. I understand it is by the power of your magic that all this uncanny disruptive change has come about within the kingdom of Benebento."

Cagliostro nodded slightly. "What has occurred thus far has been neither my design nor my intention," he replied. "But, yes. Unquestionably it indeed has resulted in part from a facet of magic brought here by me."

"Thus far, Cagliostro?" asked the Chancellor with some concern. "Is there yet more strangeness to ensue…?"

Having furled the map and replaced it back into his belt-pouch, Truffaldino had now made his way to Cagliostro, arriving with one arm lovingly around Smeraldina, and with Smeraldina holding passionately on to him, tightly gripping him and his clothing, both shoulder straps of her dress having gleefully abandoned her shoulders and now draping with loose uselessness down the sides of her arms as if in ecstatic relief and mischievous celebratory abandon.

"Master—" Truffaldino began.

One large powerful hand emerged from beneath Cagliostro's robes as he gestured toward Truffaldino.

"Truffaldino," he said swiftly. "Hold a moment, please…"

"Master…?" said Truffaldino with sudden unease.

"It has begun…" Cagliostro said vaguely.

"What has begun, sir?" asked Truffaldino, his unease growing.

"Something with a power far greater than my own…" said Cagliostro.

The enchanter looked around, scanning the expanse of the fog-obscured gardens, until his gaze abruptly stopped. Next to him, Truffaldino, Smeraldina, Lord Pantalòné, Sir Balzanno, and the stag in the body of Tartaglia all turned their heads to follow the direction of where he was looking, which now was directly at Tartaglia in the body of the hermit.

As Nicoletta stood closely at his side with her eyes closed and her head nestled against his shoulder, the body of the hermit with Tartaglia inside was giving off an increasingly bright luminous blue-green glow.

A sound started to fill the gardens, a noise like large water, and increasingly it seemed to be emanating from Tartaglia in the body of the hermit.

Nicoletta opened her eyes at the rising sound and saw the steadily intensifying blue-green light that now was clearly radiating from the body of the hermit.

The eyes of the hermit closed, and the hand of the hermit that was not holding Nicoletta's hand let go of the tree-bough cane, which toppled to the flattened-grass of the ground, bouncing slightly once and partially rolling to one side before coming to lifeless rest.

As if afraid Tartaglia in the body of the hermit might die or magically disappear—so soon, too soon after she had only just been able finally to confess to him her heart, to share with him her love— Nicoletta let go her grasp of his hand and threw both her arms around him in a loving protective embrace and held him tightly, as though by holding on to the body he now inhabited she might somehow keep her beloved Tartaglia with her forever.

Within Nicoletta's embrace, the arms of the hermit now dropped limply to his sides as the blue-green light grew brighter. The glowing radiance spread out wider and wider, faintest at the body of the hermit and brightest at the ever-expanding outer limit of the luminance, stretching outward in elastic illumination with an escalating sound like a towering ocean wave pulling back water at the shoreline and curling upward, coiling energy inside itself, rising up, swelling with power and poised ready to crash breaking onto the shore.

And then the elastic snapped, and the outward expanding glow suddenly zipped inward in an implosion of brilliant light, pulling itself in an instantaneous rush back into the core epicenter of its source, the body of the hermit, with a fast fleeting splashing crash, and then dissipating to silence like falling sea-spray, leaving in its noiseless and lightless wake a transformative change.

The body of the hermit was still the body of the hermit, but no longer was it ancient or bent with age. It was youthful and beardless and strong and upright. It was the body of who Cigolotti may have been when first he had become a young man. It was handsome and healthy, and it was alive with vitality.

Tartaglia opened the new young eyes of the hermit, and the first thing he saw was the loving look of Nicoletta gazing up him in relief and love. She appeared uninterested his new youth, filled only with joy that her beloved had not been taken from her.

"Tartaglia, I love you..." she breathed quietly.

In the transformed body of the hermit, Tartaglia made no move to examine or explore or test the newness of youth which in the span of moments had so utterly altered the body he had so recently become permanently relegated to exist within. He seemed aware of the change, but only to the extent that it affected his interaction with Nicoletta. Precipitous healthful youth itself did not appear to interest him. But the freedom it bestowed—that was what had truly transformed him, releasing him not from any incarceration of age, but from the prison of being forced to say no. It was the liberation from that confinement which seemed to have now infused vibrant new life into his very essence.

"Nicoletta," he said quietly in the soft smooth youthful voice of the strong young hermit. "Your love is the greatest gift I have ever known. You, Nicoletta, are treasure more precious to me than anything in existence. You are more precious to me than my own life."

"Will you stay with me...?" Nicoletta asked, her tear-filled eyes wide with hope and apprehension. "Will you be with me always...?"

Tartaglia nodded with the handsome dark-haired head of the young hermit. "I know not what I have ever done to deserve your love, Nicoletta," he said softly. "But if you wish it, I will with gladness and joy be with you, and stay with you, if you will have me, happily for ever after…"

"Oh, my Tartaglia…" Nicoletta whispered to him, too filled with emotion to speak further, and the two of them embraced and closed their eyes and clung to each other with boundless relief and gratitude at the sudden miraculous bliss delivered to them by a universe whose workings they could not and had no need to understand.

The present populace of the Palace Gardens was speechless and immobilized with amazement, saturated with incredulity to the point of numbness. The ability to adequately process all they had been witnessing had been exhausted.

"Master—" Truffaldino began.

Cagliostro again held up his large powerful hand. "Truffaldino," he admonished with gentleness and solemn gravity. "Whatever it is, it is not over. It has only begun…"

And now the same blue-green luminescence could be seen coming from the bodies of the stag and the parrot. As it had with the body of the hermit, it started slowly at first, with only a faint light emanating from every part of their bodies. But it soon followed the same course of intensifying, as both animals' bodies progressed to radiating an increasingly bright glimmering blue-green glow.

From both bodies, two discrete sounds blended together from their disparate locations across the gardens, as the two separate emanations of blue-green light grew brighter. The glowing radiances spread out wider and wider, faintest at the bodies of the stag and the parrot, and brightest at the ever-expanding outer limits of each luminosity, stretching outward in elastic illuminations with escalating sounds like two towering ocean waves pulling back water at the shoreline and curling upward, coiling energy inside themselves, rising up, swelling with power and poised ready to crash breaking onto the shore.

Like an effulgent shooting star, the parrot now flew from its banquet-table perch atop the candlestick and streaked through the air toward the center of the flattened-grass area, a comet-tail of blue-green luminance trailing behind it in a splendor of glistering brilliance as it raced like a rainbow-archer's flaming arrow through the foggy air to land in an expanding glow of light on the ground at the feet of Cagliostro.

And then the elastics snapped, and the outward expanding glows suddenly zipped inward in two separate implosions of dazzling light, pulling themselves in instantaneous rushing back into the core epicenters of their source, the body of the stag and the body of the parrot, with fast fleeting splashing crashes, and then dissipating toward silence like falling sea-spray.

Directly in front of Cagliostro, the transformation of the parrot appeared to take even the enchanter by surprise, and it was only the great stag in the body of the Prime Minister who had had the presence of mind to respond with swift anticipatory action in recognition of what no one else had seemed to realize—that what had been the glowing parrot was unmistakably becoming a glowing full-sized fully-grown young woman who was not wearing any clothing. Before she was fully visible as a young woman, before all traces had faded away of the luminous blue-green glow which had served to shield her from everyone's eyes as she had transformed, the stag in the body of the Prime Minister had swiftly and gallantly swept off of his own shoulders the long black cloak from the Prime Minister's dark flowing robes, and in the same motion wrapped it with billowing fluidity around the shoulders and over the body of the otherwise unclothed young lady who moments earlier had been an unclothed parrot.

For a moment, no one moved and nothing stirred.

The young woman now draped in the Prime Minister's cloak stood motionlessly before Cagliostro, breathing with exhilarated passion and smiling intently up into the shocked face of the enchanter.

"Cagliostro," said the tall lovely young lady, whose voice sounded nothing like a parrot and was as lovely as her appearance. "Cagliostro…"

"What…" the enchanter faltered as the young lady gazed adoringly at him. "What manner of enchantment is this…?"

The young lady reached up to put her hand affectionately on Cagliostro's arm, a motion which put the protection of her cloak-of-modesty precipitously at risk. She did not seem particularly interested in the cloak staying on, and seemed as unconcerned with it slipping off as the cloak's smooth fabric seemed disinclined to stay in place, and Cagliostro found himself having to quickly and carefully grasp the two front folds of the garment to pull the sides of the cloak back together and safely closed.

"Might I entreat you," Cagliostro said awkwardly, "to please put your hand here and hold this closed…?"

The young lady smiled and nodded, but made no move to comply. "Please forgive me. I'm not used to wearing anything," she said, never once taking her eyes from the eyes of the enchanter. "I'm not used to wearing anything."

"Yes…" the enchanter replied, evidently more uncomfortable than ever. "Yes, I understand… With your permission, may I use a brief spell to dress you? In whatever garb you prefer?"

"Can the spell be undone?" the young lady asked with some concern, but with perhaps even more passionate adoration in her gaze.

Cagliostro nodded awkwardly. "At your wish… Of course… Any time…"

"For now then, yes. You may. Something colorful please," she said, reaching up to place her other hand as well on the enchanter's other arm. "Something colorful please."

"Thank you," Cagliostro exhaled with some relief. "Thank you…"

There was a distant sound like wind chimes as a nearly invisible swirl of twinkling points of light momentarily winked and danced in the air around the young lady's body. As they faded away, a smart and cheerily colorful dress appeared to have manifested beneath the cloak-of-modesty.

Cagliostro seemed as unable to take his eyes from the eyes of the young lady as she was devotedly adamant in keeping her eyes gazing into his. Without looking away, the enchanter in a smooth fluid motion slipped the cloak off of her, a disrobing which the cloak seemed to have been only too readily on the verge of doing anyway. Cagliostro distractedly handed the cloak back to the great stag in the body of the Prime Minister without once looking at him, and the young lady never once released the hold of her two hands on the enchanter's arms.

"Oh...!" she exclaimed softly with quiet happiness, trembling for a moment in her vivid new dress as a slight shiver appeared to go through her. "That was exciting. Can we please do that again? Can we do that again?"

"For the moment..." Cagliostro began, faltering. "For the moment, I would ask you to please tell me who you are..."

The young lady stepped closer to Cagliostro and held affectionately on to his arms with more firmness. Her lustrous hair was all smoothly-blended gradient swathes of subtle hues, pastel versions of colors which had resided vibrantly within her feathers as a parrot—pastel oranges and pastel reds merging into pastel pinks, pastel purples and pastel blues merging into pastel greens. Ethereally chromatic, her sleek iridescent hair was not long but it flowed with slight waves and sporadic gossamer points that seemed to change shape and texture with the ambient light, framing the radiance of her face like a silken rainbow seen though mist from far away, an arc of excitement and promise curving toward home.

"I am Parrotina," she said. "Lord Cagliostro, I have been in love with you for many years. Once, long ago, I was taken from my father and my sister by the witch Fatta Morganna. She put an enchantment upon me, and then gave me to you as a present with wicked intent. You stopped the wickedness of her spell, but you could not see who I really was. But I could see who you really were. I fell in love with you, Cagliostro. I have been in love with you ever since. With each passing day, I have loved you more. But I could never escape from the enchanted transformation put upon me by the witch. But now the evil in Benebento at last has been ended. And with the ending of that evil, my enchantment is over. My enchantment is over."

"Parrotina!" exclaimed the voice of Avogadro. "Parrotina!!" And from one direction, the wise man raced across the flattened-grass, his long whitish hair bouncing with each quick heavy step, the multicolored robes of his fanciful raiment flowing in his wake as he ran to where she stood with the enchanter, while from another direction, Nicoletta hastened to make her way with the transformed new young Tartaglia toward the same destination.

Only the bonds of a loving family and the joys of reunion with a long-lost family member could have been sufficient to induce Nicoletta and Parrotina—albeit only momentarily—to each briefly relinquish their hold on their true loves, and father and daughters were all three swept up in a flood of tears and overflowing elation as they embraced.

"Oh…" Nicoletta breathed in an ecstasy of quiet happiness. "My beautiful sister… Father and I have felt such painful yearning emptiness without you… How I have longed for you to come home… For so long I have dreamt of the day you would return to us…"

"Oh, my Parrotina," Avogadro cried happily. "You're all grown up! You've turned out so lovely! You're as lovely as your mother was… Her heart would swell with joy to see you so. Just as my heart overflows with gladness to behold you and have you back home at long, long last…!"

"Oh, Father," Parrotina said, full of emotion. "How I have missed you and Nicoletta… My little Nicoletta… How you have grown… And how beautiful you are… Beautiful does not even begin to describe your extraordinary beauty… Oh, my sweet little sister, your beauty takes my breath away… There must be no one on earth more beautiful than you… But what takes my breath away most is my happiness to be back together with you and Father! At long last, our family is restored. Our family is restored."

And even as the reunited family rejoiced, Nicoletta's hands by themselves found their way back to the hands of the transformed new young Tartaglia, and of their own accord the hands of Parrotina found their way to one of the enchanter's arms where they wrapped themselves tightly with adamant affection and ardent passion.

A commotion of voices from the guards made everyone turn suddenly toward the litter.

"Behold…!" one guard cried out.

"It has wings…!" another guard exclaimed.

The stag has wings…!! exclaimed another.

Cigolotti in the body of the stag was standing atop the litter, slowly and experimentally flexing the two massive wings that now extended from the muscular shoulders of the stag's broad back, wings that were now as innately integral a part of his body as were his legs. The body of the stag was over two-and-a-half meters long, and the span of each new wing extended to nearly twice that length. The wings resembled the wings of a falcon in every way except size. Where they grew from the stag's shoulders, the feathers were the same deep red-brown as the coat-hair of the stag. The feathers became white toward the ends, were black at the outermost wingtips, and the feathers on the underside were of lighter hues than those on the leading edge and the outside.

The powerful wings stirred a strong wind as Cigolotti tested them, and the dense fog was swirled in an agitated whorled vortex around the tip and trailing edge of each wing as they stretched and flexed.

"I wasn't asleep!" Cigolotti insisted adamantly with the voice of the stag.

From where he was standing near Cagliostro, Pantalòné nodded kindly at Cigolotti. "No, no, my friend," the Chancellor agreed. "Of course you weren't."

"Look!" Cigolotti exclaimed happily. "I've got wings!"

"You certainly have," said Pantalòné.

"And," Cigolotti went on in the voice of the stag. "I thought getting used to four strong legs was difficult to coordinate… This wings business is going to really take some coordination. They feel quite natural, though. It's a bit like waving my arms around. Except, of course, I no longer have arms. Who needs arms when you're a stag with four strong legs. And two strong wings. And no cane!"

"Cigolotti…" the Chancellor began with some concern.

"Okay, I learned how to use the legs by running, so I suppose I shall learn how to use the wings by flying. Wish me luck…!"

"Cigolotti, hold a moment…" said Pantalòné with more urgency.

But Cigolotti had already taken flight, lifting off from the surface of the litter and lumbering with surprisingly graceful motion upward and away toward the lofty height of the top of the gardens' courtyard piazza, and disappearing into the fog.

All with heads tilted back, everyone in the gardens had been transfixed in rapt fascinated awe at the ascent of Cigolotti. Avogadro, too, had been intently watching the body of the now winged stag as it had taken flight. But the wise man had turned his mystically contemplative gaze to the new young body of the hermit with Tartaglia inside, and then to his daughter Parrotina.

"The prophecy…" Avogadro said so suddenly, it was almost a whisper.

"Prophecy?" asked Parrotina, looking away from the overhead thickening fog to her father while holding more tightly than ever with both arms onto Cagliostro's arm. "Prophecy…?"

"Father!" exclaimed Nicoletta, holding tightly with both arms onto Tartaglia in his new young body. "Father, the prophecy…!"

Avogadro closed his eyes and touched a hand to his forehead as he recited the prophecy. "*New wings shall bring the gift of flight, an old man shall become young, a bird shall disappear, a daughter shall return.*"

The wise man opened his eyes and lifted his hands with

numinous grandeur toward the heavens, extending his arms wide into the descending fog, toward the night sky that was somewhere unseen far above, and toward the greater universe far beyond.

"It has come true!" he pronounced with transcendent significance. "It has all come to pass. The prophecy has been fulfilled."

Chapter 32

The Connections
and
The Names

King Theramo and Angiolina, holding each other's hand tightly and connected to each other with the same loving passion that so blissfully and inextricably bound Nicoletta and the transformed new young Tartaglia, made their way to the group gathered around the enchanter and the wise man in time to hear Cagliostro responding to the information they had all just received from Avogadro.

"I was not aware there was a prophecy..." said Cagliostro, perplexity furrowing his brow.

"It was given to my father when Parrotina was taken..." said Nicoletta quietly.

Avogadro nodded. "She speaks the truth," he said simply.

"I see..." the enchanter replied vaguely. "This all begins to become less unclear..."

"Cagliostro," King Theramo said in polite grateful greeting.

"Your Majesty," Cagliostro said respectfully, bowing slightly.

"Cagliostro..." the King went on hesitantly. "I... We... Cagliostro, there is much I wish to speak of with you..."

The enchanter nodded. "And I with you, Your Majesty," he replied. "However, such discussion would best be deferred until this all is over."

This remark caused several raised eyebrows and turned heads.

"Enchanter," said the great stag in the former body of the Prime Minister, still holding the cloak draped over one arm. "Do you mean to suggest the magic and mayhem of this day has not reached its end?"

Cagliostro nodded. "I do. It continues as we speak. It is not over. It has not yet travelled the full distance of its path."

"Good heavens…" exclaimed Sir Balzanno.

"Truffaldino," said Smeraldina, finding a way to hold herself somehow even closer to him. "What's going to happen now?"

"My master needs to collect some more information," said Truffaldino.

Cagliostro nodded slightly. "Truffaldino is of course completely correct," he said, a compliment which caused Truffaldino to inconspicuously beam with pride and even less conspicuously pull Smeraldina closer to him, which caused Smeraldina to smile in a way that was not the least bit subtle.

"First, however," Cagliostro went on. "Your Majesty, though it is not my place to suggest, perhaps Lord Pantalòné ought to briefly address the guards, toward less divisive positions."

King Theramo nodded, and for a moment seemed absently surprised that he did not need to adjust his crown. "Well thought, and well proposed, Cagliostro," he said to the enchanter, and then turned to the Chancellor. "Pantalòné…?"

Pantalòné nodded swiftly with quick understanding. "Yes, Your Majesty."

The Chancellor stepped forward from the circle of personages surrounding Cagliostro and Parrotina to be seen as clearly as possible through the fog and more clearly heard by all the guards currently assembled in the gardens.

"Good men," he began, addressing the host with confidence and volume that carried across the expanse. "Your King requests that you remain alert. The procession of extraordinary events occurring here has not yet reached its end. However, as you are presently arrayed, you remain positioned in a stance of two different factions. Good men, all of you are on the same side. As you have already demonstrated, there is among you no one who loves your King or your kingdom differently.

"The foundation of the kingdom's security and safety is our military. That is you. You are the fortification that allows us all to conduct our lives free from fear. You are our foundation. And as such, you must be solidly together and indivisible. I therefore direct you now to merge your two positions into one. Join together, just as you are all united in a single loyalty—your unwavering devotion to protect and preserve the goodness of our kingdom, and the welfare of our King. Long live the King."

"Long live the King!" the guards all responded loudly with a single voice. The six elite guards thereupon moved toward the loyalist guards, and the loyalist guards moved toward the elite guards, and within moments, their steadfast martial discipline and deeply-rooted brothers-in-arms camaraderie had brought them all together in noble single-mindedness of purpose. While coming together ideologically, they simultaneously moved apart spatially, spreading their ranks out with more strategic tactically-advantageous wider coverage throughout the part of the gardens which had been the locus of the day's action thus far.

This seemed to adequately address concerns that apparently had been troubling Leandro. With the issues evidently now resolved, he turned and made his way with Clarìcé across the flattened-grass area toward Cagliostro and the others. It was likely that Leandro and Clarìcé desired to be as entwined with each other as the several other affectionately coupled pairs currently populating the gardens. But with the gaze of all his fellow guards now constituting even through the fog a gauntlet of scrutiny, he and Clarìcé—apparently as unified in mind as they were in their hearts—seemed to have tacitly agreed upon a more privately discreet and less unrestrained public interaction, and simply walked side-by-side, the desire and love between them clear while not clearly displayed.

As he and Clarìcé arrived at the group, Leandro quickly addressed the Chancellor. "That was well spoken, Lord Pantalòné," he said.

"Thank you, Leandro," replied Pantalòné. "Significant credit is due His Majesty and the enchanter."

"Understood," said Leandro, bowing respectfully to the King and to Cagliostro.

The fog was still thickening and descending into the gardens with ever more heavily-drifting roiled cloudiness, and visibility was beginning to become significantly compromised.

Cagliostro now turned his focus to Parrotina, who remained at his side with both her arms securely wrapped around one of his.

"With your permission," he said to her. "I would ask to—for a brief moment—take hold of one of your hands."

Parrotina's smile widened and another shiver of excitement seemed to go through her.

"Yes, please," she said with soft eagerness.

Cagliostro appeared uncomfortable. "Please do not misunderstand," he attempted to explain. "I need to collect some information."

Parrotina nodded, making no attempt to disguise her happiness. "Yes, of course," she said. "I completely understand."

"Lady Parrotina—" he endeavored to say.

She reached up to his mouth with one hand and put a single extended finger onto his lips to stop him speaking.

"Cagliostro," she said firmly. "You may call me Parrotina. You may, if you would like, make up a pet name for me. But you may not call me 'Lady'. That is formal, not familiar. And if you have an alternate position, I shall be very much more than glad to wrestle with you about it later."

The enchanter appeared more uncomfortable than ever.

"Very well," he managed to say. "Parrotina. You are the link in the chain of the Prophecy that seems to reach back in time the farthest. I am hoping that residing within you are strands of connection which will fill in for me crucial remaining unknown details of what at present remains a confusing picture."

Parrotina forced herself to let go of his arm, and positioning herself directly in front of him, she coyly held up one hand. "I'm all yours, Cagliostro," she said smiling deeply into his eyes. "Do with me what you will."

Parrotina was tall, though not as tall as the enchanter. Her hand was very much smaller than his, and it disappeared into his grasp as he gently took hold of it. Parrotina closed her eyes for a moment, trembling with excitement, while Cagliostro appeared to now be focused only on her hand, and his face took on the look of someone distractedly lost in the depths of thought, as though trying to find the right words to precisely convey a sentiment, or trying to recall a persistently elusive memory.

There was a distant sound like wind chimes as a nearly invisible swirl of twinkling points of light began to wink and dance around Parrotina's hand where it was being held by Cagliostro's. For a moment nothing else happened, and then Parrotina's entire body flashed for an instant the same blue-green glow from her transformation. The light radiated out and then vanished inward with the speed of an eye-blink. Parrotina's still-closed eyelids fluttered with fast tremulous ripples, and reaching unsteadily forward she placed her other hand on top of where the enchanter's hand was holding hers.

And then whatever had happened was over, and Cagliostro released her hand and looked at her intently.

"Are you alright?" he asked her.

Parrotina gradually opened her eyes and seemed dazed, but she nodded her head. "I... I'm fine..." she said slowly. "I... I've just never felt anything like that before..."

Cagliostro nodded apologetically. "I am deeply sorry if it caused you any discomfort," he said with concern.

Parrotina shook her head. "No, really... No discomfort of any kind... Just... Just a bit overwhelming, that's all... Did... Did you find out what you needed to know...? Did you find out what you needed to know...?"

Cagliostro nodded. "Yes," he said. "Yes, I did. Thank you. Parrotina."

Still looking not quite awake, she forced her eyes more fully open and looked up at him. "I like the way you say my name," she said quietly.

The enchanter looked uncomfortable again, and shifted his focus to Parrotina's father.

"Wise man," Cagliostro began with polite purpose. "Do you know of the existence of an enchanted hundred-year spring in the Forest of Aldente?"

Avogadro nodded. "There is a tarn. I have never with my own eyes seen it, and I know not where it is. It can be found only with magical means. I have never sought to find it. It is dangerously powerful. It possesses power greater than yours, enchanter."

Cagliostro nodded. "The power associated with this Prophecy is indeed greater than mine," he confirmed.

The disappearance of the fog had begun unnoticed as Cagliostro had been getting information from Parrotina, and its dissipation was now accelerating. Near the grounds of the gardens, the fog was simply dematerializing. Higher up near the tops of the loftier trees and the wide-open squared boundary of the piazza where the vast courtyard met the sky, the fog was flowing away as if being pulled by the suction of a forceful wind. But there was no wind. Only the precipitous clearing of the air, and the rapid disappearance of fog which only mere moments before had so thickly and opaquely pervaded the entirety of the Palace Gardens.

King Theramo was meanwhile looking at the enchanter with concern. "Cagliostro," he said apprehensively. "Is there something we must do to protect the people here? To protect the palace? To protect the kingdom? What did you learn from Parrotina about the Prophecy?"

Before Cagliostro could answer, a commotion of voices began to rise from some of the guards, all of whom could—in the new absence of fog—now be seen distinctly.

"It's coming back…!" exclaimed the voice of a guard.

"The winged stag! It returns…!" another guard exclaimed.

All faces now turned to gaze overhead, up toward the wide night sky high above the Palace Gardens. The fog was gone without a trace, and the view upward revealed the faraway sparkle of countless clear pinpoints of nighttime stars, a glittering backdrop for the bright radiant orb of the full moon, across which there now glided a moving silhouette—the shadowed outline of an elegant creature with wide wings, appearing larger and larger as it descended.

Perhaps more out of habit than from preference, the winged stag chose to land back on the litter. He touched down with surprising and impressively effortless grace, his two hind legs first, followed by his forelegs, his massive wings sweeping wide and downward in slow elegant motion to smoothly decelerate the end of his descent.

Upon coming to landed-rest atop the gleaming gold surface, the stag flexed his wings a last time and then pulled them folded and compactly closed to his flanks, settling them tidily and naturally to his sides with the avian ease of a fastidious raptor returned from a foray, and then sitting down on his haunches like a proud collie who had just successfully herded all his sheep, looking regal as a statue.

"That was easier than I thought!" the winged stag announced with delight. "Anyone want to go for a ride?"

"Perhaps later," answered Italo, who still was standing in close proximity to the litter and seemed genuinely interested in taking the winged stag up on his offer.

Unseen by anyone except Cagliostro, upon the return of the winged stag, three momentary motes of blue-green light had materialized, one each at the body of the winged stag, the new young Tartaglia, and Parrotina, all three of whom appeared utterly unware of what was transpiring. The three nearly indiscernible points of illumination had darted undetected through the air, each one making contact with each of the three recently transformed bodies in a lightning-quick salvo of ricochets, then had raced to the triangular center of the space between, colliding and brightening, and then separating into two new minute masses of dimly-glowing blue-green light. The pair of new luminous masses had then drifted away from each other toward opposite ends of the flattened-grass area, where they now hung suspended and nearly invisible in the air.

"I'm a new person," the winged stag continued. "And I'm not even a person! This calls for a change of name. Henceforth, I shall no longer be Cigolotti. I am now Cervolatto, the winged stag!" He declared his new identity with emancipated joy and exhilaration, proudly pronouncing his new name as *chair-voh-LAH-toh.*

Pantalòné and Sir Balzanno stepped closer to Cagliostro to confer with the enchanter confidentially.

"Cagliostro," the Chancellor said in a discreetly quiet voice. "I'm concerned about the stag flying. Cigolotti…er…Cervolatto has the sleeping fits. And if they come upon him while he is in flight, it could be disastrous. Can you cure him?"

Cagliostro shook his head. "I have no power over life and death," he replied with an equally discreet low voice. "Nor do I have power over any manner of health, whether of mind or of body. However, though your apprehension is out of kindness and your concerns come from your heart, your fears are unwarranted."

"I don't think so," Sir Balzanno disagreed. "If he falls asleep in flight, it will be bad for him and worse for anyone who happens to be under him when he falls out of the sky…"

"Cigolotti…Cervolatto is free of the sleeping fits," said Cagliostro. "They left him when he transformed."

Sir Balzanno shook his head. ""No," said the knight. "That is not accurate. He fell asleep for a long time even after he had been switched into the body of the great stag."

Cagliostro nodded. "You are not wrong, but that is not the transformation of which I speak. The Prophecy has a power which is far-reaching. When Cigolotti transformed into a winged stag, with the arrival of his wings his sleeping fits left him. He is free to fly as he desires, and free to sleep only when he chooses. He now not only slips the bonds of earth, he has flown free from ills he knew not of."

Cervolatto meanwhile was looking happily around at the various populace of the gardens as though everyone there had assembled there solely for the purpose of hearing him speak.

"Life is good," he explained with earnest enthusiasm. "If you don't have your health, you have nothing. But if you have your health, and you have good strong wings to fly, then life is good indeed!"

Cervolatto looked down at his nearest audience member, who happened to be Italo.

"This is a splendid golden platform you've gotten for me. It was very thoughtful of whoever arranged it."

Italo shook his head. "It is not intended to be a platform, Cervolatto," the squire explained. "It is to transport and display gloriously felled carcasses."

"Well, that seems needlessly gruesome," replied Cervolatto. "I think it should be re-purposed as a landing pad. The gold surface is eye-catching and easy to spot from the air, I can assure you. And that way, its gilded splendor can be appreciated guilt-free by anyone and everyone!"

"Italo!" called Sir Balzanno loudly from the group around Cagliostro and Parrotina. "Come here this instant! And fetch that Bi-Scepter device lying over there in the grass, and bring it along with you!"

With quick obedient diligence, Italo dashed from his conversation with Cervolatto, located and retrieved the Bi-Scepter from where it lay in the flattened-grass after the new young

Tartaglia had dropped it, and hurried over to where Sir Balzanno was impatiently awaiting him.

Cagliostro, meanwhile, with surreptitious attentiveness was observing the progress of the two luminous masses. Still at opposite ends of the flattened-grass, they were floating waist-high in the air, slowly spinning and fluctuating, and only gradually gaining size and brightness and opacity. They were as yet still too nascent in their appearance or process to be observed or noticed by anyone other than the enchanter, who continued to silently eye them with wary but for the moment unspoken vigilance as they proceeded to inexorably evolve toward whatever they were going to be.

"Cervolatto is right," Sir Balzanno was now saying to Italo with conviction. "Sometimes it is time for a new name…"

Standing before the knight, Italo was looking perplexed and worried. "Sir…?" he asked anxiously.

Sir Balzanno extended one hand forward toward the young squire. "Hand me that Bi-Scepter, Italo."

Italo nodded quickly and handed the device to the knight's expectant hand.

Sir Balzanno seemed uninterested in any examination of the Bi-Scepter, and looked meaningfully at Italo. "Kneel, please, squire," he instructed.

Italo knelt down on one knee before Sir Balzanno.

Sir Balzanno grasped the double-shaft of the Bi-Scepter by the hinged end and raising it high in the air, brought it down lightly onto Italo's shoulders, first on one shoulder, then the other.

"With Heaven and your King as witnesses, I hereby dub thee a fully-vested knight of the kingdom. Arise Sir Italo of Benebento…"

Italo was astounded nearly to the point of immobility. He slowly stood to his feet, his face a mixture of incredulity and wonder and exhilaration.

"Sir…" he faltered. "Sir Balzanno… I…"

Sir Balzanno nodded. "Come along, knight. You must pull yourself together. You'll be facing far more challenging scenarios than this, I can promise you."

"Sir…" Italo managed to say. "Thank you, Sir… I… I've always wanted…"

Sir Balzanno nodded again. "I know you have, lad," he said. "I as well have always wanted this for you."

"Oh, Sir!" said Italo, filled with emotion. "It… It's like a dream…!"

For the third time, Sir Balzanno nodded. "Better to live a dream than a nightmare." He turned toward the new young Tartaglia who stood with Nicoletta, their arms still tightly wrapped around each other. "Isn't that right, Tartaglia?" Sir Balzanno added.

The new young Tartaglia exchanged a friendly glance with Sir Balzanno, then looked back down into the loving eyes of Nicoletta. "Indeed, Balzanno…" he said quietly. "Much better to live a dream…"

"Of course, no knight," Sir Balzanno went on, returning his attention to Sir Italo, "is truly a knight without a horse. Therefore, on the morrow, at daybreak before the start of the wedding, you and I, Sir Italo, shall go to Cavalli's Stables in town, and I shall buy for you a steed that you can be proud of."

Sir Italo was in an overwhelmed ecstasy of gratitude and awe. "Oh…" he struggled to say. "Sir… Oh, Sir Balzanno, I shall become a noble and great knight, worthy of the confidence you have placed in me. I shall make you proud of me, Sir."

"You already have, my boy," said Sir Balzanno. "You have been a good squire. You will be a great knight. And after you choose your horse and I have completed its purchase, I shall present you formally with your riding spurs and sword."

"May…" Sir Italo began. "Sir, may I continue to study knighthood with you, under your direction and with your guidance?"

Sir Balzanno smiled. "I would be honored," he said. "Sir Italo."

"Oh, Sir…" exclaimed Sir Italo, kneeling again in appreciation and respectful honor before Sir Balzanno. "This is the greatest day of my life."

"Arise, Sir Italo," replied Sir Balzanno, smiling and extending a hand to the newly-dubbed knight. "Even greater days lie ahead. First, however, we must all somehow make our way through the rest of this day…"

Cagliostro saw it first, but within moments the guards had seen it as well, raising their weapons and their voices in warning outcry as one of the hovering and tumbling luminous masses of light had suddenly grown large enough to be plainly visible. The radiant blue-green shape expanded its size with abrupt speed, stretching both higher and to the ground, taking on the outline of a full-grown person. In an instant, the light zipped inward and completely away, leaving behind a tall imposing figure standing defiantly on the flattened-grass.

Chapter 33

The Confrontation
and
The Reunion

"**W**ho is that fascinating-looking woman…?" asked the stag in the former body of the Prime Minister, transferring the draped cloak to his other arm.

"It's the witch…!" exclaimed Sir Italo. "The potion has worn off! I remember everything now…!"

"That is Fatta Morganna," said Avogadro reproachfully, making no effort to mask his animus.

Cagliostro glanced for a moment toward the opposite end of the flattened-grass at the other suspended undulating mass of blue-green light, but it remained as yet unchanged and unseen by anyone.

Spread out in their newly-taken tactical positions, and all formidably in plain sight in the wake of the fog's departure, the King's guards all around the flattened-grass area of the gardens could be clearly seen holding their weapons steady, all aimed at Fatta Morganna.

Fatta Morganna looked around with irritated impatience at the military presence arrayed around her.

"Oh," she said with annoyed sarcasm. "A welcoming party. How quaint."

King Theramo leaned toward the enchanter to speak to him in a low voice. "Cagliostro," he asked with concern. "Does the witch pose a danger?"

Cagliostro shook his head slightly. "She does not," he replied in an equally low voice. "Your guards' alert protective concern is understandable, but not necessary."

King Theramo nodded, and turned to Sir Balzanno. "You may order your men to stand down, Sir Balzanno."

With the fog gone, Sir Balzanno could be clearly seen by the guards. He made a signal first with his fist and then his open hand, an instruction which evidently was understood and immediately implemented as all the guards in the gardens lowered their weapons.

The ornate rings of one of Fatta Morganna's long white fingers glinted in the light from the overhead full moon and the gardens' pole-torches as she pointed at the King, the long tapered sleeve of her dark gown dripping down from around the myriad cryptic bracelets encircling her narrow wrist.

"Well," she said with scorn. "If it isn't Benebento's bundle of goodness himself. King Theramo. Back in your own body, I see. Oh, yes, I have my ways of keeping track of all the ridiculous nonsense that goes on in this palace."

"Witch!" Sir Italo called out to her. "I have my memory back!"

"Congratulations, chivalrous dolt," she replied. "Yes, my potion wore off when Tartaglia lost his evil."

"And you were wrong!" Sir Italo went on. "Look at me! Sir Balzanno has knighted me!"

"Well," said Fatta Morganna, "you look exactly the same, only possibly more pathetic."

"The sun has set," Sir Italo continued. "And it has set on you. Your plan has failed. You will not regain your evil powers at the expense of our great kingdom!"

"At least I'm not a knight," replied Fatta Morganna derisively.

The witch's unseen feet seemed to be not touching the ground, and she rotated slightly as if on an invisible turntable as she now shifted her focus to the enchanter.

"Oh, and look," she went on contemptuously. "It's Cagliostro, the famous goody-good. It figures you would be behind all this. I see you've been busy meddling again. Thanks to you, these confused idiots can't even keep track of whose body they're in. And just look what you've done to poor Tartaglia. You've ruined perfectly good evil. He doesn't even seem like himself anymore."

Draped below her low-cut plunging décolleté, the eerie chain of her necklace glimmered dimly, its enigmatic symbol pendant seeming to glow like the moonlight.

"Well, enchanter," she demanded irritably. "What is it you want from me? To prove to me my fabulously evil scheme didn't turn out as planned? To show me all these stupidly happy couples? You must have brought me here for some reason."

Cagliostro shook his head. "It was not I who brought you, Fatta Morganna. You are here by the workings of your own magic."

"Ha! Idiot! I have no powers! They were taken from me!"

"The tarn," replied Cagliostro. "The spell you put upon the wise man's daughter after you abducted her, that selfsame spell found its way to the spell you cast with the waters of the hundred-year spring. This is your doing, Fatta Morganna. It is the trailing ends of your magic that have brought you here, for reasons I do not know."

"Ha!" she laughed disdainfully again, the dusky gems of her black headdress glittering in the arrayed rows of their ornamental finials. "The 'great' enchanter…! You see, Cagliostro? You don't know everything after all!"

Cagliostro nodded. "There are a great many things I do not know," he said. "But I have learned some important things about you, Fatta Morganna."

Against the pale complexion of Fatta Morganna's face, the deep crimson of her lips seemed to glow as they spread into a triumphant smile. "So!" she replied victoriously. "You finally know I exist! What a delicious delight to see your insufferable arrogance hobbled at last!"

"Fatta Morganna," said Cagliostro, glancing for a fleeting moment at the still unnoticed second tumbling mass of blue-green light. "Do you remember a time when you were not evil?"

"How dare you!" she said indignantly. "I've NEVER not been evil!"

"Explain now how Tartaglia became evil," the enchanter went on. "These people need to know, and Tartaglia deserves to know."

"It's a happy story with a sad ending, enchanter," she said. "It was going so well for so long. It was foiled by that double-crossing Bi-Scepter toy of yours. I was sure it was going to be the perfect means for Tartaglia to succeed. Right up until that idiot stag saved the King's miserable life. People hunt animals for thousands of years.

Then finally an animal gets a chance to settle the score. And what does he do? He helps the people! Animals are idiots. That's why we have them for dinner."

"Fatta Morganna," said Cagliostro. "You are the one who caused Tartaglia to change. It was your magic that caused the darkness to come to life within him, and to grow to its terrible proportion."

"Of course it was me! Who else would be clever enough to think up that brilliant plan?! Who else would be clever enough to find and use the power of the hundred-year-spring so deviously?! Of course it was me!"

The enchanter nodded. "Tartaglia himself was never evil. He was only the unwitting host to the dark seed you implanted within him."

"I know! Brilliant, right!? No one knew! Tartaglia himself didn't even know!"

"Fatta Morganna," Cagliostro went on. "There is a power far greater than yours, and far greater than mine, and greater even than the waters of the hundred-year spring."

"If you say it's 'The Power of Love', I'm going to throw up."

The enchanter shook his head. "Love should never be underestimated," he said. "However that is not the power I refer to. I am speaking of something very old, and very powerful, and with a strength of enchantment that far exceeds my ability to understand. I do not know what name truly identifies it, but it has been referred to by the wise man as 'The Prophecy'."

"If you're going to say it's 'The Power of Fate', I'm going to throw up again."

"No, it is not Fate. It is not 'prophecy'. It is The Prophecy. I refer to it that way because I do not know the sound or symbol or appellation that truly names it. The Prophecy is not the words the wise man received, nor is it the outcome those words ensured. It is a kind of entity. The Prophecy plays with people's lives the way you played with Tartaglia's soul. It rearranges and adjusts and intervenes and orchestrates. I do not know the origin of its power, I do not know its motivation, I do not know what satisfaction it derives from its manipulation of people's lives. Fatta Morganna. You have been used by The Prophecy. It has been using you the same way you used Tartaglia—as a means to certain ends, and possibly with some cruel enjoyment along the way. Like Tartaglia, you are not truly evil, you have merely been envenomed with evil. Like Tartaglia, your evil does not originate from you, it merely resides within you. Like Tartaglia, you were not born evil, the evil in you was put there."

"You're just jealous," Fatta Morganna replied spitefully. "You resent being a goody-good, but you can't help yourself, and secretly wish you could just let loose and use all your overrated magical powers to be fabulously fantastically evil. Like me!"

"What an extraordinary woman…" the stag marveled with quiet appreciation from the mouth of the former Prime Minister.

"Witch," said Avogadro. "There are two ways to be fooled. One is to believe what isn't true. The other is to refuse to believe what is true."

"No," said Fatta Morganna dismissively. "That's not how it goes. Fool me once, shame on you. Fool me twice, and I'm obviously an idiot. What is wrong with you people? You can't change someone's identity just by describing them differently. Stop trying to change me. I'm perfectly happy being evil. Cagliostro, you're the goody-good. Doesn't goody-goodness include having 'special feelings' like 'tolerance' and 'acceptance'? Why won't you just let me be who I am? Why can't you simply accept the fact that Fatta Morganna is evil? Stop bothering Fatta Morganna! What do you even want from me?"

"Fatta Morganna," said Cagliostro. "Look around. No one here wants or needs anything from you. Anywhere you look within these gardens, you will see people who are going to live happily ever after. They didn't dare to believe it might come true, or they never even dreamt of such things coming true, but it somehow miraculously has all come true."

"Even for you, enchanter?" she said accusingly. "Are YOU going to live happily ever after? Are you going to admit aloud what is so obvious to everyone else, that you're in love with a parrot?"

"You stole from me," Parrotina said to the witch. "You stole years of my life that I never got to have with my family."

"And," replied Fatta Morganna, "in return you now are with the love of your life. Admit it, parrot-girl. You would never have met the enchanter if it hadn't been for me. Would you trade, parrot-girl? If you had the chance, would you take back the lost years with your family and lose the love of your life?"

Parrotina looked down and said nothing.

Cagliostro reached over and took hold of Parrotina's hand, but he wasn't looking at her. He was looking at the second blue-green light. It was changing and beginning to grow in size.

"Fatta Morganna," said Cagliostro. "Your evil has no place here. You are correct, your evil has strangely played a crucial role in bringing about goodness. The King called upon my services because of goading from Tartaglia, whose urgings arose from the evil implanted in him by you. My arrival in Benebento set many events into motion, but it was ultimately by your hand that I came here. The paths we have been put on by you have not all been pleasant or easy. But those paths have all led to happiness. We can object to your motivation, and we can object to your interference, but we cannot object to the outcomes. We all have our resolutions, and they all have resolved well. Better than well. But you yourself have been put on a path, Fatta Morganna. You are not at this moment here because I summoned you. You have been brought here by something else. There is no action for any of us to take. The rest of what is about to take place here affects you, and you alone."

Again there were suddenly outcries of warning from the guards as the second luminous mass of light abruptly grew large enough to be plainly visible. The radiant blue-green shape expanded its size with sudden speed, stretching both higher and to the ground, taking on the outline of a full-grown person. In an instant, the light zipped inward and completely away, leaving behind a figure standing immobilized with confusion on the flattened-grass near the parrot's banquet table.

The guards had raised their harquebus long-guns and leveled their aim at the shape as it had become visible, while it still had been a fluctuating apparition of undetermined light. But they now all lowered their weapons upon recognizing that what had at last materialized before them was a harmless-looking young lady holding a wooden serving tray with mugs of ale.

"Who is that young lady...?" Sir Italo asked in a quiet voice. "She's very pretty..."

"I know her, Truffaldino..." said Smeraldina, whispering into Truffaldino's ear. "She works at the taverna..."

Truffaldino nodded. "That's Bèllabrèzza," he said. "She's my friend."

The current populace of the gardens was now staring in silent expectation at Bèllabrèzza as she looked around in shocked apprehension and astounded bewilderment.

"Truffaldino," Smeraldina whispered again. "She looks like she could use a friend right now..."

Truffaldino nodded, and as he and Smeraldina reluctantly but swiftly released their affectionate hold of each other, Truffaldino made his way with rapid haste toward where Bèllabrèzza was standing.

Fatta Morganna was staring at Bèllabrèzza with a peculiar look on her face. "What is the meaning of this, enchanter...?" she demanded. "Why have you brought that girl here...?"

Cagliostro shook his head. "I have neither hand nor role in this," he said. "She was brought here not by me, but by the power of The Prophecy."

Fatta Morganna rolled her eyes. "Oh, please. You're always blaming. Why don't you just take some responsibility?"

Relief and recognition came over Bèllabrèzza as Truffaldino

arrived at her side. She hastily placed onto the nearby banquet table the tray of beverages she had been in the midst of serving at the taverna and threw her arms around Truffaldino's neck.

"Oh, Truffaldino…!" she breathed into his ear. "I'm so happy to see you…!"

"Hi, Bèllabrèzza!" said Truffaldino in friendly reassuring greeting.

"She has such a nice smile…" Sir Italo said quietly.

Bèllabrèzza unwrapped her arms from Truffaldino's neck and took firm hold of one of his hands. "Truffaldino, what's happening?" she whispered anxiously. "What's going on…? What is this place…?"

"You're inside the castle," Truffaldino explained quietly. "This is the Palace Gardens."

"What am I doing here…?" asked Bèllabrèzza. "How did I get here…?"

"You were brought here by a Prophecy," said Truffaldino.

"Seriously…?" said Bèllabrèzza.

Truffaldino nodded at her. "Truly," he said.

Bèllabrèzza grasped Truffaldino's hand more tightly. "Okay…" she said, nodding slowly back at him, her expression a mixture of excited interest and perplexed anxiousness.

On the other side of the flattened-grass, Cagliostro was nodding gravely at Fatta Morganna.

"Unquestionably," he was saying to the witch, "I do have now a responsibility. It falls to me to remind you of something you may have forgotten, either by your own choice or because by design of The Prophecy it has been clouded over in your memory…"

"Truffaldino…" Bèllabrèzza whispered to Truffaldino. "Who is that tall handsome man…?"

"That is my master, the enchanter Cagliostro," Truffaldino said with quiet pride. "I trust him with my life. I have trusted him with my past, and with my present, and I trust him with my future. Bèllabrèzza, you can trust him too."

Across the flattened-grass, Fatta Morganna was addressing Cagliostro, but she was apparently unable to stop looking with mounting anxiety at Bèllabrèzza.

"Don't kid yourself, Cagliostro," she said dismissively. "You're just meddling. You're always meddling. You just want to put your imprint on everyone's life."

"Truffaldino…" Bèllabrèzza whispered to him. "That woman keeps staring at me… Who is she…?"

"That's the witch," Truffaldino whispered back to her. "That is Fatta Morganna."

Bèllabrèzza looked back intently across the distance of the flattened-grass into the gaze of Fatta Morganna, and suddenly a slow smile of happiness began to spread across Bèllabrèzza's face.

"Twenty-three years ago, Fatta Morganna," Cagliostro went on, "you gave birth to a baby girl. But the infant was taken from you by enchantment as punishment for your evil ways. The child was raised with love and kindness and decency here in this kingdom, within the community of a Benebento guild of artisan wheelwrights and blacksmiths. That child's goodness does not bely her origin—she is not good *despite* the mother who gave birth to her, she is good *because* of the mother who gave birth to her. Her mother is—at her deepest core—also good. Her mother's goodness over very many years has been hidden and suffocated beneath layers of darkness and bitterness—evil that was not ever innately part of who she was, but rather had been implanted into her by the power of an external force. But that goodness yet resides someplace deep within her. Fatta Morganna, that mother was you. That mother *is* you."

With his large powerful hand, Cagliostro now pointed a single finger toward the opposite side of the flattened-grass.

"Fatta Morganna," said the enchanter. "That young woman is Bèllabrèzza. She is your daughter."

A gasp came from Avogadro. "The prophecy…!" he exclaimed. "*A lost daughter shall return*…! It wasn't only meaning Parrotina…!"

Cagliostro nodded. "I was not until this day aware of the Prophecy or its manifold significance…"

Fatta Morganna was fighting with her emotions. "See, Cagliostro!? You're not so smart… You don't know everything…" Her voice was faltering, and she still was unable to take her eyes from Bèllabrèzza.

Cagliostro nodded. "I am not all-knowing," he agreed. "But I am knowing enough to understand how much I am unaware of. Wise Man, is this not so, is it not the true emblem of wisdom to recognize how much one does not know?"

Avogadro put his hand mystically to his forehead. "I'm getting something…" he said significantly. "Something that starts with a 'T'… It… It is… TRUTH. The enchanter speaks the Truth."

Her eyes still on Bèllabrèzza, Fatta Morganna was shaking her head adamantly. "No…" she contended. "No, he does not speak the truth…"

Avogadro shook his head. "Everything the enchanter has told you is true."

"You cast a very powerful spell, Fatta Morganna," said Cagliostro. "I expect even you do not fully realize how powerful a Finders-Keepers spell is. That spell causes you to randomly encounter what you are seeking at a time when you do not know what you are looking for. You thought finding the tarn was the result of that spell. It was a result, but it was not the ultimate result. This is the ultimate result. By the power of your spell, you now have what you truly wanted, even though you did not know what it was. What you did not know you were looking for is now here. It is your daughter."

"No!!" Fatta Morganna declared with distraught vehemence. "It is not so. It is impossible. It cannot be. Fatta Morganna is an island. She is her own self-made island of evil. My wickedness and my magic are all I need. My evil sustains me. I have no one. I need no one! I need no one!!"

Bèllabrèzza was continuing to smile earnestly at Fatta Morganna. She let go of Truffaldino's hand and started walking across the flattened-grass toward Fatta Morganna.

With mounting fear and dread, Fatta Morganna watched her approach. "Stay back…! Keep away from me, beer wench…!"

Bèllabrèzza continued her approach, smiling more happily with each step that brought her closer.

Fatta Morganna was beginning to tremble. "Stop where you are…! Keep away from me, girl…!"

Bèllabrèzza continued walking until she reached Fatta Morganna and came to a calm stop directly in front of the witch. Fatta Morganna was tall, but Bèllabrèzza was nearly the same height, and their faces were now only inches apart.

Fatta Morganna had raised her hands in defensive protest and now held them threateningly up in front of Bèllabrèzza. "No…!" she cried out. "I shall punish you…! I shall transform you…! You shall become… You shall become…"

Bèllabrèzza's radiantly smiling face was bathed in a glow of glad recognition and adoration. "I know you," she said gently.

"No…!" Fatta Morganna insisted desperately. "No… You don't…! You can't… You were too…"

"I would know you anywhere," said Bèllabrèzza. She slowly lifted her hands and lightly took hold of Fatta Morganna's wrists, lowering them and carefully pulling them closer to extend behind her own waist. She then gently put both her own hands on either side of Fatta Morganna's face and gazed into the witch's eyes.

"Look at you…" Bèllabrèzza said quietly, beaming. "You're beautiful… I wish I had more of your beauty…"

She reached up and lovingly traced with her finger the curved edge of Fatta Morganna's headdress where it came to a stark point in the middle of her high pale forehead.

"The enchanter speaks the truth…" said Bèllabrèzza with soft conviction. "I see it in your eyes. I see a part of myself in your eyes… I see who you really are…"

Fatta Morganna could not speak. She gazed back into Bèllabrèzza's eyes and continued to tremble.

Bèllabrèzza's smiling eyes glistened with happiness. "I don't care about any wrong you've done... Even if you don't want to be my mother... I want to be your daughter... I am your daughter..."

Bèllabrèzza put her own arms around Fatta Morganna and hugged her with kindness and affection and unconditional love.

Fatta Morganna was frozen—terror and anger and confusion contorting her pale face. And then she broke. Her arms that had been stranded and bewildered helplessly in the air behind Bèllabrèzza now slowly closed as Fatta Morganna fearfully, tentatively, and at last gently put one arm around Bèllabrèzza's back and shoulders, and with the other hand gently cradled the hair of the back of Bèllabrèzza's head. Fatta Morganna's eyes closed, and a single tear escaped and trickled glistening down the pale skin of her gaunt tormented face. She could not speak, and her eyes remained closed, and she did not loosen her hold of Bèllabrèzza.

There was a sound like distant wind chimes. Around Fatta Morganna and Bèllabrèzza at the ground by their feet, a nearly invisible swirl of twinkling points of light began to wink and dance, and then a sudden garden rose up growing from the ground around them, rich with myriad Spring color and floral fragrance. In a moment they could no longer be seen behind the newly-grown screen of lovely plants and flowers that had grown to a height of several meters and spread across with a span equally wide.

"We all now shall leave those two be," Cagliostro announced. His tone had become adamant, and the deep power of his voice now irresistibly filled the entirety of the space. "Though these gardens have of late been the site of momentous spectacle, that event is not for us. It is for those two, and those two alone."

No one said a word. Everyone remained transfixed by what they had seen, and what they now were feeling.

"I ask you all," Cagliostro went on, "to keep in your minds this one thing I now tell you. Evil must sometimes be met with overwhelming force, and perhaps even unwavering destructive annihilation. But at times, the true remediation of Evil is Goodness. Goodness is not a weapon. It is an answer. It is never too late for someone to change, it is never too late for someone to transform or be transformed. And it is never too late to trust and to have faith in someone who has fallen. It is never too late to extend a hand in help to someone who you believe can change. And so I have now restored to the witch her lost powers. It was not I who took them from her, but I do have to the ability to give them back to her, and I have now done so. I ask that you will all trust me that this is the right thing to do."

Chapter 34

The Offers
and
The Assurances

King Theramo took a cautious respectful step toward Cagliostro.

"Is it over?" the King asked the enchanter.

Cagliostro nodded. "Yes, Your Majesty. The Prophecy has reached the end of its current path. I expect there are other paths. However, this particular path has been fully traversed and is completed. All that The Prophecy had orchestrated to occur along this path now has come to fruition and has fully resolved."

King Theramo nodded and turned in the direction of Avogadro.

"Avogadro," said the King. "Are you in agreement with Cagliostro?"

Avogadro closed his eyes with mystical significance and nodded with slow sagacity. "I am," he said with sapient certitude. "All which was arranged by The Prophecy to happen has now happened."

"Thank you, Avogadro, my good, good friend," said King Theramo earnestly.

The King turned back to Cagliostro.

"It..." King Theramo began. "It has been quite a day..."

The enchanter nodded again. "It has indeed," he agreed.

"The past two days, in fact," King Theramo added, "have been a deluge of extraordinary experiences and events that are beyond my ability to yet fully comprehend…"

"You are not alone in feeling that way, Your Majesty," Cagliostro said contemplatively.

The King nodded in wordless accord.

The new young Tartaglia gently and reluctantly disconnected himself from Nicoletta and stepped over toward where King Theramo was standing with the enchanter.

"Your Highness…" he began, looking an unlikely mixture of robust healthful fitness and ragged tatters which had been right-sized for the frail ancient body of the hermit but were a poorly inadequate fit for the hardy new young Tartaglia. "Your Highness, I…"

King Theramo held up a kind hand to stop him attempting to articulate whatever he was struggling to express.

"Tartaglia," said the King warmly. "You have always been my dearest and most trusted friend. That has not changed. You are changed, and I am changed, and so many of us here in these gardens tonight find ourselves profoundly changed. But in my mind, Tartaglia, our friendship has not suffered. I would like to believe it has become stronger."

The new young Tartaglia nodded and smiled. "I am beyond grateful for your words, Your Majesty," he said humbly. "I have now three aspirational dreams, all of which I am aware will require not only my unwavering commitment and determination, but also necessarily the passage of time. One is to be worthy of the miraculous love I have been blessed with from my beloved Nicoletta.

The second is to beg forgiveness and make amends with my sister Clarìcé. The third is to be worthy of your friendship, Your Highness, which is and always has been so very dear to me."

"I am hopeful," King Theramo replied, "that you will aspire toward yet a fourth dream, Tartaglia. It is my ardent wish that you will agree to continue on in your position as my most trusted Prime Minister. For me to be the best king that I can be, I need to have you by my side."

The young Tartaglia smiled with deep appreciation and respect for his King. "Your Majesty's goodness," he said, "is not merely what all your subjects proudly acclaim as the best thing about the kingdom of Benebento. Your Majesty's goodness *is* the best thing about the kingdom of Benebento. Yes, Your Highness, if you will have me, I would be honored to continue on in the position of your Prime Minister. Thank you, Your Majesty…"

King Theramo was filled with emotion. "Thank you, Tartaglia…" he breathed with appreciation and relief. "Thank you…"

The King, still struggling to collect himself, turned back toward the enchanter.

"Cagliostro," he began. "I have learned much these past two days about the power of magic. With firm conviction, I respect that magic is never to be sought or employed frivolously or impulsively. However, would it be an acceptable and not inappropriate request for me to ask if you might bestow upon Tartaglia clothing that would better suit his new self? I feel there remain yet many words to be exchanged between those of us here in the gardens just now, and I would wish for my Prime Minister to neither leave our midst merely for the purpose of seeking more fitting habiliments, nor feel needless awkwardness at being so incongruously garbed."

"This is a night of exceptions, Your Majesty," replied Cagliostro. "Under different circumstances, I would respectfully decline. However, I believe at the moment I can accede to your request, so long as it is acceptable to the Prime Minister."

"I am humbled by the kindness from both of you," said young Tartaglia. "I will gratefully accept the generous and thoughtful gift."

"And," King Theramo added, "while I am able to elicit affirmatives from you, Cagliostro, is there a possibility you would be willing to do me the honor of attending on the morrow my marriage to Angiolina?"

"Your Majesty," replied Cagliostro. "I am confident Truffaldino will happily attend with Smeraldina, if he is given the honor of being added as a wedding guest. For myself, Your Highness, I must respectfully decline."

King Theramo nodded. "I understand," he said. "I hope you will not think less of me if I perhaps in an underhanded manner attempt to solicit the help of another, in the effort to change your mind…"

"You must do as you see fit, Your Majesty…" the enchanter replied vaguely, and then looked for a moment at young Tartaglia.

There was a sound like distant wind chimes. Around the healthy young body of the Prime Minister, a nearly invisible swirl of twinkling points of light began to wink and dance, and the ragged tatters which once had clothed the old hermit blurred and dissolved away, replaced with modest palace finery, perfectly fitting, unexceptional, but with subtle touches of higher office, and with a color gamut less somber than what had once been characteristic of the Prime Minister's garb, but nevertheless infused with the tastefully understated gravitas duly suited to the rank of the King's most trusted advisor.

Young Tartaglia extended his arms for a moment, inspecting—to the extent he could—the new apparel he was suddenly clothed in.

"Thank you, Cagliostro," said Tartaglia. "I am grateful and appreciative. I would be more in awe of your extraordinary abilities, but—if you would be so kind as to forgive me—still nothing awes me as greatly as my beloved Nicoletta's love for me. All other miraculous occurrences are, for me, simply fine brightness amidst the greater illumination which gives me new life—the sunlight of my Nicoletta's love.

The enchanter nodded in understanding acknowledgement.

"Thank you, Cagliostro," said King Theramo with appreciative gratitude. Still in awe of any manifestation of the enchanter's magic, the King did not appear to share his Prime Minister's sentiment of comparatively diminished amazement at Cagliostro's abilities. What the King did, however, share with the young Tartaglia, was the blissful wonderment and reverent thankfulness of being abruptly immersed in the out-of-the-blue sublimity of True Love. As it so closely mirrored what King Theramo shared with Angiolina, what the young Tartaglia now shared with Nicoletta evidently resonated recognizably with the King, and the expression of empathy on King Theramo's face was unmistakable. And as the enchanter's eyes apparently could not stop themselves from glancing for a fleeting moment in the direction of Parrotina, it seemed increasingly likely that Cagliostro as well may have privately been able to empathize with both the King and the Prime Minister in this regard.

"Your Majesty," said young Tartaglia. "Though I recognize there is nothing which could be done, I am nevertheless filled with concern that Cervolatto will harbor understandable resentment and bitterness that, while his former body has been given extraordinary youth, he no longer resides within it to enjoy the fruits of such miraculous rejuvenation. It does not seem fair, and I am distressed at the unfairness to him of how this crucial aspect of our new paths has resolved…"

The King nodded. "We shall ask Cervolatto about his feelings on this. As you observe, there is nothing which could be done. I am hopeful that somehow he finds himself preferring with no caveats his new path. With all the extraordinary goodness which has precipitously been bestowed upon us here, it would be—as you say—a cruel and unwelcome anomalous inequity if he is not as fully glad and thankful at all aspects of who he now is and what his new life now offers him…"

The young Tartaglia wordlessly nodded his accord.

"Tartaglia," King Theramo went on. "On the subject of another matter, I would like to offer the great stag a position within the hierarchy of the palace. However, I will not do so if your counsel deems it unwise or unwarranted, and I especially will be disinclined to do so if the peculiarities of the great stag being in attendance on an on-going basis will be a source of discomfort for you in any way…"

The young Tartaglia nodded in understanding. "Your Majesty," he replied. "I believe I recognize much of what impels your thinking in this matter, and I feel it is both appropriate and desirable to offer the great stag a position of noble influence in the palace. And I humbly thank you for your concern, but please be assured the presence of the great stag will cause me no discomfort whatsoever. I confess, Your Highness, it will indeed be peculiar to regularly see across from me the very body of my former self... However, I believe it shall serve as a not unwelcome continual reminder of where I have come from, where I once was, to ensure that I will never fail to be duly grateful for where I am, where this new path has permitted me to now be. Deep gratitude, new love, and fresh wonderment are said to be sensations and feelings with cannot help but fade over time. I am determined to defy that axiomatic inevitability. Regularly seeing and interacting with the palpable image of my former self I believe will help me to attain and maintain that objective. Your Majesty, I believe I had previously articulated to you four objectives for myself. Please accept my adding of this fifth aspiration to my personal list."

King Theramo smiled. "Tartaglia," he said. "You fill my heart with energy and joy. You are as good as the best of your former self, and your new and better self already inspires me and fills me with elation and optimism. I am not only proud to call you my best friend, Tartaglia. I am also lucky."

The King and the Prime Minister extended a right hand to each other, each clasping the forearm of the other in a confirmatory bond of unity and kinship, a connective joining whose tradition and history was rooted firmly in their own immediate present, and in the time of their parents, and the time of their parents' parents.

The two best friends ended their mutual grasp, and then the young Tartaglia demonstrated an urge and impulse and need with which King Theramo and his own happily-distracted preoccupation with Angiolina could easily empathize. Tartaglia seemed as unwilling and unable to be apart from Nicoletta as she was unwilling and unable to be apart from him, and in his freshly-fashioned garb the Prime Minister hastened his way back to Nicoletta's side where their gladdened limbs once again enwrapped each other with quietly desperate and thankful fond affection and relief.

King Theramo stepped over to where the great stag in the body of the former Prime Minister was standing.

"Great stag," said the King. "It is only by the grace of your bold intervention that I was not killed at the clearing in the forest. I owe you my life, and much more... I do not know what to do or say if you feel only resentment that—after the heroic and noble act of preserving my life—you are repaid with the insult of being trapped in a body that is not your own, a vessel you never asked to be permanently poured into, leaving your own body forever inhabited by one who is not you."

The great stag held up one hand of the former Prime Minister to stop the King from having doubts. "Your Highness," the stag replied from the mouth of the former Prime Minister. "I had no complaints as a stag, and I regret nothing about my former life. I was not seeking to amend or alter any aspect of my life as a stag. But momentous events so often occur without warning or summoning or readily apparent reason. I have now been given the gift of human speech, and I now possess the gift of being permitted the extraordinary opportunity of getting to experience life in another form, one which I find intriguing and exhilarating and desirable. Yes, it is hard to get used to walking on only two legs. But all change requires acclimation, and even the challenging process of acclimation is exciting and enriching. I am pleased and happy with my sudden new life, and far from harboring any resentment or recrimination toward the individuals or circumstances which have set me on this new path, rather I am filled only with thankful appreciation for whoever and whatever ultimately has been responsible for where I now quite happily find myself.

"And it pleases me immensely to see how my previous body has been transformed externally with its magnificent enhancement of glorious wings, as well as internally by the identity of Cervolatto, both in his persona and as well with his re-naming of himself to suit his new being and new body. I could not be content here in my own new body if I believed Cervolatto was unhappy with his new situation. However, seeing him so exultant and happy, I am gratified not only for his sake, but selfishly for my own sake as well, as it frees me to proceed with the living of my new life untroubled by any guilt or regret on Cervolatto's behalf.

"Likewise, I would be deeply troubled if the new young Tartaglia were to be distressed in any way at my continued presence. However, since he has so graciously and articulately expressed that it will not be of concern for him, it therefore will not be of concern for me, and I am grateful to him for freeing me from that burden."

King Theramo nodded. "It is not only from the debt of gratitude I owe you," the King proceeded, "but as well because of precisely the kind of noble thought and deeply wise consideration you possess—which even just now you demonstrated in all aspects of your response—that I would like to offer to you a role of authority and significance in the hierarchy of the kingdom. I propose to create a new position, the Minister of Greater Goodness, and to appoint you take on the charge of its function and responsibility—to set the highest moral and ethical and behavioral standards for the kingdom, standards we all should emulate and aspire to live up to. If you are willing...?"

The head of the former Prime Minister nodded in assent as the great stag smiled widely with the former Prime Minister's mouth. "I choose to humbly and formally accept your generous offer," he said with the voice of the former Prime Minister. "And like Cervolatto, I should like to establish via a new name the right identity for my current new self. I have not given it sufficient thought to yet determine a name which suits me. However, for the nonce you may refer to me as Minister Great-Stag, until such time as I am able to understand who I now am enough to successfully formulate and chose for myself a new name that most ideally fits the new me."

King Theramo smiled. "All aspects of your answer give me great gladness, Minister Great-Stag," he replied happily. "I am delighted and honored that you willingly accept the position and its charge, and I am elated at the prospect of the benefits we all will enjoy as a result of your presence and influence."

"Thank you, Your Highness," replied Minister Great-Stag. "I recognize that with hard work and dedication, one can often achieve sought objectives. However, if a gift is handed to you by good luck, you must then apply hard work and dedication to preserve and maintain the great gift you have been given. I vow to commit the very best hard work and dedication to my new responsibilities. And depending upon the magnitude of authority Your Majesty chooses to bestow upon the new position, I would seek Your Highness's approval and authorization for two new proposed policy changes. The first is to abolish and end for all time the peculiar and barbaric ritualistic practice of The Hunt. Lord Mirino and his huntsmen would be given the task of employing their extensive knowledge of wildlife and wilderness to protect and preserve the animals whom they heretofore have been so proficiently expert at killing."

King Theramo nodded in agreement and empathy. "Minister Great-Stag. Having been in your shoes…er…your former shoes… er…your former hooves, I know all too well that being hunted for sport or food is no picnic. You have my assurance that what you propose will become law by decree. Never again shall there be a Royal Hunt."

"Thank you, Your Highness," replied Minister Great-Stag. "The second proposal is to amend the Royal Trophy Hall. The animal heads currently and grotesquely mounted and displayed will be removed. The trophy heads of all killed animals will be taken down from there, and from anywhere they may now hang upon the palace walls. All trophy heads will then be given proper funerals, and all will be reverently buried with respectful solemnity. Upon the walls in their place will be installed art— tapestries, paintings, and sculpture representing, depicting, honoring, and informing about animals, celebrating the glory and goodness of animals, accentuating their rights as living creatures, and emphasizing their greater value to all when left alone to exist in Nature, peacefully and unaccosted by people, free to live their natural lives in their own habitat without being hunted or mistreated or unappreciated. This of course will necessarily be accompanied by a formal declaration of commitment to preserving the habitat wherein any manner of wildlife makes its home within the bounds of the kingdom."

King Theramo smiled with pride and approval. "You are as politically agile and fleet-of-foot on two feet as your body once was on four, Minister Great-Stag," the King said with admiration. "Your kindness and decency and civility are precisely why I envisioned the new position, with you as its standard-bearer. I applaud your two policy changes, and I hereby bestow upon you whatever authority is required to implement both immediately."

Minister Great-Stag beamed. "Thank you, Your Majesty. I can see it is going to be a great pleasure for me to serve in my new position at the pleasure of the King."

"Verily!" the King agreed with cheerful high spirit.

King Theramo now made his way toward Cervolatto. As he passed closely by Angiolina, without his forward progress ever pausing or slowing, their hands found each other and momentarily clasped tightly in adamant affection, trying to extract and savor an hour's worth of contact from an instant of touch, and then reluctantly relinquished their hold as the King's striding momentum carried him past and on toward the large ornate ceremonial gilded litter.

Cervolatto still sat like a picturesque statue on his haunches, wings folded with compact elegant neatness against his flanks, his majestic array of antlers towering skyward, his noble head aimed downward as he conversed in casual affability with Sir Italo who was standing before him.

"And so, Sir Italo," Cervolatto was saying. "Shall we agree to a ride, then? On the morrow? After the wedding?"

"Yes, Cervolatto," said Sir Italo firmly. "If the offer still stands."

"It does indeed," Cervolatto confirmed happily. "I look forward to it."

"As do I," replied Sir Italo with excited anticipation.

"Cervolatto. Sir Italo," King Theramo began as he arrived at the site of the litter.

"Your Royal Highness," said Sir Italo, bowing respectfully.

"Your Majesty," said Cervolatto with respectful courtesy.

"Please forgive my interruption," the King proceeded. "Firstly, Sir Italo I would like to formally congratulate you on your ascent to knighthood."

"Your Highness is extremely kind," replied Sir Italo. "I am honored by your good wishes, Sire, as I am honored to be a knight of your realm, and a knight of our glorious kingdom."

"I am proud of you, Sir Italo," said King Theramo.

"Thank you, Your Royal Highness," said Sir Italo, bowing again.

The King then turned toward Cervolatto.

"Cervolatto," King Theramo began. "I would like to extend an invitation. I wish to make you an offer of residency. Would you like to make your new permanent home here in the palace?

There is a southeast courtyard near the Vitaian Gate. It is open to the sky, sheltered and protected along the perimeter, it enjoys lovely sunlight in the mornings, and a clear view after dark of the night sky. If you choose to live there, it can be modified to function more suitably as a dwelling for you. You could come and go to and from the castle as you please by air, or on foot…er… on hoof by way of the skybridge of the Hanging Gardens, and in and out of the central palace by way of a courtyard archway passage."

Cervolatto dipped his great head further downward in a gesture of respectful assent. "Yes, Your Majesty," he replied. "It would well behoove me to accept your gracious offer, and so I do. I believe I would enjoy that very much, and I thank you for your thoughtful generosity. I have a single request, if it please Your Majesty. If you would be so kind, please have this gilded litter moved this eve to my new dwelling area. I have become rather fond of it. It makes an outstanding launch and landing platform. And the sight from the air of its golden surface reflecting the moonlight will be a pleasant and welcoming familiar beacon to my first landing at the site of my new home in my new life."

King Theramo smiled and nodded. "Of course. I shall order arrangements to ready your new dwelling post haste, and I shall ensure that priority is given to expediting your gilded litter there directly. I… I assume you do not wish to be carried on it as it is transported thither…?"

"No indeed," agreed Cervolatto cheerily. "I intend to now go for another flight. Flying is the most extraordinary sensation. I thought existing in the body of the stag was the most exhilarating sensation I had ever experienced, until I felt my new wings lifting me up into the air. I love flying!"

"Cervolatto," King Theramo went on. "Tartaglia has expressed a grave concern…"

"Is he afraid I'm going to fall asleep?" asked Cervolatto. "Because if that's what he's worried about, you can just tell him I ONLY SLEEP WHEN I FEEL LIKE IT."

King Theramo shook his head quickly. "No, no, Cervolatto. Rest assured, no one believes your sleeping habits are anything other than your own explicit deliberate choice."

"Yes," said Cervolatto. "That's right. It's about time people finally figured that out. It's a very strange social shortcoming for people to randomly accuse someone of having been asleep."

King Theramo nodded. "I am in complete agreement," he said resolutely. "However, the Prime Minister does have a valid deeply-felt worry. He is concerned you might be understandably bitter that your former body is now young, and you do not get to enjoy the benefits of the transformation."

"Well," replied Cervolatto. "That is very thoughtful of him. Please assure him he should now let that worry leave his mind forever. I am beyond happy with this body that is now mine, this new life that is a continuation of my past life. I never want to go through my youth again. It was lovely and wonderful, but it is in my past, and there is where it belongs. That body is who I once was. This body is who I now am. With all my heart and with every fiber of my soul I desire to proceed with my life upward and forward in this body which I now celebrate and cherish as my own. I have been given the rarest of gifts, the opportunity to start over while still being myself."

King Theramo was smiling. "That is quite wonderful to know, Cervolatto. So many of us here this eve feel blessed by the new paths we now find ourselves on. It is a gift. And all our gifts are made more dear if you too feel that you have only benefitted."

"I do," confirmed Cervolatto. "Should I be concerned the great stag might be upset with how things have turned out? This magnificent body which formerly was his is young and strong, with a whole full life ahead of it, only now it has wings. And quite fabulous wings, I might add. Does the great stag wish it were him instead of me?"

King Theramo shook his head. "As you have instructed me to advise Tartaglia, I shall advise you. Let that thought go from your mind forever. Minister Great-Stag is as joyfully happy and content in his new body as you are in yours."

"That is uplifting information, Your Majesty," said Cervolatto. "So uplifting, that I intend to now take off on my next flight. To go from having every slightest motion an ordeal of effort in an elderly body, to having every muscle restlessly eager to be exercised to its fullest strength and capacity is a sensation that fills me with such happy excitement, I cannot resist—and have no interest in resisting—the impatient urge to go, to move, to use the power and flexibility of my body. To fly. To fly! You will all forgive me, I hope, Your Majesty, if I do not stay to socialize and celebrate with everyone. I've always been a bit of a loner, and to be honest I've always preferred it that way. Which is not to say I'm not capable of being social, because I am. I'm fairly good at listening, and I'm exceptionally good at talking. I can talk at great length when given the opportunity. And I do like people. I just prefer to not have to always be around them. I wish good luck to one and all, and my thanks to the enchanter and the witch, without whose intervening actions I most certainly would still be a happy hermit with but a short path of life left to travel before me. Now my path is the limitless sky. I am happy and grateful. And now, I must fly...!"

Cervolatto stood from sitting, unfolding his massive wings from his sides and stretching them open. With a single powerful flex, they lifted him airborne as first his front legs and then his hind legs left the surface of the litter. He rose into the air, again lumbering with surprisingly graceful motion, upward and away toward the lofty height of the top of the gardens' courtyard piazza. Silhouetted against the perfectly round radiance of the moon, he appeared smaller and smaller as he ascended and cleared the height of the uppermost limit of the gardens' boundary walls.

With heads tilted back, everyone in the gardens had once again paused to look up in fascinated awe at Cervolatto's ascent, and they now watched a few moments longer as the high-above slow majestic movement of his wide wings carried him out of sight and off into the nighttime.

Chapter 35

The Amends
and
The Elucidations

When Nicoletta had declared her unequivocal love for him, Tartaglia had transformed and his enchantment of evil had been dispelled. With the evaporation of his evil—and with the enchanter's subsequent grasp of The Prophecy by the hand of Parrotina—the fog had lifted, and in its place had arrived the smell of evening springtime, warm and sweet and exciting, and full of promise and romance and possibility. In the absence of fog, the gardens had brightened. The light of the rising full moon bathed the courtyard piazza in beneficent white radiance, and the yellow-red-orange flickerings of the sentry pole-torches had become crisply vivid, casting their tightly-dancing illumination reassuringly across the growth and foliate complexity of the vast space.

And now the sounds of natural-life-in-progress were returning to the gardens. Aurally layered onto the simple trickling and gradual flow of tumbling water spilling its way gently down the tiers of the fountain, the staccato trilling of crickets and the soothing continual quietly clattering racket of cicadas pervaded the ambient air, joined by conversant rhythmic ribbits of frogs from water features deeply recessed in the farthest corners of the elaborately landscaped expansiveness of the gardens.

With Nicoletta at his side, Tartaglia now made his way to where Claricé and Leandro were standing together. Even though the new young Tartaglia outwardly appeared to be an utterly different person, out of too-long accustomed habit Claricé with reflexive apprehension hastily let go of Leandro's hand which she had been holding as her brother approached.

"Please..." Tartaglia began. "My sister. Do not relinquish your loving hold of good Leandro. I am writhing inside to see how my mistreatment of you has affected your freedom to be yourself. Claricé. My sister. I understand if you can never forgive me... But still I beg of you... Forgive me my egregious failings... If you can find it within your heart..."

"Oh... My dear brother..." Claricé struggled to speak, filled with emotion.

"Claricé, my beloved sister..." Tartaglia managed to continue. "You are, and for much time have been, old enough and utterly entitled to make decisions for yourself, to decide the path of your own life. I neither deserve nor desire control over your life, and it is an outrage—of which I am deeply ashamed—that I ever presumed to do so. I can never forgive myself..."

"Oh, Tartaglia..." said Claricé, taking hold of her brother's hand, her eyes filling with tears.

"Leandro..." Tartaglia went on. "Good Leandro... I beseech you... Both of you... Stay your hearts no longer on account of the evil I once embodied. I suffer too many bitter regrets at recollections of who and what I had become... Most acutely stinging is how much of your lifetimes I have robbed you of by keeping you apart.

Please… I entreat you… Be together as your hearts desire… Good Leandro, be with your beloved Clarìcé, with my blessing, with my deepest sorrow for having ever sought to keep the two of you apart…"

Tartaglia and Clarìcé embraced with tearful reconciliation, and then Tartaglia and Leandro shook hands with mutual forgiveness and mutual new respect.

Clarìcé and Nicoletta embraced each other, and Clarìcé whispered into Nicoletta's ear. "We have been given miracles…" she breathed softly.

"Oh, Clarìcé…" Nicoletta said quietly into Clarìcé's ear. "My sister has come home. My beloved Tartaglia loves me at last… I could never have dreamt of such happiness… We are so lucky…"

"We are so lucky…" Clarìcé whispered back, nodding her head against Nicoletta's.

Giddy still-incredulous relief was spreading among the current populace of the gardens. Emotions were releasing themselves and flowing free. Bodies were beginning to drift closer together, and rich soothing waves of impassioned voices now rose and fell as everyone was talking at once.

Truffaldino and Smeraldina came over to the group gathered around Tartaglia, and Smeraldina joined the embrace of Nicoletta and Clarìcé. Moments later, Angiolina had joined them.

"Lady Angiolina…" Tartaglia began. "I… I am so ashamed…"

Angiolina turned for a moment from her friends and took Tartaglia's hand, clasping it tightly with both of hers. "Prime Minister Tartaglia," she said. "Just look at how happy you have made Nicoletta. Just look at how happy you have made your sister Clarìcé. Just think how overjoyed Theramo is to have his greatest true friend back in his life. All darkness now is behind us. You are a decent and greatly good person, Tartaglia. The witch's spell did not tap into any inherent evil of yours. You had no evil at all, only what she forced into you. All evil came from her spell. And now you are free. You are once again who you once were."

"I am better than I once was, Lady Angiolina," replied Tartaglia, nodding in appreciative gratitude. "And I shall yet be an even better person…"

Nicoletta wrapped her arms in loving affection around Tartaglia.

Near the marble walkway, King Theramo had been speaking with some of the guards, several of whom had nodded and bowed and left the gardens, while several others had nodded and bowed and proceeded to the gilded litter, which they hefted and raised to their shoulders before marching it back the way it had come, out of the gardens and presumably on its way to the dwelling site of Cervolatto's new home in the southeast courtyard by the Vitaian Gate.

The remaining guards were at ease and seeming relaxed, though by the looks on their faces they apparently still were working in their minds to process all they had witnessed. Apart from the King, everyone else had ended up gathered together around young Tartaglia near the center of the flattened-grass, between where Cervolatto's litter had been and the still-growing Privacy Garden. Everyone except for Cagliostro—who seemed manifestly averse to being without a task and amidst a crowd, even a small one—and

Parrotina who, far from leaving his side, seemed only delighted at the opportunity to be at least somewhat alone together with her enchanter.

King Theramo made his way back across the flattened-grass toward the group. As he approached, his gaze found the gaze of Angiolina, and he nodded affirmatively at her, smiling.

Angiolina returned his nod with an even larger happy smile, and she mouthed the words 'thank you' to him across the flattened-grass.

"Brother," Claricé was saying admiringly to Tartaglia. "What a lovely new outfit. You look quite dashing."

Tartaglia nodded appreciatively. "The enchanter has good taste in clothing," he agreed.

"He certainly is an enigmatic and charismatic individual," observed Smeraldina. "Parrotina is going to have her hands full with that relationship…!"

Angiolina nodded at Smeraldina. "It seems even an enchanter isn't immune to falling in love," she said.

"Are you sure?" asked Claricé.

"Have you seen his eyes when he looks at her?" replied Smeraldina, flipping her shining red hair over one shoulder. "He's in love alright…!"

"Well," said Pantalòne. "Either way, that is indeed a smart new outfit, Prime Minister."

"Thank you, Chancellor," said Tartaglia with respectful appreciation.

King Theramo came over to Angiolina, and they smiled excitedly at each other and eagerly clasped hands for a moment, before Angiolina forced herself to let go and moved to grab the hands of Smeraldina and Clarìcé.

"Come with me for a moment," she said conspiratorially, cajoling the two of them each away from Leandro and Truffaldino. "Nicoletta," she continued. "Would you mind terribly coming with us for just a few brief moments, for a girls-only chat?"

Nicoletta smiled, squeezed Tartaglia tightly, and then reluctantly let go of him to step aside with her friends.

"We have so much to talk about…!" Angiolina whispered to them in a thrilled quite voice once the four of them were out of earshot from the rest of the group. "So much has happened…!"

"Angiolina," whispered Smeraldina in kindred hushed excitement. "Can we invite Parrotina and Bèllabrèzza to our all-girls slumber party?"

Angiolina grinned and nodded enthusiastically. "Of course!" she whispered eagerly.

"How wonderful!" whispered Clarìcé excitedly.

"If they want to come…" Angiolina added hopefully. "But listen," she went on, still speaking softly. "I think we should postpone our sleepover to tomorrow night. Tonight, I think we may all want to spend some time alone with… Well, I asked Theramo if everyone can spend the night here in the palace, in the Royal guest suites. And he has agreed!"

"Oh, Angiolina!" Smeraldina exclaimed, barely able to keep her voice volume low and grabbing Angiolina's hand in excitement. "Angiolina, you're amazing! Thank you!!"

"Thank you, Angiolina!" whispered Clarìcé happily, also

grabbing Angiolina eagerly and gratefully by the hand. "Thank you!!"

Nicoletta smiled radiantly and wrapped a hand in grateful appreciation around one of Angiolina's arms.

"But Angiolina," Claricé whispered. "Shouldn't tomorrow night be your honeymoon…?"

Angiolina smiled slyly. "I think," she whispered, "we're going to have our honeymoon tonight…!"

Claricé put her hand to her mouth in shocked delight.

Nicoletta smiled wider and squeezed Angiolina's arm more tightly with happy excitement.

Smeraldina grinned approvingly. "These past two days have been such a lot to deal with," she whispered. "I think we're all entitled to have desert before dinner!"

"But just remember," whispered Angiolina. "We all still have a wedding to attend first thing in the morning…!"

The four friends pulled themselves close in to each other for a moment and put their heads together, laughing and giggling in mischievous joyous alliance.

Back at the gathering, Avogadro was gazing up at the night sky high overhead.

"Behold," he reported with mystical significance, raising one open-palmed hand and extending it toward the heavens. "From our perspective, we are observing above us the moon fully illuminated. Moments ago, its waxing ceased. And moments from now its waning will commence. For this one present instant, we enjoy the sight of a full moon. This month has not ended. Yet at the start of this month, those gazing skyward would have seen then also a full moon. As the second such lunar phase within the same calendrical month, the glorious heavenly display now in its fullest splendor amid the celestial tapestry high above our heads is therefore a blue moon. You will notice its light is white. Blue is not its color. Blue is given to its name to signify its rarity. It is a good omen. We should be duly and humbly thankful."

With heads once again tilted back, the populace of the gardens paused to take in the full-orbed luminous beauty of the soundless faraway spectacle.

Moments later, King Theramo made his announcement.

"Arrangements have now been made," the King declared happily. "Please consider this a formal invitation. The castle has more than enough Royal guest suites to accommodate everyone, and you are all welcome to overnight in the palace as guests of the Crown. After all, we are all going to be attending the same wedding on the morrow…!"

"That is exceedingly gracious and generous, Your Highness," said Lord Pantalòné. "Thank you."

"How exciting!" said Smeraldina with coy exhilaration and re-wrapping her arms around Truffaldino as the four young ladies returned to the gathered group. "All of us spending the night together in the palace!"

"Thank you, Your Majesty!" said Clarìcé enthusiastically, taking hold of Leandro's hand, and unable to resist—for the most fleeting of moments—the indecorous impulse to reach up and run an affectionate finger through the single long curl of Leandro's ink-black hair, half coiled across his forehead, uncontained by his guardsman's helmet.

Nicoletta was still smiling as she returned closely to Tartaglia's side and took hold of one of his arms with both her hands.

Angiolina stood next to Nicoletta and appeared to be doing her best to practice the tricky art of queenly restraint by not immediately rushing to her King's side while he was in the midst of a public address.

"In the meantime," King Theramo went on, "I have sent instructions to the Master of the Kitchen. Food-and-drink refreshment is on its way to us here in the gardens. So if you all can endure a few minutes longer with mere conversation to sustain you, more substantive sustenance will rescue us all from hunger and thirst in but a very short while from now."

Further heartfelt thanks were respectfully offered, and with the prospect of luxurious accommodations awaiting invitingly whenever the urge for bed might manifest, and with the knowledge that refreshment fit for a King would arrive any minute, the social atmosphere of the gardens shifted to something much more palpably informal and relaxed and festive. With the warmth of a rising tide of voices, everyone resumed talking to each other with the social enthusiasm and gregarious animation that comes with shared experience and communal exhilaration.

"Cagliostro," said King Theramo as he stepped over to the enchanter. "If young Parrotina would forgive me, I would ask to have few words of discussion with you."

Cagliostro nodded. "Of course, Your Majesty," he said politely.

"Thank you, Your Majesty," said Parrotina, "for your wonderful invitation. It is such a lovely gesture. Such a lovely gesture."

"It is truly my pleasure," replied King Theramo. "It is truly my pleasure."

In the reassuring luminance of the sentry pole-torches and the blue moon, the King and the enchanter walked together across the lush grass of the gardens until they were sufficiently separated from the cheery talkative mingling of the others.

King Theramo took from the pockets of his robes the rivet spectacles and the Bi-Scepter and handed them to Cagliostro.

"I…" the King struggled to begin. "I will never be able to thank you enough for helping me…"

Cagliostro took from the King's hands the two magical objects and put them away somewhere within the folds of his own robes.

"What someone wants reveals who they truly are," said the enchanter. "I helped you because of what you wanted. You wanted someone who loved you. That mattered more to you than all else. And you wanted someone who loved you so that you could be a good king. Those aspirations are noble and laudable and rare. That is why I chose to help you.

"And consider what you did with the power you were given. You did not want the most beautiful. Had you been looking for beauty, you would have looked no further than Nicoletta, who would have made an exquisite queen, one who was fair and decent and wise and good. You did not want the most attractive. Had you been looking for attractiveness and allure, you would have looked no further than Smeraldina, who would have been the most appealing queen in the history of the kingdom, one who was fair and decent and wise and good. Had you been looking for devoted goodness, you would have looked no further than Claricé, who would have made a strong and dedicated queen, one who was fair and decent and wise and good. But those are not the qualities which spurred your search. You wanted the one person who was right for you. That was who you desired to find."

"I wanted someone who loved me," said the King. "And I wanted someone I truly loved. And I wanted to know the Truth. I needed to know for sure that if she said she loved me, that she genuinely did love me. And you gave me what I needed most—the power to find that person."

"With respect, Your Majesty," said Cagliostro. "It was your desire to find that person which made the difference. Had you not gone to such lengths to find a love that was true, you would never have given to the one person who loves you beyond all others the freedom and the opportunity to declare to you her love."

King Theramo nodded thoughtfully. For a moment, from habit his hand started to reach up to adjust his crown, but it somehow needed no adjusting.

"Why did you send me the parrot?" asked the King.

"I apologize for that," said Cagliostro. "I was curious. I had confidence in you, but I wanted to see how you would succeed. And I confess, I wanted to know if at some point along the way you would be perilously in need of further help. I would not have intervened. And indeed, in your most dire moments, I did not intervene. But I wanted to learn if my judgement with your situation was sound.

It is important to me to learn from what fails, and learn from what succeeds. I affect the lives of many, and the responsibility I have is too significant for me to ever cease from continually learning how to become better at what I do."

"You are very good at what you do," said the King.

"I thank you for those generous words, Your Majesty," said the enchanter. "However, like everyone else, I ultimately succeed or fail by luck. I try to learn how best to put myself on a path where Good Luck will have an opportunity to find me."

King Theramo nodded. "Because of you, Good Luck found me," he said. The King glanced for a moment in the direction of Parrotina, and looked back at Cagliostro. "Perhaps," King Theramo added, "Good Luck has found you as well."

"Perhaps..." the enchanter replied vaguely.

They turned to make their way back to the group gathered on the flattened-grass, and Cagliostro paused for a moment.

"Your Majesty," the enchanter said. "Yesterday you paid a high compliment to Truffaldino and asked me to convey to him your gracious sentiment."

King Theramo nodded and smiled, remembering. "That seems like so many years ago..." the King said thoughtfully.

"Indeed," agreed Cagliostro. "I have not yet shared your thoughts with Truffaldino, but I will do so, as I promised. I look forward to enjoying with him that conversation. And I now would make of Your Majesty a request, one which is only distantly similar in nature. If you would be so kind, please convey at an opportune discreet moment to Minister Great-Stag my gratitude for his alert and swift chivalrous action regarding his cloak. It… It was a gesture for which I am very much appreciative."

King Theramo smiled. "Cagliostro," he replied. "It is not my place to say, however I will speak it nevertheless. If you love her even only one one-hundredth the magnitude of the love she so clearly has for you, you two are both as blessed and lucky as any of the blissful pairs of people present in these gardens this night who have been brought together in ecstatic happiness, either directly or indirectly by the work of your hand. Yield, Cagliostro. You are permitted to be happy. She is permitted to be happy. You both are entitled to live happily ever after. And yes," the King added as an afterthought. "I of course will at an appropriate moment convey to Minister Great-Stag your sentiments of appreciation. You might, as a manner of thanks, consider orchestrating for him an opportunity to…er…to have plausible cause for meeting and speaking with Fatta Morganna."

"It has become a veritable epidemic, Your Majesty…" observed Cagliostro.

King Theramo smiled. "I can think of worse widespread occurrences," he said. "And I cannot think of any sudden rampant happening which would be preferable."

"I will not disagree with you," Cagliostro replied vaguely as the two of them resumed walking back.

Chapter 36

The Envoys
and
The Avocations

Ahead of the King and the enchanter at the gathering on the flattened-grass, Angiolina had ushered Parrotina into the assembled group, leading her with welcoming friendliness by the hand and formally introducing her to everyone present.

"And," Angiolina was saying to her. "There is to be a special evening event, tomorrow night after the wedding. We're having an all-girls sleepover. Claricé and Smeraldina and your sister and me. Parrotina, we were hoping you might want to come, too. If you would like to join us, we would very much enjoy having you be with us."

"Even though it is only for close friends?" asked Parrotina.

"Parrotina," said Angiolina warmly. "You would be there with your sister Nicoletta. But more importantly, we would like you to *become* one of our close friends. And this seems like a fun and perfect way for us to all get to know one another better!"

Parrotina smiled and nodded. "Nicoletta is so lucky to have such friends," she said with quiet enthusiasm. "Thank you, Angiolina. How kind of you to want to include me. Yes, I would very much enjoy being there with all of you. Thank you. Thank you."

"Wonderful!" exclaimed Angiolina. "Wonderful! And we're

hoping Bèllabrèzza will come, as well. We just need to figure out a way to let her know she's invited."

"You would like Bèllabrèzza," Truffaldino said to Nicoletta. "She's like you. She's beautiful on the inside. She helps people, and she makes everything better."

Nicoletta smiled. "Thank you, Truffaldino," she said quietly. "If you like her, then I'm sure I will like her, too."

"I thought of you when I met her," said Truffaldino. "She helped me, even though she didn't know me. Like you did. You're a really good friend, Nicoletta. Smeraldina's the love of my life, but you're my best friend in Benebento. I always think about how you helped me. It made a permanent impression on me."

Nicoletta nodded fondly at him. "You've made a permanent impression on *me*, Truffaldino," she said with quiet ardent gladness. "Our friendship makes me happy."

"If a message of invitation needs to be conveyed to Bèllabrèzza," said Cagliostro, as he and the King arrived at the group, "perhaps Sir Italo would be willing to act as messenger."

Sir Italo looked suddenly flustered. "I… I would of course carry out to the best of my ability any duty His Majesty the King directed me to undertake…"

Cagliostro looked for a moment toward the new garden he had by enchantment and good-will cultivated. It had grown and was thriving. Its ongoing enlargement was not serving to confine or trap the two occupants it enveloped, but rather was simply and thoroughly and successfully providing them the intended privacy of its purpose. The only outward indication of the unseen mother and daughter reunion and re-acquaintance taking place was the very continued growth of the garden itself, expanding to the proportions of a grove as if were becoming a kind of living floral manifestation of the new familial love blossoming within and the vernal growth of their new lives. There was an aura of permanence about it, as though even after whenever the mother and daughter currently inside the lush enclosure chose to leave its flourishing midst, the grove garden itself would afterward remain as a newly enduring feature of the Palace Gardens.

"Would it be acceptable," the King asked the enchanter, "to dispatch an envoy into the Privacy Grove Garden at this time?"

Cagliostro nodded. "I believe such a mission would not constitute an unwelcome intrusion. Both mother and daughter as yet remain. However, with her powers restored, Fatta Morganna easily possesses the ability to—in the span of an instant—relocate them both to another place, and it may thus be expedient for Sir Italo to proceed directly."

King Theramo looked at the newly knighted knight. "Sir Italo," he said. "Might you employ your resourcefulness and reliability to immediately locate the young lady and convey this invitation to her? Would you be willing to proceed as emissary post haste?"

"Yes, Your Majesty," said Sir Italo, dutifully doing his best to conceal keen enthusiasm and bowing respectfully.

"If I might suggest, Your Majesty," the enchanter went on. "Perhaps Minister Great-Stag would be willing to go along as well. The Minister could, if necessary, engage Fatta Morganna in courteous dialogue as Sir Italo formally conveys the message of invitation to her daughter. The prestige of the Minister's presence would perhaps well-complement the gallant chivalry of Sir Italo, as the two act in concert as respectful ambassadors of the Crown."

"Minister Great-Stag," inquired King Theramo. "Would you be amenable to participating in such an embassy?"

Minister Great-Stag cast a fleeting glance of appreciative acknowledgement at the enchanter before turning his focus back to the King. "Yes, Your Majesty," replied the Minister, nodding in respectful assent. "It is my humble honor to serve at the pleasure of the King. Ought we," he added, "extend, as well, wedding-ceremony invitations to both mother and daughter?"

"Historically," Avogadro interjected with sagacious gravity, "it has proven ill-advised to not invite to a wedding a witch with connections to the parties involved."

"The wise man speaks the truth," pronounced Cagliostro. "In addition to the invitation conveyed by Sir Italo to the witch's daughter for the ladies' event on the morrow-night, it is well-advised and appropriately courteous that invitations from the Crown to the morrow's wedding ceremonies be proffered to both mother and daughter by Minister Great-Stag in his role as ambassador. Your Majesty need not harbor any concerns about the witch's attendance—she will choose to not attend. However, it would indeed be imprudent not to extend to her the invitation."

"Very well," King Theramo said with decisive accord. "Just when I thought this day could deliver no further gifts of great goodness, I have here received uniquely judicious counsel from an array of wise minds to make any monarch acutely envious. I am deeply grateful to you all for your vital guidance."

As he was leaving, Minister Great-Stag turned to the enchanter. "Thank you, Lord Cagliostro," he said. "A gracious exchange of courtesies indeed. A return gesture of parity was neither expected nor needed, but it is greatly appreciated nonetheless."

Cagliostro nodded in silent affable acknowledgement.

Sir Italo and Minister Great-Stag thereupon proceeded together to the Privacy Grove Garden, and soon had disappeared from view into the lush fragrant density of its burgeoning floral splendor.

Cagliostro was again contemplatively studying the Privacy Grove Garden. From within its luxuriant oasean midst, a pair-tree was now growing, two arboreal stems entwined in a helix and rising together enwrapped as a single trunk. The upward-spiraling thriving two-fold tree had already risen high above the topmost floral limits of the grove, and like the subtle expansive growth of the grove itself, the growth-in-progress of the tree was nearly discernable.

The nascent double-sapling evidently was some kind of fruit tree. Amidst its verdant foliage and colorful-petaled blossoms could now be seen drupes of appealing enigmatic fruit, appearing as healthy and vital and ripe and succulent as they were exceptional in form and color.

"That is a species I recognize," said Cagliostro thoughtfully. "It is an ensorcellment tree. It thrives off of proximate magical energy the way other trees thrive from water and soil nutrients and sunlight. There may be some peripheral effect from my current presence here, but what is occurring there at this moment is the result of far more than whatever my influence might be, even when combined with the considerable dynamic-core reservoir of Fatta Morganna's restored powers. I would venture to presume there is a strong likelihood that Bèllabrèzza is a witch.

"It is probable the father, whoever he may have been and whatever may have become of him, did not possess any magical powers or abilities—which would account for Bèllabrèzza being unaware of powers she may possess, that have been hiding dormant and thus far unaccessed somewhere deep within her. I would not be surprised if any or all of this day's events and occurrences may now serve to awaken within Bèllabrèzza her latent powers and her awareness of their existence. It is fortuitous she now has a parent in her life and at her side—and indeed the very parent who is responsible for Bèllabrèzza possessing magic—who can support her through her transition and acclimation to the significant personal changes which will affect every aspect of her life from this point forward."

"That…" King Theramo struggled to express. "Cagliostro, that is truly extraordinary…"

Avogadro nodded, gazing in grateful awe at Parrotina. "May the blessed reunion of a long-lost daughter with her parent prove to be an extraordinary gift that shall smile upon them both," he said empathetically.

King Theramo turned for a moment to Parrotina.

"Parrotina," the King began. "I wish to give you great thanks for the words of encouragement you gave me at the clearing in the forest when my faith had failed. When we are on the verge of submitting to defeat and failure, there often is nothing to hold on to and nothing to help us pull ourselves back from the brink of the abyss. But you were there for me. You gave me the glimmer of forward-looking hope I needed to pull myself together, to refuse to submit, to refuse to give in, to refuse to accept defeat. Under the right circumstances, we are all capable of refusing to accept defeat. But too often, it is not the right circumstances. You rescued me. You helped me to summon the will to fight back. You showed me the way to recover. You saved me. You made me see that the only failure is acceptance of failure. You helped me to refuse to fail. You saved my life. You saved my future. You saved my world. I can never adequately repay you. I will be grateful to you forever."

Parrotina bowed with respect and humility before the King. "I am humbled and honored by your words, Your Highness," she said quietly.

"Parrotina," King Theramo went on, glancing momentarily at the enchanter. "Should the opportunity present itself, I would ask if you might move the mind of Cagliostro and persuade him to honor me and Angiolina with his—and of course your own—presence at our wedding."

Parrotina was a colorful picture of poise and aplomb. "Out of the greatest respect and reverence for Your Majesty," she replied, "I will in good faith attempt to sway the enchanter's mind on this matter. However, as I believe I am not alone in recognizing, Cagliostro's own unique reasoning underlies all his decisions, and that reasoning usually is as inscrutable as it is immovable. But for you, Your Highness, I will do my best. I will do my best."

The glint of a smile broke for an instant to Cagliostro's face before being sent back the way it came.

"Thank you," said King Theramo, nodding cheerily with understanding and approving admiration of her finesse. "Thank you, Parrotina. I fully grasp what you have so artfully articulated, and I appreciate all of its import."

"Your Majesty," said Leandro, bowing slightly with full respectful courtesy. "With so much that has occurred, and with so much sudden change affecting so many aspects of the palace, is there anything of singular immediacy Your Majesty needs attended to?"

King Theramo gazed with fondness and appreciation at his most trusted palace guard. "No, good Leandro," he said warmly. "The remainder of this evening is for enjoyment and appreciation, to be with those we love, to celebrate the miraculous gifts we have been given. The work of the day is ended. Not only is it permissible once-in-a-while to exhale and unwind after an ordeal, it is in fact properly respectful to Providence to acknowledge a miraculous gift by pausing to celebrate what has occurred, and to celebrate the joy of life itself."

Leandro glanced sideways for a moment and stole a shared loving glance with Claricé before formally responding to his King.

"Fully understood, Your Majesty," Leandro said with respectful courtesy and grateful appreciation. "Thank you, Your Majesty."

As the gathering once again began to entropically rearrange itself into smaller conversational groups, Chancellor Pantalòné and Sir Balzanno stood together with Avogadro.

"Balzanno," said the Chancellor. "What would you say to some games of tabula-backgammon in the Royal Dining Hall? With trencher bread and ale?"

"To resume from the previous rounds?" asked Sir Balzanno.

"I should think not," replied Pantalòné. "A fresh round of games. A new competition."

"That," said the knight, "sounds a most enjoyable and consequence-free final chapter to these past two days of whirlwind tumult. I heartily accept your appealing offer."

"Excellent," said Lord Pantalòné. "Avogadro? Would you care to join us?"

The wise man put his hand to head and closed his eyes for a moment before opening them and answering. "Thank you for your social inclusivity," replied Avogadro. "But I already know who is going to win."

"Come along, Avogadro," chided Sir Balzanno. "The victory is simply the outcome. It is the playing of the game wherein the true enjoyment resides."

Lord Pantalòné nodded in accord. "Winning," the Chancellor said, "is what we strive for as we play. But it is not the objective. The point of the game is the playing."

The wise man again put his hand to his head for a moment before slowly nodding in agreement. "You both speak the truth," he acknowledged. "Wanting to know what happens impels us through the reading of a book, but it is the experiencing of the story and the telling which are the true enjoyment. Getting my daughter back was not the reward. Life proceeding, with her now back in it—that is the reward."

Sir Balzanno nodded. "We celebrate you having your family restored, Avogadro," the knight said earnestly.

Avogadro nodded. "I am at last and once again a happy man," he said. "Thank you for your kind sentiment."

"Then you will join us in gaming at the dining hall?" asked Lord Pantalòné. "Or, perhaps you wish to remain here in the gardens to festively socialize?"

"It is too long ago for me to remember," replied the wise man, "when last I was at work in my atelier sanctum with peace in my mind and undiluted joy in my heart. To have your family, and for that to be ordinary—that is a gift. Eventful can be exciting, but uneventful can be bliss. The lull that settles in the wake of excitement can be blessed euphoria, and featureless calm is most exhilarating when infused with anticipation of a greatly good excitement yet to come. I relish this sudden new peacefulness, wherein I can cast my mind forward in glad expectations of spending time with both my daughters together. And so, with the gifts of this day in my thoughts, I intend to proceed thither, to my sanctum, and enjoy my work in a way I have not enjoyed it for many heavy years."

"I respect your mind, Avogadro," said Pantalòné. "It is a wise man who knows what manner of celebration and thanksgiving truly suits his own soul."

Verily," agreed Sir Balzanno. "I wish for you, Avogadro, that the remainder of this day will bring you fulfillment of great goodness in your heart and mind."

Avogadro had once again closed his eyes and put one of his hands significantly to his own forehead. "I'm getting something…" the wise man announced, his brow furrowed with concentration. "Something that starts with a 'G'… And it's… Guests." Avogadro opened his eyes. "The wedding guests in the Royal Banquet Hall will soon be wending their way here to the Palace Gardens."

"Nothing about imminent food and beverage refreshment, eh?" suggested Sir Balzanno.

Avogadro nodded. "The one invasion shall follow in short order upon the other," he said. "The minions of the Master of the Kitchen will be arriving with their onslaught of culinary offerings to infiltrate rearward of the initial wave of wedding guests."

The wise man paused for a moment and placed his hand to his head again with mystical significance. "Did I mention the arrival of minstrels?" he asked.

"Then come now, before they all arrive," said Lord Pantalòné. "There is food and drink aplenty in the dining hall, and the sumptuous peace of far fewer fellow celebrants and far more traditional music fare. Walk together with us, Avogadro, even if only as far as the cypress grove, as all our paths flow in parallel at least as far as the inside of the castello."

And after briefly conveying the intentions of their plans to their daughters, the Chancellor and the knight and the wise man walked together, sharing their words and their company as they made their way across the flattened-grass toward the marble walkway and tall trees of the cypress grove.

Chapter 37

The Ends
and
The Beginnings

At the same time, Cagliostro was standing alone together with Truffaldino farther into the gardens just past the outer limit of the flattened-grass.

"Sir," Truffaldino was saying. "Is it wrong that I still find the wise man annoying?"

"Many people are annoying, Truffaldino," said Cagliostro.

Truffaldino sighed. "He is the father of Nicoletta and Parrotina, two people I like very much," he said disconcertedly.

"Life is not simple, Truffaldino," replied the enchanter.

"Master, I don't want to be apart from Smeraldina," said Truffaldino. "I love her with all my heart, and I hope to marry her. But I don't want to stop being your assistant. Ever. Master, nothing is more important to me than being your assistant. So, I don't know what to do…"

"Truffaldino," said Cagliostro. "You know it is your destiny to marry Smeraldina."

"Yes," said Truffaldino. "That's what you've always told me. And I even think if you hadn't told me, I might not ever have even recognized her when I saw her. You were right, Master. You're never wrong."

"Truffaldino," the enchanter said sternly. "Seeking to never be wrong is not an aspiration, it is an affliction. To never be wrong is an impossibility. To aim to never be wrong is a malady of a deeply misguided mind. To believe that you never are wrong is to sever yourself from reality and humanity. You have known me a long time. Longer than anyone. Truffaldino, I am often wrong. It is important to accept being wrong, and it is essential to never expect or even wish to never be wrong. Without mistakes, true learning is not possible."

"Then I must be a very good learner, Master," Truffaldino said glumly.

"Truffaldino. You *are* a good learner. Not just because of your mistakes. And in the same way that you must be able to learn from your mistakes, you must also not let yourself be weighed down by them."

"Master, is it your destiny to marry Parrotina?"

Cagliostro paused with long contemplative hesitation.

"I confess, Truffaldino," he said at last, "that I am utterly at sea about all things having to do with Parrotina. It is my job to always be able to see the entirety of a landscape. Yet I was never able to see Parrotina anywhere in either the past or the future, or even for years right in front of me…"

"Are you in love with her, Master?"

The enchanter did not seem unwilling to answer, as much as he appeared unable to answer.

"She's in love with you, Master," said Truffaldino.

Cagliostro nodded. "Yes, she is…" he said slowly. "I am

lucky beyond my ability to understand or describe. Thank you, Truffaldino…"

"Master," said Truffaldino with a burst of enthusiasm. "You have given me an idea. You and Parrotina will often want time to be alone together, and Smeraldina and I will often want time to be alone together. So, you and I could spend some of our time being apart from each other and being each with the love of our life, and then we could spend some of our time being together, with me being your assistant and helping you and learning from you. That is… If… If you still want me to be your assistant…"

Cagliostro smiled warmly. "Truffaldino," he said with firm emphatic adamance. "I will never want another assistant other than you. I think your idea makes excellent sense. I think that is exactly what we should do."

"That makes me very happy, Master." Truffaldino said, beaming. "Very very happy."

Truffaldino paused for moment, his face revealing a whirlwind of thoughts and feelings reeling in his heart and in his mind.

"Master…?" he said at last.

"Truffaldino?"

"A lot of happiness all at once can be overwhelming," said Truffaldino, awash in emotion.

Cagliostro nodded. "Until today," he said, "I have had no experience with having to manage that enviable problem. You and I will have to teach each other what we learn about how to deal with such moments of overpowering happiness."

"I like it when we work on things together, Master."

Cagliostro smiled. "Truffaldino," he said. "I made a promise to King Theramo that I would like to make good on now. He paid you a compliment, and I assured him that I would tell you what he said. When I told the King I would not be remaining in Benebento to assist him with the magical gifts, he was understanding and said he supposed that he must seem a bit like my assistant Truffaldino—promising me he would not in my absence get into any trouble. I told him, 'Your Majesty, you and Truffaldino have in common only one thing, and that is that I care very much about you both.' Whereupon King Theramo replied, 'That is a kind sentiment indeed. If you would be so good as to please convey to your assistant that I am honored to be in his company in this regard.' And I answered him saying, 'That is very gracious of Your Majesty. I will of course share your thoughts with Truffaldino. It will mean a great deal to him, I am sure.'"

Truffaldino beamed. "What the King said DOES mean a great deal to me, Master. What YOU said means even more to me. Thank you, Master."

"Few things are as important as family," said Cagliostro. "Truffaldino, I consider you and me to be family."

Truffaldino was smiling in exhilarated happiness. "That's how I feel, too, Master."

"And," the enchanter went on, "our family has suddenly become quite unexpectedly larger. We shall have to make some changes, and in light of your idea, I believe all those changes involve us spending a great deal of our lives now here in Benebento. Truffaldino, you and I have an unbreakable bond that connects us. And we now have yet another strand to that connection—Benebento now binds us all together. And Parrotina... Parrotina has much time she has missed away from her family. She will want to spend as much time as she can with her father and her sister. We will all of us henceforth necessarily be spending a great deal of time in Benebento."

"Nicoletta was my first friend in Benebento," said Truffaldino. "She's a really good friend. I will be happy if we are all together more. And maybe I'll even get to spend time with Bèllabrèzza. And mostly, being in Benebento means being with the love of my life Smeraldina. And best of all, now it also means you and me still being together as family. Master, this has been a very long day...! But it is ending very wonderfully!"

"Take a breath, Truffaldino," said Cagliostro. "The remainder of this night is yet ahead of us..."

Truffaldino smiled at Cagliostro. "Do you see what I mean, Master," he said enthusiastically. "You're never wrong!"

While this conversation was taking place, some distance away on the flattened-grass King Theramo and Angiolina were standing closely together and having a discussion of their own, and in a moment of unsuppressed relief and emotion, they had cast aside Royal decorum and thrown their arms passionately around each other.

"Oh, Angiolina..." King Theramo breathed in quiet desperation into her ear. "I thought I would never again hold you in my arms..."

"Oh, Theramo," Angiolina whispered back, near tears. "I... I'm so ashamed of how I could not put my arms around you when you were suffering so, when you most needed comfort… Yet I—your true love, and you my true love—even I could not bring myself to embrace you as you were. I was weak, and I am ashamed… True Love endures all, pushes through all difficulty… Yet I could not… I did not… How can I be worthy of your love, when the force of True Love was not sufficient inside me to do what true lovers do—be there for each other, no matter what, at all times, in any circumstance… Is that not what True Love is…? I am so ashamed…"

"No, my dearest beloved sweet Angiolina," he whispered into her ear, holding her more tightly. "Do not be ashamed. I love you as you are. You were, in that dark moment, not perfect. I do not desire you to be perfect. I desire you only to be yourself. I desire you as you are. I desire you very much. I do not need you to be pure, or to be breathtakingly beautiful. You are perfect to me. You are perfect for me…"

Angiolina nodded against the side of her King's head, but she was quietly crying into his shoulder. "Theramo…" she whispered. "I believe Nicoletta is an angel. She does not trap a person to their body. She loves Tartaglia for who he is on the inside. But I could not do that… You, my Theramo—your body needs to have you in it. I need to have you yourself in your body. For me, you in your own body is who you are. I would always love you, but I will now always give thanks that you are you in your own body where you belong, where you have always been ever since I first fell in love with you, where you were when you for the first time told me you loved me…"

"Oh, how I love you, Angiolina…" the King whispered.

"Theramo," she whispered, trying to collect herself. "I want to not ever again be a person who cannot embrace and give unconditional help to someone who needs aid and comforting because they are in some kind of troubled circumstance. No matter what that circumstance is. Who you really are emerges in an extraordinary circumstance or a crisis. I… I don't like the me who emerged when you needed me most, my dearest love… And I am determined to change that me to better match what I expect of myself, to become more of a better me, to become more of the real me that I believe is who I really am…"

"One cannot learn how to see in a single day," King Theramo whispered into her ear. "Even a single extraordinary miraculous day. In a single day, one cannot even learn to see how much one is unable to see. Angiolina, say you will love me, and you will be with me, for all the days—for that is how long it will take for me to truly become a better King, a better man, a better husband, one who is truly worthy of his throne and his humanity and his Queen…"

Angiolina nodded emphatically, holding herself closer to her true love. "I will love you, my Theramo," she whispered fervently. "And I will be by your side, and be blissfully in your arms for all the days, happily ever after…"

Some distance away, at the edge of the flattened-grass, Truffaldino was now standing alone together with Smeraldina who was holding tightly to his clothing, pulling herself closer to him and gazing with bright adoration up into his face.

"Truffaldino," she said giddily. "Are you excited that we will be overnighting together alone in our own suite?"

Truffaldino nodded, smiling. "We have not been alone together since we met," he said.

Smeraldina smiled back at him, her eyes sparkling. "Your eyes are lovely to look into, Truffaldino," she said.

"You have green eyes," said Truffaldino. "Like me. We have the same color eyes."

"That's because we have the same color dreams," explained Smeraldina.

Truffaldino nodded. "I've dreamt of you all my life, Smeraldina," he said. "But even in my dreams, I've never seen you. But I always knew I would recognize you."

"You smell good," said Smeraldina dreamily, pulling herself closer. "You smell clean and delicious."

"My master Cagliostro is very particular about good personal habits," said Truffaldino. "He always says that a clean body helps you to have… to have… oh, yes, I remember—a clean body helps you to have a sharp mind."

Smeraldina giggled happily. "You have a lovely mind, my funny and wonderful Truffaldino."

"Your breath smells good, Smeraldina," said Truffaldino. "I noticed it when we first met. It smells natural and clean and sweet. It's a smell I would like to keep inhaling forever."

A look of momentary pensiveness crossed Smeraldina's face.

"Truffaldino," she said. "Nicoletta has always loved Tartaglia. Even when he was in a different body, she still loved him. I could never be me in a different body. My body is too much a part of who I am. I could only ever really be truly me in my own body…"

Truffaldino nodded. "Nicoletta is unlike anyone," he said. "She's like an angel on earth."

"Truffaldino, do you still love me?"

Truffaldino smiled widely. "Smeraldina," he said. "From the moment we met I've been madly in love with you. That will never change. Except, I think I might love you even more now than I did yesterday. You're the love of my life, Smeraldina. I will always be madly in love with you."

"Madly passionately crazy in love with me?"

Truffaldino nodded happily. "Madly passionately crazy in love with you, Smeraldina."

"I don't understand it…" she said, putting her arms around his neck. "The more I'm around you, the more in love with you I am… Are you using magic on me?"

Truffaldino shook his head. "I have not advanced far enough along in my studies for my master to teach me any magic yet. And he himself would never use his powers for such a purpose. He is like King Theramo. The Truth is more important to him than anything else. And Smeraldina, even if I did have such a power, I would never use it. That's not what magic's for, and it's certainly not something I would ever want to use magic for. You and I didn't have to make each other fall in love with each other, Smeraldina. We fell in love with each other because we're meant for each other."

"Truffaldino, being in love with you *is* magic," she whispered into his ear.

At the same time, someplace beyond the flattened-grass, Cagliostro and Parrotina were now standing alone together, facing each other. Parrotina was not as tall as the enchanter, but she was tall enough that their faces were almost level with one another. She appeared to be making a semblance of effort to stand not too close, but her efforts were not being particularly successful.

"Parrotina…" Cagliostro was struggling to say. "I… I deeply regret having… Having used you to observe and listen from a distance to situations which I placed you in expressly for that purpose…"

Parrotina smiled up at him with adoration and unconcern.

"You must not fault yourself, Cagliostro," she said earnestly. "You thought I was a parrot."

"You *were* a parrot," said Cagliostro.

Parrotina giggled and leaned forward slightly. "Yes," she agreed. "I was. And I was delivered to you as a booby-trap, rigged against my will and against my knowledge as an engine of spying for the witch. A spell which you immediately recognized and disabled."

"I did not manage to recognize that you had been enchanted into being transformed…" said the enchanter.

"If you had," said Parrotina, "you would have transformed me back, and I would never have been able to spend all that time with you, getting to fall in love with you."

"That likely is true…" said Cagliostro hesitantly.

Parrotina smiled. "No, it's not. Of course it's not true. I fell in love with you the moment my eyes beheld you. Not because of how dashingly handsome and charismatic you are. And you are dashingly handsome and charismatic. But that is not why I fell in love with you in an instant. I fell in love with you because every part of me recognized you. We had never met or ever been together, and yet in the blink of an instant I recognized you. I knew right away who you were. You were the love of my life. You *are* the love of my life. It was not a choice. It simply was. I needed no time to realize it. But I did end up having years afterward to think about it.

"I do miss my wings now. And I'm going to terribly miss flying. But for all those years, I very much missed having hands. I'm so very glad to have hands again. And they're my hands. I'm me again. It makes me feel so happy and so alive. Like how being with you makes me feel."

"Parrotina," said the enchanter. "I am like Fatta Morganna. I am an island. I need no one, I want no one…"

Parrotina smiled. "You're a good enchanter, Cagliostro," she said. "But you're a terrible liar. You couldn't endure life without Truffaldino. He is more to you even than a son is to a father. Your love for that boy is so beautiful and so present, it's like a lovely aura in the air that I could run my fingers over."

"Parrotina, what I do…"

"I know what you do. You listen for the sound of people in trouble. You go to where you're needed. You help people. You change people's lives for the better. You bring about extraordinary change and you orchestrate it all so that it seems like you didn't do it. You arrange for people to feel as though they themselves are responsible for how much better their lives have become. I've been seeing you do it for years. I've even at times helped you."

"That particular truth troubles me profoundly," said Cagliostro, his face clouding with vexation and self-recrimination. "In future, when next a need arises where my vigilance is warranted or required, an utterly different means of surreptitious surveillance and observation—as yet unconceived or devised—shall be utilized instead of peering and listening through a living entity. That method I now recognize as being unseemly and abhorrent, and not in any way appropriate to the situation or to the invasion of privacy it constitutes upon the living entity unknowingly enlisted to be the conduit for such ill-gotten reconnaissance…"

"I was not unknowing," said Parrotina reassuringly. "I was fully aware, and I was happy to be helping you. My only unhappiness was that I was unable to tell you that I was in love with you. And that unhappiness has ended."

"Parrotina… I… I promise you, I will never again have the power to see through your eyes or hear what you hear. Your life is your own, as it should be."

"Then," said Parrotina, "I will tell you what I see. What I see is the love of my life standing before me. And I wish to hear what I have wished to hear for so long. I have always wished to hear you say those words to me. I dreamed, but I didn't dare to believe. Cagliostro, please say it. Say you're mine forever. Say you're mine forever."

"Parrotina…" the enchanter struggled again to say. "Parrotina…"

"It was very romantic of you," Parrotina went on, "to orchestrate for Sir Italo and Minister Great-Stag an opportunity for them to talk with Bèllabrèzza and Fatta Morganna."

"Opportunity is no assurance of a successful result," said Cagliostro.

"But you can't have a successful result without an opportunity," replied Parrotina.

"I…" the enchanter faltered. "I owed a bit of a return-thank-you gesture to the Minister…"

Parrotina moved closer. "It would have been perfectly lovely if he hadn't been so gallant," she said brightly, her eyes glittering with excitement.

"Not in public, it wouldn't have…" said the enchanter.

Parrotina giggled giddily. "O Cagliostro, my Cagliostro," she said with exhilarated delight. "That is the most romantic thing you have ever said to me."

Cagliostro appeared more flustered than ever.

"I… I didn't mean…"

"Cagliostro," she said. "I once saw and heard you say to Truffaldino that everyone has—somewhere—someone who is exactly right for them, and the two of them are exactly right for each other."

"That… That is correct…"

"Cagliostro, are you and I exactly right for each other? Am I exactly right for you? Cagliostro, are you in love with me?"

The enchanter returned the intensity of her look, gazing as deeply into her eyes as she was gazing into his. Once again, he seemed unable to answer, rather than unwilling to answer.

"Lord Cagliostro," she said gently. "Would you please hold my hand again? You can get more information from me if you'd like."

"I…I believe I already have all the information I need…"

Parrotina took hold of his hand anyway. "You never know what you don't know," she said. "You never know what you might want to learn. You never know what you might find out."

At the same time, both of them glanced to one side as the noise of some manner of commotion began rising from the direction of the cypress grove.

Word travels fast in a castello, even one the size of the Castle Delprego. It had not taken long for news of extraordinary goings-on in the Palace Gardens to reach the Royal Banquet Hall, where so many post-hunt revelers and night-before-the-wedding guest-celebrants had been boisterously and joyously feasting and carousing.

The guards currently deployed in the Palace Gardens did not appear to have any standing orders to stop nobility or other guests from entering, and so the initial trickle of wedding guests milling their way in through the cypress grove in no time had become a flood of incoming happy people. And it was not only the wedding-guest nobility and aristocracy. Castle servants and palace staff were also apparently keen to not miss out on any kingdom-changing momentous extraordinary events, the likes of which had become strangely commonplace over the course of the past two days.

And along with the now increasing inflow of guests arrived the minions of the Master of the Kitchen, fabulously dressed as festive jesters and jubilant harlequins, and all armed with broad trays spread with a spectrum of food and beverage refreshment profferings which they wasted no time in circulating with zealous expert presentational proficiency, as they made their way fluidly through the growing crowd of celebrants. A spontaneous cheer had gone up as the minions had arrived, and the entirety of the Palace Gardens now erupted to sudden vigorous life with animated festivity and gregarious common joy and vibrant universal celebratory elation.

"The minstrels will arrive any moment…" observed Cagliostro.

"Ideal for dancing," said Parrotina. "Ideal for dancing."

"Indeed," agreed Cagliostro. "Indeed."

"Cagliostro, isn't it wonderful?" said Parrotina cheerfully. "Look how happy everyone is."

The enchanter nodded. "The only thing happier than happy people is happy people with food and drink refreshment."

Faint new wisps of smoky vapor had begun to reappear swirling around Cagliostro's robes, as if he might be on the verge of dematerializing, or in some other way about to vanish.

"Are you happy, Cagliostro?" she asked.

The enchanter turned his focus back to her and again appeared unable to resist gazing into her eyes.

"I'm happy," she said, smiling widely. "Because I'm with you. I only want to be with you, no matter where we are or what we're doing, or what is going on around us."

"Parrotina…" he faltered again. "I… I do not like crowds. I… I shall be taking my leave of the Palace Gardens."

"Shall we escape together?" she said excitedly. "To the suite offered by the King?"

"Parrotina, I—"

Parrotina put a finger softly to his lips to firmly stop him speaking.

"I'm sorry," she said. "Did that come out as a question?"

"Parrotina…"

She took hold of both his hands. There was a long hesitation. And then his fingers interlocked with hers.

With their hands clasping each other, Parrotina pulled herself close and stood on her toes, bringing her eyes nearly parallel to his.

"Just talking," she said gently. "Nothing else. I promise. I promise."

"Do you really?" asked the enchanter skeptically. "Do you really promise?"

She moved her face closer to his and nodded emphatically.

"I do not desire to attend the wedding on the morrow," said Cagliostro quietly. "As I have said, I do not like crowds…"

Parrotina smiled happily and continued nodding in accord. "I understand," she said. "I will go with Nicoletta and our father and Tartaglia. But you and I can discuss these things together in our suite."

"How are we to know," Cagliostro said with dubious uncertainty, "which suite is intended to be designated as ours?"

"Truffaldino says you know everything."

Cagliostro shook his head. "I do not. There are far more things I cannot do than there are things that I can do, and there are far more things I do not know than there are things I do know."

Parrotina nodded obligingly. "Do you know which suite is to be ours?" she asked.

"Yes…"

She affectionately squeezed his hands more firmly and moved her eyes somehow even closer to his.

"Work your magic, please," she instructed softly. "Work your magic."

There was a distant sound like wind chimes as a nearly invisible swirl of twinkling points of light began to eddy about the bodies of the enchanter and the former parrot, a whorling cloud of barely perceptible sparkling glimmers that winked and shifted and danced, before sparking apart like tiny fireworks and fading into invisibility as Cagliostro and Parrotina disappeared.

Amidst the increasing celebrations whose joyful sounds and gregarious activity flurried like buffeting gusts of Spring afternoon wind, out from the recesses of foliage somewhere in the verdant piazza emerged the two scribes, efficiently wielding their parchment sheaves and inkwell rings, their unsheathed quill pens poised, their faces as bright and delighted as the boisterous merriment jubilating throughout the gardens all around them.

"All they ever do is eat!" declared Pentimento, flipping open the cap of his ingenious inkwell-ring and dipping his quill.

"If you are what you eat, these people are everything!" agreed Graphiare, flipping open his own inkwell-ring.

"The witch was right," observed Pentimento. "That enchanter is always meddling in other people's business!"

Graphiare nodded, dipping his quill and scribbling busily. "Moral: Sometimes meddling helps solve problems!"

Pentimento nodded, the feathered end of his own quill now waving industriously as he wrote. "Moral: Sometimes Goodness overcomes Evil!"

Graphiare paused the activity of his ink-stained fingers and looked up in quizzical dissatisfaction. "That can't be right…!"

Pentimento paused to look up, nodding in dissatisfied assent. "Too maudlin…!"

"Too sentimental…!" agreed Graphiare.

"Not enough blood…!" concluded Pentimento.

Graphiare dipped his quill again and bent his head zealously back to his scribbling. "Moral: Sometimes there's not enough blood!"

Pentimento dipped his own quill and energetically resumed writing. "Moral: Sometimes prophecies come true!"

"Prophecies ALWAYS come true!" clarified Graphiare.

"That's a tautology!" Pentimento exclaimed gleefully.

"That's right, because it's correct!" contributed Graphiare.

"So much Truth!"

"So much switching bodies!"

"So much romance!"

The two scribes paused and looked at each other.

"Way too much romance!!" they both chorused emphatically.

"So many new paths!" narrated Graphiare, bending his head back to his writing.

"All roads lead to romance…" narrated Pentimento, his quill again scratching briskly across the vellum as he wrote.

"Seriously!" Graphiare agreed with vigorous astonishment. "What is wrong with these people?!"

"And so much happily ever after!"

"And they're just getting started!"

"We'd better transcribe this tale quickly…!"

"Before the next tale begins…!"

"It will take great pictures to illustrate it all!" declared Pentimento eagerly.

"The pictures will need captions to explain them all!" Graphiare added with excited enthusiasm.

"Because it's all so complicated!"

"But all in all, it will make for a good story."

"If we write it well."

"Which we will!" they declared together in proud unison, lifting their inky quills with gleeful exultation triumphantly in the air toward the moon and stars of the overhead nighttime sky.

"Good luck to all!"

"Good will to all!"

"Good life to all!"

"Benebento, să-lū-té!"

With duly fastidious idiosyncrasy, they now swiped the nib ends of their quills against the fold of linen each had affixed to the outer rim of their quill-quivers to wipe away excess ink. Deftly stowing their quills and flipping closed the caps of their inkwell-rings, they speedily shuffled and straightened their vellum folios, and turned to each other with collaborative gleeful smiles of jaunty accomplishment.

"And that is THE END," concluded Pentimento.

The two scribes grinned and nodded at each other, then turned and scurried off as they animatedly narrated in moonlit unison:

"For now…!"

VERITAS GRATIA VERUM AMORIS

Cagliostro the Enchanter
THE SECOND TALE IN THE SERIES

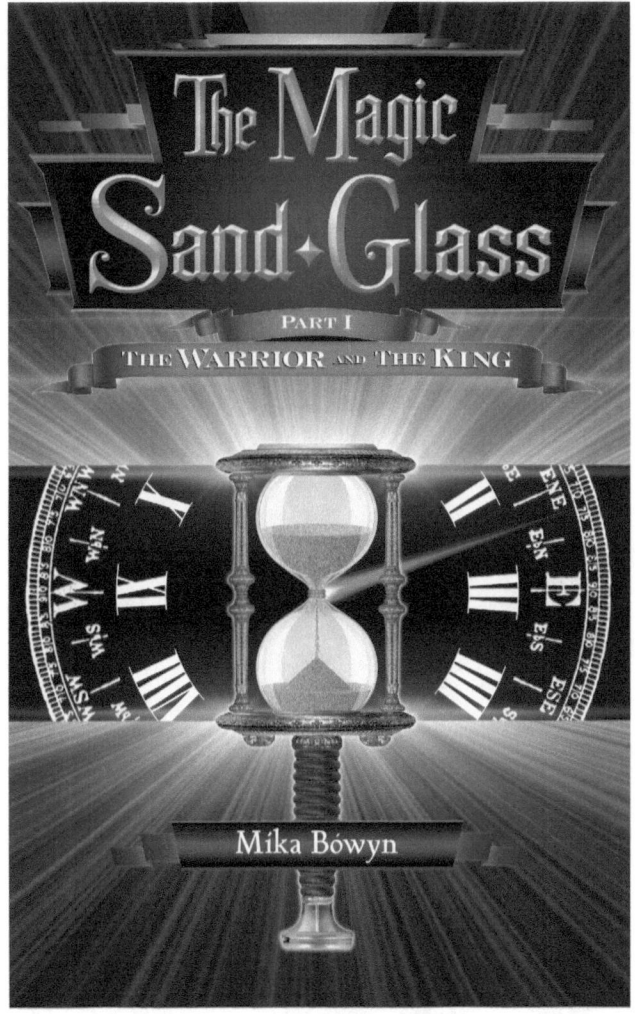

Two missions.
A young warrior on a crucial journey planned for her since before she was born.
A young king on a crucial journey to save his kingdom from destruction.
An extraordinary race against time filled with magic and peril and adventure.

ALSO BY MIKA BÓWYN

FOUR GREEK MYTHS
FROM
ANCIENT GREEK MYTHOLOGY

MIKA BÓWYN

THE MYTH OF **ARACHNE**
THE MYTH OF **PANDORA**
THE MYTH OF **PERSEUS**
THE MYTH OF **THE GOLDEN APPLE** AND
EVENTS LEADING TO THE START OF THE TROJAN WAR

A
MacKenzie Milles
ADVENTURE

THE TREASURE OF SANTA CATALINA ISLAND

MIKA BÓWYN

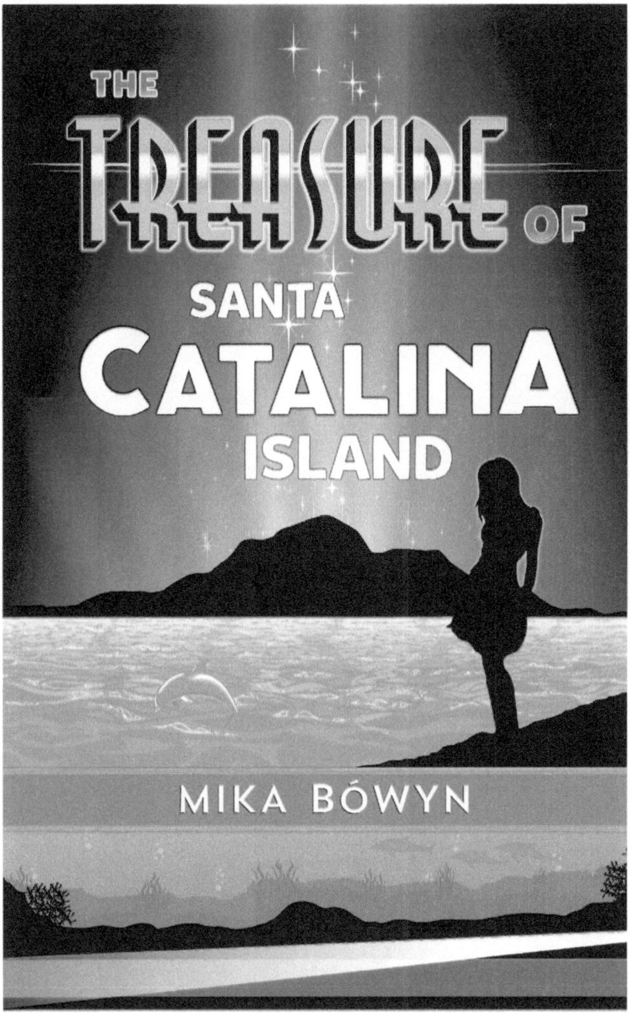

In the summer of 1993
a girl named MacKenzie Milles did something bravely heroic
and made an extraordinary secret discovery
about the Island of Santa Catalina.